KT SALVO

Idol Minds

JETSPACE STUDIO

First published by Jetspace Studio 2023

Copyright © 2023 by KT Salvo

All rights reserved. No part of this publication may be reproduced, stored or transmitted in any form or by any means, electronic, mechanical, photocopying, recording, scanning, or otherwise without written permission from the publisher. It is illegal to copy this book, post it to a website, or distribute it by any other means without permission.

This novel is entirely a work of fiction. The names, characters and incidents portrayed in it are the work of the author's imagination. Any resemblance to actual persons, living or dead, events or localities is entirely coincidental.

Designations used by companies to distinguish their products are often claimed as trademarks. All brand names and product names used in this book and on its cover are trade names, service marks, trademarks and registered trademarks of their respective owners. The publishers and the book are not associated with any product or vendor mentioned in this book. None of the companies referenced within the book have endorsed the book.

First edition

ISBN: 979-8-9855022-9-9

Contents

Content Warnings	v
Blossom	vii
01	1
02	15
03	30
04	47
05	60
06	72
07	86
08	101
09	118
10	132
11	147
12	164
13	177
14	191
15	203
16	218
17	234
18	248
19	262
20	275
21	286
22	300

23	311
24	322
25	334
26	346
27	356
Acknowledgments	365
About the Author	366

Content Warnings

This book contains brief descriptions of mild physical violence and mentions of homophobia, racism, emotional abuse, abusive parents, and teen suicide.

Blossom

When I see you, my heart starts to race
Every time you smile, it lights up your face Your eyes
sparkle like the stars in the sky
I never knew love could be this sweet, oh my

I'm so happy you're mine
You look at me, and I cry
And our love's blossom burns
Like the fires in my mind

Every moment feels like a dream come true Never want
to wake up, just wanna be with you Your love holds me
like a warm embrace
Never want to let go, just wanna stay in this place

I'm so happy you're mine
You look at me, and I cry
And our love's blossom burns
Like the fires in my mind

When I'm with you, I feel alive
Your love is all I need to survive
I'll cherish every moment we share
Because I have you I could ever want or need

I'm so happy you're mine
You look at me, and I cry
And our love's blossom burns
Like the fires in my mind

01

Jason strode across the dusty warehouse floor, grit and loose gravel loudly crunching under the soles of his heavy boots. Ahead, a bloom of tiny dust motes danced in the single shaft of light slicing through the dusky gloom. He stopped where he knew the light would strike the sharp planes of his angled face just right. The bloody sweat on his brow begged to be wiped off, but Jason ignored the irritation, curling his lip into a vicious sneer. Then he pointed his katana at the shadowy figure looming before him, his sword's gleaming blade catching the light to throw off a dazzling shine. "Looks like it's down to just you and me, Nomura. One way or another, this ends here."

The dark figure spread his arms wide, revealing the matching tantos in each hand. He took a single step forward and flashed a malicious grin. "Then let it end, Shoda," the figure growled. "Let it end now."

"Cut!" The director lowered the headphones she'd been holding to her ear. "Circle that one. It was perfect. What's next?"

Jason let his arm fall. Another few seconds and it would've started to shake. It turned out period-accurate Japanese swords were heavy when you held them for hours. Hopefully, they'd be wrapping for the day soon. Jason's arm felt like a noodle.

The prop wrangler, a gruff, older white guy with a scraggly beard and a growing midsection, came to collect the katana from Jason. What was his name again? Ralph? Carl? Not that it mattered. He'd probably always be "prop guy" the few times Jason even bothered to think of him.

A droplet of red-stained sweat fell from Jason's brow, narrowly missing his eye. He nearly wiped his forehead before remembering his hand was just as filthy. "Hey, can somebody please come wipe this shit off my goddamn face?"

One of the production assistants rushed to Jason's side, bearing a small plastic tub full of baby wipes. Jason quietly seethed while the PA attempted to clean the worst of the fake dirt and blood from his face. But Jason angrily waved them away when they tried to wipe off his chest. "No, damn it. Leave that. I need a shower, not a fucking sponge bath."

The PA mumbled an apology and quickly stepped back. Jason rolled his eyes. They weren't gonna make it in the business very long if they couldn't handle an actor who was tired and cranky after a long day of filming.

"Hey, I'll take some of that." Tommy Yoshida walked over, still holding his fake tantos down by his sides. While his face was just as dirty and sweat-stained as Jason's, wardrobe had given him a black scarf to wear as a headband. And the dirt may have been fake, but the sweat was real. The Sherman Oaks warehouse where they'd been filming was a sweltering hot box. Jason would've gladly traded the expensive replica sword for working A/C. "Nice work there, Park. Seriously. I really felt that one."

Jason shrugged. "Yeah, whatever." Compliments were all

well and good. But Jason was in no mood to get his ass kissed. He was tired and really needed a drink.

Tommy shook his head as the PA tried wiping the artfully applied dirt and grime from his face. "Jesus, Park. I was trying to be nice. You don't have to be an asshole."

Jason snorted. "And you don't have to jerk me off after every scene. Nobody's winning any awards for this shit."

Tommy frowned but bit back any other replies he might've had. He was undoubtedly well aware of Jason's reputation. That was fine. Tommy was just a glorified stuntman, anyway. His toned, athletic body and martial arts expertise were strong enough to cast him as the villain. But Tommy's emotional range was limited to angry sneer and angry frown. Not to mention that Tommy could barely remember his lines half the time. Jason hardly needed his praise.

Then Penny, the 2nd AD and only person on the set who seemed to know what she was doing, finally called out the magic words. "That's a wrap for today, everyone. But FYI, the EP just called for a full cast and crew meeting."

Jason groaned. The Executive Producer hadn't set foot on set since they started shooting three weeks ago. "What now?"

Penny shrugged. "Your guess is as good as mine. Just be there." She walked away without further explanation, leaving Jason alone with a silently stewing Tommy and a nervous PA whose name he didn't know. Jason softly chuckled. He liked Penny, at least. She didn't take any shit from him.

Jason walked off without a word, finally giving Tommy and the PA the freedom to exchange their knowing glances about working with an asshole like Jason Park. Whatever. He made a beeline to the nearest exit door and stepped outside to the stifling, late afternoon heat. It was an absolute scorcher in the Valley. No wonder the warehouse was a fucking oven.

Jason mindlessly patted his pocket before remembering that he was still in wardrobe. "Shit."

"I got 'em, J."

Startled, Jason nearly jumped out of his boots. "Jesus, fuck, Lil. Where the hell did you come from?"

Lily Garcia, Jason's 27-year-old assistant and handler, smirked as she held out a pack of cigarettes and a lighter. Her rosy brown skin glistened with a sheen of sweat despite being dressed for the heat in simple white shorts and a black t-shirt with her long, dark hair pulled back into a tight ponytail. "I waited for you in there, but you walked right past me."

Jason huffed. A proper studio would've hired an on-set assistant, so he didn't have to bring his own. Then again, Lily was one of the few people on set that Jason could even stand. It's not like he was working with a proper studio anyway, just the pretend production arm of BigCloud's streaming service making another schlocky direct-to-streaming action flick. Jason grabbed his pack, pulled out a cigarette, and stuck it in his mouth. "Sorry. Long day."

Lily snorted. "You're telling me? We were supposed to wrap more than an hour ago." She lit his cigarette before handing Jason his lighter. "And what was that I heard about an all-hands meeting?"

"Can't be anything good." Jason took a long drag and frowned. Then he turned away to exhale. "You got my phone?"

Lily nodded as she pulled a phone from the tote hanging off her shoulder. "Here."

"Thanks." Jason took it and thumbed the power button. He had a handful of message alerts but nothing major. Jason sighed and looked at Lily. "Come on. I need to wash this shit off."

A couple years ago, Jason would've never considered doing a throwaway, low-budget action movie. After all, he was Jason fucking Park, award-winning actor and former teen idol. He'd single-handedly carried the hit *Monday Night Club* teen movie franchise while he was still a teen himself. And that was before he became the youngest-ever Best Actor winner for his role in Lodestar Studio's *The Moon Shines Madly*. But work was work. And after his famously well-documented on-set blow-up cost Jason his lead in Lodestar's next film, followed by a few too many drunken confrontations with paparazzi and fans, work was increasingly hard to come by. At the tender age of twenty-four, Jason's reputation for being problematic and hard to work with already overshadowed his status as an award-winning actor. At least BigCloud had given him his own trailer.

After a cigarette and a shower, Jason stood in the icy cold breath of his trailer's roof-mounted A/C unit wrapped in a damp towel. He took a swig from the nearly empty bottle of Kingston whiskey sitting on his kitchenette counter before offering the bottle to Lily.

"I'm good," Lily replied without looking up from her phone.

"Suit yourself."

Jason set the bottle on the counter and checked his reflection in the full-length mirror mounted by the door to ensure he'd washed off all the dirt and prop blood. He leaned in close to check his face. Even with all the pancake scrubbed away, his golden-brown skin looked smooth and clear. Jason smiled. He honestly had no right to have such good skin with all his smoking and drinking. Score one for good genes.

Jason looked down at his torso, frowning when he caught sight of his abs. Three weeks of twelve-hour days had taken their toll on his workout schedule, and he was already losing definition. Jason flexed his chest. Was he losing mass there, too? He needed a week in the gym and at least three days laying out in the sun to get back to normal. Thankfully, they'd already shot his nude scenes. Jason smiled when he remembered how great his ass had looked in the dailies. Way better than his scene partner Maggie's, if he was honest.

Lily snorted. "You want me to leave you two alone for a while? The way you're eye fucking your reflection, I feel like a third wheel here."

"You mean fifth wheel, Lil. And, no. I want you to start packing up my trailer."

"What? Why?"

"So you don't have to do it tomorrow." Jason ran his hands through his too-short, thick black hair before dressing in the skinny, black jeans and tight gray v-neck t-shirt he'd worn to set that morning. "And tell Naomi to set a meeting with my agent."

"Why? You really think they'll pull the plug?"

Jason nodded as he pocketed his phone, wallet, and keys. He'd been in the industry long enough to know something was up. Production usually only called everyone together in the middle of a shoot for one reason. "Yeah, I do."

"Shit." Lily frowned. "Maybe I will have that drink."

Jason chuckled. "You're welcome to it. Just make sure you get everything that's mine out of here before they strike the trailer."

Jason went outside and lit another cigarette. He took a long drag and held it until the nicotine hit his bloodstream, mingling with the alcohol to take off a bit of his edge. Everyone was probably waiting on him in the production trailer, so Jason strolled toward the double-wide they'd brought in to use as an office. It was barely big enough to hold the whole cast and crew. And Jason was the last to arrive, so he stood near the door. The A/C already struggled to keep up with the sudden influx of body heat, so he didn't want to stand there for a moment longer than he had to. Jason suspected it wouldn't be a long meeting anyway.

One of the Associate Producers stood and waved to get the group's attention. "I want to start by thanking you for all your hard work on this picture. But BigCloud has recently made some changes to their funding priorities. Unfortunately, that means they shifted the budget away from this project. So we're officially on hold for now."

The room erupted into a burst of surprised, angry chaos. But Jason just chuckled. On hold? Like hell. Just like "for now" almost always meant forever. He shook his head as he turned toward the door. Jason wanted no part of the unfolding mess. So he quietly slipped out to stand on the scorching black pavement. He pulled out another cigarette and lit it before heading for the parking lot. Then he winced as he heard the trailer door slam behind him.

"Hey, Jason!"

Jason groaned before turning around to see Maggie Zamora hurrying toward him. His co-star's wavy black hair was still pulled back in the ponytail she'd gotten from hair and makeup that morning. Her soft, pouty face was flushed with the same surprised anger Jason had heard from everyone else in the meeting. He took a slow drag on his cigarette and blew it out while he waited. "What's up?"

Maggie shook her head. "I don't know. What does on hold even mean?"

Jason shrugged. Maggie's soft frown and slumped shoulders probably meant she was looking for emotional support. But they didn't have that kind of relationship. And Jason was the last person you wanted for that, anyway. Maggie was just another in a string of co-stars who mistook Jason's fiery attitude for emotional investment. When would they ever learn?

Still, Jason couldn't help feeling bad for Maggie. It was her first big role. Hopefully, it wouldn't be her last. But Jason knew well enough how hard it was to find work in Hollywood as an Asian actor. Unless you managed to achieve crossover audience appeal, you usually ended up in lazily written, direct-to-streaming action flicks about modern-day ninjas like the one they'd just been fired from. Hell, neither of them was even Japanese. Jason was Korean, and Maggie was Filipino. Tommy was probably the only actual Japanese person in the whole cast. But the studio didn't care about shit like that. To white audiences, Asian was Asian.

Maggie wasn't Jason's responsibility anyway. It was hard enough for him to find work as it was. And, in their business, it was everybody for themselves. "Don't know, Mags. Don't care."

Maggie's surprised reaction almost made Jason laugh. "What do you mean you don't care? Aren't you worried about getting paid?"

Jason snorted and shook his head. "Nope." Then he smiled. "I already got paid, babe."

Maggie scoffed. "You're such an asshole."

Jason rolled his eyes as Maggie walked away. Then he took

another drag from his cigarette before throwing it to the ground and stomping it out. With the money gone, there'd probably be no one left on set to clean up the butt. But that was no longer Jason's responsibility either.

Jason felt his phone buzzing as he neared his car. He pulled it from his pocket and saw that his business manager Naomi was calling. At least Lily was still doing her job. He tapped the answer button.

"Yeah?"

"What the hell, Jason? Lily says you just got fired. What did you do?"

Jason snorted. "Fuck you, Naomi. I didn't do a damn thing. BigCloud pulled the money."

"Oh. Shit. Sorry."

"Don't sweat it, Ms. Bell." Jason heard the doors unlock as he approached his jet-black Ficaro Monaco convertible. He pulled the driver's door open and climbed inside. "Check my contract and see what they still owe me. And get me a meeting with Evan."

"Yeah, sure. I'll put a call in." Naomi paused long enough that Jason thought he'd dropped the call. "What are you gonna do now?"

"I'm gonna get the hell off this goddamn set." Jason started the engine and revved it loud enough so Naomi would be sure to hear it.

"You know what I mean, Jason. If you're thinking of–"

"I'll be fine, Naomi."

They both knew what Jason was thinking of doing. But Jason wasn't about to let his business manager mother him. He'd just been fired from his first real job in nearly a year. He wanted a real fucking drink.

9

"Yeah, whatever. Just try to stay out of trouble."

"Trouble's my middle name. Talk to you later."

Jason ended the call before Naomi could protest. He slipped on the overpriced designer Japanese shades he'd gotten from some award show party gift bag and pulled out of his reserved parking spot for the last time. Jason wordlessly handed over his parking pass at the gate before turning onto Van Nuys. Since he was all the way out in the Valley, Jason decided to pay another visit to the little dive bar on Van Nuys that he'd been frequenting while filming in Sherman Oaks. It was dark, out of the way, and had generous pours. Plus, Jason had never seen any paparazzi there, and the staff let him park in the back. There was no way he'd park his Monaco on the street.

Although it had been a long day for Jason, it was still early enough that plenty of parking was available behind the bar. The car's alarm chirped as Jason locked the doors on his way to the bar's rear entrance. He'd only ever used the front door once. Jason wasn't sure he even remembered what the front of the place looked like.

Cool darkness enveloped Jason as he stepped inside. The back door led past the restrooms, so the A/C chilled air smelled like cleaning fluid and urinal cakes. Jason had been surprised to discover the place tucked between a taqueria and pet food supply store in one of the endless streams of Sherman Oaks strip malls. The decor said roadside biker bar, but the music was strictly Top 40. And there wasn't a star fucker in sight.

Josie nodded as Jason emerged from the back hallway and sat on an empty stool. Then she pulled the bottle of Kingston Premium Bourbon Whiskey from the shelf behind her, poured three fingers into a low ball, and set them both on the bar in front of him. "You look like hell."

Jason nodded. A single insult was usually the extent of Josie's banter. "Long day." He tossed the whiskey down his throat, set the glass down, and tapped the rim with his finger. Josie frowned and poured him another three fingers. Then she moved off to talk to someone else but left the bottle behind. Jason smiled. That was his idea of bottle service. Let all those silly, miniskirt-clad starlets sip their overpriced, small-batch tequila in a private booth in some flashy Weho club. Jason just wanted a dark, quiet dive bar and a bottle of Kingston.

Jason swallowed his second whiskey and helped himself to a third. The liquor finally hit his system, wiping away another layer of the tension he'd carried in from the set. It helped that Jason hadn't eaten since he hit the craft services table during his early lunch break. Food just got in the way of his buzz.

Jason pulled out his phone and went online, sipping his Kingston while he looked to see if news of his canceled picture had hit the Hollywood blogs yet. He would've been surprised if it had. A dozen projects more noteworthy than Jason's got shit-canned every day. There was nothing about his to make it newsworthy. But Jason caught a story about Sophie Gibson, one of his costars in the *Monday Night Club* movie series. Despite her character's wholesome, all-American girl vibes, Sophie had been even messier than Jason. She was the one who'd turned him onto Kingston in the first place.

"Don't bother with all the expensive shit," Sophie had once told Jason after snorting a thousand dollars worth of coke off the tiny dining table in her trailer. "Just stick with the basics."

Apparently, Sophie had just announced another engagement. Good for her. Back then, the blogs kept posting rumors that the pair were dating. But the closest they'd ever come was when Sophie offered to blow Jason in his trailer before rushing off to the toilet to throw up. Hopefully, this engagement worked out better than the last three times she'd tried it. But Jason doubted it would.

"Hey. Are you Jason Park?"

Jason swallowed his automatic groan before turning to see a bleached-blond, spray-tanned surfer boy who'd probably never set foot on an actual surfboard. Was he a hustler? No. He was cute, but his teeth weren't white enough. Probably not a wannabe actor, then, either. Jason's eyes flicked up and down as he gave Surfer Boy a once over. No, the guy was probably nobody except a beach boy poser whose entire personality revolved around his horse cock.

"No. I'm not."

Surfer Boy frowned. "Are you sure? I've seen all his movies, and you look just like him."

Was he a genuine fan? Too bad. After a few more shots, Jason might've entertained the thought of taking him back to the restroom and sucking him off. He was certainly pretty enough for a white boy. But Jason was definitely not in the mood to smile for some dumbass loser's poorly-lit selfie just so he could brag to his perpetually disappointed girlfriend about meeting the Jason Park.

"Are you seriously suggesting I don't know my own fucking name?"

Surfer Boy's frown morphed into a scowl. "Hey, you don't gotta be an asshole about it."

"Says the asshole standing there bothering me while I'm trying to sit here and have a drink."

Surfer Boy squared up his shoulders. Jason saw the veins

on his biceps pop out as he squeezed his hands into fists. "Did you just call me an asshole?"

Jason smiled. He could see where things were going from a mile away. If he couldn't blow the guy, then maybe he could kick his ass instead. And the whiskey coursing through his system told him that was a good thing. Jason slowly sat forward, pushing his face just a little too far into Surfer Boy's personal space. "Awe. Pretty and stupid? That's always a dangerous combination, my friend."

Surfer Boy stood there, breathing too heavily while deciding what to do. Come on, dumbass. Take a swing. But he shook his head instead. "Whatever." Then he turned and took a step away.

Jason snorted. Surfer Boy might've been done with their little chat. But Jason was just getting started. "That's right, dickhead. Walk away."

Surfer Boy halted midstep. Jason watched him curl his hands into fists again, telegraphing every move he was about to make. The poor asshole had no idea the fight was already over. The thing about being an Asian actor is that producers always expected you to know martial arts. So Jason had trained in several, including taekwondo, aikido, and the three weeks of kenpo he'd just suffered through learning how to hold that fucking sword. Jason was no super ninja like the character he'd just played, but taking down Surfer Boy wouldn't require anything like that.

Jason was already moving by the time Surfer Boy threw his first punch. The Kingston hadn't dulled Jason's reaction time enough to miss the obvious move. And it relaxed him enough to make his motion feel fluid and easy. Jason slid off his stool in time for the punch to hit nothing but air. He slipped to his left and double-thumped Surfer Boy's exposed midsection with a pair of low fists. Then he swept Surfer Boy's legs with his foot, sending him tumbling to the floor.

Surfer Boy's brown-haired clone charged toward Jason from the pool table, brandishing his pool cue just like Jason's period-accurate katana. "You're dead meat, asshole."

Jason quickly ducked under Surfer Clone's swinging pool cue. Then he smiled. Swinging a fist at Jason would get you knocked down. But swinging a weapon at him would get you pummeled. Jason lunged at him, knocking him back with an off-hand punch to the face and following up with a right-hand roundhouse. Surfer Clone stumbled, dropped the pool cue, and fell to the floor. Jason was on top of him in a second, straddling his pelvis in a lurid display of dominance before punching him in the face. Once. Twice. Bang!

Startled, Jason looked up to see Josie leaning over the bar with a mahogany bat in hand. The thing could've been made of steel the way she'd just smacked it on the bar top without even cracking it. Grim-faced, Josie tipped her head to the side, and Jason looked around to see a dozen bar patrons standing out of range, phones in hand, filming the whole scene.

Shit.

02

Tae Hyun stood before the mirror mounted next to his sister's front door and practiced his smile. It had been nearly two years since he'd stood before a mob of cameras, so he was well out of practice. He knew the old habits would eventually come back. But he didn't have time for eventually. He was about to ask for the moon and a star, so his smile needed to be perfect.

There was a science to Tae Hyun's smile, built from careful measurement of his head and face by his early handlers at KBR. He was fortunate enough to have already been graced with the strong chin and cheekbones that his corporate masters had paid for many of his fellow trainees to acquire. His nose was a little too wide but not enough to require any plastic surgery. A little contouring sufficed.

Tae Hyun turned his head slightly to the right to emphasize the curve and deemphasize the width of his nose. Then he lifted his chin just so, making his pouty lower lip appear that much more prominent. When he spread his mouth into a broad smile, he let his eyes nearly close to achieve the anime character look that was all the rage when he was last on tour. There it was–the smile he'd spent countless hours practicing in front of the mirror in his trainee dorm room until it eventually ended up on the cover of fashion and culture magazines worldwide.

His unit's many duty rotations outside under the sun had deepened Tae Hyun's formerly sandy brown complexion. But a little brightening powder worked wonders on that. At least his skin was still smooth and clear. Tae Hyun's already broad shoulders had only grown larger under his enforced fitness regimen. And his narrow waist was 2.5 cm smaller than before he'd joined the Army.

Tae Hyun still wasn't sure about his outfit. His younger sister had offered it to him to celebrate his discharge. Yun Seo assured Tae Hyun that it was what all the other idols were wearing. He thought the oversized sweatshirt and tight pants made him look top-heavy. But his only civilian clothes were two years out of date, so Tae Hyun had to take his sister's word for it.

"It's so weird watching you do that, oppa."

Tae Hyun resisted the urge to frown, focusing on his smile instead. "Then don't watch me."

Yun Seo walked up behind her brother and put her hands on his shoulders. The pair looked so much alike they were often mistaken for twins, even though she was two years younger. Of course, her dark hair fell well past her shoulders. Tae Hyun's hair was only a month from his last military haircut. "You look fine. And you're going to be fine."

Tae Hyun sighed. "That's easy for you to say."

"Only because it's true," Yun Seo said with a wink. "Now, turn around and let me fix your makeup."

Tae Hyun huffed. "My makeup's fine. It's just a meeting. I don't–"

Yun Seo grabbed Tae Hyun's shoulder and turned him to

face her. "Your makeup's fine for a trip to the market. But this is important. And you never know who you'll see out there. I can't have my Tae Hyun going out without a perfect face."

"Alright." Tae Hyun pouted. "Sorry."

Yun Seo rolled her eyes before setting her makeup bag on the nearby side table. "I can't believe your skin is still so good." She leaned forward and squinted. "Do you even have any pores?" Tae Hyun ignored the jab as he allowed his sister to touch up his foundation, eyeliner, and lip color. When she was done, Yun Seo lifted her brother's chin to point his face at the light. "There. That's the idol I know and love."

Tae Hyun smiled. "Thanks."

"Do you think you'll see him?"

Him could only mean one person. "No, Chang Min won't be there. It'll just be Managing Director Choo and me."

"Do you think he knows you'll be there?"

Tae Hyun had wondered that already. But he shrugged. "I have no idea. I don't see why he would."

Yun Seo nodded. "Well, if you see him, kick his ass for me."

Tae Hyun snorted, but it was only a bluff. Sure, it had been two years since he'd last seen Chang Min. That night had spelled the end of their secret romance. And also, despite Chang Min's many frantic apologies, the end of their working relationship as two of the three members of *XTC*. But Tae Hyun's anger at his former lover and group member hadn't cooled so much as it had hardened and sharpened. Back then, it was a sledgehammer. It had since become a knife.

A knock on the door stole Tae Hyun's attention from his sister. Was it already time? Tae Hyun looked through the peephole to see the driver KBR had sent. "Looks like I gotta go, Yun Seo."

Yun Seo nodded and pulled Tae Hyun into a hug. "Have a great day, oppa. Knock 'em dead."

When they arrived at the KBR headquarters, the driver pulled into the garage, saving Tae Hyun from having to walk in the main entrance. But it wasn't entirely for Tae Hyun's benefit. KBR didn't want to make his return public until everyone had decided what it would actually look like.

"Oh. I almost forgot." The driver reached over, opened the glove box, and pulled out a small box. "Here. This is for you, courtesy of Director Choo."

Tae Hyun took the box and looked at it. "A new phone?"

The driver nodded. "Back on the leash, I'm afraid. It's already set up with your social media account access."

Tae Hyun shoved the box into his sweatshirt pocket. "Thanks."

Tae Hyun got out of the car and went to the garage elevator entrance. Unlike the lobby, which featured a squad of uniformed security guards and a formation of tastefully dressed hosts meant to sweep aside anyone whose visit was for something other than business, the garage only had a pair of uniformed guards. Neither moved a muscle as Tae Hyun walked by. Despite his nearly two-year absence, Woo Tae Hyun was still a known quantity at KBR. Besides, he had an appointment. Even if the guards didn't know who Tae Hyun was–an unlikely event–they certainly would've been informed of his arrival.

KBR Managing Director Choo Ji Hoon's office was on the twelfth floor–high enough to afford him a decent view of the Gangnam skyline but not high enough to catch a glimpse of the Han River. Tae Hyun didn't recognize his manager's assistant when he stood and bowed.

"Hello, sunbae-nim!" the assistant exclaimed. "I'm Jang Min Jun, Managing Director Choo's assistant. Welcome back."

"Thank you. Is he ready?"

Min Jun nodded. "Please, go in, sir."

Ji Hoon's door was already open, but Tae Hyun still politely knocked on the doorframe.

"Director Choo, sir?"

Ji Hoon looked up from the tablet on his desk and smiled. "Tae Hyun! Come in, come in."

Tae Hyun smiled and bowed before stepping into Ji Hoon's office. It had hardly changed since the last time he'd set foot inside. The plants were different. The office chair was a newer model. And there was an updated photo of his wife and two children on the counter next to Choo's wet bar. His children looked like they might be nearing their teens. "Thank you, Director Choo." Tae Hyun sat in one of the chairs facing Ji Hoon's desk.

"What's with all this formality, Tae Hyun? Did the army's brainwashing erase our friendship while you were away?"

Tae Hyun smiled and shook his head. "No, sir. But it will probably take more than a few weeks to erase all those habits."

Ji Hoon nodded. "Of course. I remember it well. And I'm glad to see you looking so well, too. I assume you enjoyed your time off?"

"I did, sir. Thank you. Although I still find myself waking with the dawn."

Ji Hoon chuckled. "That's not necessarily a bad habit to keep."

"No, Director Choo. I suppose it's not."

Ji Hoon briefly frowned at Tae Hyun's insistence on using formal language. Although Ji Hoon's military training comment was accurate, Tae Hyun deliberately used it. He had a good idea of what his manager wanted to talk about. Despite Ji Hoon's insistence that they were old friends, Tae Hyun didn't imagine it would be a friendly chat.

"I suppose we should get to business, then."

"Please, sir."

Ji Hoon nodded. "I met with CEO Pak this morning. One of the topics we discussed was your return to the KBR fold. And he was very interested in an *XTC* comeback reunion."

Tae Hyun was careful to keep his face composed despite the surge of annoyance from hearing his old group's name. He'd only been eighteen when the eventual K-pop supergroup debuted their first album, *Almanac*. Their first single, *Random Geography*, hit a perfect all-kill on the Korean charts before reaching overseas to dominate the Americas and Europe. But that had been five years ago. "Respectfully, Director Choo. But, no."

Ji Hoon sighed and shook his head. "Come on, Tae Hyun. It's been nearly two years. Surely things have changed since then?"

Tae Hyun frowned. Did he honestly think Tae Hyun would forget why he'd left the group in the first place? If Ji Hoon wanted informal, he'd get informal. "Of course, things have changed, sir. But not how I feel. I told you I'm not working with Chang Min ever again. Certainly not if I have to pretend things are fine between us." Tae Hyun angrily shook his head. "Things will never be fine between us."

Ji Hoon clucked his tongue. Had Tae Hyun already pushed things too far? Not that it mattered. Song Chang Min could go to hell for all Tae Hyun cared. Tae Hyun had opened himself to his fellow group member in ways he'd never imagined he ever would. They'd spent a glorious year secretly flirting until their flirtations became something more. Something real. Tae Hyun and Chang Min had spent many secret nights engaging in behavior that the average fan would be shocked to discover. But Tae Hyun had only been imagining it was something real. He learned that the hard way when he discovered Chang Min getting fucked by some nameless Japanese moneyboy in their shared Tokyo hotel suite. Tae Hyun hoped that night had cost Chang Min dearly. It had certainly cost Tae Hyun.

Between his unexplained anger and secret heartbreak, Tae Hyun refused to ever work with Chang Min again. The leadership at KBR was understandably upset and confused. They may or may not have known about two of their top idols sleeping with each other. Unofficially, of course. Officially, those sorts of liaisons were strictly forbidden. Korean idols were trained from the start to be idealized versions of themselves. Attractive but pure. Alluring but chaste. Approachable but untouchable. It was important for fans to think their idols were just one stolen glance away from running away with them. Otherwise, no entertainment executive would invest hundreds of billions of won in their development.

That was why Tae Hyun opted to enter his compulsory military service. It gave both him and KBR a chance to save face. Of course, KBR had hoped that cooler heads would prevail after all the time away. But they'd get no such thing from Tae Hyun.

Ji Hoon sighed again, then spread his hands out in a surprisingly apologetic gesture. "And what would you have us do? Replace Chang Min?"

"Would you?"

Ji Hoon snorted. "Of course not. Then it wouldn't be *XTC*."

As if they couldn't find another trainee in their stable whose romanized name started with C. "Then you have my answer."

Ji Hoon leaned forward, his expression almost fatherly. "Be reasonable, Tae Hyun." Ji Hoon was really pouring on the charm. "We gave you the time away for your military service. And then we gave you another month to get back on your feet. But your contract says that you still owe us three albums. And CEO Pak wants you to rejoin *XTC*."

Tae Hyun remained silent for a few moments, letting the tension between them linger. After years of training and performing, he knew a few things about manipulating tension. "Let me go solo, sir."

Ji Hoon almost shook with surprise. "You want to go solo?"

Tae Hyun nodded. "Yes. I want to record a solo album."

"Are you serious?"

"Of course. Why wouldn't I be?"

Ji Hoon frowned. Tae Hyun stayed quiet, letting the offer dangle while his manager considered the possibilities. He already knew the answer Ji Hoon would give him. Tae Hyun had been the strongest vocalist and dancer in the group. Choreographers and photographers always put him in the middle of the lineup. Yes, his initial was also in the middle of the group's name. But Tae Hyun was more than the group's leader. He'd carried that group on his back. Besides, Xiang and Chang Min had been allowed to craft solo projects while Tae Hyun was away. Why couldn't he have one as well?

"I see," Ji Hoon finally replied. "I assume you expect us to keep waiting while you write this album?"

02

Tae Hyun shook his head. "No, sir. It's already written."

Ji Hoon's further shock was evident. Tae Hyun was disappointed that his manager would expect him to ask for something like a solo album without already having it written. "Well, I can't make that call. KBR invested heavily in the *XTC* brand. I'm not sure they're ready to let that go." Tae Hyun nodded, making subtle eye contact with his manager as he did until Ji Hoon finally nodded back. "Fine. I'll bring this to CEO Pak. I'll have to let you know."

Tae Hyun hid his smile all the way past Ji Hoon's assistant. Ideally, his manager would've loved the idea of a solo album. But he hadn't expected that. Tae Hyun expected what actually happened–that his manager would pass it up the ranks for approval. At the very least, it bought him some time before he was forced into a decision he didn't want to make.

"What's that sneaky grin all about?"

Tae Hyun turned in surprise at the unexpected sound of an all-too-familiar voice. "Yoo Mi? I can't believe it! What are you doing here?"

Sang Yoo Mi smiled, the brilliant flash of her bright white teeth highlighted and offset by a shade of scarlet lipstick so dark it was nearly black. She'd paired the lipstick with a short dress in nearly the same color–a dress that also highlighted her impressive cleavage with a not-quite-plunging neckline. Yoo Mi's hair was longer than Tae Hyun remembered it. She'd also gone back to her natural, dark hair color. But she still wore the same perfume. "I'm here on business, of course. But you're looking good, Tae Hyun. I'd say military service agrees with you."

Tae Hyun chuckled. "If you say so. And you look amazing. I love that color on you."

Yoo Mi feigned a bashful smile, brushing some hair behind her ear. "You were always the best flatterer. Are you back to work now? I hadn't heard."

"That remains to be seen. How've you been? Congrats on your engagement, by the way. He's a lucky man."

"Thank you." Yoo Mi playfully snorted. "Although I'd prefer if you could at least pretend to be a tiny bit jealous."

Tae Hyun smirked. "Would it be any more convincing than when I pretended to be in love with you?"

Yoo Mi laughed. The bright musical tones sounded just like Tae Hyun remembered. Although their year-long romance had been a sham, conjured by Yoo Mi and her management to squash some unpleasant rumors about Yoo Mi's dating habits, the two had grown close enough to be good friends. Yoo Mi was also one of the few people besides his sister and a few carefully chosen lovers who knew Tae Hyun's secret. Well, them and one poorly chosen lover. But Chang Min wasn't about to spill it anyway—not when he stood to lose just as much as Tae Hyun. "I miss you. We should get a drink."

"Right now? Won't your fiance be jealous of you getting a drink with your ex?"

Yoo Mi moved to stand beside him and take his arm. "Don't be silly. Besides, you know how the press will eat it up. And you could use the publicity."

A highly regarded model and actress, Sang Yoo Mi was by far the better of the two when it came to managing her public image. She insisted it was a necessary evil if they wanted to be successful. Their fanbase was finicky and prone to quickly changing interests. But an idol who was good at keeping fans on their toes would always be popular. During their fake relationship, Yoo Mi had even gone as far as creating public quarrels between them. Fights that Tae Hyun would invariably end with some grand display of affection and an expensive gift.

Tae Hyun finally nodded. "Alright. I would enjoy a chance to catch up."

Yoo Mi delightedly clapped her hands. "See? There's the fun-loving Tae Hyun I remember." She had Min Jun arrange for a driver to take them to Veil, a high-end club in Cheongdam-dong that had opened the year prior. The club owners had hit on a particularly successful business model—offering private dining rooms for the ultra-wealthy and a semi-private mezzanine where celebrities could dine in view of but away from the general public. Many dating rumors had been started and squashed on the Veil mezzanine. And the Veil host was only too happy to accommodate Yoo Mi's last-minute request for a mezzanine table, especially when he discovered who she was drinking with. The distant shutter clicks started up when their server brought their drinks.

"Tricky," Tae Hyun observed.

Yoo Mi grinned. "It's not my first time, darling. Places like this have made things so much easier. They let me do my face time without talking to anyone except my date."

"And now I'm your date?"

Yoo Mi quietly chuckled. "You're my ex, recently back from his military service, who offered to buy me a drink to celebrate my impending marriage." She reached out and put her hand on his. "At least, that's what my publicist will say."

"Are you ever not working?"

Yoo Mi shrugged and pulled her hand away. "It's the life of an idol. Speaking of which, I assume they want you to get back with *XTC*."

Tae Hyun nodded. "Obviously."

"And I assume you told them to go to hell."

Tae Hyun smiled. "You still know me so well."

"We fake-dated for a year, darling. Of course, I know you."

Tae Hyun laughed. Then he felt a wave of melancholy, which he did his best to hide with a smile. Yoo Mi had been one of the first people Tae Hyun secretly ran to after the incident with Chang Min. And she'd let him cry on her shoulder, despite having told him that sleeping with Chang Min was a mistake. Tae Hyun had thought she meant the inevitable scandal if they were found out. It was only later that he realized she'd been talking about Chang Min being a cheating asshole.

"Have you talked to him?"

"No. Have you?" Tae Hyun shook his head. "The asshole's even worse now. I think he's dated every model at my agency at least once since then."

Tae Hyun snorted. "That sounds like a lot of very disappointed women."

Yoo Mi laughed. "You have no idea. I'm surprised he managed to keep you satisfied."

Tae Hyun made a half frown. "If you want me to look happy, we should probably change the subject."

Yoo Mi waved off his concern. "It's far past time you got over him, Tae Hyun. I bet every KBR publicist hates him. I know ours sure do. He's lucky he's so good-looking."

"You should look up the pics of his old nose that mysteriously leaked online."

Yoo Mi's jaw dropped. "You didn't?" Tae Hyun allowed himself a brief smirk. "You little demon. I had no idea you had that in you."

Tae Hyun casually shrugged. "I was angry and heartbroken back then. I'd never do something like that now." Then he forced himself to smile. "And I am over him. But that doesn't mean I want to start working with him again. I carried that asshole for years. I'm not doing it anymore."

"You're not lying about carrying him. I assume you haven't listened to his album." Tae Hyun shook his head. "It's shit. He's got no charisma at all. And I don't think it even cracked the Top Forty."

"What's that old saying? You reap what you sow?"

Yoo Mi snorted. "Aren't you just the fucking philosopher. And, from what I've heard, Chang Min hasn't exactly been doing much sowing. What about Xiang? Have you talked to him?"

Tae Hyun nodded. "We talk here and there. To be honest, we're not all that close, considering how much time we spent together. Xiang's always been so private. But I know he was disappointed when I left the group."

"Do you think he knew about you and the asshole?"

Tae Hyun shrugged. "He never said anything if he did. I mean, he had to, right? I don't know how he could've missed it. I don't know how anyone missed it."

Yoo Mi shook her head. "You weren't nearly as obvious about it as you think." She flashed Tae Hyun a mischievous grin. "Not that it stopped half your fans from shipping you two, anyway."

Tae Hyun snorted. "Please, don't remind me."

"Don't get all straight and narrow on me now. You were just starting to get fun."

"I am who I am."

"More philosophy? Boo. Fine. You want to change the subject? Then let's talk about something interesting. What are you planning to tell KBR?"

Tae Hyun smiled. "I requested to become a solo artist."

"You want to go solo? Now that's interesting. Do you think they'll go for it?"

Tae Hyun shrugged. "Maybe. They did for Xiang and the asshole. But that was just while they waited for me to come back." Tae Hyun sighed. "At least Director Choo didn't outright tell me no."

"He'd be a fucking fool if he did. Xiang and Chang Min always held you back. You'll be three times the performer on your own."

Tae Hyun felt his ears warming from embarrassment and knew they were turning pink. "Maybe. I suppose we'll have to wait and see." Tae Hyun took a breath to center himself. "What about you? We've talked about me this whole time."

"What about me? I didn't disappear from the public view for two years."

Tae Hyun rolled his eyes. "But you disappeared from my view. How are you? Are you happy?"

Yoo Mi silently regarded him for several moments. Then she nodded. "Yes. Very. Surprisingly, I love him."

Tae Hyun frowned. "You're surprised about that?"

Yoo Mi smiled. "I'm surprised I fell in love. I never thought I'd have the chance. But I'm not surprised that I love him. He's kind, thoughtful, and a good listener. Everything you were, really. But he's also got a tongue that can make me scream." Tae Hyun nearly choked on his drink, making Yoo Mi chuckle. "Seriously. Every time I cum, it feels like the first time all over again."

02

Tae Hyun laughed. "If only we could all be so fucking lucky."

Yoo Mi reached out and put her hand on top of his. "I know you'll find someone wonderful, Tae Hyun. And I don't just mean someone who makes you scream when he tongues your asshole."

Tae Hyun laughed. "Not that I'd say no to that. This well has been dry for way too long. But I'm happy for you, Yoo Mi. And I only wish the best for you." He picked up his chilled vodka and offered a toast. "To your happiness."

Yoo Mi lifted her glass of chardonnay. "To both of our happiness. And to your future solo career."

03

Jason lounged on his sundeck, his eyes closed, as he soaked up the bright sunshine under an astonishingly blue sky. The offshore winds had blown the city's smog out to sea, creating the kind of day you usually only saw in drone-shot b-roll footage of Los Angeles. The sun's warmth felt glorious on his oiled skin, helping him sweat out all the drama from the day before. Well, the sun and the cut crystal low ball of Kingston warming on the small table next to his lounge chair.

Then a shadow fell over his face.

"Well, aren't you just the picture of Hollywood Hills bliss?"

Jason immediately recognized the voice of Naomi Bell, his business manager and sometime surrogate parent. He didn't have to open his eyes to know the expression on her face. "This is my first day off in three weeks. I've earned it."

"Mm-hmm." She didn't sound convinced. "Where's Lily?"

"No work today, so I sent her home. Plus, I couldn't stand her withering looks of judgment." Technically, Lily worked for Jason's company, which Naomi managed. But that didn't matter. Jason was still the boss.

Naomi laughed. "Then you're in for a real treat from me."

"I can stand your withering judgment just fine."

"Mm-hmm. Look, could you please physically join this

conversation? I feel like I'm about to scold my Thanksgiving turkey."

Jason sighed and opened his eyes. Naomi hovered uncomfortably close, holding out Jason's sunglasses. She looked great, as always. Her mahogany skin glistened in the afternoon sun, offset by the orange and cerulean, sixties-style mini dress she wore. Naomi had pushed back her naturally poofy black curls with a matching headband.

Jason took his sunglasses and put them on. Then he sat up and swung his legs to the side of the lounge chair. "Better?"

Naomi took a seat at the nearby patio table. "I'd feel better if you put some clothes on."

Jason scoffed. At only 37, Naomi wasn't old enough to be his mother. But she certainly acted like she was. "I invested a lot of effort in this body. I'm not gonna hide it." He pointed his thumb over his shoulder at the panoramic view of the LA basin. "If you don't want to look at me, look at that."

Naomi sighed, but she didn't look away. "$250 thousand."

One of Jason's well-manicured eyebrows peeked out from behind his sunglasses. Although she hadn't said so, he knew Naomi was talking about how much it cost to buy his way out of any potential lawsuits from his fight at the Sherman Oaks dive bar. He technically hadn't started it. Surfer Boy swung first. But Jason was a wealthy celebrity, so it didn't matter. And that was a lot of money. At least it wasn't his. "Are you serious?"

Naomi shrugged. "Paps are expensive."

"There were no paparazzi there. Josie would've beat them with her bat if she knew."

"Hence the secrecy. But your father wanted me to tell you how much your little stunt cost him."

Jason scoffed. "Why are you even talking to him? You work for me."

"Because you're not answering his calls. And because he showed up at my office this morning."

Jason frowned. A surprise visit from Gerald Park was rarely a good thing. "Shit. Sorry."

"Yeah. So next time you keep ignoring his calls, think about that."

Jason rolled his eyes. "What else did he say?" He held up his hand. "No, wait. Don't tell me. Stain on the family name? Wasted potential?"

Naomi chuckled. "Something like that."

Jason didn't bother admitting that he'd answered his father's initial call but hung up after the usual lecture on filial piety veered into one of his father's unhinged homophobic rants. Jason's parents had adopted a don't ask, don't tell policy regarding his being gay–a policy that he frequently and willfully violated. The resulting melodrama often felt like the only times his parents recognized who he really was or acknowledged their part in causing his trauma.

Jason picked up his Kingston, swallowed the rest, and stood up. "Want a drink?"

Naomi smiled. "Hell, why not?"

Jason carried his glass over to the bar cart under the shady overhang. He half-filled it with whiskey. Then he mixed Naomi a gin and tonic on the rocks and brought it over before sitting across from her.

"I assume ignoring your calls is what brought you here."

Naomi picked up her drink and took a sip. "It worked well enough for your father."

Jason snorted. "How did you get in, anyway?"

"I'm your business manager." Naomi smiled. "I have keys to everything your company owns."

Of course, she did. Jason sighed. But Naomi also made it sound like he couldn't be trusted to handle his own possessions. "Is this visit about BigCloud?"

Naomi took another sip of her drink. "Among other things. This is good, by the way."

Jason nodded. "Of course it is. I've been mixing them since I was ten."

"You've been drinking since you were ten?"

Jason scoffed. "No, I'm not a degenerate. I didn't start drinking until I was sixteen. It was for mom. Dad preferred a Manhattan. Let me know if you want one of those next."

"I'm fine. So, do you want the good news or the bad news?"

Jason sipped some of his Kingston. "The good news, obviously."

"BigCloud exercised your contract buyout."

Jason sighed. "Well, when it rains, it pours. So, what next?"

"That's just it." Naomi frowned. "I'm not sure what else is next."

Jason shook his head and sat back in his chair. He knew the view of his crotch stuffed into tiny black swim briefs would probably make Naomi uncomfortable. But he didn't care. "How is that even possible? There must be something else. I'm only 24, for fuck sake. I'm charming, handsome, and wealthy. Not to mention a damn good actor.

"Sure. Except you won't be wealthy for much longer."

"What?"

"I manage your books, remember? Even with the buyout, half of which they advanced you anyway, you're down to maybe a year left of this glorious lifestyle."

Hearing that felt like a slap in the face. A year? There was no way that could be true. He still had the residuals from his movies coming in. Was he really that bad with his money?

Jason swallowed the rest of his whiskey. He hadn't intended to drink that much, but it was turning into that kind of day. "Well, shit. So, now what? Commercials in Japan?"

Naomi shrugged. "I don't know, Jason. You need an image makeover yesterday. Especially yesterday." She turned away to look at the skyline view. "This city is full of young, charming, handsome actors. And right now, no one wants to hire you. Hell, even your agent won't take my calls now."

Jason scoffed. "Fuck Evan. I need a new agent anyway." Jason took a deep breath, forcing himself to calm down. "And that's the good news? Do I even want to hear the rest?"

"No. But I'm going to tell you anyway. Your father wants you to know that yesterday was the last incident he's paying for. Any more, and you're on your own."

Being cut off wasn't exactly the worst thing in the world. It's not like Jason lived on his father's money. But Gerald Park was the one who always bailed him out. Sometimes literally. If it wasn't for his father's quarter million, Jason would be looking at some seriously unflattering press coverage and at least a pair of high-dollar lawsuits. And he couldn't afford that sort of thing. Especially not if he was running out of money. "Shit."

Naomi set down her half-finished cocktail. "Look, I'm not trying to rain on your parade here. I'm just doing what you pay me to do."

Jason huffed. "And I can afford you for another year, right?" Naomi nodded. "So fucking find me something."

"Just because you can afford me doesn't mean I'll stick

around that long." Jason's jaw dropped. "What? Don't get all dramatic on me now, Jason. If you can't turn things around, I've got to think about my future. I'm coming up on forty soon. And, let's face it. You're not exactly a glowing reference." Naomi reached out and put her hand on Jason's knee. "I'm sorry to hit you with all this at once, honey. But we're at that point." She lifted her hand and sat back in her chair. "Honestly, commercials in Japan isn't a bad idea. They gave Summer Redding seven figures to do that campaign for that awful coffee soda." Naomi paused. "And there's always Seoul."

Jason shook his head, remembering his childhood trip to Seoul, fumbling over his half-remembered Korean while his family and their friends laughed and shook their heads. "No fucking way I'm subjecting myself to that. Just–" Jason stopped. He was breathing too heavily and needed to calm down. "Just find me something, Naomi. Please. I'll even sell a shitty Japanese soda if you can get me seven figures. Hell, even six."

"Alright, I'll keep looking." Naomi pushed her chair back and stood up. "But I've got to go. And I'm taking your car keys."

"What? Why?"

Naomi nodded toward his empty low ball. "If you're already day drinking, I don't want you anywhere near a driver's seat."

"What if I want to go somewhere?"

"Call me. I'll send a driver." Naomi turned and walked toward the open window wall that led to his upstairs lounge. "Don't bother getting up," she said with her back to Jason. "I'll show myself out."

Jason was tempted to pour himself some more bourbon. He settled for finishing off Naomi's gin and tonic instead. And he had another idea anyway. As appealing as drinking away his day sounded, Jason figured it was time to scratch another long-neglected itch.

Jason went inside and grabbed his phone off the coffee table. His father hadn't called again since that morning. And Naomi had only called twice before coming over. He opened his messages and scrolled down till he found the thread with Diego. Had it really been six months? Damn. Jason clicked into the message thread and started typing.

Hey sexy! You around today? I know it's last minute, but I could use your company.

To Jason's surprise, Diego started typing his reply right away. It showed up a moment later. *Hey J! It's been too long. Sure, I'm free today. I can be at your place in a couple hours.*

Maybe his luck was turning around? Catching one of the city's most sought-after and exclusive escorts on an off day like that was rare. *I'm so down. See you then.*

Jason smiled. Just the thought of their last hookup started Jason's blood flowing. His hand automatically went to his cock as it hardened in his tight swimsuit. No! Jason quickly pulled his hand away. If he was gonna drop five figures on a fuck, there was no way he was jerking off first. Jason went to his bedroom instead. He changed into workout clothes and went downstairs to his gym to spend an hour working off some of the booze. Then he spent the next hour trimming, cleaning himself, and taking a long, thorough shower. Diego didn't much care what his clients looked like. But he had high standards when it came to cleanliness. He wouldn't sleep with just anyone. It was part of his allure.

Diego arrived almost exactly two hours after his last message. Even though Jason had seen him many times, he was still blown away the moment he opened his door. Diego was simply gorgeous. He had a lustrous walnut complexion with skin so smooth his pores must've been microscopic. Diego's trim, athletic build made him look fabulous, clothed or naked. His deep brown eyes lit up every time he smiled. And Jason's eyes lit up as he imagined Diego's round, tight ass and perfectly-sized cock. Best of all, Diego was skillfully verse, so Jason never had to worry about whether he wanted to top, bottom, both, or neither.

Diego flashed Jason his winning smile. "Hi, baby." His thick, black hair was a little longer than the last time Jason had seen him. And his chin was covered in the faintest hint of a beard.

Jason sucked in his thick lower lip and bit down. "Damn. How do you always look so hot?"

Diego laughed. "Says the teen idol movie star. May I come in?"

"Shit, sorry. Yeah, please come in." Jason stepped back from the door to allow Diego room to come inside. "Do you want a drink? Or are you in a hurry? We can–"

Diego stepped forward and silenced Jason with a finger on his lips. "Shh. I've got plenty of time."

Jason nodded. "Okay, yeah." He glanced around his foyer as he hunted for something to say. "Then, I guess, maybe we can–"

"Are you okay? You seem nervous today."

Jason sighed. Did he? "Maybe. It's, um–" Nervous wasn't really his thing, But he was definitely acting scatter-brained. Jason lifted his hand to gently massage the back of his head. "It's been a rough couple of days."

Diego's thick lower lip poked out in a playful pout. "Ah, I see." Jason shivered as Diego softly ran his fingertips along

Jason's jawline. "Is that why you reached out? You need to blow off some steam?"

Jason slowly nodded, already caught in Diego's spell. "Yeah. I, uh–" He briefly shook his head to clear his thoughts. "I don't know. It's been so long, and I, uh–" Then he snorted. "Shit, Diego. You're making it hard to look cool here."

Diego chuckled. "Why are you even trying to look cool? It's me."

"I don't know." Jason frowned. "I guess I was hoping you could–"

"I think I get it." Diego reached out and took Jason's free hand. "Why don't you let me take charge this time?" Jason nodded. "Good. I assume the bedroom's in the same place?"

Jason chuckled. "Yeah."

Diego smiled as he gently tugged Jason's hand. Jason eagerly followed him through the upstairs lounge to the hall that ended in his bedroom suite. He had a moment of panic when he noticed he'd forgotten to make his bed. But Diego didn't say anything about it. He simply took Jason to the bed and gently pushed him down to sit on it.

"Take your shirt off."

Jason nodded, lifted his t-shirt over his head, and set it down on the bed.

"Now, take my pants off."

Jason nodded again, unconsciously licking his lips as he reached out and undid the button on Diego's pants. Then he slowly pulled the zipper down, revealing a thick mat of bushy, black hair. Jason smiled as he tugged on the waistband, pulling Diego's pants down and exposing his perfect cock.

Of all the people Jason had slept with–truth be told, it wasn't nearly as many as most people thought–he liked Diego's cock the best. It was an ideal length–six, maybe seven inches–and girth. It was easy to deep throat and felt great inside him. And it was already partly hard. Jason opened his mouth and–

"Ah, ah. Not yet, baby." Diego tapped his thigh. "You still have to take these off first."

Jason chuckled. "Sorry." He grabbed the waistband again, slid Diego's pants all the way down, and held on while Diego stepped out of them. Where were his shoes? Diego must've taken them off on the way inside.

"Okay. Now you can do it."

Jason smiled, biting his lower lip again as he savored the moment. Then he opened his mouth and leaned forward, taking in Diego's cock until his pubic hair brushed the tip of Jason's nose. Diego immediately let out a long, quiet moan. And Jason lightly suckled as Diego got fully hard in his mouth. He breathed in through his nose, inhaling Diego's sweet musk and the slightly woodsy scent of his body wash. Then Jason pushed Diego's foreskin back and ran his tongue over the tip, tasting the salty sweetness leaking out. Diego moaned as Jason swirled his tongue around and slowly rubbed the shaft with his hand. Then Jason felt Diego's hand on his head.

"Alright, baby. Now it's my turn."

Diego lifted his shirt off, revealing the ornately colorful phoenix tattooed across his chest. Jason watched the firebird settle before him as Diego knelt, undid Jason's fly, and gently yanked Jason's pants down. Jason also wore gray sports briefs–he hated going commando, especially in jeans–and expected Diego to take those off next. But Diego leaned forward and put his mouth on them, gripping Jason with his lips, warming him through the cloth with his hot, moist breath. Jason groaned and put a hand on Diego's shoulder.

He almost came right there. Maybe he should've jerked off after all.

Diego chuckled as he got back up. "Okay, maybe we'll hold off on that. Why don't you turn around and get on all fours?"

Jason eagerly nodded, sliding his briefs off before climbing on the bed and pointing his ass at Diego as instructed. It was clean and freshly trimmed. Jason was surprised at how much he'd let things go down there. Diego approvingly purred as he leaned in and pressed his tongue between Jason's cheeks. A delirious vibration shot up Jason's back as Diego's tongue danced and twirled. Jason's arms almost buckled, but he fought to stay upright as Diego worked his magic. Just when Jason thought he couldn't stand it anymore, Diego stopped and leaned back.

"My turn."

The two switched places. Diego's efforts had already steadied Jason's jangled nerves, so he eagerly returned the favor with his tongue, pressing and prodding it against Diego until he felt Diego's legs quiver.

Diego loudly groaned. "Oh, fuck yes. Get that tongue in there, baby." He abruptly reached back, gripped Jason's head, and yanked him forward until his neatly trimmed hair tickled the inside of Jason's bent nose. Diego grunted in time to Jason pulsing his tongue, pushing it into Diego again and again. And Jason ached with desire as Diego squirmed and moaned, his movements orchestrated by Jason's tongue. "Holy shit, Jason! You better fuck me right now. Right. Fucking. Now."

"Yes, sir."

Jason stood and reached for the bottle of lube he'd left on his nightstand. After lubing himself and Diego, Jason positioned himself against Diego and pressed the tip inside. His knees nearly buckled as his foreskin was pushed back, and another wave of ecstasy danced up his spine. He bit his lip, determined not to cum yet, and gently pushed himself all the way inside. Diego moaned low and deep as Jason pulled back and slowly pushed in again, building up his rhythm and speed until he felt his balls smacking Diego's backside. The pair grunted and moaned in a synchronous rhythm to Jason's thrusts. And Jason knew that he couldn't hold off much longer.

"I'm gonna cum, Diego."

"Do it!"

"I'm serious. If you don't want–"

"I said fucking do it!"

And then Jason came, loudly crying out as he emptied himself inside Diego, holding onto Diego's hips for balance as his body spasmed. "Holy shit, dude."

Diego laughed. "You're telling me." He glanced back at Jason, smiling, while Jason was still inside him. "Now it's my turn."

Jason smiled. "Yes, sir." He slowly pulled out, twitching each time his sensitive post-cum cock sent another electric buzz through his body. Jason grabbed a clean towel from the short pile on his nightstand and handed it to Diego. Then he grabbed a second towel to wipe himself down. "Do you want to keep going now, or do you need a minute?"

Diego grinned. "Oh, we keep going now. I'm a pro, remember?" He lay down on his back, stretching his arms out and dropping his legs over the side of the bed. "I know I'm in charge, but I'm gonna cheat a bit. I want you to sit on it."

"Yes, sir."

Jason grabbed the lube and squirted a generous amount

onto Diego. Then he poured some on his fingers and lubed himself as much as possible. Diego was the last person to fuck him, but that had been six months ago. Jason wasn't taking any chances. He climbed onto the bed, got on his knees, and straddled Diego's hips. Then he reached back to grab Diego's cock and slowly lowered himself onto it. The pressure was almost too much until Diego brushed against Jason's prostate, sending a torrent of dizzy bliss through Jason's body. He slowly let himself down until Diego was entirely inside him. Then he closed his eyes and savored the feel of Diego's perfect cock. When he was ready, Jason opened his eyes and looked down at Diego's handsome face.

Diego smiled. "Are you ready?"

Jason nodded and began to pump himself up and down until he relaxed. Then he leaned into the motion, increasing his speed until he bucked against Diego's hips, overcome with furious desire. Each of Diego's thrusts rang Jason's prostate like an alarm bell, sending jolt after tantalizing jolt through his body until he knew he'd cum again soon.

Diego seemed to notice and chuckled. "You're gonna shoot again?"

Jason nodded, breathless and nearly unable to speak. "Yeah. You?"

"Just waiting on you, baby."

"Show off," Jason huffed. "Better make it a good one."

Diego laughed, grabbing Jason's hips to take over, and pounded Jason until he could no longer hold off. Jason howled as he came all over Diego's chest. Diego kept thrusting until he finally cried out and unloaded inside Jason. Unable to stay upright, Jason finally collapsed onto Diego, panting as he tried to catch his breath. The two of them lay there, hot, sweaty, and contented, chest upon chest, until Jason finally shifted and rolled onto his back. He began to sit up, but Diego stopped him with a hand on his chest.

"I've got it." Diego got off the bed, grabbed another pair of towels, and handed one to Jason. "Is it alright if I go clean up?"

Jason nodded as he wiped himself down. "Of course."

Diego smiled as he went to Jason's bathroom. Jason got off the bed and went to the closest guest bathroom to clean off and shower. The cool water felt delicious, running over his warm and flushed skin. He always felt so calm and relaxed after Diego visited. That wasn't even the best technical sex they'd had. But it was more earnest and genuine than anything Jason had experienced in a long while. Once he was finished, he wrapped a towel around his waist and returned to his bedroom. Jason found Diego sitting in a towel on the bed, looking at his phone. But he smiled and put the phone down as soon as Jason walked in.

"You know," Diego admitted, "I enjoy my job. For the obvious reasons, of course. But I even surprise myself with how much I enjoy some of my clients. So, thanks for that."

Jason bashfully smiled. "You don't have to say that."

"I know."

Of course, he did. "Can I ask you something?"

Diego patted the space on the bed next to him. "Only if you sit down."

Jason chuckled as he sat next to Diego. But Diego scooted back and got onto his knees. Then he put his hands on Jason's shoulders and started working his thumbs into the muscles. "I noticed your shoulders tensing up a lot. This will help. Now, what did you want to ask me?"

Jason closed his eyes as Diego kneaded the knots from his shoulders. That's why you always go to a pro, he reminded himself. He didn't even realize how bad the muscles were. "Am I an asshole?"

Diego briefly stopped his massage. "Hmm." Then he quickly resumed. "I don't know that I can honestly answer that."

Jason sighed. "I guess that's a yes."

"No, it's not. You've never been an asshole to me. So if that's what you want to know, then no. You're not."

It was hard to ignore the unspoken end to that thought. "But?"

"But, it's a small town, Jason. I know others haven't been so lucky as me to experience this side of you."

Jason let out a slow breath. It wasn't quite a sigh because he knew he couldn't deny what Diego said. If Jason counted up all the people he was a dick to in the last twenty-four hours, it would take more than all his fingers.

"Have you thought about just coming out?"

Jason nodded. "Of course. I think about it every day. Hell, right now, it might even help my career."

"Oh, wow. Are things that bad?"

Jason chuckled. "I'm down to Japanese soda commercials at this point."

Diego quietly laughed. But Jason knew it was friendly. He didn't think there was a malicious bone in Diego's body. Then he wondered, as he usually did after hooking up with Diego, why they never dated.

"Well, that's better than Broadway."

Jason laughed. "Or dinner theater."

"Or cruise ship variety shows."

Jason snorted. "Cruise ships? For real?"

"Don't ask." Diego moved his thumbs to Jason's neck, gently working them over the stiff muscles holding his head aloft. "Look, I know I'm paid to say this, but I genuinely like you, Jason. You're great in bed, you take good care of yourself, and you take good care of me. I can't tell you how many rich assholes think I'm less than a person after I make them scream with the only pleasure they've probably felt in a year. Or try to bargain my prices down like they're doing me a favor."

Jason nodded. "Cheap fuckers. Like my dad says, you don't get rich by spending money."

"Then I'm glad you're my client and not him." Diego lifted his hands from Jason's shoulders and moved to sit next to him again. "Are you hungry? I'm hungry."

Jason turned to Diego in surprise. "Are you asking me out?"

Diego chuckled. "No, I'm offering to eat something with you. Off the clock."

Jason took a deep breath while he considered the idea. He liked Diego and would probably enjoy having dinner with him. But they'd have to order in. There was nowhere they could go together without being seen. And Naomi would kill him for being seen in public with an escort, no matter how much Jason liked him. If his father didn't first. That's why they never dated. "No, I've got something I need to do. But it was good to see you again."

Diego nodded. "Fair enough." He leaned over and kissed Jason on the cheek. "You know my number if you change your mind."

Diego got off the bed, picked up his pants, and stepped into them. Jason grabbed his phone from the nightstand and transferred the money for their session into Diego's account. Even knowing he was eating away at a tiny chunk of his remaining funds, it was money well spent.

04

Tae Hyun wasn't very surprised by the accuracy of Yoo Mi's prediction. The press totally ate up their Veil outing. So many bloggers and reporters were waiting for them when they'd finished their drinks that KBR had to send over a PR team to corral them all. The PR team also insisted that Tae Hyun make a statement sharing how happy he was about Yoo Mi's engagement just to limit the speculation about them getting back together.

And the press wasn't the only one eating it up. Yoo Mi was ecstatic. While Tae Hyun had no doubt that she honestly wanted to catch up with her old friend, he also knew how calculated she could be. And he was impressed that Yoo Mi had worked all that out just by running into him in the corridor outside Ji Hoon's office. Tae Hyun wondered if someone at KBR had tipped off Yoo Mi that he was there. But it didn't matter in the end. Tae Hyun had enjoyed talking with her, and his public presence had been given a welcome boost.

Ji Hoon called Tae Hyun the next morning and invited him to a meeting with KBR CEO Pak. So much for delaying things. Tae Hyun had only managed to put off the process by less than a day. Ji Hoon also had the style team send over an outfit for him to wear. The shirt was a purple so dark it was nearly black, reminding Tae Hyun of Yoo Mi's scarlet-black dress and making him wonder if it was a new fashion trend. Tae Hyun would've been more grateful for Ji Hoon's generosity if he didn't already know that it was just the KBR way. They wanted their idols to look good. But they didn't always want their idols to choose their own clothing. Thankfully it fit with Tae Hyun's tastes. He'd hated some of the flashier clothing he'd been made to wear, especially early on in his *XTC* career. Putting on his military uniform for the first time had almost been a relief. But the new shirt looked good on him, especially once he paired it with the dark gray skinny jeans that came with it.

KBR sent a car to collect Tae Hyun for his meeting. The driver met him in the car park below Yun Seo's apartment building. Tae Hyun was happy no one in the press had figured out he was living there yet. He was seriously out of practice dealing with the press and the public. And he knew KBR would want to work out his lingering contract issues before they set him loose on the world–at least on anything more than a very short leash.

When Tae Hyun saw Ji Hoon waiting in the KBR garage, it confirmed his suspicion that it would be a serious meeting. That didn't bother him as much as he'd expected. He'd spent years with Ji Hoon and his team by his side, managing nearly every aspect of his life. In many ways, it made adjusting to life in the military that much easier for him. In some ways, military service had given Tae Hyun more freedom.

Ji Hoon smiled as Tae Hyun climbed from the back of the car. "Tae Hyun! I knew you'd look good in that shirt. Have you eaten?"

Tae Hyun offered his manager a short bow as thanks. "Yes. You know me so well, Director Choo."

Ji Hoon clucked his tongue. "Again, with the formality? I suppose that's fine today since we're meeting with CEO Pak. But I'm serious, Tae Hyun. I may be your manager, but I've known you since you were sixteen. I'd say that has to count for something."

Tae Hyun smiled. "As you say, sir."

"Smart ass." Ji Hoon snorted. "Let's get you upstairs. We've got twenty minutes with the CEO, and I don't want to waste a moment of it." He led Tae Hyun into the waiting elevator and pressed the button for the sixteenth floor. "Speaking of which, I see you wasted little time catching up with Yoo Mi."

Tae Hyun nodded. "It was nice to see her again. I'm glad she's doing so well."

"Nice, indeed."

"You didn't have anything to do with our surprise meeting, did you?"

Ji Hoon grunted. "I may be a miracle worker, but even some things are beyond my control."

Tae Hyun chuckled. "Fair enough."

They arrived at the CEO's office just as he finished a meeting with another KBR staffer Tae Hyun didn't recognize. But Tae Hyun had no time to ask about them before CEO Pak's receptionist ushered them into his office. The CEO had his phone to his ear but still waved them in to wait as he finished his call. Publicly gregarious, Pak Jun Ho was a ruthless manager when it came to KBR's interests. Educated at a prestigious California university, Pak's ingenious combination of Korean-style business and American-style entertainment was often credited as one of the initial boosters of Hallyu, or the Korean Wave.

Ji Hoon and Tae Hyun silently waited until Pak finished his call. Tae Hyun tried his best not to look at the clock on the table behind Pak's desk, keeping his focus pointed at a random building in the distance outside Pak's expansive office windows. But Pak wrapped up his call a moment later and set his phone down next to his tablet. "Thank you both for waiting. My apologies for the delay."

Ji Hoon and Tae Hyun bowed. But Tae Hyun let Ji Hoon speak first. "Good morning, CEO Pak, sir. Thank you for taking the time to meet with us."

Pak dismissed Ji Hoon's greeting with a wave. "Yes, yes. Please sit. We have business to discuss, and I have a tight schedule today."

Ji Hoon and Tae Hyun both nodded in acknowledgment. Tae Hyun waited until Ji Hoon was seated before taking his seat.

"You received my proposal, sir?" Ji Hoon asked.

Pak nodded. "I did. I must admit, I was intrigued." He turned to Tae Hyun. "The Director tells me that you refused our request for an *XTC* comeback reunion, Tae Hyun."

Tae Hyun bowed his head. "Yes, CEO Pak, sir. I'm sorry."

Pak snorted. "If you were truly sorry, you would've said yes. But that's not why we're here. I don't know what happened between you and Chang Min. And, frankly, I don't want to know. But I also don't want to throw all the money we invested in you down the drain."

Tae Hyun nodded. "Of course not, sir."

"But I appreciate your request to record a solo album. And that little stunt you pulled last night with Sang Yoo Mi shows me that your fan base is still alive and well."

"As you say, sir."

Pak frowned. "But here's my dilemma. You've been away for nearly two years. Conservatively, we're looking at an additional six months to a year before seeing a new album from you. And I can't have that. Time is money, as they say. And we should use that time to our advantage. So here's what I propose. We put you in a movie."

Tae Hyun was stunned. He'd never expected something like that. "I don't understand."

Pak huffed. "Don't play coy with me, Tae Hyun. You understand perfectly. You're just surprised." He sat forward in his chair and placed his hands on his desk. "KBR has been looking to expand into long-form visual entertainment, and we've recently been given a chance to produce a movie. Yes, a movie role would require a certain portion of your time. But it gives us something to promote while you work on your album. And it keeps you in the public eye."

Tae Hyun felt the sudden urge to bite his lip, a habit he thought he'd kicked years ago. He gripped the arms of his chair instead. "Respectfully, sir, I'm no actor. I never even received any acting instruction as a trainee."

"That may be true. But how hard could it be? You acted as Yoo Mi's boyfriend for a whole year."

Tae Hyun felt the first flickers of concern creep through his composure. Of course, Pak would've known that the relationship was false. But Tae Hyun was suddenly unsure what else CEO Pak knew about him, his previous admission not to know notwithstanding. Was that a veiled threat? "Respectfully, sir, but–"

Pak loudly huffed. "Enough with all that. Speak plainly, Tae Hyun."

Tae Hyun wasn't sure he even could speak plainly with the CEO. But a command was a command. "You have to know that propping up a sham relationship through a few public appearances and social media posts isn't the same, sir. If I were to do a poor job acting in this movie, it would damage my public image more than help it."

Ji Hoon quietly cleared his throat. "If your concern is a lack of training, Tae Hyun, let us train you. We could find you an acting coach. The movie isn't scheduled to begin filming for a few months."

Pak nodded. "That's right. That would address your concern, yes?"

"As you say, sir." Tae Hyun took a slow breath while he found the courage to say the next thing on his mind. "And if I still decline to do the movie?"

Pak sat back and crossed his arms. Tae Hyun didn't find the move very encouraging. "Then you and KBR will part ways, Woo Tae Hyun. And I will wish you the best of luck in your future endeavors."

Tae Hyun had also considered that possibility. Going truly solo was a dangerous option. Sure, another company might be willing to take him on based on his history. But, without having an album ready, it could be a tough sell. Or, Tae Hyun could produce the album himself. But that would still require an income. Or backers. And Tae Hyun could just as easily spend a year finding that money on top of the time it took him to record the album. Not to mention the costs of a studio, recording engineers, studio musicians, and all the other perks that came with being part of KBR. Or, Tae Hyun could give up performing altogether. Of course, he wasn't trained for anything else beyond the food service he'd done in the army.

Tae Hyun was begrudgingly impressed with his CEO. While ostensibly agreeing to Tae Hyun's request to go solo, KBR still backed him into a corner. And Tae Hyun didn't see any way around it. "Of course, CEO Pak, sir. I accept."

The meeting had only used twelve of their allotted twenty minutes, so Ji Hoon opted to claim the additional eight minutes for himself. Tae Hyun excused himself, promising to wait for Ji Hoon in the third-floor private staff lounge. KBR also had a popular public cafe and lounge on the ground floor. They frequently used it as a controlled space for their idols to interact with the public. When *XTC* was rumored to be recording their second album, members of the *XTC Dream* fan club would wait in line for hours to sit with an overpriced coffee and pastry in hopes of catching a glimpse of Xiang, Tae Hyun, or Chang Min.

Tae Hyun grabbed a coffee and a packet of biscotti to consume while he waited for Ji Hoon. He'd picked up the practice while *XTC* had been in Italy on their first European tour. Several Korean biscuit companies had rushed their version of biscotti to market when they found out, hoping to catch a potential craze before it started. Since Koreans love their coffee, the idea took off like a rocket. Tae Hyun softly chuckled as he recalled being served biscotti at every press function for a year before he complained to Ji Hoon.

"Well, that's a laugh I haven't heard in a while."

Tae Hyun looked up to see Sun Se Yoon, one of KBR's choreographers and dance instructors, standing at his table. Tae Hyun quickly stood and bowed his head. "Se Yoon! I didn't know you'd be here."

Se Yoon laughed and clapped Tae Hyun on the shoulder. "Where else would I be, Tae Hyun? I'm not the one who mysteriously left."

Tae Hyun snorted. "It was hardly mysterious." He gestured to the empty seat next to him. "Join me? I'm stuck here waiting for Director Choo."

Se Yoon shook his head. "Sorry, I'm only here for a bottle of water. But I'll be in the studio all day if you want to stop by." Se Yoon smirked. "It's still in the same place too."

Tae Hyun chuckled. "Maybe I will."

Se Yoon winked as he walked away, leaving Tae Hyun standing alone in wonderment. It wasn't the first time the choreographer had gone out of his way to make friendly physical contact like that. But Tae Hyun was never sure if Se Yoon was being overly affectionate or actually flirting. He didn't even know whether Se Yoon was gay. But Se Yoon was undeniably gorgeous. He had a strong, flexible dancer's body, of course. And Tae Hyun was a sucker for broad noses and thick, kissable lips like Se Yoon's. What if the dancer really was flirting? Was that something Tae Hyun would even pursue? His head told him no. But a long-neglected stirring in his pants suggested otherwise. Still, it didn't matter. Tae Hyun was stuck waiting for his manager.

Then Tae Hyun's phone buzzed with a message from Ji Hoon.

Sorry, I have many arrangements to make. Take the rest of the day for yourself. I will meet with you again soon.

And, just like that, Tae Hyun was off the leash again. Or, at least, he'd been switched to a much longer leash. Tae Hyun dumped his untouched coffee and biscotti in the trash and went off to find Se Yoon's dance studio on the second floor. Although he hadn't been there for two years, Tae Hyun had been there many times before then. So he knew the way.

04

Tae Hyun peeked through the window in the door to see a dance practice still in session. Se Yoon, standing opposite the door, noticed Tae Hyun and waved him inside. Tae Hyun carefully opened the door and walked in, hoping to avoid disturbing the practicing performers. Once he heard the song, Tae Hyun knew they were the *DoubleDown Boys*, another KBR group about to make their official debut. Ji Hoon had sent Tae Hyun an advance copy of their debut EP *DoubleTrouble*. Tae Hyun really liked it.

DDB was six performers to *XTC*'s three. And they had another six dancers backing them up. Tae Hyun was a little envious as he watched the next generation of idols practicing, remembering his long-ago excitement for *XTC*'s debut. Their song was catchy, and their moves were fluid and tight. Tae Hyun was sure they'd do just fine.

Se Yoon stopped the playback when the dancers hit their final pose. "Good job, everyone. That was almost perfect. Jeong Mun, you still need to watch your footwork during the second chorus."

One of the performers nodded. "Sorry, seonsaeng-nim."

"Don't apologize. Just practice." Se Yoon smiled and looked at Tae Hyun. "And it looks like we've been joined by some KBR royalty."

Tae Hyun waved as everyone turned to face him. "Hello, everyone. That was a great routine. I can't wait to see it on stage."

After a series of bows and handshakes, Tae Hyun spent a few minutes meeting and chatting with the *DDB* performers. They all looked so young to him, even though he was only two years older than their oldest member. But they'd already mastered that tricky balance of polite, playful, fun-loving, and respectful that everyone expected of their favorite idols.

Tae Hyun posed for a few group photos before Se Yoon finally shooed everyone from the studio so they could get on with their packed schedules for the day. That left him alone with Tae Hyun. The dancer had already stripped off his sweatshirt, wearing only a loose, sleeveless t-shirt and a pair of black sweatpants. Tae Hyun caught himself checking out Se Yoon's smooth, tight body and forced himself to make eye contact.

"Those guys are excellent."

Se Yoon nodded. "That's because people like you set the bar so high. What happened to your meeting?"

"Canceled." Tae Hyun grinned. "Why? Has your invitation to visit already expired, seonsaeng-nim?"

"You know you're always welcome in my studio." Se Yoon smiled, grabbed a towel from the stack on a nearby table, and mopped up the sweat on his brow. "How long has it been since you last performed?"

Tae Hyun snorted. "You know the answer to that as well as I do."

Se Yoon smiled, making a show of giving Tae Hyun a blatant once-over. "Still, you look like you've kept yourself in shape."

Tae Hyun smiled at the compliment, wondering again if Se Yoon was just being overly friendly or if he was actually flirting. "I've done my best. But I'm nowhere near the shape I was in back then."

"Maybe you'd like a personal session?"

Tae Hyun carefully considered his response. Flirting was a delicate art form, and he was long out of practice. Se Yoon was his senior, and saying the wrong thing could easily offend him. Tae Hyun had always known his dance instructor to be cheerful and friendly. But you could be cheerful and still be straight. Fuck it. Tae Hyun took a step forward. "That depends on what the lesson is for today."

Se Yoon's face gave away his mild surprise. But Tae Hyun didn't see any anger. "You've been away for a long time. You must be out of practice."

Tae Hyun nodded. "I am. But I'm anxious to change that."

"Anxious?" Tae Hyun nodded. Se Yoon draped the towel over his shoulder as he walked across the studio, his bare feet hardly making a sound on the wood floor. He stopped when he was barely a hand's width from Tae Hyun's face. "How anxious, exactly?"

"Very."

Se Yoon let the silence between them linger for a long, delicious moment. Then he grabbed Tae Hyun's hand.

"Come."

Tae Hyun let Se Yoon pull him across the studio toward a door opposite the mirrored wall. Se Yoon opened the door and pulled Tae Hyun inside the spotlessly clean washroom. Then he let go of Tae Hyun's hand, grasped him by the arms, and pushed him against the tiled wall.

"Still anxious?"

Tae Hyun gulped and nodded. Se Yoon smiled. Then he leaned in and put his mouth on Tae Hyun's, making Tae Hyun's heart flutter. He parted his lips to allow Se Yoon's probing tongue inside and breathed in the dancer's warm, slightly musky scent. It drove him wild. All the while, Se Yoon kept his hands on Tae Hyun's arms, holding him in place. Being there, knowing that someone could walk in and discover them at any time, felt dangerous and wrong. And it made Tae Hyun feel alive.

Se Yoon moved from Tae Hyun's mouth to his neck, gently kissing the spot just below Tae Hyun's ear. A shiver of excitement rippled through Tae Hyun's body and made his cock jump.

"Oh, hyung," Tae Hyun softly moaned.

Se Yoon chuckled but didn't stop. He let go of Tae Hyun's arm so his hand could wander down Tae Hyun's stomach to his crotch. Tae Hyun almost jumped when Se Yoon took hold of his cock through his pants, but he fought the urge to squirm and push Se Yoon away. What they were doing was definitely wrong. But Tae Hyun didn't want to stop.

After one last kiss on Tae Hyun's neck, Se Yoon dropped to his knees. He undid Tae Hyun's pants and pulled down his underwear. Tae Hyun's erection sprung out, already dripping wet. Se Yoon lightly gripped it, gently pulling back the foreskin before running his tongue along the tip.

Tae Hyun's eyes rolled back as he fought to keep his knees from buckling. He groaned, all thoughts of propriety suddenly forgotten. Then he took hold of Se Yoon's head, guiding it toward him as the dance instructor took Tae Hyun into his mouth.

"Fuck."

Se Yoon let Tae Hyun take control, guiding his head forward and back until Tae Hyun was fucking Se Yoon's warm mouth. Then Se Yoon used his tongue to tease the head until Tae Hyun knew he'd climax soon.

Tae Hyun tried to push Se Yoon away, but Se Yoon wouldn't let him. "Hyung, I'm about to cum."

Se Yoon grabbed Tae Hyun's hips and forced Tae Hyun all the way into his mouth. Tae Hyun tried to keep from cumming, but the sensation was too much. He let out a muffled animal cry as he erupted onto the back of Se Yoon's throat. Then he nearly collapsed. Only Se Yoon's hands on his hips kept him upright.

Se Yoon backed off Tae Hyun's cock. Then he smiled and made a show of swallowing Tae Hyun's cum. "I've waited a long time to do that, Tae Hyun. Thank you."

Tae Hyun felt the familiar wave of guilt wash over and threaten to overwhelm him. It was impossible to avoid, drilled into him growing up the child of conservative parents in a conservative society. But Tae Hyun tried to push the feeling away. He'd done nothing wrong. Their illicit liaison was only wrong in the eyes of others. Between them, it was fine. Tae Hyun finally managed a smile, focusing instead on the welcome feeling of bliss that also came after release. "I've always wondered. But I had no idea. You should've said something."

Se Yoon chuckled. "You know as well as I do why I never did." He took the towel from his shoulder and handed it to Tae Hyun. "But I'm glad you finally said something. And if you ever feel anxious for another private session, I hope you'll think of me."

05

Jason climbed from the back of the chauffeured SUV into the lingering, late summer heat, stopping to check his reflection in the blacked-out window after he closed the door. It had been more than a week since he'd last been on set, and the haircut he'd gotten from the production's stylists had finally grown to an acceptable length. Jason had repeatedly told them it was too short, but they obsessively kept it that length anyway. He actually liked the haircut otherwise–a skin fade on the sides and back blending into a chunky razor cut that looked good gelled into spiky anime-hero peaks or slicked back and wet. But he'd known it would look better if it was just a little longer. A week's worth of growth proved him right.

Jason flashed himself a quick smile before tapping on the window to let the driver know he was done using it as a mirror. He didn't recognize the driver, but they'd obviously chauffeured enough celebs around to know not to pull off until told. Then he turned around and walked to the entrance of the Century City office building where his company leased its office suite.

Naomi had texted Jason that morning to tell him she was sending a car at eleven. Be ready, she instructed him in no uncertain terms. After spending a week sequestered in his Hollywood Hills home, Jason was more than ready for an outing. Even if it was just to his business office. He'd spent his days down in his gym or out on the sun deck. He'd spent his evenings with a bottle of Kingston while he rewatched all his old movies. It would've been pathetic if it also hadn't helped keep him from wallowing in whatever funk he was stuck in. And Jason didn't have anywhere else to go that felt safe anyway. His father may have bought his way out of a front-page picture on the *Flipside Magazine* gossip blog. But Jason had been a troublemaker long enough to know that the paps would still smell the blood in the water and be out in force, waiting for him to make another appearance and fuck something else up. And Jason knew himself well enough to know that he absolutely would.

Jason's housekeeper had gotten so irritated with him always being around that she kept finding something to clean on the opposite side of the house. And Lily had quit twice. The first time, she'd walked in on him after he'd passed out on the couch in the upstairs lounge wearing only a jockstrap. The second time they'd gotten into a screaming match about his refusal to answer any of her calls. Then she called him a royal asshole, told him to go fuck himself, and stormed out. Jason assumed that was why Naomi had summoned him to her office. Hopefully, she'd at least give back his car keys.

Jason ignored the building receptionist as he crossed the lobby and went straight to the elevators. After a brief moment of confusion, Jason guessed that his office was on the eleventh floor and hit the button. Thankfully, he'd guessed right. His company's suite of offices was at the end of the corridor.

"Good morning, Mr. Park. Ms. Bell is expecting you."

Jason didn't recognize the receptionist sitting at his front desk. Had it really been that long since he'd been to the office? But he was cute for a white guy, with lightly tanned skin, short, light brown hair, bright hazel eyes, and a great smile. Jason was tempted to ignore him just like he had with the receptionist downstairs. But this one actually worked for him, and Jason really needed to stop being an asshole to his employees. "Thanks, uh–"

"Steven."

An easy name to remember. Even easier to forget. Jason decided to pull out the charm. He frowned, bashfully rubbing the back of his head just like his character from the *Monday Night Club* movies. "Oh, yeah. Sorry, Steven. It's been a rough week."

Steven nodded. "It's alright, Mr. Park. Ms. Bell told me what's been going on."

Jason let his mouth curl into the slightest grin. "Enough with that mister business. It's Jason."

Steven smiled. "Ms. Bell also told me that if you ever did that thing with your hand on the back of your head, I should remind you that I'm not here to sleep with you. Jason."

Jason chuckled as he lowered his hand. He had no doubt that Naomi had him pegged. But that was a little too on the nose, even for her. And it only made Jason want to try harder. He liked it when they didn't make it too easy.

Jason leaned forward and put both hands on Steven's desk. While he was careful to stay out of Steven's personal space, Jason still gave him a perfect view of his chest and torso through the unbuttoned opening at the top of his shirt.

"And do you always do as your told, Steven?"

Steven kept his expression neutral. But Jason still caught the downward flicker of his eyes. And he definitely saw Steven lick his lips. Then Steven nodded. "Always."

Jason grinned. "That's what I like to hear." He stood up and made a show of brushing some nonexistent dust from the side of his pants, knowing that it would drag Steven's gaze downward to his crotch. "Keep up the good work. I'll just show myself in."

Steven nodded again, staring at Jason as he walked to Naomi's office door and let himself in. "Knock, knock."

Naomi's office had originally been Jason's. But they quickly realized he had absolutely no need for an office. So she took it over, and they sublet the extra space to the company next door. The retro wood paneling and olive green shag carpeting suited her style much better than Jason's anyway. And Naomi had style to spare that day in her melon silk crepe jacket with its matching silk blouse.

Naomi smiled when she saw Jason. "Right on time."

Jason nodded as he sat in a chair facing her giant white desk. "So, Steven seems nice. Is he new?"

"Seriously, Jason?" Naomi snorted and shook her head. "You're such an asshole sometimes. Steven's worked here for a year."

"For real?" Jason shrugged. "What can I say? I'm a shitty boss. Speaking of which, I assume Lily called you."

Naomi nodded. "I already deposited her final paycheck."

Jason raised an eyebrow in surprise. "She's not coming back?"

"No, not this time. But that's not why I asked you to come in." Naomi smiled. "I received an offer for you and wanted to discuss it in person."

Jason winced. "That bad?"

Naomi shook her head. "No, not a bit. Remember when you said you'd do a Japanese commercial for seven figures?"

Jason laughed. "No way. Did you really find me one?"

"No." Naomi smiled. "This is better. You'll be an acting coach."

"Wait." Jason's smile disappeared. "What?"

"You said it yourself, right? You're a damn good actor." Naomi shrugged. "So why not put those skills to work?"

Jason shook his head. "I still don't get it. Please spell it out for me like I'm a day-drinking actor who's somehow washed up and over the hill at twenty-four."

"Fine. Your uncle called me. They have an idol in Seoul that they want to put in a movie. But they want him trained first."

An idol in Seoul? That didn't sound right. Or, like it had anything to do with Jason. "Don't they have acting coaches in Seoul?"

Naomi shrugged. "You know how it is with your family. Your uncle called your father. Your father gave him my number. Your uncle called me."

"Which uncle are we even talking about? You know they use that term a little more loosely than we do."

"Ji Hoon Choo. Or Choo Ji Hoon, I suppose. I believe he's married to your mother's sister. And he's a managing director at KBR."

"No shit. Uncle Ji Hoon?" Jason had vague memories of meeting someone who was an up-and-coming manager at KBR when he last visited. But that had been a decade ago. "So, that's what this is? More nepotism?"

"Sure, but it's six-figure nepotism. And it's only a three-month gig."

Jason huffed and let his head fall back as he slid down in his chair. "Three fucking months in Seoul?" He grabbed his chair's arms and pulled himself upright. "No fucking way, Naomi. I already told you. I mean, I could maybe do a commercial there. Or even a K-drama guest spot. But three months? Hell no."

"Stop being such a baby. You spent almost that long in Hungary filming that horror movie."

Jason shrugged. "Budapest is hella fun. And why can't they fly him here? If he wants a Hollywood acting coach, shouldn't we do it in Hollywood?"

Naomi frowned. "Look, Jason. I already hear you whining and shying away from a real opportunity. So, let me be frank. You need this gig. It's an actual paying job. And it's more money than you've made in the past year to do something you're good at. Without this money, I'll have to start looking into liquidating some of your assets."

"What?"

Naomi shrugged. "I told you yesterday you're running out of money, Jason. That's why I didn't try talking Lily into coming back. But this money could buy you at least another year. Maybe more." She sat forward, clasping her hands on her desk. "And the change of scenery might actually do you some good. Have you even left the house since I last saw you?" Jason shook his head. "See? You already know how it is out there. This will get you out of town long enough for the paps to forget about you and focus on some other self-destructing young starlet." Naomi paused in that parental way, waiting to be sure her tough love message hit home. Then her expression softened. "And is Seoul really that bad? It's the new entertainment capital of the fucking world."

Jason started chewing on his lower lip. Naomi was probably right. No six-figure deals were waiting for him at home. Just a string of failed movies and expensive habits. Jason felt like he didn't have much choice. Like Naomi said, it would buy him some more time. But he had a complicated relationship with Korea in general and Seoul in particular that Naomi wasn't fully aware of. Still.

"How much are we talking about?" Jason's jaw dropped when Naomi told him.

"I know, right? He didn't even try to bargain." Naomi shook her head. "I should've asked for more. But it's half up front, half at the end."

"Who's the idol?"

"Tae Hyun Woo."

The name sounded familiar. But Jason wasn't as much of a K-pop groupie as he used to be. "I don't think I know him."

"Sure, you do. He was the T in *XTC*.

"No way!" Jason definitely knew who *XTC* was. He'd scored VIP tickets and a meet and greet for their first LA concert. Jason had actually shaken Tae Hyun's hand. And he jerked off to pictures of him for a week afterward. "I thought he quit the group?"

"He did. Supposedly to perform his military service. But that's over now. And KBR is looking to drum up some publicity for him while he gets back into music."

Jason snorted. He'd often wondered how things would've turned out if his parents hadn't come to the States. Would he have become another cog in the Korean entertainment machine? Jason knew the stories. Yeah, your company took great care of you. But they asked for fucking everything in return. And Jason didn't imagine he would've survived something like that for very long. It was bad enough hiding his sexuality from the US press. But at least he could still fuck pretty much whoever he wanted to. As long as he was careful. Sure, Korea had come a long way when it came to being queer since—Wait.

"Supposedly? Do you know something here that I don't?"

"About this?" Naomi shook her head. "No, not a damn thing. It was just an awfully convenient situation. I mean, who drops out of a world-famous pop group during its fucking prime to head off to feed orphans or whatever?"

Jason chuckled. "So you think there's maybe something there?"

"Of course there is." Naomi snorted. "We've both been in the business long enough to know there's always something there."

Jason had a hundred more questions. Who would watch the house? What about his cars? Did he need a work visa? Where would he stay while he was there? And Naomi patiently answered all of them. In the end, Jason couldn't think of any good reasons to pass it up beyond his stupid stubbornness regarding a promise he'd made to himself when he was fourteen. Even after a decade to soften and mellow, the memories of his last visit to his parent's homeland were still sharp enough to cut. Never again, Jason had told himself. He'd never return. And yet, here he was arranging to do just that.

After Jason signed the contract, a visibly excited Naomi sent him on his way with a promise to deal with all the necessary arrangements. Of course, she was excited. Naomi had bought herself another year of employment while sending her asshole boss overseas for three months. And she still hadn't given him back his car keys.

Jason lit a cigarette as soon as he was back outside. He really wanted to get a drink, but he couldn't think of anywhere in Century City that was dark and seedy enough. There had to be somewhere, right? Plenty of shady backroom deals happened in Hollywood's shadow. He briefly entertained the idea of heading back to the Sherman Oaks dive bar to see if those poser surfer bros were back. But that would be stupid, even for him. The last thing Jason needed was to end up in jail when he was supposed to be winging across the Pacific. Besides, Jason was willing to bet a chunk of his new money that Naomi had instructed the driver to take Jason home no matter what he said. That was probably for the best.

Once he was back in the SUV, Jason popped his earbuds in and pulled up the music video for *XTC's* final single, *Blossom*, on his phone. The music totally banged, and the video was stylish and, honestly, ahead of its time. The group had just hit its peak, both in popularity and performance ability. The choreo alone was enough to make Jason sweat. And Tae Hyun was the obvious centerpiece. With his narrow waist and broad shoulders, Tae Hyun was just twinkish enough to be called a boy next door without really being all that boyish. And he could really fucking sing. Tae Hyun's vocals were tight and sharp. His voice was smooth and sultry with immense power.

Jason smiled, shaking his head. He couldn't sing for shit, despite the vocal training his parents had insisted on when he was a preteen. Then he replayed the video, intently watching the boys' near acrobatic dance moves. Jason didn't realize they'd stopped at his house until the driver said something. He offered the driver a mumbled apology and thanks, not taking his eyes off his phone until he stood at his front door.

Jason tore himself away from his essential research long enough to change into shorts and a t-shirt. Then he grabbed a beer from his refrigerator and sat on the couch in front of the giant TV in the upstairs lounge. Jason pulled up the video streaming app, found the *Blossom* video, and played it again. Then he worked his way through *XTC*'s impressive video catalog. They had a lot of music for a group that had only performed for a few years. KBR must've poured a ton of money into video production.

After finally exhausting their supply of music videos, Jason watched all the interviews he could find with the group and with Tae Hyun alone. He was regularly surprised by how much different musicians were during their interviews than when they were onstage. That's where the personality differences between the three guys were more noticeable. Or at least the differences between their *XTC* personas. Jason knew well enough that the public persona of an actor, musician, or any other performer was rarely how they were in private. He was a prime example of that himself.

Even in their interviews, Tae Hyun was still the group's centerpiece. His friendly, infectious smile made him seem light-hearted and joyous. Xiang, who always sat on the left, was the serious one. He always seemed ready to roll his eyes at what the other two said. Chang Min was the bad boy, cracking jokes and poking fun at the others. Of the three, Jason was sure Chang Min's public persona was most like his real personality. This seemed even more apparent when Jason found a fan service video with the boys on a camping trip on Jeju Island. As the three played several drinking games on camera, Jason noticed that Chang Min drank far more heavily than the other two. His behavior got a lot worse throughout the video, to the point where even the perpetually good-natured Tae Hyun was clearly getting irritated. Jason was surprised that KBR had even put the video out until he noticed that it was uploaded by an apparent *XTC* fan, who must've pirated a copy before KBR deleted it.

Then Jason was startled by his doorbell. He'd gotten so far into the weeds watching behind-the-scenes and fan service videos that he hadn't noticed the sun falling low enough to cast a blushing glow throughout the room. He glanced at his beer to see that he'd hardly touched it. Damn. But who was at his door? Jason used the remote to activate the door's security camera. Steven? What the hell was that boy doing at his house?

Jason went to the door and pulled it open. Steven stood on Jason's doorstep, eerily mimicking Diego's pose from a week ago. He'd changed out of the suit and tie he'd been wearing at the office into a mesh tank top and tiny running shorts. Steven had looked older in his business attire. But Jason could see that Steven was actually younger than him in his twink outfit. Was he even twenty-one?

"Hey, Steven. What's up?"

Steven smiled and held out a set of car keys. Jason's keys. "Naomi asked me to get these to you."

Jason frowned as he reached out and took the keys from Steven's hand. "Really?" He supposed Naomi wasn't above asking her receptionist to do a little legwork. Especially since Lily was no longer on the payroll. Still. "That's weird."

Steven's smile turned a little bashful. "Well, to be honest, she didn't ask me to bring them myself. But I thought I'd do it anyway."

05

Ah, of course. Jason had flirted with Steven at the office. And Steven used it as an excuse to visit Jason's house. "I thought you always did what you were told?"

Steven seductively narrowed his eyes. Then Jason caught him licking his lips again. Did Steven do that on purpose? Did he even know he was doing it? "Well, sometimes it's important to know when to break the rules."

Jason couldn't help but smile. It took a lot of guts to show up at your employer's house uninvited, dressed in your best fuck-me shorts. Had Jason spent the afternoon drinking as he'd intended, he had no doubt that he'd entertain little Steven's movie star fantasy despite the risk of what Naomi would say. Or, worse, what Steven's friends would say when he told them he'd gotten fucked by Jason Park.

But Jason had spent the afternoon getting hooked on a particular K-pop performer and had Woo Tae Hyun on the brain. "Sorry, Steven, this is definitely not one of those times. But, thanks for bringing me my keys."

Then Jason shut the door.

06

The flashbulb storm erupted before Tae Hyun even opened his mouth. But his smile never faltered. Momentarily blinded by the lights, Tae Hyun focused on where he imagined the reporters' faces would be until he could make out the video cameras filming him.

"Of course, I'm thrilled to be here. The *DoubleDown Boys* are super talented, and I've really enjoyed listening to *DoubleTrouble*. So I was excited to be invited to their release party."

"Tae Hyun! You were just seen out with your old girlfriend, Sang Yoo Mi. What can you say to fans who've suggested that you two might be getting back together?"

The press at KBR's event had all been vetted, so Tae Hyun expected the question and had an answer ready. "I can say that I care for Yoo Mi very much, and I'm happy I finally had a chance to congratulate her on her engagement." Tae Hyun's PR team had carefully constructed his answer so that it didn't include an actual denial, leaving fans free to ship him with Yoo Mi in their blogs and fanfics. But it was still an honest answer. "I wish the couple happiness and good fortune."

"Tae Hyun! When will you announce your next project? So many *XTC* fans are hoping for a comeback reunion."

"I love all my fans. And I love the *XTC Dream*. I can't wait to announce what's coming up next for me, but I have to for now." Tae Hyun playfully pouted and held up a finger heart. "I'm sorry. Please don't be mad."

Several reporters laughed, but it sounded good-natured. Tae Hyun enjoyed the chance to flex his charm a bit. Despite his initial worries, he'd quickly slipped back into the old rhythm KBR had drilled into him with years of training. Then another reporter called out his name, but Tae Hyun held his hand up. "I'm so sorry. I love talking to you all, but I have to share this time with many others. And to the *Dreamers*, I love you!"

Tae Hyun stepped toward a pair of waiting handlers, who ushered him behind a nearby curtain while the next idol was given a chance to speak to the press. Ji Hoon waited for him backstage.

"That was excellent work, Tae Hyun. You haven't lost your touch."

Tae Hyun smiled and offered a slight bow. "Thank you, sir. I was worried right up until I got my first question. Then all the old habits came right back."

Ji Hoon patted Tae Hyun on the back. "See? You're still a total professional."

Tae Hyun knew Ji Hoon was being extra nice to him because of his blow-up during their meeting earlier that day. That's when Tae Hyun learned who his new acting coach would be. He wished he'd reacted a little better to the news. But Tae Hyun was who he was. And asking questions, even if they were uncomfortable, helped him understand what he was dealing with.

"I'm sorry, sir, but why an American?" Tae Hyun frowned.

"Are you telling me you couldn't find any Korean acting coaches?"

Ji Hoon impatiently clucked his tongue. "Jason is Korean, if not by birth, then by heritage. And his manager assures me that he speaks Korean with near-native fluency. Besides, you speak English, too."

Tae Hyun nearly scowled and fought to keep his expression neutral. It was bad enough being forced into a movie role. But to be trained by an American actor whose name he didn't even know? That was pushing things. "But—"

"Jason's experience makes him particularly suited for this position, Tae Hyun. And I'll remind you he's my sister-in-law's son before you say anything careless."

"Yes, Director Choo, sir." Tae Hyun's words were respectful, but his tone was ice-cold.

Ji Hoon huffed. "Oh, don't start with all that again." He threw his hands in the air, obviously annoyed with Tae Hyun's frequent complaints. "Honestly, I'd think you'd consider showing a little more gratitude! You're getting exactly what you asked for, remember? And all it's costing you is a chance to boost your profile even further. Maybe you should consider that."

Tae Hyun knew he'd pushed things too far and immediately bowed to Ji Hoon. "I'm sorry, Director Choo, sir. You're right. I'm being ungrateful."

Tae Hyun's contrition seemed to mollify his irate manager, at least for the moment. "That's better. Because we haven't even talked about the movie soundtrack yet. Don't you think KBR would want you to perform at least a few songs on it?"

Tae Hyun hadn't considered that. He'd been so focused on how much he didn't want a movie role. Of course, he'd want to contribute to the soundtrack. At least, once he'd seen the script. That part still bothered him a bit. Tae Hyun thought it was unusual to cast him before they'd even told him what the movie was. All he knew was that it was a period romance. But he didn't have any experience in the film industry, so he could've been wrong. It wasn't like he'd had any say in the songs on *XTC*'s first album. And Tae Hyun reminded himself to trust Ji Hoon and CEO Pak. They wouldn't push him into something they didn't think he'd be successful at. It didn't make good business sense.

Tae Hyun returned his attention to the backstage mirror, checking his hair and makeup for the final time before getting ushered into the event. A KBR stylist had transformed his grown-out military cut into something edgy and cool, shortening the sides and artfully distressing the top with a razor. Then they'd bleached a section in the front to add a purple streak. It had been so long since Tae Hyun wore that much makeup that he almost didn't recognize himself. He looked at least two years younger than he had that morning. And he loved how the eyeliner and mascara made his lashes look so lush and thick.

But the best part was the suit. Tae Hyun had worried that his stylists would try fitting him into something loud and flashy like he'd worn back in his *XTC* days. But his new style was a little more mature. Tae Hyun wore tight black pants over chunky black combat boots and a dark purple jacket woven with a subtle black pattern paired with a black turtleneck. Would purple be his new signature color? That wouldn't be so bad. And he loved how the jacket over-emphasized his broad shoulders, giving his body a nice v-shape. The stylists finished Tae Hyun's look with a chunky, silver, curb-link chain necklace and simple silver hoop earrings. Unfortunately, they had to re-pierce his ears for those.

Once he was out among the crowd, Tae Hyun grabbed an unknown cocktail from a server's tray to carry around. KBR's idols had strict limits on their alcohol consumption, as much for the calorie count as for the potential for trouble. Those rules technically didn't apply to Tae Hyun anymore, but he'd learned early on that public events were no place for excessive drinking. Better to do it in private, if at all. But appearances mattered, so he'd sip from his drink every few minutes just to look like he fit in.

Tae Hyun began working the room, starting on the near side and making his way across. KBR had rented one of the ballrooms at the giant Park Grand Hotel near their headquarters in Daechi-dong. Their event team had worked their magic with hidden lights and giant video projections, turning the room into a hip, stylish nightclub for the night. And a DJ he didn't recognize spun a deep, soulful house remix of *Sapphire Emblem*'s recent single *You Make Me Weep*. Tae Hyun could feel the pounding bass in his chest.

A large crowd had already gathered in the ballroom. Tae Hyun knew some of the people in attendance, including Viki and Min Ji from *Cherry Squad*, who he ran into right away. The all-girl group launched a few months after *XTC*, so they were contemporaries.

"Hi, Min Ji," Tae Hyun said. "Hi, Viki."

Min Ji and Viki still wore their trademark cherry red hair color. Min Ji wore hers as a wig cut into a bob, although it looked expensive, and matching false eyelashes. Viki wore cherry red extensions threaded into her tightly braided black hair. Viki, who was from the Philippines, had been discovered during KBR's annual *Treasure Idol* TV competition. She was also half-Black and one of the rare Black faces in an industry that borrowed heavily from Black American culture.

"Tae Hyun!" Viki replied and lightly tugged at one of his sleeves. "You're looking totally fresh. I love this look on you."

"Yeah," Min Ji agreed. "It's much more grown-up than what I remember you wearing before."

Tae Hyun felt his ears warming from their praise. "Thanks. It's my new style era, I suppose. Have you two been here long?"

"A little bit," Min Ji replied. "We've been hiding out over here to avoid those jerks from *DAZ3*."

Viki laughed. "Don't listen to her. She's just mad that Do Hyun keeps hitting on her."

Tae Hyun snorted. "I'm surprised. After what happened at the Video Music Awards that one time–"

"Right?" Min Ji huffed. "They never fucking learn."

Tae Hyun nodded. "Why are they even here? I thought this was a KBR event."

"Who knows?" Viki shrugged. "Maybe KBR is buying their label."

That would've been interesting, given that they were also expanding into film production. Did they somehow come into a lot of money while Tae Hyun was away? But it would help explain why the *DoubleDown Boys* had scored such a lavish release party for a debut. All in, Tae Hyun guessed that at least a dozen groups and their handlers and reps were in there. Including the press, the many KBR staffers, and the handful of other celebrities and superfans in the room, the party held at least two hundred people.

Tae Hyun spotted Xiang standing nearby, so he excused himself from the *Cherry Squad* girls to walk over.

"Hyung! I can't believe you're really here."

Tae Hyun smiled as the former *XTC* maknae pulled him into a hug. Xiang was dressed in a sharp black and white plaid jacket over a red shirt and white tie, with red leather pants and white boots. He looked great. And thankfully, he was dressed nothing like Tae Hyun, so there were no subliminal reminders of *XTC*. But Xiang had never been much of a hugger. Was it a new thing for him? Or had Xiang been drinking?

"Of course, I'm here. Didn't Ji Hoon tell you I'd be coming?"

Xiang let go and stepped back. "Are you kidding me? I've hardly seen our illustrious manager at all this week." He winked. "Apparently, some hot new idol's been taking up all his time."

Tae Hyun smirked. "I have no idea what you're talking about. How've you been? What have you been up to since we last talked?"

"I've been shooting a music video, actually. We decided to do a separate video for the Chinese-language version of my last single." While Xiang was Korean by birth, his parents had come from China, so he also spoke fluent Mandarin. And he'd recorded Chinese-language versions of all the songs on his last album so KBR could take advantage of the booming Chinese pop market. "What about you? You look great, by the way."

"Thanks! So do you. And I've been up to absolutely nothing yet. It's been nice having some time to myself. But I think that'll change soon." Tae Hyun took a careful sip of his drink.

Xiang grinned. "So then the rumor I heard about you going solo is true?"

Tae Hyun nearly did a spit take. "Where did you hear that? It's supposed to be secret."

Xiang laughed. "I didn't hear a damn thing. I was just guessing. But now I know it's true."

"Damn it, Xiang." Tae Hyun frowned. "That's not fair. I didn't want you to find out like this."

"It's fine. Really. I never expected *XTC* to get back together anyway." Xiang shrugged. "And I'm totally okay with it. My solo stuff is doing really well."

Tae Hyun let out a relieved sigh. "Well, I still wanted you to hear it from me. Just, not like this."

"Yeah, I know. But you have to know it's not really me you need to worry about, right?"

Tae Hyun snorted. "Whatever. Chang Min is the least of my worries."

Xiang smiled. "Good. Because he's coming over here right now."

"What? You'd better not be–"

"Well, hello, boys!" Chang Min stepped up next to them. His hair had been bleached and colored a fiery orange-red. His stylist had also dressed him in a plaid jacket. But Chang Min's plaid was red and black tartan, and his jacket had small metal spikes on the shoulders. His stylists had given him heavier eyeliner than Tae Hyun's and some contouring to sharpen his round cheekbones. As much as Tae Hyun wanted to punch Chang Min in the face, it was still a handsome face. "Are you two starting the comeback reunion without me?"

Tae Hyun could smell the alcohol on Chang Min's breath. Of course, his glass was already empty. Tae Hyun had often suspected that Chang Min was one of the inspirations behind the no-alcohol rule. He frowned despite himself. Tae Hyun hadn't seen or spoken to Chang Min in nearly two years. And he'd known that his fellow idol and former lover would be at the party, so he'd spent an hour on the treadmill at home to burn off some of his anticipated anger before the event. But, even then, Tae Hyun could barely contain his mounting rage.

Something over Tae Hyun's shoulder seemed to catch Xiang's interest more than the storm quickly brewing in front of him. "Oh, look. There's someone way over there that I should talk to right now. I'll see you both again soon, I'm sure."

Chang Min frowned as Xiang walked away. "What was that about? Were you two talking about me?"

Tae Hyun shook his head. "No, we were only saying hello. Despite how much you might believe it, the world doesn't revolve around you."

Chang Min snorted. "Damn, hyung, I was only kidding. Did you leave your sense of humor at home?"

"No, I left my sense of humor in a Tokyo hotel room. Or did you forget about that?"

"Shit." Chang Min let out an exasperated sigh. "That was two years ago, hyung. How long will you hold that over my head?"

"I'll hold it over your head forever. And stop calling me that!"

Chang Min's face fell. Tae Hyun hadn't meant to sound so forceful. But at least it scored him a point. "I'm sorry, sunbae-nim. Just like I'm sorry about that night. And for everything. You know I'll do whatever it takes to make it up to you for our comeback. I promise."

"There's not going to be a comeback. We haven't announced it yet, but KBR is going to release my solo album."

Chang Min's jaw dropped. "What? Are you fucking with me right now?"

Tae Hyun shook his head. "No. Now, I've got to–"

Chang Min grabbed Tae Hyun by the arm. "You can't do this to me, hyung. I need–"

Tae Hyun jerked his arm from Chang Min's grip. "I told you not to fucking call me that. Now get your shit together. We're in front of a hundred people and a hundred cameras right now."

Chang Min stood dumbfounded while Tae Hyun walked away. As bad as he'd expected their reunion to be, it had been so much worse. Not that he thought Chang Min would be okay with the news about their comeback. But he definitely hadn't expected Chang Min to call him hyung like everything was okay between them. And then make a fucking scene in front of everyone, too. What an asshole.

Tae Hyun set his drink on the bar as he walked by and escaped into the washroom. He hadn't realized how warm the party had become until he was hit by a wall of ice-cold air. His turtleneck may have looked great. But it was fucking hot. He needed to splash some water on his face, but he didn't want to ruin his makeup. So Tae Hyun settled for washing his hands in cold water.

Chang Min burst in just as Tae Hyun ran his hands under the wall drier. "Sunbae, please."

Tae Hyun groaned. "Look, if you want to talk about it, fine. But not here."

Chang Min stomped over to Tae Hyun's side. His expression hovered somewhere between despondent and furious. "Well, I want to talk about it now, damn it. I've already waited for two fucking years."

"Then another day or two won't matter. Because I'm not doing this now."

"You don't understand, hyung. I need this." Chang Min reached out and put his hand on Tae Hyun's shoulder. "I need you."

Tae Hyun grabbed Chang Min's wrist, yanked it behind his back, and shoved him face-first into the shiny white tile wall. "I already told you," Tae Hyun growled. "I'll never work with you again after what you did."

Chang Min struggled, so Tae Hyun twisted his arm enough to get him to stop.

"Look, I know I fucked up. But it was one time. It was just a mistake."

"One time?" Tae Hyun leaned in close to Chang Min's ear. "I'd have to be an idiot to believe anything you say." Tae Hyun relaxed his grip on Chang Min's arm but didn't let go. "I'm going to walk out of here now. Don't follow me. And don't speak to me here again. Understand?"

Chang Min nodded, so Tae Hyun let him go. Then he turned away from his ex-lover, put a smile on his face, and returned to the party. Someone had already cleared his drink away from the bar, so Tae Hyun grabbed another from a roaming server. Then he drank half of it in one gulp.

"That bad, eh?"

Tae Hyun lowered his glass to see Yoo Mi standing before him. She'd pinned her long hair up in an elaborate knot with a pair of Chinese-style Ji. And her body-hugging, fire-red gown was embroidered with golden dragons. "Wow. You look stunning."

Yoo Mi smiled and offered Tae Hyun a slight bow. "Thank you. But are you alright? I saw the asshole follow you into the restroom just now."

"He did." Tae Hyun snorted. "Did you come to rescue me?"

"If necessary. Or help you hide the body."

Tae Hyun laughed. "Neither is necessary. But I appreciate the thought. Are you here alone?"

Yoo Mi shook her head. "No, I'm here with Seong Woo, of course. He's around here somewhere." She playfully slapped Tae Hyun on the shoulder. "But stop changing the subject. What happened with Chang Min?"

Tae Hyun snorted. "What do you think happened? He asked about our comeback reunion and pretended everything was somehow fine between us now."

"But you set him straight? So to speak?"

Tae Hyun chuckled. "I did. Then he followed me into the washroom for another go. He tried apologizing, but he only sounded anxious and desperate. I think he was genuinely surprised to hear that there won't be a comeback."

Yoo Mi nodded. "Well, you didn't hear this from me, but word has it that KBR is about to cut him loose. His solo material hasn't been selling at all despite some really aggressive marketing."

"Ah." Tae Hyun nodded. "Of course. And he was waiting for me to come rescue his career. Well, that's too fucking bad."

"Are you sure you don't want to get back together with me?" Yoo Mi smirked. "I like this evil side of you. It's hot."

Tae Hyun shook his head. "I'm not being evil. I just don't care if he succeeds or fails. Either way, I'm not about to sacrifice my happiness for his success."

"Coming from someone who sacrificed his happiness for my success." Yoo Mi lifted her glass. "Thank you."

Tae Hyun clinked her glass with his. "That was hardly a sacrifice. And you never lied to me." Then he took a sip from his drink instead of a gulp. Yoo Mi had calmed him enough that he didn't have to get drunk anymore. "Oh, I almost forgot. Do you know the American actor Jason Park?"

Yoo Mi nodded. "From the *Monday Night Club* movies? Sure. I actually met him once at a fashion show in New York. Why? Are you boyfriend shopping already? Because I don't think he's your type."

Tae Hyun scoffed. "Hardly." He wanted to share the news about his movie role, if only to commiserate with Yoo Mi. But he didn't want to ask her to keep yet another of his secrets. The news would come out soon enough anyhow. "Apparently, he's Ji Hoon's nephew."

"Oh, that's interesting."

Tae Hyun frowned. "Why is it interesting?"

Yoo Mi shrugged. "Well, he's American, for one. And he's well known for being a bad boy. But he was nice enough when I met him. And he's a good actor. You know he won the Best Actor award for *The Moon Shines Madly*?"

Tae Hyun remembered that movie well. It was about the son of poor Korean immigrants forced to deal with American racism, aging parents, and his own mental illness. It had done well in Korea for an American film that didn't have any superheroes in it. And Tae Hyun thought Park's performance was powerful and moving. He'd talked about it for weeks afterward–enough so that Chang Min even got jealous. He'd even wondered after the fact if it was what spurred Chang Min's cheating. But, no. It turned out Chang Min had been cheating on him the whole time. Still, Tae Hyun was surprised he hadn't made the connection when he heard Jason's name from Ji Hoon. "No. I didn't realize that was him. And what do you mean by bad boy?"

Yoo Mi rolled her eyes. "Oh, you know. Parties, drinking, getting into fights, and getting bailed out by his wealthy father. The usual American movie-star stuff."

Tae Hyun struggled to reconcile that with what he remembered of Park from the film. At least it was a sign that he was indeed a good actor.

The room's lighting slowly shifted as the background music faded out. Tae Hyun glanced at the performance area to see people gathering nearby. "Looks like it's time for the show. Are you staying?"

Yoo Mi shook her head. "No. This is only our first stop tonight."

Tae Hyun smiled. "Look at you, as busy and in demand as ever. But I'm glad I ran into you again."

"Me, too." Yoo Mi leaned in and gave Tae Hyun a small peck on the cheek. "Take care of yourself. And if you end up needing help hiding the body, call me."

07

Jason was surprised by how quickly he made it through customs at Incheon. After the hassle of dealing with an international departure at LAX, he'd expected it to be much worse. Jason had enjoyed a relatively painless fourteen-hour flight, half of which he slept through thanks to his personal cocktail of Kingston, a sleeping pill, and a muscle relaxer. He'd spent the other half getting so worked up flirting with one of the flight attendants that he had to make a special solo trip to the first-class lavatory. And his arrival at Incheon was a model of ruthless efficiency, dumping him on the South Korean side of immigration control barely twenty minutes after getting off the plane.

Jason's first challenge was navigating the unfamiliar airport using the dual Korean/English signage. Naturally, being in Korea surrounded by other Koreans, Jason's brain reverted to some base programming that favored Korean signage over English. Unfortunately, Jason was terrible at reading Korean on the fly. He could speak it and understand it just fine. But reading it required concentration and effort, neither of which Jason was particularly in the mood for. And by the time Jason found his luggage carousel, he was thoroughly annoyed. At least no one there seemed to recognize him. Jason had narrowly avoided a notorious reporter from the *Hollywood Hush* blog outside the LAX international terminal. But he still ended up signing a handful of autographs and posing for a pair of photos inside. Jason blended in better in Korea. And he wasn't nearly as famous as he was back home.

Jason found Ji Hoon waiting outside the arrivals area next to a black-suited staffer holding a tablet that said J. Park. Jason quietly chuckled, guessing there were probably a dozen other J. Parks on his flight. But it was the only sign he saw in English, so it was clearly meant for him. And Jason recognized Ji Hoon from the picture Naomi had given him anyway. He vaguely remembered meeting his uncle when he was last in Seoul. Dressed in a sharp, gray double-breasted suit, Ji Hoon looked every bit the successful executive. But he definitely looked older than Jason remembered him.

Ji Hoon smiled when Jason approached him. "Welcome to Korea," he said in English. "I trust you had a smooth flight?"

"Smooth enough." Jason offered Ji Hoon his hand, then quickly pulled it back. "Wait. Do we shake hands? Or am I supposed to bow?"

Ji Hoon laughed and gave Jason a friendly clap on the arm. "Either is fine, but don't worry about that for now. Let's just get you to the car, shall we?"

Ji Hoon had brought along a second helper in addition to the sign-holder, also wearing a black suit. The two handled Jason's luggage, leaving him free to follow Ji Hoon unencumbered to the exit doors. Jason reached for his cigarettes the moment he stepped outside.

"Ah." Ji Hoon shook his head. "I'm sorry, that's not allowed here."

Jason frowned. One of his childhood memories of Seoul

was how everyone seemed to be smoking. "Where is it allowed?"

Ji Hoon turned and pointed to an outdoor shelter near the taxi stand. "There, I believe." Then he gestured toward a glossy black sedan pulling up to the curb. "But our car has already arrived."

"Shit." Jason shook his head and stuffed his cigarettes back into his pocket. He was closing in on eighteen hours without one. Another hour wouldn't kill him. "I guess then maybe I'll wait."

Ji Hoon's helpers loaded Jason's bags into the car's trunk while Jason and Ji Hoon climbed into its tastefully opulent rear seats. As they pulled away from the curb, Jason took a moment to turn his phone back on. It had been off since he took off from LAX the day before. Once it finally connected to the local wireless network, Jason received a handful of notifications, mostly from Naomi, giving him the final updates on his trip. As annoying as Naomi could sometimes be, Jason was grateful to still have her as his business manager. She was every bit as ruthlessly efficient as Incheon customs. Jason would've never agreed to spend three months overseas without her handling things back home. He replied to Naomi's message asking him to let her know he'd made it to Seoul safely. Then Jason stuffed his phone back in his pocket. When he glanced at Ji Hoon, Jason saw him doing the same thing. Like uncle, like nephew, right? Not that they were actually related. Or, really, alike in any other way. Unless Ji Hoon also really wanted a drink.

"So, it's been a while since we've seen each other, eh?"

Ji Hoon looked up from his phone and smiled. "Indeed it has. You were but a boy then. But I remember it well. Even then, I thought you would turn out to be someone special." Jason smiled despite being sure that Ji Hoon was blowing smoke up his ass. He'd already signed the contract. There was no reason to make a thing out of it. "Have you truly not been back to Seoul since then?"

"That's right." Jason didn't feel like explaining his vow to never return. At least to someone like Ji Hoon. Especially after he'd just broken it. "I got that part in the first *Monday Night Club* movie a few years later. And I've been working ever since."

Ji Hoon nodded. "So I've heard. When I spoke to your father, he couldn't say enough about what a fine actor you've become. I'm sure he's very proud of you."

Jason snorted. So, Ji Hoon was gonna blow smoke up his dad's ass, too? "I appreciate you wanting to speak so highly of my father. But we both know him. I don't think we need to pretend he's someone he's not."

"Of course. Honestly, I don't know him all that well, except by reputation. But, as you might say, that reputation is what it is."

Jason nodded. Gerald Park's reputation as a cunning, ruthless businessperson was well deserved. After he and Jason's mother had emigrated to California, Gerald had taken a small nest egg and turned it into a vast fortune. As a result, Jason had grown up highly privileged and wanting for nothing. Except for a loving family.

"So, when will I get to meet Tae Hyun?"

"Very soon. We're on our way to the office right now."

"Right now? Don't I get to clean up and settle in first?"

Ji Hoon smiled. "There'll be plenty of time for that later. I'm anxious for you to meet Tae Hyun right away."

Jason didn't like being thrown in feet first like that. But he was at Ji Hoon's mercy for the time being. Or, at least, for as long as he was riding in Ji Hoon's car. "Alright, fine. Naomi said you'll handle my accommodations?"

Ji Hoon nodded. "That's correct. I thought it would be best if you stayed with Tae Hyun. At least initially."

Jason frowned. "I thought I was coaching him, not babysitting him."

"I'm sorry, I don't believe I know that particular phrase."

Based on his flawless English, Jason highly doubted Ji Hoon was being truthful. But he didn't know how to say babysitting in Korean either. And he didn't have the energy to bother explaining it. "Never mind. It's not important."

"Very well. It would be best if you got used to speaking Korean as soon as possible. I assume you're tired from your flight, which is why I'm speaking English now. And Tae Hyun also speaks English. But the film and script will be in Korean, of course."

"Naturally. I haven't actually seen the script yet. What's the movie?"

Ji Hoon smiled. "We're filming a Korean remake of *The Long Evening Sunset*."

Jason scoffed. "You're kidding, right?"

"I'm not." Ji Hoon frowned. "You disapprove?"

"Disapprove?" Jason took a deep breath as long-suppressed anger threatened to upset his already unstable mood. "You're lucky I don't have you turn the fucking car around right now and take me right back to the airport."

Ji Hoon's frown deepened. "I'm afraid I don't understand."

Jason fought the sudden urge to just throw himself out onto the highway. There was no way he'd just signed a three-month contract and flown halfway around the world to teach some Korean idol how to act in a Korean remake of a movie he'd been famously fired from. Fresh off winning his Best Actor award, *The Long Evening Sunset* was supposed to cement Jason's transition from teen comedies to dramatic leading roles. Instead, it had become the beginning of the end of his career. "I don't know what you're playing at here, Ji Hoon. But I seriously don't like it."

Jason could see that Ji Hoon was flustered from the apparent redness in his cheeks. Did he really not know why Jason was upset? "I'm sorry for my confusion, Jason, but I assure you we meant no offense. Your prior experience with the role was one reason we could pay you so well."

"Are you honestly telling me that you didn't think hiring me to work on the Korean remake of a movie that ruined my career would be upsetting? Is that what you're saying right now, Ji Hoon?"

"I am." Ji Hoon's expression was neutral enough that Jason couldn't tell if he was being sincere. "I'm sure that after you–

Jason held his hand up. "Don't. Just–" He sighed, unsure if he wanted to scream or cry. Of all the movies they could've picked, it had to be that one? "Don't. We can talk about this again later when I'm not so filthy, tired, and hungry. Just take me to your office, give me a drink, and introduce me to Tae Hyun."

Jason turned to the window without waiting for Ji Hoon's response, knowing that if he looked at Ji Hoon again, he was liable to do or say something he couldn't come back from. Instead, he pulled out his phone and fired off another message to Naomi.

I already hate it here

Jason was surprised to see Naomi typing a response right away. It had to be the middle of the night in LA. She must've deliberately stayed up, knowing that Jason would have some sort of complaint.

Suck it up and do the job

Jason frowned. Of course, Naomi would say that. It was probably in her quick replies list.

The movie is The Long Evening Sunset

Jason waited as the typing indicator flashed on and off before a quick series of replies appeared.

Shit

I'm sorry. I didn't know

They must've changed the title

Of course, Naomi hadn't known. There was no way she would've dumped Jason into that mess unprepared if she had. But that didn't change the fact he was still in that mess. Jason started to reply when another message came through.

I know you probably don't want to hear this but maybe this is your second chance to get it right

Jason sighed. Naomi was right. He didn't want to hear that. But Jason didn't want to admit that Naomi was also probably right about the other thing. So he put his phone away and looked out the window, staring at the passing scenery as they drove toward Seoul. Jason wondered about bailing on the whole deal right then and there. Sure, the contract probably had some penalty clause in it. Naomi would know. But she'd already told him to stick it out. And it was a lot of money. But was it worth it? The universe was clearly fucking with him, throwing him into a scenario where he'd finally have to reckon with his past actions. Hell, that story would probably make an even better movie. Look at the failed Hollywood golden boy who'd somehow managed to pull the rug out from under his own career! Then again, was it really that much worse than a Japanese ad campaign for a coffee-flavored soda or flashy sports drink? Fuck it.

By the time they pulled into the garage under the KBR building, Jason had managed to calm down enough that he thought he could at least carry on a civil conversation. Since no one came to open his door, Jason opened it himself and stepped out.

Ji Hoon joined him a moment later. At least his lingering concern looked genuine enough. "Is everything alright, Jason?"

Jason shrugged. "It is what it is." He nodded toward the car. "What about my bags?"

"They'll be waiting for you at Tae Hyun's apartment. Shall we head upstairs? I believe you said something about a drink?"

Jason forced himself to smile. "Now you're speaking my language, Ji Hoon."

Ji Hoon led Jason into the elevator and took him to the twelfth floor. KBR's headquarters was stylishly efficient for an office building. Glossy posters and vivid digital displays covered the corridor walls, showing off KBR's impressive catalog of bright young pop stars. Despite being well into the evening, plenty of people were still hard at work. Global entertainment was a twenty-four-seven business, after all. Ji Hoon's office had a decent view of the Gangnam district, which felt more like Manhattan than LA. Jason hated Manhattan. At least Ji Hoon's office also had a wet bar. Ji Hoon gestured toward a seating area just inside his office while he went to his bar.

"Please, have a seat. What will you drink?"

Jason plopped himself in a soft, upholstered chair. He was finally sitting still for the first time in what felt like forever. "Do you have Kingston?"

"I'm afraid I have no bourbon. The closest I have is scotch whiskey."

"That'll work."

Ji Hoon nodded as he poured Jason a generous serving of an unknown scotch from a crystal decanter. At least Koreans had a strong drinking culture. If they'd been in LA, it would've been just as likely for Ji Hoon to offer Jason a fucking smoothie. Ji Hoon smiled as he handed Jason his drink. "Tae Hyun should be here soon."

Jason nodded before swallowing a mouthful of scotch. "Fantastic. I can't wait to–"

"I'm here now, actually."

Jason looked toward the door in surprise to see the famous Woo Tae Hyun. Jason had enough experience meeting other celebrities to know they rarely looked the same in person as they did in touched-up photos or videos. But, even after an entire day of watching his performances and interviews, Jason found Tae Hyun to be the rare exception. If anything, he looked better in person, dressed in a simple gray button-down and expensive jeans that showed off his narrow, athletic frame. Tae Hyun's jaw was stronger than Jason remembered. His cheekbones were sharper. Tae Hyun was taller than Jason expected, too. And the fresh purple streak in his recent haircut made him look edgy without looking emo.

Jason had thought Tae Hyun was hot since they'd first shaken hands. Standing in Ji Hoon's office doorway, Tae Hyun was more than simply hot. He was a gorgeous creature sculpted from talent, passion, and drive. But he looked angry.

No, not angry, exactly. Reserved? Maybe. Or stoic. Jason couldn't peg his exact expression, but stoic seemed to fit. Unlike the many videos Jason had watched, where Tae Hyun had been cheerful and effortlessly charming, his expression was pure ice. That couldn't be a good thing. And they were supposed to live together? Suddenly Jason was even less sure that would work out.

Still, Jason knew he had to play nice. KBR had thrown a lot of money his way for Tae Hyun's benefit. And if Jason was really gonna use that as a chance to right some past wrongs, then he'd better do it right. He set his glass down on the nearby side table, stood from his chair, and offered his hand as he walked over to Tae Hyun. "Hi. I'm Jason."

Tae Hyun gave Jason an obvious once-over and frowned. Jason had clearly failed to meet the pop star's expectations, whatever those may have been. Maybe Jason wasn't the only one in the room upset about his coaching gig. Tae Hyun ignored Jason's hand, offering him a simple bow instead. "Hello. I'm Tae Hyun. It's a pleasure to meet you."

Jason almost laughed. Nothing about Tae Hyun's frosty tone or stiff body language said their meeting pleased him. Jason couldn't remember the last time he'd gotten such a chilly reception from someone who didn't already know him. Unless he did. Jason reached out with his extended hand and patted Tae Hyun on the arm. "We've actually met before."

Tae Hyun recoiled so hard from Jason's touch he nearly fell backward. "We have?"

Something had that boy wound up tighter than a drag queen's corset. Jason tried putting a little warmth in his smile. "Yeah, when you were still with *XTC*. It was backstage at your first LA concert during the VIP meet and greet."

Tae Hyun frowned, accentuating his thick, pouty lips. "I'm sorry. I don't remember that."

Of course, he didn't. It was years ago. Jason probably would've forgotten about it, too, had their positions been reversed. And Jason knew that was when he should let it go. But it was the first sign of emotion he'd gotten from Tae Hyun, good or bad. And the long flight to another country, the news of the movie they'd be working on, and Tae Hyun's adorably irritating standoffishness had conspired to push all of Jason's troublemaker buttons. "It's alright." Jason tilted his head and flashed a devilish grin. "I do."

Tae Hyun quickly composed his face, returning it to a carefully neutral expression. It would've been maddening if he wasn't so damn pretty. And Jason would have to work a little harder to crack Tae Hyun's icy shell. But it was Tae Hyun's move, and Jason wasn't about to break first. So the pair stood in awkward silence, letting the tension build for several long moments while Ji Hoon anxiously hovered nearby. Then Tae Hyun finally spoke again.

"I appreciate you coming all the way to Seoul."

Jason shrugged. "It's no problem. I'm not filming anything at the moment."

Tae Hyun nodded. "Yes, I read that your latest project was recently canceled."

Oh, so Tae Hyun really had come to play after all. "Did you?" He smiled again and carefully stepped into Tae Hyun's personal space. "Been reading up on me, have you?"

Tae Hyun didn't move, but his expression didn't change, either. "Yes."

Jason snorted. He rarely met someone so immune to his charms. It was annoying and delightfully challenging. Jason had already gone too long without any satisfaction. That would have to change.

"Tell me. Are you always this much of a dick? Or is this warm and cozy welcome meant just for me?"

Tae Hyun pushed his well-shaped brows together. "Excuse me?"

Jason smiled and took another small step forward. "You heard me."

Ji Hoon suddenly swooped in. He probably would've jumped between them if there had been room. "Tae Hyun," he said in Korean, "I'm sure he only meant–"

"I know what he meant," Tae Hyun snapped, switching to Korean. "I can speak English." Tae Hyun dramatically frowned as he shook his head. "I'm sorry, sir, but I don't know what you expect me to learn from this American except for poor hygiene and bad manners."

Jason chuckled. "I admit that my manners are poor," he said in informal Korean, leaning in close enough that he could feel Tae Hyun's warm breath on his face. "but you can hardly hold it against me that I just got off a fourteen-hour plane ride." Jason grinned as Tae Hyun's mouth fell open. "What? They didn't tell you I can speak Korean?"

Tae Hyun huffed and leaned in close enough that their noses were almost touching. Finally, Jason was getting a genuine reaction from him. The tension between them was so electric that Jason almost couldn't stand it. "If you're so Korean, you should know to address me with respect."

"Is that what you want?" Jason lifted his chin in a deliberate show of disrespect. "Do you want me to order you around like my little hubae? Because, if you do, then I could make this really interesting."

Tae Hyun pressed his lips together so tightly they turned an even brighter shade of red. He leaned back and turned to his manager. "This isn't going to work, sir. Please find me someone else." Then Tae Hyun turned his back to them and stormed out of the office.

Jason remained there for a few moments, silently savoring his victory, before returning to his chair. "Well, that went well," he said, reverting to English. "Now what?"

Ji Hoon closed his eyes and gently massaged the bridge of his nose. Then he walked over to Jason and sat in the chair next to him. "May I be frank with you, Jason?"

Jason shrugged. "Sure."

"Although I didn't anticipate your reaction, I understand you're upset after learning about the movie. For that, again, I apologize. But I know enough about your situation to know that you need this to work out as much as I do. And your behavior isn't helping things."

Jason snorted. "My behavior? After seeing all that from mister stick up his ass, you think my behavior was the problem?"

Ji Hoon shook his head as he clasped his hands and sat forward in his chair. "Are you telling me you haven't been contrary and argumentative since I picked you up at the airport?"

Jason frowned. Uncle or not, who was Ji Hoon to talk to him about his attitude? He hadn't flown all that way to get lectured by another surrogate parent about being nice to his bratty cousin. Jason could've stayed home for that. But the fact remained that Ji Hoon was probably right. Jason had been spoiling for a fight even before Tae Hyun had set him off. And Jason had deliberately taunted Tae Hyun just to get a rise out of him. "Alright, fine. Maybe I came on a little strong."

Ji Hoon nodded. "I agree that Tae Hyun's behavior was unfortunate. While this doesn't excuse his actions, I know he's guarded because he's quite sensitive. He had a falling out with one of his former group members that was serious enough to permanently change both their career trajectories. Naturally, he'll be cautious when meeting someone new."

Of course, he'd be. Jason still didn't know what had happened to Tae Hyun that made him leave his group and join the military. But he knew a thing or two about guarding himself. And, as Naomi has said, there had to be something there. "I see."

"And," Ji Hoon frowned, "I suspect that Tae Hyun mistakenly believes he's older than you."

"Older than–oh. You think so?"

Ji Hoon shrugged. "As I said, it's only what I suspect. Normally, as a foreigner, your use of informal language is something most of us would overlook. But you look and sound Korean. And were you actually from Korea, what you said would be very insulting. "

Jason sighed. Sure, he'd gotten what he wanted. But his satisfaction had quickly faded, replaced by a pang of sudden guilt. Naomi told him to suck it up and do that job. Maybe he should? Maybe it really was a second chance for him to get it right. And he was already doing his best to get it wrong. "Fine. What should I do?"

"You could start by apologizing. And being more open-minded."

"So I should bow and call him sunbae?"

Ji Hoon shook his head. "No, that's not what I mean. You're

his elder, so it wouldn't be appropriate. But a little respect would still go a long way." Ji Hoon stood, went to the wet bar, and poured himself a drink. Then he swallowed it in one go before wiping his mouth with the back of his hand. "Honestly, if I'd known you both would fight me so hard on this, I might never have arranged it. Not that I have any right to be surprised. On a certain level, you're both very much alike."

Jason snorted. "You think so?"

Ji Hoon nodded as he poured himself a second drink. "You're both talented. You're both charming and hot-headed. And you're both willing and able to weaponize your charm to get what you want."

Jason chuckled. "Ouch."

Ji Hoon shrugged before sipping from his glass. "I've been in this business a long time, Jason. And, yes, I know that sounds cliché. But the fact remains that Tae Hyun needs this as much as you do. So maybe you could remind him of that, too. Nicely."

08

After his angry march from Ji Hoon's office, Tae Hyun found himself in the private staff lounge. He wasn't sure why he'd gone there or even how he'd gotten there. He'd been so upset that he hadn't paid attention to where he was going. At least it was late enough in the evening that the lounge was mostly empty. Tae Hyun hated stewing in front of others, and he had a lot of stewing to do. So Tae Hyun hotly paced back and forth, ignoring the curious glances from the few KBR staffers who were present.

Some of Tae Hyun's anger was directed toward Jason. But he was mainly upset with himself. Why had he acted like that? Sure, the American actor had an impressive ability to get under Tae Hyun's skin. But Tae Hyun had not only let it happen. He'd provoked it. Jason may have been rude, brash, and forward. But he was also right about one thing. Tae Hyun had been a dick.

After hearing Yoo Mi's take on the actor, Tae Hyun did some research. She'd been right about Jason's reputation as a Hollywood bad boy. Tae Hyun had found a dozen or more unconfirmed reports of drunken fights Jason had been involved in. He also read many news reports and blog posts about Jason's role in *The Long Evening Sunset*. But Tae Hyun wasn't some ordinary, ignorant fan. He knew that the value of an unconfirmed rumor in some blog article was worth the paper it was printed on. So he'd gone into the meeting with an open mind. Or, at least, he'd tried to.

But something about Jason had immediately rubbed Tae Hyun the wrong way. It could've been his cocky swagger. The way Jason had arrogantly inserted himself into Tae Hyun's personal space hadn't helped. That was when Tae Hyun had caught a whiff of Jason's scent, a potent mix of musk and deodorant with a hint of whiskey and cigarettes. Did Jason smoke? Just remembering it made Tae Hyun stop in his tracks.

Here was someone who'd flown all that way just for him, and instead of welcoming him, Tae Hyun had been an asshole. He didn't know why he'd done it beyond his sudden and undeniable attraction to Jason. No, that was a lie. There was nothing sudden about his attraction. Tae Hyun had fallen hard for Jason's character in *The Moon Shines Madly*. Of course, the real Jason Park was nothing like his character. Was that why Tae Hyun had been such an ass?

"Tae Hyun?"

Tae Hyun turned around to discover that Jason had somehow found him in the lounge. Perhaps Ji Hoon had guessed where he might go? But something about Jason seemed different. His brash cockiness was gone. Jason's expression was calm and sincere. "Jason?"

Then Jason did something unexpected. He bowed. "I'm sorry. Could we try starting over?"

Tae Hyun snorted before he could stop himself. "So you do know how to bow?"

Jason smiled. "I never said I didn't know how."

"How did you find me?"

Jason's chuckle was light and pleasant. It was almost like he was a different person. "Are you kidding? I could hear your angry pacing up on the twelfth floor."

Tae Hyun laughed despite himself. "Well, I appreciate your apology. And I'm sorry, too. You're our guest, and I've been an awful host." Then he nodded. "So, yes. Let's start over." He offered Jason his hand. "I'm Woo Tae Hyun. I think you're a fantastic actor, and I would appreciate it if you taught me how to act."

Jason smiled, calmly stepped forward, and took Tae Hyun's hand. Tae Hyun's breath immediately caught in his throat. Their connection was electric. Even Jason seemed to notice it, pausing before he finally spoke. "I'm Jason Park. I think you're a talented and charismatic singer and performer. It would be my pleasure to teach you how to act."

Jason's grip was firm but gentle. His hand was surprisingly warm. And Tae Hyun caught a glimpse of Jason's *The Moon Shines Madly* movie character in his smile. Then Tae Hyun realized it had to be the other way around. That was a piece of the real Jason he'd shown through the character.

"Good." Tae Hyun finally let go of Jason's hand. "Do you want to get out of here?"

"Shouldn't we check in with Ji Hoon?"

Tae Hyun shook his head. "No. Let him wonder. And I'm sure your luggage is already at my apartment by now."

Jason frowned. "About that." He grinned and bashfully rubbed the back of his head. "Maybe it's better if I stay in a hotel. I don't want to put you out any more than I already have."

Jason suddenly looked adorably boyish and vulnerable.

Tae Hyun couldn't imagine just putting him on the street looking for a hotel. "No!" Tae Hyun felt his ears warming from embarrassment and knew they were turning red. He anxiously shook his head. "I mean, you don't need to stay in a hotel. At least not for tonight. You're the reason they even gave me the apartment. The second bedroom is yours."

Jason nodded. "Okay. If you're sure."

"I am."

"Good."

Tae Hyun called Ji Hoon's assistant to arrange for a driver to take them to his apartment. Ji Hoon would learn of their plans that way, but that was fine. They met the KBR driver in the lower-level garage, who took them the short distance to Tae Hyun's building. As expected, Jason's luggage was waiting inside the apartment door. Tae Hyun frowned. Some KBR staffer must've let themselves inside to deliver it.

"My manager has keys to my house, too," Jason suddenly shared. "She actually has keys to everything I own." He chuckled at some private joke. "And she's not afraid to use them." Then he grabbed a pair of his bags. "Where do these go?"

Tae Hyun grabbed the other pair. "This way." He led Jason from the entryway through the main room to a bedroom off the main hallway. Tae Hyun set Jason's bags down next to the closet. Then he gestured toward the bed. "I just made this up today, so everything's fresh."

Jason nodded, looking around the room. "It's very minimal."

Tae Hyun frowned. "I'm sorry. I haven't been in here very long."

Jason playfully tapped Tae Hyun's arm with his fist. "I'm not criticizing you. As long as there's a place to charge my phone and rest my head, I'm good." He made a show of sniffing under his arm. "Is it alright if I take a shower? I smell like two airports and a fourteen-hour flight."

A potent mix of musk and deodorant with a hint of whiskey and cigarettes–

"You smell fine." Did he really just say that? Tae Hyun knew his ears must be turning red again. "But, yes. The shower's this way."

Tae Hyun couldn't believe how flustered he was by having Jason in his apartment. His subtle, knowing grin didn't help. Jason picked up one of his small bags and followed Tae Hyun to the bathroom. Tae Hyun showed him the small linen cupboard with the towels and washcloths. Then he opened a pair of empty drawers near the sink. "You can put your toiletries in these if you want. If you decide to stay."

Jason tilted his head like an adorable puppy. "You're really okay with me staying here?"

Tae Hyun nodded. "If you are, yes." He briefly looked away. "I'm not used to living by myself. So it's no problem." He looked up at Jason, whose face showed his obvious amusement at Tae Hyun's awkwardness. Tae Hyun guessed that he'd just have to get used to having warm ears whenever Jason was around. "Anyhow, I'll let you shower." He turned to walk from the bathroom but stopped in the doorway. "Do you have any food allergies?"

Jason laughed. "Am I showering in food?"

Tae Hyun shook his head without turning around. "No. I was planning to make something to eat."

"Oh, of course. No, I can eat pretty much anything."

Tae Hyun walked away without saying anything else. It

took all his effort just to keep himself from running off. Tae Hyun shook his head again. If he was going to be like that for the next few months, then maybe it would be better if Jason stayed in a hotel.

While the apartment was still sparsely furnished and decorated–minimal, as Jason pointed out–the kitchen was the exception. Tae Hyun loved cooking, especially if it was for someone else. Once he decided what to make, Tae Hyun started the rice cooker and quickly pulled out the necessary ingredients. Then he turned on the burner under his skillet and started chopping and slicing.

Jason emerged from the bathroom while Tae Hyun was reheating the seasoned ground beef he'd been storing in the refrigerator. "Wow, are you making bibimbap?"

Tae Hyun nodded as he turned to Jason. "Yes, I thought–" Jason stood there, still a bit damp from his shower, wrapped in one of Tae Hyun's white bath towels. The overhead kitchen lights reflecting off the water droplets on Jason's smooth, golden-brown skin almost made him sparkle.

Tae Hyun had seen Jason without a shirt before. There'd been a long scene in his movie where he only wore a pair of undershorts. But seeing Jason like that in person was another thing entirely. Even without the body makeup accentuating his muscles, Jason still looked incredibly fit. Tae Hyun was no slouch when it came to working out. But Jason's body–from his prominent chest muscles to his tight, rippled abs–was a work of art. His arm and shoulder included literal art, too, in the form of an intricate dragon tattoo.

Tae Hyun swallowed. "I, uh. I thought since it's your first night in Seoul, you'd like to eat something Korean." Tae Hyun almost winced at how silly he'd just sounded. And he could feel the rising heat in his ears right away.

Jason quietly chuckled as he smirked. "That's so thoughtful. I think I'd definitely like to eat something Korean."

Tae Hyun swallowed again and nearly choked on his spit. Was Jason flirting with him? Could it be possible that Jason Park was gay? Tae Hyun quickly turned back to his frying meat and nodded. "Great. This will be ready soon. You should go get dressed."

But Jason didn't go. Tae Hyun felt him walking closer before seeing the movement in the corner of his eye. Then Jason stood right behind him. Even standing before a hot skillet, Tae Hyun could feel the heat from Jason's body as he leaned in and looked over Tae Hyun's shoulder. Jason deeply inhaled through his nose. "That smells amazing. Almost as good as it looks."

Tae Hyun stood motionless, afraid to move or even breathe and accidentally touch Jason's naked body. Why was he standing so close like that? Was Jason really gay? And a shameless flirt? Or was he simply comfortable in his own skin, and Tae Hyun was projecting? Not knowing made Tae Hyun extremely uncomfortable.

Then Jason finally stepped back. "Okay. I'll be right back."

Tae Hyun held his breath until Jason was out of sight, then slowly let it out before giving the ground beef a final stir. He shook his head as he grabbed two bowls from the cupboard and filled them each with a scoop of rice. Then he began arranging the vegetables on top of the rice.

What was he going to do? Whether or not Jason was really flirting, Tae Hyun's attraction to him was getting out of hand. They'd hardly been together more than two hours, and Tae Hyun was already totally flustered. He seriously needed to get his shit together.

The problem was that Tae Hyun was supposed to spend the next three months closely working with Jason. And the last thing he needed was another workplace romance. Of course, that hadn't stopped him from visiting Sun Se Yoon. But that didn't really count. And Tae Hyun hadn't dated anyone since Chang Min. At first, he'd been too hurt and angry to consider going to the trouble. By the time he was comfortable enough to think about it again, he was in the army, which made it nearly impossible. It was something Tae Hyun had come to terms with early on in his idol training. While gay sex was legal, Korean society still generally looked down on it, especially from their idols. A few actors and performers had come out and built decent followings. But Tae Hyun was an idol with one of the Big Four entertainment companies. Coming out just wasn't an option. And Tae Hyun now had a gorgeous, charming, charismatic Hollywood actor staying in his apartment.

"Can I help with that?"

Startled, Tae Hyun looked over to Jason standing nearby in gray sweats. Tae Hyun's gray sweats. "Are those mine?"

Jason looked down at his outfit. "Yes. These were sitting out, and I wanted to wear something comfortable. I'd have to dig through my bags to find mine. But I can take them off." Jason lifted the sweatshirt, giving Tae Hyun another peek at his toned torso.

"No," Tae Hyun blurted. "It's fine."

Jason nodded and pulled the sweatshirt back down. "Alright. But you never answered my first question. Can I help? You looked stuck."

Tae Hyun quietly sighed. He'd gotten so lost in thought

that he'd stopped putting together the bibimbap bowls. "No, I've got it. It's just–" He forced himself to smile. "It's been a weird day."

Jason snorted. "You don't have to tell me that. I hardly even know what day it is. And I'm standing in a virtual stranger's apartment wearing his clothes."

Tae Hyun laughed. "It's Tuesday."

Jason chuckled. "There. That's one less weird thing. We're practically back to normal. Do you have anything to drink?"

Tae Hyun nodded. Jason had said drink, as in consuming a beverage. But Tae Hyun knew he really meant drink, as in alcohol. That might've been the first mistake he'd made speaking Korean to Tae Hyun. "There's soju in the refrigerator."

Jason shrugged. "It's not Kingston. But that'll work." He walked into the kitchen, opened the refrigerator, and pulled out a bottle of soju.

"Kingston?"

"It's American whiskey. Bourbon, actually."

Tae Hyun nodded as he scooped a serving of meat and a fried egg into each bowl. "Oh. I'm sure we can have some delivered." He nodded toward the cupboards to his right. "The cups are in there."

Jason poured them each a cup of soju while Tae Hyun transferred everything to the table. Tae Hyun took the seat facing the kitchen to give Jason the benefit of the apartment's city view. He waited until Jason took his first bite before eating, anxious to know how his guest liked the food.

"Oh, shit. This is so good!"

Tae Hyun grinned. It had been so long since he last cooked for someone outside of a mess hall. Having another person to share his meal with was a pleasure. "Do you like it?"

Jason nodded. "For sure. I haven't had good bibimbap like this in a long time."

"Not since your mother's?"

Jason snorted. "Are you kidding? My mother never once cooked for me. No, I was thinking of this little hole-in-the-wall place in–" Jason stopped for a moment, looking unsure. "In a neighborhood in LA."

"Koreatown?"

Jason laughed. "I guess you've heard of it. I wasn't sure if you'd know it. Or how to say it."

Tae Hyun nodded. "We did an appearance at a record store there. And your Korean is excellent. I can hardly hear your accent."

Jason chuckled. "Thanks. It'll get better with more practice. But I'm pretty used to being scolded in Korean. And apologizing. That might be why it's been so easy for me so far."

Tae Hyun snorted, imagining a young Jason being dressed down by his Korean parents. "Nothing like an angry mother to bridge the cultural divide."

Jason downed the rest of his soju and poured himself another. He tilted the bottle toward Tae Hyun, who shook his head. Jason shrugged and set the bottle down. "May I ask you a question, Tae Hyun?"

Tae Hyun nodded as he took a sip of his soju. "Of course. And you really don't have to be so formal. It was wrong for me to insist on it."

"I don't mind it so much. I'd even call you sunbae, but I'm actually older than you."

"You are?" Tae Hyun winced. Of course. He'd compared

his Korean age with Jason's American age. "I'm so sorry. Why didn't you tell me before?"

Jason shrugged. "Because I was being an asshole before. And things seem better between us now. It's not a big deal anyway since I didn't grow up like that. But I wouldn't mind if we could speak informally. Speaking in formal Korean sounds too much like I'm talking to my parents."

"You're the senior. It's your call."

Jason chuckled. "If it's up to me, we'd stick with English."

Tae Hyun snorted. "That's also your call. But your Korean, formal or informal, is much better than my English."

"Fair enough."

"What was your question?"

"What? Oh, yeah. Whose idea was it to bring me here? I mean, don't get me wrong. But I'm guessing it wasn't even your idea to get an acting coach."

Tae Hyun sighed. Then he picked up his soju, swallowed the rest, and set his glass in front of Jason. Jason chuckled as he poured Tae Hyun another glass.

"It's like that, is it?"

Tae Hyun nodded. "It wasn't even my idea to do a movie. I wanted to–" Tae Hyun stopped. Did he even want to tell Jason that story?

Jason picked up the hint right away. "Hey, you don't have to explain it. I know we hardly know each other."

"But this is how we get to know each other, right?" Jason nodded. It was weird to have the movie star sitting across from him. Jason had probably met and befriended countless famous people. Tae Hyun only knew the other idols from his company, along with the people he'd met through Yoo Mi. "How about this? Do you know the truth game?"

Jason frowned. "Is that where you drink if you refuse to answer a question or perform a task?"

"There are only questions, no tasks. That's a different game. But yeah, otherwise."

Jason smiled. "That's bold, Tae Hyun. Okay, I'm game."

"Since you already asked the question, it was our CEO's idea to put me in a movie. But it was Ji Hoon's idea to hire you. "

"Ah, okay." Jason nodded. "So that makes it your turn to ask me something."

Tae Hyun hoped that he wasn't about to worsen things between them. "What's one personal detail about you that I couldn't find online?"

Jason sat back and smiled. "That's it? Shit. So, anything?" Tae Hyun nodded. "Okay. How about this? I got my first blow job and lost my virginity on the same night but with different people."

"Whoa."

Jason laughed. "Now it's my turn. Still want to play?"

"Of course. I can always drink if I don't want to answer."

Jason leaned forward, a devilish grin on his face. "Okay, here it comes. What's your favorite movie?"

Tae Hyun had expected a tougher question. But it still wasn't a question he wanted to answer. He reached forward to grab his glass, but Jason was faster, grabbing it and pulling it from Tae Hyun's reach.

"No way. That was a totally easy one. You can't drink on it."

Tae Hyun felt his ears warming and looked down at the table. "I'm embarrassed to admit it."

"Come on." Jason chuckled. "It can't be that bad. Have I

even heard of it?"

Tae Hyun nodded. "I'm sure you have. You were in it."

"Oh, wow." Jason's grin briefly disappeared before returning as a bright smile. "Are you serious? I'm honored."

Tae Hyun nodded again. "Of course. That's why it's embarrassing."

"It shouldn't be." Jason shrugged. "You already know I've been a fan of yours for a long time. I was at your first US concert."

"Oh, yeah. Sorry again that I don't remember that."

Jason waved off Tae Hyun's concern. "Don't be. You think I remember everyone who's shaken my hand? But you can make it up to me." He leaned forward, smiling, and slid Tae Hyun's glass back. "Tell me what you liked about my movie?"

"That's a second question, and it's my turn."

"Fine, I'll give you two questions if you answer mine."

"Okay." Tae Hyun was sure his ears would be permanently red by that point. "I don't watch many American movies. My English is pretty good, but I still miss a lot of context. Especially slang. But *The Moon Shines Madly* was different. I was so moved by the story and your performance. The scene where you sat in your bedroom with the gun, contemplating suicide? I cried so hard when I watched it."

Jason smiled again. But it wasn't his usual, goofy smile. It was serious. It had weight. "I really appreciate you saying that. I put a lot of myself into that role." Then his smile melted away. "And that was a hard scene for me. It was so easy to fall into certain parts of the character like that. And it was hard to put it away afterward."

Hearing Jason say that was something of a revelation. Tae Hyun knew well the struggles of maintaining his public persona versus his authentic self. Some idols spent so much time being their public selves their private selves disappeared. And some struggled with being their public selves so much that it broke them. So the stories of Jason's troubles, drinking, and all that made a little more sense. Tae Hyun couldn't imagine what it was like to live somewhere he'd have to deal with people discriminating against him just for being Asian. Even being gay in Korea was different. That he could at least hide from everyone else. "Thank you for doing it."

"I'm glad it meant something to you. That's what makes it all worth it." Jason grinned and refilled his glass. "I believe it's your turn."

"How old were you when you started acting?"

"I was sixteen when I got cast in my first big-time movie role. But my first official acting gig was in a commercial a few years before that."

That was surprising. Tae Hyun had never imagined Jason acting in anything other than films. "Wow. What was the commercial for?"

Jason narrowed his eyes. Tae Hyun couldn't tell whether it was in suspicion or annoyance. Then he reached for his glass. "I don't think I–"

Tae Hyun reached out and took Jason's glass. "Oh, no. You made me answer the movie question."

Jason frowned and lightly shook his head. Then he sighed. "Fine. It's not like you probably couldn't just look it up online anyway. It was for CheezyFish."

"Wait. You don't mean–?"

Jason nodded. "I'm afraid so. Can I have my glass back?"

Tae Hyun slid the glass toward Jason, thinking back to– "I've seen it! I remember that commercial!" He'd only been a kid back then, but he somehow still remembered a young Jason stuffing a handful of the cheese-flavored snack crackers in his mouth.

Jason chuckled before swallowing a mouthful of soju. Tae Hyun smirked when he noticed that Jason's cheeks had reddened. "I'm sure you do. It fucking ran for at least a year." Then he smiled and patted his stomach. "Get in my tummy!"

Tae Hyun laughed. "I can't believe that was you. So, you started acting in Korea?"

Jason shook his head. "Ah-ah. You've already had two. It's my turn to ask a question." Tae Hyun gestured for him to go ahead. "Why did you become an idol?"

Tae Hyun scratched his chin as he thought about what to say. His answer to that could be complicated. "I think mostly it was the usual childhood fantasy. An idol's life seemed so glamorous and exciting. So I begged my parents to let me study dance. And take voice lessons. And I got so much shit from my friends who were convinced I'd never make it."

Jason smiled. "You certainly showed them."

Tae Hyun grinned. "I sure did."

"But you said mostly. Is there another reason?"

"I believe that's a second question. "

Jason snorted. "Fine, fine. Maybe we should just change the rule to two questions each?"

Tae Hyun shrugged. "As you wish, sunbae-nim."

"Don't start with that, please. The power will definitely go to my head." Jason winked. "Just answer the question."

Tae Hyun nodded. "I'm the oldest of two children–me and my younger sister. And my parents put a lot of pressure on me to be successful. This seemed like the best way for me to do that." That wasn't the whole story, of course. Because, deep down, Tae Hyun had a third reason, too. Becoming an idol allowed him to escape from his parents.

"Oh, I know a little something about parental expectations."

Tae Hyun chuckled. "Yeah, I suppose you do."

Jason refilled both cups before taking a drink from his. "And now it's your turn."

"When was the last time you were in Seoul?"

Jason pursed his full lips, and, for a moment, Tae Hyun thought he might not answer. "My parents brought me here for a summer when I was fourteen."

"Ten years? How come it's been so long?"

"Is that your second question?" Tae Hyun nodded. Jason shrugged. "It wasn't a good visit."

Tae Hyun frowned and shook his head. "If you don't wanna give me a real answer, then just drink."

Jason snorted. "That was the truth. But, fine." He picked up his glass and took a drink. "Happy?"

Tae Hyun shook his head. "No. I don't understand why you're okay telling me that you got blown by someone else the night you first had sex but not why you waited until now to come back to Seoul?"

Jason leaned forward. "I don't mind telling you that sex story because I wouldn't really care if it ended up in some Hollywood blogger's newsfeed. But the reason I've waited this long to come back to Korea is very personal. And I don't know you well enough to trust you with something like that."

Tae Hyun looked down, suddenly ashamed that he'd pushed Jason so far. "I'm sorry."

"Don't be." Tae Hyun looked up, surprised to see Jason smiling at him. "I don't have many boundaries, Tae Hyun.

You just happened to find that one right away."

Tae Hyun nodded. "Okay, I understand."

"Good." Jason winked. "Now, I believe it's my turn."

09

Jason knew he'd ruined the mood by refusing to answer Tae Hyun's question. Tae Hyun couldn't have known how Jason would react. But that's what happened, and there was nothing more to be done about it. There was no way Jason was telling a virtual stranger like Tae Hyun one of the most personal stories from his past. Tae Hyun would have to earn that if he wanted it.

They'd traded softball questions after that, talking about favorite places to visit, funny concert stories, and shit like that. Tae Hyun remained friendly and charming, and the evening was pleasant and even a little fun. But, charming or not, Tae Hyun's walls had slammed back up after Jason had managed to get them down just a little. And that was frustrating. Tae Hyun, the idol, was fine. But Jason liked the tiny glimpses he'd gotten of the real Tae Hyun better. Especially when Tae Hyun got embarrassed or flustered and his ears turned red.

It hadn't taken many more glasses of soju before Jason could see that the wind had gone out of Tae Hyun's sails. So he called an end to their truth game and offered to help Tae Hyun clean up the dinner mess. Tae Hyun refused, of course. So Jason asked where he could smoke. He'd done well going so long after his flight without lighting up. But the soju, his stress, and the day's general weirdness had finally caught up with him.

Since it was a non-smoking building, Jason had to go downstairs and head outside. But Tae Hyun gave him the extra keys to the apartment so he could let himself in. It was still warm out, and he was wearing Tae Hyun's sweats. So Jason changed into his own shorts and t-shirt before heading down.

The sidewalk was busier than Jason would've expected. You rarely saw folks out walking around in LA, especially at night. Jason got a few curious glances as people walked by. But he wasn't worried about being recognized. Jason was so far from his beaten path it wouldn't occur to anyone that he was an American movie star. It was more likely that the passers-by wondered if Jason was one of the wealthy people that lived in the building. Jason wasn't quite sure where in Seoul he even was. He was pretty sure they were in Gangnam. They hadn't traveled very far after leaving the KBR building. But where in Gangnam was a mystery. Maybe Nonhyeon-dong? He'd have to remember to ask.

Tae Hyun had apparently gone to sleep by the time Jason went back upstairs. Jason was tired, too—at least his mind was—but his body hadn't figured out it was time for bed. So he sat on the couch, figured out how to turn on the TV, and watched a slick but cheesy Korean action movie. Jason resisted the urge to turn on the English subtitles, forcing himself to follow along with the Korean dialog. The movie finished after midnight, which meant Naomi would be awake. So Jason pulled out his phone and called her. Naomi picked up on the second ring.

"Figured I'd be hearing from you."

"Fine, thank you," Jason sweetly replied. "And you?"

Naomi snorted. "Yeah, yeah. Good morning, good night, whatever."

"It's morning here now, too. A different day, though. I think."

"Fantastic. So, tell me? How'd everything shake out?"

Jason sighed. "Well, after an obviously rough start and a less than warm welcome from our favorite K-pop idol, I'm sitting in the living room I share with Tae Hyun as we speak. And I'm fat and contented from eating the second-best bibimbap I've ever had."

"That sounds like maybe good news, then? Can I stop worrying about you?"

Jason laughed. "Not as long as I'm paying you, no."

"You know what I mean." Naomi sighed. "Are you gonna do the job?"

Jason didn't know how to answer that yet. He could see himself getting along well enough with Tae Hyun. But that was only part of the equation. "I think we're down to fifty-fifty odds that I fuck off and go sit on a Thai beach for three weeks."

Naomi snorted. "That sounds like better odds than when you texted me before."

"It is. You know, honestly? I don't mind it here so much. It's been long enough that everything feels different. When I went outside to smoke a little while ago, no one recognized me. And I haven't seen a single white person since I left the airport."

Naomi laughed. "I could get used to that real fast."

"But I'm not sure where things stand with Tae Hyun. I think I like him. He's got some serious walls up right now, but I got a few glimpses behind them. And I think I can work with what's there." Jason sighed. "That only leaves the fucking movie. Can I really do this?"

"You're the only one that can answer that. But the Jason I know and love can do it."

Jason chuckled. "Awe. You love me?"

"It's a figure of speech. But I know you've been carrying those demons around a long time. I think this is when you let them go."

"Well, I love you, Naomi."

Naomi snorted. "That's harassment."

"No, harassment is your twink receptionist showing up at my door in fuck-me shorts and a mesh tank top."

"Steven really did that?" Naomi sighed. "Shit. No wonder he's been so mopey. I hope you let him down easy."

"I let him down. That's as easy as I get."

"Good boy. Is there anything you need out there?"

"Yeah. I can't stand soju. Please get me some fucking Kingston."

Naomi groaned. "Get KBR to send you some. Or, better yet, take your ass to the store and get it yourself."

"Then no. I'm good for the time being."

"Fantastic. By the way, how would you feel about doing a commercial while you're there?"

"What? For real?"

"It's nothing right now. But one of the feelers I put out before you signed this deal is making a little noise. And, since you're already in Seoul–"

"I already told you I love you. Now you just seem desperate."

Naomi snorted. "So what should I tell them if they make an offer?"

"Tell them you'll run it by me first. By the way, am I officially here yet?"

"No. KBR will officially announce the project on Friday. Before then, it's probably best to lay low."

"Low and slow. Got it. I'm gonna try sleeping for a bit. Talk to you later."

"Okay. See ya."

After hanging up with Naomi, Jason headed for his temporary bedroom, took one of his sleeping pills, and lay down on the surprisingly comfortable mattress. But, even so, he only managed a few hours of sleep. He finally gave up and got out of bed around five AM. He thought about heading downstairs for another cigarette, then decided it wasn't worth the trouble. Instead, Jason crawled out of bed to visit the bathroom. He passed Tae Hyun's closed door along the way. His host was probably still asleep. Tae Hyun had mentioned the night before that he was usually awake early. But he'd also had enough soju to start slurring before going to bed. So Jason gave him even odds to sleep late.

Since he was alone and restless, Jason dug through his luggage and found workout shorts, a shirt, and running shoes. Then he went downstairs to the building's fitness center and spent forty-five minutes on the treadmill. When he was done, Jason stepped outside and finally had his first cigarette of the day. The nicotine made his heart thump–not quite giving him a buzz, but definitely making him light-headed. Unlike his nighttime visit, the street in front of Tae Hyun's building was nearly deserted in the early morning.

"Excuse me, sunbae-nim."

Jason nearly jumped at the sound of the stranger's voice. He whirled around to see a young man approaching him from a nearby parked car. He had a conservative haircut and handsome face and was dressed in a sharp suit. He also looked familiar. Had Jason seen him at KBR? It had to be that. No one else in Seoul would know who Jason was. "Do I know you?"

The young man nodded and offered Jason a quick bow. "I'm Jang Min Jun, Managing Director Choo's assistant. I apologize for bothering you, but Director Choo told me–"

"It's fine. Do you, uh, want to come up? I don't know if Tae Hyun is awake yet, but–"

Min Jun shook his head. "No, that won't be necessary. I'm simply here to drop off your copies of the script and deliver a message."

"A message?"

Min Jun nodded as he handed over a thick envelope he'd been holding. "These are your scripts. Director Choo also wanted to let you know that you'll have a free hand in coaching Tae Hyun, but he expects the idol to be ready for his first table read in three weeks."

The idol? Jason snorted. Which of them was referring to Tae Hyun as an object. Ji Hoon? Or Min Jun? "He does, does he?"

"That's what he told me, yes."

"Fine. Please thank Ji Hoon for me. And tell him not to worry. The idol will be ready."

"I will." Min Jun stood in awkward silence for long enough that Jason wondered if he was supposed to bow or something. Then Min Jun affected a slight wince and spoke again. "Sunbae-nim, is it alright if I ask for a photo? I'm a big fan of yours."

Jason snorted. So much for no one recognizing him. "Sure,

why not. Just make sure you don't post it until after KBR announces the movie."

"Of course."

Jason set his cigarette down as Min Jun pulled his phone from his jacket pocket. Min Jun stood next to Jason and held the phone out to take a photo. Jason took a moment to check his hair–it looked surprisingly good considering he was still covered in sweat–before putting his arm around Min Jun's shoulders. Then he grinned while Min Jun took a few pics. "Good?"

"Yes, thank you. I should get back to the office."

"Alright. See ya."

Min Jun bowed again, then turned and walked away.

Jason watched Min Jun long enough to finish his cigarette. When he got back upstairs, Tae Hyun's door was still closed, so he showered and changed into Tae Hyun's sweatpants and a t-shirt before heading to the kitchen to make breakfast.

The kitchen was serious business compared to the spartan state of the apartment. Jason found ground coffee and a large french press, so he boiled some water in the kettle. Then he rummaged through the refrigerator, pulled out fresh eggs and the leftover veggies from the bibimbap, and started mixing them to make omelets. He quietly chuckled. Tae Hyun was the first guy Jason had ever made breakfast for. And they hadn't even slept together.

Tae Hyun finally appeared as Jason poured the first omelet onto the hot skillet. "You're already awake?"

Jason looked over to see Tae Hyun wearing the shorts and t-shirt he'd apparently slept in. His bedhead was adorably messy, and his long, graceful legs were clearly those of a dancer. "I am. Couldn't sleep."

Tae Hyun walked closer to get a better view of Jason's cooking. "What are you making? It smells delicious."

"Since you already cooked for me, I'm treating you to an American breakfast to return the favor. I'm not just a pretty face, you know." Jason winked at Tae Hyun. "Although my face is stunning."

Tae Hyun chuckled. "Whatever. Do you want to get started with the coaching today? Or do you still need some time to settle in?"

"We may as well get started right away." Jason nodded toward the thick envelope sitting on the kitchen island counter. "Ji Hoon's assistant delivered our copies of the script after I finished at the gym."

Tae Hyun's eyebrows floated up in surprise. "You've already been to the gym?"

Jason shrugged and expertly flipped the omelet. "It feels like the middle of yesterday afternoon to me. It's gonna take me more than a day to adjust to the time difference."

"Of course." Tae Hyun stretched, treating Jason to a surprise peek at his smooth, flat torso. Jason had to stop himself from licking his lips. "Do I have time for a quick shower?"

"Yeah." Jason almost offered to help. Why was he suddenly feeling so flirty? He'd never known jet lag to make him horny. "As long as it's quick."

Tae Hyun nodded and walked away while Jason slid the finished omelet onto a plate before starting the second one. He needed to be more mindful around his host. Sure, a little friendly flirting was probably okay, especially if it helped bring Tae Hyun's wall down. But pushing things too far too fast would no doubt ruin any chances of the two getting along.

When he finished, Tae Hyun still hadn't returned. So Jason

put some more butter in the pan and made skillet toast. He wished Tae Hyun had bacon. After the toast was ready, Jason poured two cups of coffee and set them on the table. Then he grabbed the envelope, opened it, and slid a pair of scripts out. As Ji-hoon had promised, they were written in Korean.

Jason took one of the scripts to the table to read it. They'd gone literal with their retitle, calling the film *Lover's Time Soul's Journey*. The original movie, *The Long Evening Sunset*, was the story of two lovers who'd been doomed to fall in love only to tragically die, reincarnate, and do it all over again throughout time until they finally remembered their past lives and moved on to the afterlife. The lead roles were challenging because the actors essentially had to portray two different characters simultaneously–their original selves and whoever they'd been reincarnated as. As Jason flipped through the script, he saw that the rewrite had been updated with Korean settings and events. But it looked like the translated dialogue was pretty much the same.

Jason stopped when he reached the scene where the two leads first promised their undying love for one another. It was one of the few that he'd actually filmed before getting fired. As he read through the scene, Jason was mentally transported back to Vancouver, where they'd been shooting. He recalled standing on the cobblestone street in Gastown that had been redressed to look like Victorian England, gripping his costar's hands as they stood in the freezing cold under the flickering glow of a gas streetlamp. That same night, his costar, Amber Merritt, had told Jason about–No. Jason frowned. Those feelings were still too powerful, even though it had been years.

"What do you think?"

Jason looked up in surprise to see Tae Hyun taking the seat

opposite him. He'd changed into sweatpants and a different t-shirt, leaving his freshly washed hair unstyled. Tae Hyun looked so much different with his bangs covering his forehead. A little more boyish, possibly, if not actually younger. "Hmm?"

"Of the script."

Jason closed the script and set it aside. Then he flipped on a casual grin, shoving his inconvenient anguish away for the benefit of his host. "I think I'm gonna be really good at reading Korean when we're done." Tae Hyun chuckled. "Let's eat before these omelets get too cold."

Tae Hyun nodded. He grabbed his fork, sliced off a corner of his omelet, and put it in his mouth. "Oh, wow," he said after swallowing. "This is good. Do you eat breakfast like this every day?"

"Absolutely not. It's usually coffee and a cigarette. And sometimes a smoothie. This is special just for you."

Tae Hyun's bashful smile complemented his rosy ears. "Thank you. So, do you have a coaching plan for me? Not that you have to have a plan."

"We have a lot of time–more than we'll probably need–so there's no need to rush things. But I do have a plan." That was partly true. He'd initially intended to do a table read with Tae Hyun. But Jason was no longer in the mood for that–not with the general weirdness of the past couple of days. "Before we start, I want you to tell me what you know about being in love."

Tae Hyun's startled expression was almost priceless. "I'm sorry, what?"

"I want to know what being in love means to you." Jason tapped his script. "At its heart, this film is a story of love and loss. I mean, you've been in love before, right?"

"I have?" Tae Hyun's troubled expression and bright red ears said a lot.

Jason frowned, wondering what he was stirring up. "You dated that model for over a year. Weren't you in love with her? Or was it just a fling?"

Tae Hyun let out the breath he'd been holding as he nodded. And Jason realized that Tae Hyun thought he was referring to something–or someone–else. That was interesting. Maybe Naomi had been right about him. "Oh, yeah. Of course."

"And you lost her. So you know about loss." Tae Hyun slowly nodded. But his eyes were distant. Where had he gone? "You know, I actually met her once. After a fashion show in New York, I think. Besides being gorgeous, she's got a ton of charm and charisma."

Tae Hyun smiled. "She remembered meeting you, too."

Jason laughed. "Oh, so you really did check me out?"

"Of course. Yoo Mi travels often, so I figured she'd know who you were. Ji Hoon was light on details about you."

Jason shrugged. "He may be my uncle, but we barely know each other. And everything he knows about me comes from my father, which makes it immediately suspect."

"Can I ask you a question?" Jason nodded. "Have you seen the original movie?"

"No." Jason frowned. He'd tried watching it once but couldn't get more than a few minutes into it before he had to stop. It made him too upset.

"Of course. I've read the stories about what happened."

Jason's frown deepened as he felt tension stiffening his shoulders. As much as he wanted to avoid a repeat of their disastrous first meeting, Jason didn't appreciate Tae Hyun calling him out so early. "And do you believe everything you read?"

Tae Hyun's expression returned to his carefully neutral default. "Of course not. I've dealt with the press enough to know that's probably not the whole story. And you don't have to tell me what really happened. But I'm curious." Tae Hyun frowned. "I'm sorry to bring it up like that. But with our situation, it's been on my mind."

"Has it, now?" Jason's tone was ice cold. "Because it's none of your fucking business." He was perfectly willing to write off Tae Hyun's question about his history with Seoul as innocent. The idol had no way of knowing anything about that. And he'd been drinking. But bringing up his firing from *The Long Evening Sunset* was fucked up. They barely knew each other. Despite Jason assuring Naomi that he was only half-ready to walk away, the scales were rapidly tipping toward that conclusion.

"I'm just being honest."

Jason leaned forward, allowing himself the barest grin. "Fuck you."

Tae Hyun's jaw dropped. "Excuse me?"

"You heard me. Fuck you. And fuck your honesty." Jason pushed back from the table and stood up. "It's not like you're not sitting on your own juicy secret. You want me to bring that up next?"

Tae Hyun scoffed. "I don't know–"

"Don't play fucking innocent with me. You don't think I've wondered why you quit your group? But you don't hear me asking about that."

"Why I–?" Tae Hyun stopped, frowning. And Jason knew he'd scored a hit there. "Military service in Korea is compulsory, so I–"

"Bullshit." Jason scoffed. "You think I don't know you've got years before you're required to enlist? But no, you left your group in its fucking prime."

Tae Hyun scowled. "Fuck you."

"Fuck me?" Jason scoffed. "In your dreams, hubae." He shook his head. A dozen different insults came to mind. He knew he was at a crossroads and–if he wasn't careful–was liable to say or do something that they couldn't come back from. "But you can fuck all this," he added as he turned away. "I'm out of here."

"Wait!"

Jason stopped but didn't turn around. "What?"

"Where are you going?"

"Out."

"You can't go."

Jason growled and turned around to face a shocked Tae Hyun. "Why the hell not?"

Tae Hyun gulped. Jason could plainly see the struggle on his face as he searched for a response. "You're still wearing my sweatpants."

"Are you fucking serious?" Jason shook his head as he undid the drawstring, slipped the sweatpants off, and tossed them toward the table. Thankfully, he'd put on nice underwear–of which Tae Hyun suddenly had an excellent view. "There. Happy?"

But Jason didn't wait for an answer, heading for his room instead. After putting on the first pair of jeans he found, Jason stuffed his keys and cigarettes into his pockets and left the apartment, only stopping at the door long enough to put his shoes on. Jason made it halfway down the block before he realized he had no idea where he was going. He stopped to get his bearings, but it was a wasted effort. Jason hadn't explored Seoul unsupervised in a decade. Then he lit a cigarette and kept walking, wondering if he could even smoke where he was. But it helped calm his nerves almost as much as the walking did.

Jason found salvation at the end of the second block–an open bar. He dropped his cigarette and stomped it out before pushing through the ancient wooden door into virtual darkness. It took his eyes a moment to adjust to the interior gloom. He was in a small tavern populated by a single, grizzled bartender and a pair of gray-haired seniors sitting at the far end of a bar that took up half the space. Jason smiled as he took a seat in the middle of the bar. The bartender set down the glass he was wiping and gave Jason an eyebrow-raised glance. Jason took a moment to scan the stack of bottles on the back bar shelves before finding what he was looking for.

"Kingston, neat."

The bartender nodded, grabbed a low ball from beneath the bar, and filled it with a generous pour from the dusty Kingston bottle. "American?" he asked in English as he set the glass in front of Jason.

Jason shook his head. "No. British." Then he picked up the glass and downed its contents in one go.

"You don't sound British."

Jason snorted and set down the empty glass. "And you don't sound like my mother. Yet, here we are."

The bartender frowned. But he filled up Jason's glass again before returning to his glass-wiping duties. Jason took a gulp from his refill and smiled. He'd finally found someone in Korea who really understood him.

<u>10</u>

Tae Hyun sat at the table in silence, waiting for the front door to close before letting himself sigh. What the hell just happened? He'd happened, of course. They'd been sitting there enjoying a wonderful breakfast that Jason had made. And then Tae Hyun opened his mouth. He could hardly believe he'd asked Jason about the movie incident. Not that he didn't want to know the story. But he remembered what Jason had said the night before about boundaries. Jason had been friendly enough to let him off the hook when he asked why he hadn't returned to Korea. And that was fair. He had no way of knowing it was a sensitive subject. But he'd crossed the line by asking Jason about *The Long Evening Sunset*. How could he have been so careless to think that would be okay? And Jason had struck back with the one thing Tae Hyun never wanted to discuss. Which, of course, he would.

Just because Tae Hyun wanted to know didn't mean it was any of his business. Just because they'd bonded over drinks and a game of truth didn't make them true friends. Just because Jason had made him breakfast didn't mean he considered Tae Hyun to be trustworthy. Just because–ah! Enough.

Tae Hyun loudly groaned. Then he reached out to grab

his sweatpants. That had to be the stupidest thing he'd ever said. *You're still wearing my sweatpants.* As if that somehow would've kept Jason from running away. Tae Hyun should've known better, but he couldn't think of anything else to say. *I'm sorry* probably would've worked. Or, *please forgive me*.

Still, it was the second time in as many days he'd seen Jason half-dressed. Was that why Tae Hyun was acting so strangely? Was sharing his living space with such an attractive man turning him into a babbling schoolchild with no control over his emotions? It's not like there was a shortage of handsome men in Tae Hyun's life. He was an idol. Everyone around him was attractive. But it was different with Jason. He wasn't bound by an idol's strict rules of propriety. Not that those were always followed.

Yet, for a few moments, when they'd first started eating their second meal, the setting felt comfortably domestic—just the two of them sitting across from one another enjoying a homemade breakfast like old friends. Or a couple, even. And that was over. Instead of helping Jason feel welcome, Tae Hyun drove him off.

After dumping his sweatpants in the clothes hamper and cleaning up from Jason's breakfast, Tae Hyun grabbed his phone and called the only person he could think of for advice.

"Hey, oppa. Getting settled into the new place okay?"

"That depends on your definition of okay. I, uh—I kind of fucked up."

Yun Seo dramatically sighed. "Okay. Tell me everything."

Tae Hyun explained what happened. Telling the story aloud only made it sound worse. "So, he left. But not before I made him take his pants off."

"You did what?"

"It's not important. But what do I do now?"

Yun Seo snorted. "You're asking me? I should think that's pretty obvious."

"If it was obvious, I wouldn't be asking you."

Yun Seo huffed. "Sometimes I wonder if you really are the older one, oppa. You should apologize and beg for his forgiveness."

"Should I, though?" Tae Hyun sighed. "I never wanted him as my acting coach. Maybe this is a blessing in disguise."

"Then why are you calling me? Are you looking for validation here? Because I can't give that to you."

"Why not?"

Tae Hyun could almost hear his sister rolling her eyes. "Wow. I forgot how cold you could be sometimes."

Cold? He was being realistic, yes. But cold? "Yun Seo–"

"No. Don't you *Yun Seo* me. You asked me what to do, and I'm telling you that you need to apologize. And you need to stop pushing everyone away. Just because you got hurt once doesn't mean everyone will hurt you."

"What?"

"You heard me. When's the last time you made a new friend?"

Tae Hyun snorted. "I made plenty of friends in the army."

"Oh, did you? And that's why you came to stay with me every time you went on leave? And after you were released? And called me asking for advice just now? Because you have so many friends?"

Tae Hyun felt his jaw clenching and forced it to relax. Yun Seo had seen right through him like she always did. "No. I called you because you're the only person I know who'll talk to me like that."

Yun Seo's bright chuckle took away some of the sting of what she'd just said. "That's better. I'm sorry that sounded so harsh. And you know I'd take your side if Jason was an asshole to you, right?"

"I know. And I'm sorry for being so cold."

"See?" Yun Seo snorted. "You do know how to apologize. Now turn that magic around on your sexy acting coach."

Tae Hyun laughed. "My what?"

"Come on. Jason is so hot! I mean, everyone you know is hot. But Jason is on another level entirely. Have you seen him without a shirt yet?" Yun Seo huffed. "What am I saying? You've already seen him without pants. Tell me. How big do you think it is?"

Tae Hyun nearly choked. "I'm not having this conversation with you."

"Fine. Have it with him instead. And let me know how it goes."

"Thank you."

"Of course. But I've gotta go. Next time, let's work on getting you to ask me how I'm doing, too."

Tae Hyun sighed. "Shit. I'm sorry."

"Too late. Love you, oppa."

"Love you, too. Bye."

You need to stop pushing everyone away. Was that what Tae Hyun was doing with Jason? Pushing him away? It seemed obvious to Yun Seo, but he wasn't so sure. Still, it made a lot more sense than him being thoughtless for no reason.

Tae Hyun wondered where Jason had gone. He had no idea where Jason would even go. Tae Hyun would've called him, but he didn't have Jason's phone number. Ji Hoon probably had it, but the last thing he wanted to do was lie to his manager.

Or, worse–explain the actual situation to him. No, he'd just have to wait until Jason came back. He had to come back. All his stuff was in their apartment.

Stuck with waiting, Tae Hyun decided to visit the building's fitness center and get on the treadmill. Tae Hyun's phone rang around forty-five minutes into his planned hour-long run. The call was from an American number he didn't recognize. Maybe it was Jason? Tae Hyun tapped his earbud to pause the *DoubleDown Boys* album and answer the call.

"Hello?" Tae Hyun said in English.

"Hello." It sounded like a woman's voice. Not Jason. "Is this Tae Hyun? I'm Naomi Bell, Jason's manager."

His manager? Tae Hyun was suddenly sure that Jason had quit. Why else would his manager call him? "Oh, hello, Naomi. Yes, I'm Tae Hyun."

"Oh, good. I'm sorry to bother you. And I'm sorry that I only speak English."

"It's no problem. What do you need?"

"I'm looking for Jason. I've tried to reach him, but he's not answering my calls."

Tae Hyun gently sighed. "I'm sorry, Naomi. He's not with me at the moment. I don't know where he is."

"Ah. Are you not at home? His phone locator says he's at the address he gave me for your apartment."

Had Jason come back already? If so, he'd probably started packing. "I'm not there, no. But I'm close. Let me go check and call you back."

"Okay. Thank you. And Tae Hyun, is he–" Naomi paused. Tae Hyun thought he heard a muffled sigh. "Never mind. Just let me know if you find him."

"I'll call you back soon."

Tae Hyun disconnected the call, grabbed his sweat towel, and headed for the elevator. If Jason really was back, Tae Hyun wanted a chance to apologize before the actor did something rash like leaving. He could only imagine what Ji Hoon would say if he managed to drive Jason off after one day. Not to mention CEO Pak.

Tae Hyun got himself so worked up in the elevator he was practically hyperventilating by the time he got back to the apartment. "Jason!" he called out as he burst through the front door. He didn't even bother removing his shoes, instead rushing straight to Jason's room. But no one was there. Nothing had changed since Tae Hyun had gone down to the fitness center. Was Tae Hyun too late? No, Jason's stuff was still there–including his phone. Tae Hyun frowned when he saw it sitting on the bed. So much for tracking Jason down.

Tae Hyun pulled out his own phone and redialed the last number.

"This is Naomi."

"It's Tae Hyun calling you back. Jason isn't here. Only his phone."

"He left his phone there? But he's not–Oh. Okay. Let me guess. He got mad and stormed off?"

"He–" Tae Hyun sighed. "He did. We had an argument. Is that something he normally does?"

"Storm off? That depends on whether or not he likes you."

Ah. If Jason liked Tae Hyun, he would've stayed. "Of course. I was intrusive and unkind with some of my questions."

Strangely, Naomi chuckled. "No. I meant he wouldn't bother storming off if he didn't like you. Otherwise, he'd just keep being an asshole to you until you cried."

Tae Hyun frowned. "I see. I'm concerned that he left his

phone behind. Do you have any idea where he might go?"

"Sure. Is there somewhere around there that serves liquor?"

Tae Hyun found Jason at the second bar he tried. He hadn't bothered showering, instead changing his t-shirt, putting on pants, and adding a mask and baseball cap. The mask helped him stay incognito. The cap was because his hair looked terrible.

Jason sat camped in the middle of the bar, regaling two elderly drinkers with a highly inappropriate story about his antics while filming one of the *Monday Night Club* movies. Tae Hyun doubted either of the men spoke English, but they seemed to greatly enjoy Jason's enthusiasm.

"Sunbae-nim," Tae Hyun called out. Everyone but Jason looked at him, and he grimaced. They were all his seniors. "Jason."

Jason slowly turned around. "Who's–ah! Tae Hyun! Is that you? Is this your bar, too?" His voice was brimming with drunken wonder. "Shit! I can't believe we have the same bar!" He reached out and patted the barstool next to him. "Come on and sit with me."

Tae Hyun briefly considered walking back out before relenting to the inevitable, taking a seat next to Jason, and removing his mask. "Naomi was looking for you," he said in English for Jason's benefit.

"Naomi's here?" Jason shook his head. "No way." He smiled and tapped Tae Hyun's thigh. "Are you sure you're not drunk?"

Tae Hyun smiled despite himself. Even drunk, Jason was charming. "Of course, she's not here. She tried calling you, but you left your phone behind."

Jason snorted. "She's always trying to call me. That's her

job. And I'm always avoiding her calls. That's my job." He picked up his glass and swallowed the remaining amber liquid it held. Then he refilled it with the mostly empty bottle sitting nearby. Ah, it was the Kingston bourbon Jason had talked about before.

Jason waved at the bartender, who'd been talking to the other two patrons. "A glass for my friend, please."

Tae Hyun shook his head. "No, thank you, bartender, sir," he said in Korean. "I'm fine."

"Bah," Jason huffed. "Don't listen to him," he said in Korean. "He's anything but fine."

Tae Hyun nearly laughed at the surprised look on the bartender's face. Perhaps he didn't know Jason spoke Korean too. Then Tae Hyun nodded toward the bottle. One drink couldn't hurt, right? The bartender grabbed an empty glass, poured in a small amount from the Kingston bottle, and set it before Tae Hyun. It wasn't his first time drinking whiskey. But Tae Hyun wasn't sure if he'd tried bourbon–or even what made it different from regular whiskey. He took a sip from the glass, and the lukewarm liquid burned as it went down his throat.

Jason chuckled. "Good stuff, right?"

Tae Hyun nodded. "It is." Jason watched him expectantly, so Tae Hyun took another sip. It didn't burn quite as much as the first one.

Jason smiled. "I'm glad you're here. The bartender is the only other dude here that speaks English. But he won't talk to me because I'm an American."

The bartender huffed. "You told me British."

"That was half a bottle ago. Now I'm willing to admit the truth." The bartender waved him off and went back to wiping glasses, so Jason turned to Tae Hyun. "See?"

Tae Hyun sighed. As much as he wanted to avoid the issue, he kept hearing his sister insisting that he apologize. "Jason, I owe you an apology."

"For what?" Jason frowned. "Oh, wait. Yeah. For being an asshole and asking about why I got fired." He shrugged. "Okay."

"Okay? As in, you accept my apology?"

Jason snorted. "What apology?" He shook his head. "No, okay, as in, let's hear it."

Tae Hyun nodded. "Sunbae-nim, I apologize for my questions. I overstepped."

"Back to formal, are we?" Jason huffed and shook his head. "It's fine. Don't sweat it."

Tae Hyun didn't know what that meant. He assumed from the context that he shouldn't let the matter concern him. "No, it's not fine. I'm sorry, Jason. I shouldn't have brought it up."

Jason shrugged. "Probably not, no. Then again, I wasn't exactly a sweetheart, either." He took a long swallow from his glass, then wiped his mouth on his arm. "Look, Tae Hyun, I'm sorry, too. Alright? I don't know what it is that makes us rub each other the wrong way–"

"What?"

Jason chuckled. "Sorry. That probably sounds dirty if you don't know it. It means we easily irritate or annoy each other."

Tae Hyun nodded. "Anyway. So I think it's time we put our cards on the table."

"I don't know what that means, either."

Jason frowned. "We should level with each other. Tell each other the truth."

"Oh." Tae Hyun shook his head. "No, I don't think that's–"

10

Jason suddenly put his arm around Tae Hyun's shoulder. Tae Hyun nearly jumped out of his skin. But he left Jason's arm alone, despite it making his heart race. "It's okay. I'll start. You see, the reason I got fired was–"

"Wait. I thought you didn't trust me."

Jason grinned. "I don't. But I've been thinking about that. And I guess it doesn't really matter if I do or not. I mean, what are you gonna do? Blog about it? Tell all your friends? We're in fucking Korea, dude."

Tae Hyun snorted. Then he took another drink. "Okay."

"Good." Jason lightly squeezed Tae Hyun's shoulder. "So, anyway. The reason I got fired–well, I got fired because I beat up the director. That part is true. But the reason I beat up the director was because my costar Amber told me that he got her drunk and tried to fuck her. And when she turned him down, he tried to fire her." Jason's expression turned sour. "Can you believe that shit?"

Tae Hyun nodded. Of course, he could. It happened in Korea, too. It probably happened more than Tae Hyun was even aware of. "Why didn't you tell anyone?"

Jason sighed and pulled his arm off Tae Hyun's shoulder. "Come on. Are you telling me you don't know how people would react if they found out he tried to rape Amber?"

"Oh." Tae Hyun hadn't considered that. "Yes. I guess I do."

Jason nodded. "Yeah. She made me promise not to say anything because she knew she'd get blamed somehow. And I went and kicked the shit outta that asshole anyway. Because he fucking deserved it." He frowned. "But I never said anything. And, in the end, I'm the only one who got fucked. Metaphorically speaking."

Tae Hyun wasn't sure what to say. Jason's actions had been

reckless. But his motivations were justifiable. Tae Hyun couldn't say for sure that he wouldn't have done something similar if he'd been in that position. And he could relate to going nuclear when presented with the right circumstances. He'd nearly sank his career–and Chang Min's–just from the sight of his romantic partner getting fucked on 1 million won per night hotel room sheets. Jason had sacrificed his most prominent role to date because of his actions. And he'd suffered for that choice ever since. "I'm sorry."

Jason shrugged. "Eh. It is what it is." He gently put his hand on Tae Hyun's shoulder. "But thanks for listening. Hardly anyone else knows that story." Jason smiled. "It's nice to finally talk about it with someone."

Jason's sad smile reminded him of a puppy, and Tae Hyun wanted to hug him. But he'd only known Jason for less than a day. And they were in public. "Thank you for sharing that with me. But can we leave now? Being in here makes me uncomfortable."

Jason snorted. "Why? Worried about being seen?"

"Yes."

"Oh." Jason nodded. "Yeah, okay. I get that. Just lemme settle up."

Tae Hyun waited while Jason haggled with the bartender, who didn't look like he wanted to accept his credit card. Then it turned out that Jason was trying to buy the bar's remaining bottle of Kingston, which definitely wasn't allowed. But Jason's charm–and, undoubtedly, his willingness to spend–won out.

Jason kept stumbling as they walked and almost dropped the whiskey bottle. So Tae Hyun eventually took it from him and put Jason's arm over his shoulders to help him along. The scene felt way too much like being in a drama series. All they needed was the accidental trip and fall into an unexpected kiss. But it also made Tae Hyun's heart race again.

Jason rambled as they walked back to their building, sharing stories about filming his first movie that Tae Hyun only half understood. And they thankfully avoided seeing anyone in the elevator as they went upstairs. Once they returned to the apartment, Jason announced that he needed a nap. So Tae Hyun let him go and brought the whiskey bottle to the kitchen. Then he went to Jason's room to find him lying face down on the bed. Well, mainly on the bed.

"Don't forget to call Naomi and tell her you're okay."

Jason replied with a muffled snort. Then he pushed himself over to lay on his back. "You've got her number now. You do it."

"Fine." Tae Hyun turned to leave. "I'll let you sleep."

"No, wait."

Tae Hyun turned back. "What?"

"Thank you for coming to find me." Jason tried sitting up but only managed to get up on one elbow. "I didn't realize how drunk I am. I never woulda found my way back by myself."

"You're lucky you only went two blocks away."

Jason snorted. "Where would I go? I don't know my way around. I don't even know where this building is."

Tae Hyun smiled. "Is that your way of asking me to show you around?"

Jason nodded. "Please?" He pushed out his lower lip in an adorable pout.

"Fine, I will. Now, get some sleep."

Tae Hyun returned to the kitchen, wondering if he should

call Naomi on Jason's behalf. He wasn't sure what time it even was in Los Angeles. Tae Hyun reached for his phone and remembered he still had Jason's with him, too. He pulled the other phone from his pocket and went to return it when he heard a muffled crash and thump. Tae Hyun rushed through Jason's door to see him sprawled on the floor with his pants halfway down.

"Are you okay?"

"Yeah." Jason laughed. "Just too drunk to take my pants off."

Tae Hyun shook his head. "Let me help you." He set Jason's phone on the dresser and bent over to help pull Jason to his feet. Then Jason somehow got his legs crossed and tripped, dragging them both down onto the bed.

Jason groaned. "Oh, man. I'm sorry." He tried to lift himself off of Tae Hyun's arm. But he slipped off his elbow and landed on his side, putting their faces inches apart. Jason snorted and pushed his face a fraction closer. "I've seen this K-drama before. I think this is where we confess our secret love for each other and kiss."

Tae Hyun felt Jason's warm, whiskey-scented breath on his face. He swallowed hard, unsure of what to do or say. Was Jason being serious? Or was it more drunk rambling? Because Tae Hyun suddenly wanted to kiss him. "I, uh–"

Jason snorted again. "But this is no K-drama, right?" He rolled off Tae Hyun's arm. "Although if you were ever looking to take advantage of me," he added with a wink, "now's your chance. Especially if you help me get my pants off."

Of course, Jason was just being drunk. Tae Hyun frowned and got off the bed. "Fine. I'll help you with your pants, but I'm not–"

Jason laughed. "Damn. Are you always this serious? I swear

I've watched you smile more in a two-minute interview than you have all day today."

Tae Hyun turned to face Jason seated on the bed, his pants around his ankles and his underwear-clad crotch on full display. Next to his smooth, tanned legs, the bright fabric of Jason's white briefs practically glowed. Tae Hyun swallowed hard as he stared at the shape of Jason's cock. He was suddenly sure he wanted to do more than kiss Jason. "You watched my interviews?"

"Of course! You researched me, right? And there's way more footage of you online than there is of me." Jason smirked and glanced at his naked thighs. "Now, are you gonna help me? Or are you just gonna stare at my balls?"

Tae Hyun quickly looked up. His ears warmed to the point he was sure they'd turned scarlet. "I–uh. I–"

"Relax, it's fine. I like looking at 'em, too. I'm a total hottie." Jason lay back and lifted his feet. "Help, please? I promise to stop making fun of you."

Tae Hyun groaned and nodded. After a minor struggle, he pulled Jason's jeans off and let them drop on the floor. "Anything else?"

"No. Not unless you like to cuddle." Jason winked and lay back on the bed.

Tae Hyun had just about reached his limit of Jason's sexy teasing. The whole interaction was stressful beyond the point of making him uncomfortable. "Then I'll let you sleep."

Tae Hyun couldn't leave Jason's room fast enough. Between their fall onto the bed and Jason's brazen display of his underwear-clad crotch, Tae Hyun was no longer confident in his ability to control himself around Jason. Only his certainty that Jason's drunken flirting was meant to tease Tae Hyun stopped him from responding in kind. Hopefully, Jason would sleep all that off before they started working together again. Tae Hyun decided to take a long, cold shower just in case.

11

Jason had no idea where he was when he woke up. That led to a brief moment of panic–lying in a strange bed in his underwear–before he remembered. He was in Seoul, lying in bed inside an apartment he temporarily shared with a K-pop idol turned soon-to-be movie star. An idol that he was sure was also a closeted gay.

It had been impossible to ignore how Tae Hyun stared at Jason's crotch. He had almost felt the pressure from it. Sure, he was hot enough that even straight guys looked at him that way. But it hadn't been one of the curious glances he'd sometimes get from the straight boys at the gym–sizing up the assumed competition or wondering if that old cliché about Asian dick sizes was really true. No, Tae Hyun's signposts all pointed in a particular direction. The look on his face had been pure lust. It had only lasted a moment–but at that moment, Jason decided he would fuck Tae Hyun. Maybe not soon, and certainly not that day. But the idea was already a foregone conclusion. No one he'd decided to take to bed had ever avoided that fate. And Tae Hyun wouldn't be the first.

Before he put any plans for conquest into motion, Jason knew he needed to call Naomi. He checked the time on his phone–two PM–and tried doing the mental math to guess the time in LA. Then he gave up and tapped her contact. Naomi answered by the end of the second ring.

"Do you have any idea what time it is here?"

Jason snorted. "No, of course not. Now, what was so fucking important that you sent our favorite idol out to hunt me down instead of waiting for me to call you?"

"Your dad had a stroke."

Jason nearly gasped. "What? How is he? And why am I hearing this from you?"

"He's fine. Well, not exactly fine. But he's expected to fully recover."

"Okay. And?"

Naomi huffed. "Your mom called me because she still thinks I'm your assistant."

"Seriously?" Jason chuckled. Although his mother had grown up solidly middle class, she'd adjusted to her new wealth long ago. That included considering everyone below her social station to be her servant in some kind of twisted, capitalist-infused Confucianism. "Well, I guess her plan worked. But you said he's fine?"

"Yes. I called the hospital on your behalf to check. It was a minor stroke, so they only kept him for the day. He's already home resting in bed."

Jason snorted. "There's no way Gerald Park's resting in bed. If you're up working, he's up working."

"And well on his way to stroke number two, I imagine." Naomi paused. Jason could almost hear her transformation from caring colleague to stern manager. "What happened today? Tae Hyun mentioned something about being intrusive and unkind."

"My host has been steadily testing my boundaries–"

Naomi laughed. "You have boundaries?"

"Fuck you. Anyway, today, he asked me about getting fired from *The Long Evening Sunset*."

"Ouch. But you like him, so you took off instead of letting him have it."

Jason scoffed. "Get out of my head, damn it. And I let him have it a little, too. Then I ended up telling him anyway."

"What? You're saying you told him what actually happened?"

"I did, yeah."

"Shit." Naomi took a loud breath. "Wow. That's– Well, that's–"

"Stop making it into something. It's nothing. I was drunk. And who's he gonna tell? Nobody knows me here."

"One: that's not true. *Moon Shines Madly* did really well there. And, two: I can count the number of people you've told that story to on one hand. Including Tae Hyun."

Jason huffed. "As far as you know."

"Yes. And I know everything. Or, at least, enough to say, please don't sleep with him, Jason."

"Jesus fucking christ! Would you get out of my head?"

"You say that like you're at all complicated and not just a simple, predictable, alcohol-infused man-child."

"Fuck you. I'm hanging up now."

"Fine. I'll just pass the fact that you're in Seoul to your mom."

Jason groaned. "Do that, and I'll give her your private number."

"What? How did you know–"

"You know me. I know you. Now I'm gonna put some pants on and try rescuing this day from the clutches of my alcohol-infused childishness."

"Man-childishness. I'll call if there's any more news."

"Thanks."

Jason ended the call before Naomi could pull out any more threats or scary predictions. Then he put on his pants and left his room. He found Tae Hyun sitting at the dining table reading through the movie script. He'd showered and changed into simple gray sweats, leaving his hair unstyled. It was an appealing look, despite being so dressed down. And sweatpants had long been a weakness for Jason. Then Jason noticed that Tae Hyun was humming to himself.

"That's beautiful, but I don't recognize it. Is it new?"

"Hmm?" Tae Hyun looked up from the script. "Oh." He probably didn't realize he'd been humming. "Yeah, it's a new song I wrote," he explained before returning to his reading.

"Ah." As much as Jason would've loved to hear it, Tae Hyun seemed much more distant and closed off than he had earlier. Probably best to leave it for some other time. He looked at the steaming mug sitting on the table and sniffed. "Is that coffee?"

"Yes." Tae Hyun tilted his head toward the kitchen without looking up. "I thought you might want some, so I just made a fresh pot."

Jason frowned. Why was everyone in his head lately? "Great. So. About today. Are we good?"

Tae Hyun closed the script and looked up. His body was stiff, and his face was full ice queen. Jason may have exorcized some of his demons, but Tae Hyun was still wound up tight. "Yes."

Jason's frown deepened, dragging his eyebrows together. "That's it? Just, yes?"

Tae Hyun's mouth twitched. Some emotion was bubbling beneath the surface of his frosty shell. "What else should I say?"

Jason shrugged. "Nothing. If you're good, then I'm good." He went to the french press sitting on the kitchen counter and poured some coffee into an empty mug. "What do you think of the script?"

"I think I'm in over my head."

Jason chuckled. He'd been worried that Tae Hyun's lingering tension was related to their argument. "It might feel like that, but you're really not." Jason brought his coffee to the table and sat across from Tae Hyun. "You've already got most of the skills you need from performing. And you've spent plenty of time in front of a camera."

"No." Tae Hyun shook his head. "This is different."

"It's not. Sure, it's bigger. But it's more of the same."

Tae Hyun didn't look so sure. "You really think I can do this?"

Jason smiled. "Of course. I wouldn't have taken the job if I didn't think so." He reached out and pulled the other script closer. "What page were you reading?"

"Hold on." Tae Hyun flipped through until he found where he'd left off. "Page twenty-two."

Jason nodded. It was the scene he'd read that morning that set off the whole day's events. "Yeah, that's a big scene, their declarations of love for each other. That's why I asked you about love earlier. You'll have to figure out how to express that, along with longing, hope, and sadness."

"But how do I do all that?"

"That's the big question, right? There are a few different ways that most actors use. You could use your own memories and experiences to bring up the emotions for the scene. Or you could mimic how you've seen others react to similar situations. But that only works well if you can make yourself cry on cue."

Tae Hyun frowned. "Which way do you use?"

"A little of both." Jason pursed his lips, wondering how far he could push things with Tae Hyun on his first day of acting school. "Let's try an exercise. Close your eyes and think about a happy memory from your past–something that really stands out in your mind."

"Anything?"

Jason nodded. "Anything happy. But something you remember really well."

Tae Hyun closed his eyes. He nodded after a moment. "Okay."

"Now, imagine that you're there again at that moment. And tell me what you hear."

Tae Hyun frowned. "What I hear?"

"Yes."

"Um." Tae Hyun took a slow breath. "Okay. I hear music. I hear children's laughter. I hear–" He stopped for a moment. "I hear the neighbor's wind chime."

"Good. And what do you smell?"

Jason watched Tae Hyun inhale through his nose, knowing that he wasn't really trying to smell his actual surroundings. "I smell kimchi and barbecued meat. I smell smoldering charcoal. I smell–" Tae Hyun suddenly smiled. "I smell my mother's perfume."

"Are you warm or cold?"

"Cold." Tae Hyun's smile grew bigger. "But warm in my mother's arms."

Jason smiled. "Do you feel happy?" Tae Hyun nodded, brightly beaming. "Okay. Let's try another. I want you to get angry."

Tae Hyun opened his eyes. "Why angry?"

"It's easier to start with the base emotions before you move into the more subtle ones. Shut your eyes." Tae Hyun nodded and closed his eyes. "Think of a time when you were so angry you couldn't feel anything else–a time when your anger was–" Jason paused. He wanted to say primal but didn't know the Korean word. "Intense."

Jason watched Tae Hyun's face as his smile was replaced by a deep frown and his eyebrows bunched together. Tae Hyun deeply inhaled. Then he loudly blew his breath out through his nose. "Alright."

"What do you hear?"

"I hear shouting. I hear a door slam. I hear my heartbeat pounding in my ears."

"What do you smell?"

"I smell–" Tae Hyun stopped and shook his head. "No." He opened his eyes. "I don't want to go back there."

"Then don't. Think of something else. Hell, you were pretty mad at me yesterday. Try that."

Tae Hyun shook his head. "No. I don't see the point of this."

Jason chuckled. "Are you angry now? You sound angry." Tae Hyun nodded. "That's the point. You'll need to call up these emotions on command. But you'll also need to put them away. A minute ago, you were happy. Now you're angry. But neither of those are related to what's actually happening now."

"Okay. Maybe I understand."

"Good. Let's try another. Close your eyes and think about the last time you fell in love with someone. Remember how you felt then." Jason watched as Tae Hyun closed his eyes. His face remained still. "Okay. Think about the first time you kissed each other. Now express how that felt without speaking."

Tae Hyun frowned but kept his eyes closed. "How do I do that?"

"You emote. Did it make you happy? Then maybe you'd smile. Did it make you sad? Then you'd probably frown." Tae Hyun's frown deepened. Was his first kiss that bad? No, it was something else. Jason could see the tension in Tae Hyun's neck and shoulders. He sighed. "Okay, you can open your eyes."

"I'm sorry."

Jason shook his head. "It's fine. We're just starting out, right? Switching between raw emotions like that is difficult." He pushed back from the table. "Let me show you how I'd do it. I remember most of the lines from this scene. At least, from the English script." Jason got up and walked to the open area next to the living room seating. "Come on." Tae Hyun silently considered Jason's request for a moment before getting up and walking over. "Good." Jason pointed to a spot a couple feet away from him. "You stand there, and I'll act out part of this scene for you."

Tae Hyun nodded and stood where Jason pointed. "Okay. What do I do?"

"Try to get into the scene. We're both madly into each other and pledging our literal undying love. Watch my facial expressions and my body language. Listen to the tone of my voice. Imagine the emotions I'm expressing and the emotions you'd feel. Understand?"

Tae Hyun nodded. "But I don't know the lines yet. Do I

have to–?"

"No. You don't have to say anything. Just observe. Try to feel what I'm expressing." Jason waited until Tae Hyun nodded again. Then he closed his eyes and thought back to when he stood with Amber on that brick-paved, gaslit Vancouver street. But that only pushed him toward anxiety and anger. That wouldn't do. Jason couldn't rely on real-life experience either. He'd only confessed his love for someone once, and it had ended badly. But the intensity of that memory was enough to make his heart race. It would have to do. Jason opened his eyes, and looked at Tae Hyun.

"Quickly! There's no time." Jason stepped forward and put his finger to Tae Hyun's lips. "No, don't speak. I must say this before the coming dawn steals my courage." Jason grasped Tae Hyun's hands, lightly squeezing them, never looking away from him. "I've dreamed of you since the night we first met. But I've never dared to speak of it, to open the floodgates for fear of drowning in my emotions." Jason sucked in his lower lip and lightly bit down, his breathing heavy as he stared into Tae Hyun's eyes. "To say love is to fail–for the word cannot begin to bind the ocean of my feelings. You've trapped me. You've ensnared my heart. My captured soul is yours to command." Jason felt himself tearing up. He blinked to send a tear cascading down his cheek. "I look at your face and stare into the blinding fire of a thousand suns. But I would gladly exchange my sight for a single glimpse of you, would your serene face then forever be burned into the folds of my mind." Jason reached up and gently caressed Tae Hyun's cheek. "I pledge myself to you, now and forever. All I ask in return is but a single kiss to fuel my heart's long, time-worn voyage to oblivion." Jason leaned forward until his mouth was almost close enough to touch Tae Hyun's. "A single kiss," he purred, his breath playing across Tae Hyun's lips. "Surely my love is worth at least that to you?"

Tae Hyun suddenly surged forward, pressing himself against Jason as their lips met. For a moment, Jason was too surprised to react. Was that actually happening? Then Jason felt Tae Hyun's erection pressed against his hip and knew it was real. Jason ran his hand down Tae Hyun's back as they kissed, pulling him close enough to feel his own hardening cock push against Tae Hyun's.

Jason shifted his kisses across Tae Hyun's face until he reached the top of his neck, just below his ear. He gently nuzzled that spot, then lightly kissed it. Tae Hyun moaned as Jason kissed down his neck to his collar, slipped his hands under the waistband of Tae Hyun's sweatpants, and cupped his firm dancer behind.

"Hyung," Tae Hyun hummed into Jason's ear. "Are we really doing this?"

Jason kissed Tae Hyun's collarbone again. "Do you want me to stop?" He pulled Tae Hyun's hips closer, pressing their erections together. "Because it doesn't feel like you want me to stop."

"No. Please don't stop."

Jason lifted his head and found Tae Hyun's lips again. He playfully poked his tongue into Tae Hyun's mouth as he slowly slid the idol's sweatpants and underwear down. Jason gently wrapped his hand around Tae Hyun, his tongue still exploring the inside of Tae Hyun's mouth, and slid his foreskin back to reveal a growing droplet of precum. Tae Hyun nearly bit Jason's tongue when he ran his thumb over it and smeared the slickness around.

Jason quickly pulled his tongue back to safety. "Careful."

"Sorry. I–uh!" Tae Hyun groaned as Jason stroked him, rhythmically sliding his foreskin up and down. "Hyung, wait."

Jason stopped and pulled his hand away. "What's wrong?"

"Nothing." Tae Hyun grinned. "Just something I want to do first."

Tae Hyun knelt before Jason and undid the button on his pants. Then he slid Jason's pants and underwear down. Jason frowned. He hadn't showered since that morning and had drunk most of a bottle of whiskey before his afternoon nap. But Tae Hyun didn't hesitate to take Jason into his waiting mouth.

Jason groaned as he felt himself surrounded by fiery wetness until he bumped the back of Tae Hyun's throat. He looked down and had a moment of near vertigo at the unreal sight of the K-pop idol going down on him. Jason had imagined it many times while he jerked off. But the real thing was so much better. And Tae Hyun had outstanding breath control–for a moment, Jason wondered if he was even breathing–and quickly brought Jason to the edge.

Jason grunted as he grabbed Tae Hyun's head and gently pulled him away. "Not yet," he panted as he helped Tae Hyun to his feet.

There was so much more Jason wanted to do. But neither of them had planned for what was happening, so they weren't prepared. Instead, Jason leaned forward and kissed Tae Hyun again, tasting the salt from his own precum and the musk from his crotch. Then he grabbed Tae Hyun and stroked. Jason shivered and nearly lost his balance as Tae Hyun did the same, taking Jason in his hand. And the pair of them kissed, tongues darting in and out of each other's mouths, hands on each other shoulders, as their stroking fell into a mutual rhythm. It wasn't long before Tae Hyun's moaning crescendoed, and Jason felt the sticky warmth of Tae Hyun's cum splash on his hip. Tae Hyun pulled his mouth from Jason's, taking a moment to catch his breath. Then he grinned, staring into Jason's eyes, as he resumed stroking Jason's cock. Jason closed his eyes, trying to delay the inevitable, but was powerless to do so. He soon let out a fevered cry as he splattered Tae Hyun in return.

The pair stood there for a few moments, panting, absorbed in mutual bliss, holding onto one another for balance, their softening cocks still in each other's grip. Then Tae Hyun let go of Jason and lifted his sweatshirt off, using it to wipe his fluids off Jason's hip. After wiping himself, Tae Hyun stepped out of his pants, grabbed Jason's hand, and led him to the shower. Jason got hard again as they took turns washing each other. Before Jason could stop him, Tae Hyun fell to his knees, took Jason into his mouth, and gave him another demonstration of his excellent breath control. After Jason came for the second time, Tae Hyun gently rinsed him off.

"So," Jason casually offered as the pair toweled themselves dry. They hadn't spoken since the first time Tae Hyun had blown him. "That happened."

Tae Hyun chuckled. "Don't act so surprised. You've been flirting with me since you got here."

Jason grinned. "You think I don't know I'm irresistible?"

"Really?" Tae Hyun snorted. "If only your cock was as big as your ego."

"Ouch." Jason chuckled. "I suppose I deserve that."

Tae Hyun shook his head. "No. You don't. I'm just feeling a little awkward now. I don't do this kind of thing very often."

Jason heard Tae Hyun's unspoken anymore. His excellent oral skills made it clear that Tae Hyun was at least experienced with giving blow jobs. Jason wrapped his towel around his waist and leaned against the bathroom counter. "There's no need to feel awkward. And I don't do this often, either. You're only the second person I've fooled around with in the last six months."

"Really?"

Jason understood Tae Hyun's surprise. His reputation as a bad boy was well-established. But a person's reputation wasn't always deserved. "Yeah, really. So. You're gay?"

"What gave it away?" Tae Hyun chuckled. "You are, too?" Jason nodded. "Okay." Tae Hyun sighed. Despite Jason's assurances, he clearly still felt awkward. "What now?"

Jason wasn't sure how to answer that, either. "That was the longest time we've spent together without arguing, so I suppose that means there's hope for us yet. Other than that?" Jason shrugged. "I don't know. I like you. I'm attracted to you. And I have to work with you for the next few months."

"You like me?"

Jason chuckled. "Yeah. I like you when you're open with me, like this. I don't like when you hit me with super intense personal questions without reciprocating. It's–how did you put it? Intrusive and unkind?"

"Ah." Tae Hyun nodded. "I-ah. I should just tell you."

Jason shrugged. "Now that I have some context, I think I may have a better idea of what happened." Tae Hyun's ears, already rosy, turned a bright red. "Relax. You don't have to tell me. But you already know my big secret. It's not like I'll tell anyone about yours."

Tae Hyun took another deep breath. "Okay, yeah. But I'm

going to need a drink."

"A drink?" Jason chuckled. "Don't tell me you're taking after me already."

"Please don't tease me. I'm well outside of my comfort zone right now."

After they got dressed, Jason opened the illicitly purchased bottle of Kingston, chuckling as he poured a drink for each of them. He had no idea what the dollar-to-Korean-won exchange rate was. But he was pretty sure he'd paid the bartender more than a hundred bucks for it. "At least you're not in a foreign country." Jason set down the bottle and Tae Hyun's glass and took his seat.

"I think I'd feel less exposed if I was." Tae Hyun drained his glass in one swallow and held it out to Jason.

Jason obliged him with a second pour. "Go easy on this stuff. It's not soju."

"Good." Tae Hyun took another drink but didn't finish the glass. "So. My dirty little secret?"

Jason shrugged. "Up to you if you want to tell me."

Tae Hyun nodded. "I don't know how much you know about the Korean music industry. I started as a trainee when I was sixteen. Well, fourteen, by international age. And I did well, obviously. I was eighteen when *XTC* debuted. Being an idol comes with a lot of perks. But it also has conditions–one of which is that I wasn't allowed to date."

Jason raised a questioning eyebrow. "What about that model?"

"No." Tae Hyun shook his head. "That thing with Yoo Mi wasn't real. It was a publicity thing her management arranged to help rescue her image. But we're very good friends. In fact, she's also one of the few people who know I'm gay."

"It's good that you at least have someone to talk with about that."

Tae Hyun nodded. "Yeah. But the only thing worse than a young idol dating someone would be an idol dating someone in their own group." He paused, clearly struggling with talking about the situation. "I started flirting with Chang Min when we were still trainees."

"Chang Min?" Jason shook his head. "No offense, but he always seemed like an asshole. I was sure it was the other one."

"Xiang?" Tae Hyun snorted. "No. He mostly kept to himself. At the time, I thought he was just a private person. Looking back, I think he may have felt left out." Tae Hyun shook his head. "But Chang Min and I started dating, if you can call it that, about a year after our debut. I loved him. And I thought we were in love right up until I found him in bed with a callboy in our Tokyo hotel room."

"Are you serious?" Tae Hyun nodded. "Shit, that sucks. Also, how was that even possible? Aren't you pretty much under constant watch?"

Tae Hyun shook his head. "Not as much as you'd think. Our watchers are people, too. You can bribe them. Or wait until they're looking the other way, which they frequently do. As hard as touring can be for us, it's twice as much work for them."

"Still, I'm sorry."

"Thanks." Tae Hyun took another sip, holding the bourbon in his mouth for a moment before swallowing. Maybe Jason had won over another Kingston fan. "I was livid, shouting the callboy out of the room before I turned on Chang Min. I wanted to kick his ass, but, of course, I couldn't. I wanted to

161

tell our management, too. But I couldn't do or say anything to give away our secret. I think he was counting on that to keep me in line."

Jason nodded. "I know the feeling. So, you quit instead?"

"I was under contract, so I couldn't exactly quit. But military service is compulsory, so my contract has a military clause. It was the only thing I could think of to do. KBR had to allow it, and I didn't have to explain anything to anyone."

"Do you think they knew?"

"KBR?" Tae Hyun shrugged. "I don't know. Normally, something like that would've gotten us fired. But the whole thing with Yoo Mi made me wonder. Plus, there were only three of us. Even firing one of us would be the end of the group."

Tae Hyun reached up to rub one of his shoulders, reminding Jason how Diego massaged him after their last hookup. Jason got up and walked around behind Tae Hyun.

"Here. Let me."

Tae Hyun briefly stiffened under Jason's touch. Then Jason gave his tight shoulder muscles a firm squeeze. Tae Hyun closed his eyes and moaned. "Oh, that feels amazing."

Jason chuckled. "I know." Tae Hyun's shoulders felt like there were made of iron. "But you're so fucking tense. You may need to see a professional."

Tae Hyun moaned again as Jason worked his thumbs into the sides of his neck. "You're probably right."

"If only there was some other way I could help you get rid of this tension."

Tae Hyun snorted. "I thought you weren't going to tease me."

"You asked me not to, but I never said I wouldn't." Jason

pulled Tae Hyun's head backward and looked down at him. "Besides, that's not teasing. It's flirting."

Tae Hyun held Jason's eye contact for a few moments before looking away. "I'm out of practice."

"If only there were some way to–"

Tae Hyun laughed and grabbed Jason's hands. "Already?"

"What can I say? I'm relentless."

Tae Hyun gently squeezed Jason's hands. "I can't deny that I'm attracted to you. And what we did was fun. But I'm not sure how far I want to take things. We're working together. We live together. And we've spent at least half our time together arguing and insulting each other. Let's see if we can get along first."

Jason considered that. He knew the idol was right. Jason offered Tae Hyun a single nod. Then he leaned down and kissed Tae Hyun's forehead. "You're right. We should slow down. How about we run through a different scene?"

"Okay." Tae Hyun smiled. "As long as you give me a few more minutes on my shoulders first."

12

Tae Hyun hadn't taken the metro in years–not since he was a KBR trainee. And then he was mostly shuttled around in a company van. Jason had never taken any subway, including the one in Los Angeles. Tae Hyun didn't even know LA had a subway. But the pair managed to get off at the correct Jongno-gu station, emerging at street level to the outskirts of the charmingly nostalgic Ikseon-dong Hanok Village. Tae Hyun was excited to finally return. Jason seemed more concerned with himself.

"See?" Jason gestured to the uninterested passersby surrounding them before lighting a cigarette. "No one knows me here."

Tae Hyun shrugged as he watched Jason take a long drag. While they'd both opted for baseball caps before heading out, Tae Hyun also wore a mask. Jason went with sunglasses instead. "If you say so."

"So," Jason said as he exhaled. "This is it?"

Tae Hyun frowned. "You don't like it?"

"It's not that." Jason shrugged. "It's just not what I expected. It's very, uh, quaint."

Tae Hyun breathed out a sigh through his nose. "You hate it."

Jason shook his head. "No. It's fine. It's just not what I would've chosen." He turned to face a nearby, narrow Ikseon-dong street entrance. Then he frowned. "It's also familiar."

Tae Hyun nodded. "We filmed a music video here. I always wanted to come back but never had the time."

"Oh yeah," Jason said, nodding. "I remember that one. You guys did a bunch of different period scenes and stuff, right? It was cool. And that choreo was killer."

"Thanks." Tae Hyun smiled. It was nice that Jason had been honest about being a fan. "It was fun to shoot."

Tae Hyun wondered if it was too late to turn around and go back home. Probably. Visiting Ikseon-dong had been his idea after Jason's request to see more of the city. Tae Hyun had suggested it after the pair had spent the evening casually chatting when they got tired of acting exercises. Well, Jason had been casually chatting. Tae Hyun had been mindful of asking questions he guessed might be too pushy. Jason had seemed to forget all about their earlier arguments, and Tae Hyun didn't want to remind him.

Tae Hyun had also spent most of the evening silently worried that what they'd done would make things awkward between them. But Jason was just as friendly and charming as ever, except for being a little more willing to engage in casual touch. Tae Hyun had also worried about how the night would end. Would they share a bed? Would they sleep alone? Would they fool around again? He wasn't even sure which of those he wanted. But Jason resolved that as well. When it came time for bed, he offered Tae Hyun a gentle kiss on the cheek before heading for his own room. But that still left his primary question unanswered. What were they to each other? Friends with benefits? Lovers? Colleagues who hooked up?

"Well, we're here," Tae Hyun finally said. "Want to go look around with me?"

"Sure, why not?" Jason smiled. "Let's go."

Ikseon-dong was an older neighborhood, Tae Hyun explained as they wandered, built in the early part of the previous century and mostly left unchanged since then. The Hanok Village's traditional houses were packed together along narrow, tiled lanes, forcing out any vehicle larger than a motorbike. While still primarily residential, the area had undergone some gentrification over the past decade, with various shops, cafes, and restaurants moving in.

"I'm surprised it's not more touristy," Jason commented.

"It's mostly locals that come here. Are you hungry? There's a hotteok shop here that I've been meaning to try."

Jason chuckled. "I can pretty much always eat. But remind me what hotteok are?"

"Stuffed pancakes. You'll love them."

It took a little time to find the shop. Tae Hyun's memories from his last visit included the film crew, which was absent. But he kept his eye out for the shops with lines of people waiting before spotting the hotteok shop he remembered.

Tae Hyun ignored his rising anxiety as he and Jason got in line. The more people around him, the more likely someone would recognize him. And he was way off his leash, dragging Jason across Seoul without saying a word to Ji Hoon or KBR first.

Tae Hyun ordered a pair of hotteok for himself–one with a sweet cheese filling and the other with sweet red bean paste. Jason got a traditional hotteok filled with cinnamon, sugar, and nuts and one filled with peanuts and honey.

"Oh, wow," Jason said after swallowing his first bite. "This is amazing. I don't even want to know how many calories it has."

Tae Hyun nodded as he chewed a bite from the bean paste hotteok. "It's better not to ask. Do you like sweet bean paste?" He held his out to Jason. "You should try this one."

"Okay, thanks." Jason grabbed Tae Hyun's hand, and Tae Hyun's posture automatically stiffened. "Relax. I'm not gonna bite you." Jason pulled Tae Hyun's hand close and tore a bite off the hotteok. "Wow. This is so good. Reminds me of the bean buns I'd get from the Chinese market."

Tae Hyun held his breath until Jason let go of his hand. "Uh, yeah."

Jason laughed. "Would you please relax? No one's watching us. And who cares if they are? It's not like we're making out. You're just sharing your food with me."

"I guess so." Tae Hyun nodded and blew out a long breath. "I'm sorry. I'm not used to this."

"Used to what? Going out with friends? Why would–" Jason stopped and shook his head. "No. I'm sorry. I'm being an asshole. I'll stop."

"You don't have to stop." Tae Hyun shrugged and showed Jason a reluctant smile. "I'm just not used to it."

Jason snorted. "Alright. Then do you want to try mine?"

Tae Hyun nodded, so Jason held out his hotteok. Tae Hyun leaned in and took a bite. "Delicious."

Tae Hyun felt some honey dripping down his lip, but Jason reached out to wipe it off with his thumb. Then he stuck his honeyed thumb into his mouth.

"Delicious."

Tae Hyun snorted. "Just two friends sharing food, eh?"

"What?" Jason chuckled. "I do that with all my friends."

"Sure you do. Eat up. There's another shop I really want to visit."

The next shop sold aroma diffusers, scented candles, and scented oils. Tae Hyun remembered wanting to visit when they'd filmed in Ikseon-dong. But there'd been no time. He'd even looked it up online that morning to ensure it was still there.

Jason frowned when they stopped in front of the shop. "It's a perfume store?"

"No." Tae Hyun shook his head as they walked inside. He was nearly overcome by a symphony of competing fragrances. "Scents for the home. You can mix your own and everything."

Jason snorted and rolled his eyes. "Okay, sure."

"You don't have to get anything, but I'm going to. I tried to take Yoo Mi here, but her publicist said it wasn't trendy enough."

Jason snorted. "Good thing I don't have a publicist."

"You don't?"

"You know my reputation." Jason gently elbowed Tae Hyun. "What publicist would want to work with me?"

Tae Hyun nodded, unwilling to press the sensitive issue further–especially in public. While Jason browsed through the shop, Tae Hyun went to the counter and asked about recommendations. The clerk pointed him toward an older woman seated at a small table in the back corner. As Tae Hyun approached, the woman noticed and waved for him to come close.

Tae Hyun offered her a slight bow. "Excuse me, grandmother. The clerk said you make scent recommendations."

The woman smiled. "Yes, I do. Please, have a seat and show

me your palms."

"I'm sorry?"

The woman frowned. "I said take a seat, young man."

Tae Hyun quickly sat in the empty chair. His elder had made her instructions plain, and Tae Hyun was reluctant to be rude. At least she didn't ask him to take his mask off. Tae Hyun awkwardly held his hands out, palms up. The palm reader grabbed Tae Hyun's hands, leaned forward, and began to examine them. He felt the warmth of her heavy breath on his hands. It smelled a little spicy. Then she frowned and put on a pair of reading glasses hanging from a chain around her neck.

"Interesting."

Tae Hyun tried to swallow his growing sense of unease. "What do you see, grandmother?"

The palm reader shook her head. Then she moved her thumb to a spot on Tae Hyun's right palm and pressed down. "What do you smell right now?"

Tae Hyun hadn't expected that. He sniffed a few times. "Something woody." It was fresh, bright, and clean. "Pine? Or maybe cedar?"

The palm reader nodded. Then she released Tae Hyun's right hand and pressed down on a spot on his left palm. "And now?"

Tae Hyun sniffed again, expecting to smell the same thing. But it was different–darker and spicy. He frowned. "Spices. Cardamom or cloves."

The palm reader nodded again. "I see."

"What does that mean?" Tae Hyun hoped he didn't sound as anxious as he felt.

The palm reader pressed her thumb into Tae Hyun's right

palm again. "You have great potential. You're talented and driven." Then she pressed her thumb into Tae Hyun's left palm. "But you're blocked. You're fighting against your own nature." Tae Hyun nearly pulled his hand from the palm reader's grasp. But the woman's grip was surprisingly firm. "Only when you let go and become your true self will you realize your full potential. It will still cause you great difficulty. But you're no stranger to that already, I'll wager."

Tae Hyun jerked his hands back the moment the palm reader released her grip. What the old woman said was uncomfortably close to the truth. "I don't understand."

"I think you do." The palm reader scrawled a short list into a small notebook. Then she tore the page out and handed it to Tae Hyun. "Give this to the girl at the counter. She'll mix it up for you."

Tae Hyun took the list and looked at it. Dangyuja, leather, amber, nutmeg, iris, violet, mandarin, and juniper berry. He never would've come up with that on his own. But he liked most of the smells he saw. Still, the whole experience was way too weird. "Thank you, grandmother."

The palm reader nodded as Tae Hyun got up. On his way toward the counter, still shaken, he noticed Jason talking to a shop clerk before a display of diffusers. Jason caught him looking and waved, which made Tae Hyun grin under his mask. He realized he had no reason to worry about what the palm reader had said. The more he thought about it, the more he understood that the reader's pronouncements were vague to the point that they could apply to almost anyone. Sure, Tae Hyun was fighting his true nature. But who wasn't? Jason, probably.

Tae Hyun chuckled as he handed the list to the clerk at the

counter. The clerk nodded as she read it over. "This will take me a few minutes. You should look for a diffuser while you wait."

"I will. Thank you."

Tae Hyun found Jason alone in another part of the shop. The clerk he'd been speaking to was nowhere to be seen. "Find anything?"

Jason nodded. "I did. They're wrapping it up for me now."

"What did you get?"

"You'll see." Jason smirked. "It's a surprise. How'd your reading go?"

Tae Hyun shrugged as he picked up a diamond-shaped, cut crystal diffuser. "Fine, I suppose. It was weirder than I expected."

"Weirder than an old woman telling you what smells you like from looking at your hands?"

"You saw that?" Tae Hyun snorted as he grabbed a lovely blue patterned, blown glass diffuser. He flipped it over to check the price. 60,000 wasn't bad. "And, yes. Weirder than that."

"That's pretty."

Tae Hyun glanced up to find Jason looking at him. "Are you talking about me or the diffuser?"

Jason shrugged. "Maybe you should check with the palm reader." He looked at something over Tae Hyun's shoulder. "Mine's ready. Pick up whatever you want. It's all on me."

Jason left Tae Hyun at the display to go pay for his purchase. Tae Hyun examined several other diffusers before settling on the blue one and bringing it to the counter. The clerk had already packaged his scented oil mixture. She wrapped the diffuser and added it to his bag before handing Jason his credit card.

When they were back outside, Jason excitedly turned to Tae Hyun. "Okay. Do you want to see what I got?"

"Right now?" Tae Hyun laughed. "I thought it was a surprise."

"It is. I was gonna wait until we got back to the apartment to show you, but I'd rather show you now." Jason reached into the bag he was holding, pulled out a small box, and handed it to Tae Hyun. "Here."

Tae Hyun looked at Jason's box for a moment. "It's for me?" Jason nodded, so Tae Hyun traded his bag for the box. He opened it to see a crumpled nest of purple tissue paper. Nestled inside was a white ceramic fox figurine with a purple strip painted down its back. Tae Hyun smiled as he picked up the fox and inspected it.

"Do you like it?"

Tae Hyun forgot the mask blocked his smile and quickly nodded. "It's adorable."

Jason grinned. "I saw the purple stripe and thought of you. Because of your hair. I know it's not much, but–"

Of course. The purple streak in his hair. It was so new that Tae Hyun forgot about it. But Jason had never seen him without it–at least not in person. It was such a silly, thoughtful gift. Tae Hyun almost couldn't believe it. He threw his arms around Jason and pulled him into a tight embrace. "I love it. Thank you."

Jason snorted in surprise. "I thought you were worried about what people would think."

Tae Hyun let Jason go and put the figurine back into the box. "And I thought no one would recognize you here."

"Yeah, until KBR announces everything tomorrow. Then

my ordinary person vacation is over."

Tae Hyun chuckled. "You're nowhere near ordinary, hyung. Not even incognito."

"Hyung? Are you flirting with me? Because if you are, I might have to–"

Tae Hyun caught the flash's reflection in Jason's sunglasses. A flash? Who used a flash in broad daylight?

Jason frowned. "What the hell?"

Tae Hyun quickly looked back to see where the flash had come from. He spotted the photographer but looked away before they could get a shot of his masked face. "It's fine, Jason. Don't worry about it."

Jason shook his head and squeezed his hands into tight fists. "It's not fine." He moved to step around Tae Hyun before Tae Hyun grabbed him. The last thing they needed was to cause trouble in public.

"Jason, please don't," Tae Hyun begged. "It won't help things."

Jason tried to tug his arm free from Tae Hyun's grasp. "Are you saying you want pictures of this all over the web?"

"Of course not." Tae Hyun tightened his grip on Jason's arm. "But what do you want? Because you seriously need to think about how you look right now." Jason stopped trying to pull his arm free. "Maybe you don't care about assaulting a photographer. But if people figure out it's me with you, I'll never hear the end of it."

Jason frowned. "Well, I don't like it. That asshole's got no right to–"

"Alright." Tae Hyun spun Jason around and marched him back inside the scent shop. He was done humoring Jason's prickly nature. If the actor wanted to fight someone in broad daylight, he could do it on his own time.

The girl behind the counter gave them a confused smile and half-wave as Tae Hyun pushed Jason past her toward the palm reader. "Excuse me, grandmother–"

"The back door is that way," the old woman replied and jerked her head to her right.

Tae Hyun bowed his head in thanks as they rushed past the palm reader toward the back of the shop. He spotted the red exit sign and dragged Jason through the door beneath it into the tiny alley behind the shop. Tae Hyun only stopped to press Jason against the wall behind him.

"Listen to me right now, hyung," Tae Hyun commanded. "I don't care what you do when you're alone. But you need to act right when you're with me. No running off to get drunk. No getting into fights. Nothing that will damage my reputation. Understand?"

Tae Hyun watched the grin blossom on Jason's face as he nodded. "Yes, sir. I understand."

Tae Hyun huffed. "Don't push me, Jason. I can't have you always swinging around like a big hammer. I mean it."

Jason's grin disappeared. "Oh, I believe you." He sucked in his lower lip and bit down for a moment. "It's just that you're so fucking hot when you're bossy like this. It makes me want to show you my big hammer."

"That," Tae Hyun said as he pointed his finger in Jason's face, "is exactly what I mean. I need you to behave."

Jason pouted. "You're right. I'm sorry. You'd better punish me. Thoroughly."

"Ugh. You're fucking impossible. If I didn't–" Tae Hyun's phone began vibrating in his pocket. He pulled it out to see Ji Hoon calling. "Don't move. I have to take this." Tae

Hyun tapped the answer button and held the phone to his ear. "Hello, Director Choo."

"Tae Hyun! I hope you're enjoying your visit to Ikseon-dong."

"What?" Tae Hyun frowned. "How did you know?"

"I'm looking at photos of you and Jason feeding each other on *K-Star Daily* right now. What are those? Hotteok? They look divine."

Tae Hyun felt his stomach drop. "Are you serious, sir?"

"Of course, I'm serious."

Jason frowned. "What's up?"

Tae Hyun shook his head, holding up a single finger to silence Jason. "We only just spotted the photographer and ducked into an alley behind a shop. What should we do now?"

"You just spotted him? So I guess I still have more pictures to look forward to." Ji Hoon sighed. "Find a place to hide out, and I'll send a team to fetch you back here to the office. The good news is that you're trending right now. But I want to get this situation back under control."

"I understand, sir."

"What shop are you at?" Tae Hyun gave Ji Hoon the shop's name. "Okay, there's a café near there. In fact, you may be able to reach it from the alley. Ask if the owner, Su Bin, is working and tell her you're a friend of mine. She'll keep you out of sight until we can get to you."

"I will, sir. I'm sorry."

Ji Hoon acknowledged Tae Hyun's apology with a simple grunt before disconnecting. Tae Hyun frowned and opened his phone's browser.

Jason cleared his throat. "What's up?"

"We were too late," Tae Hyun replied as he looked up the

K-Star Daily blog. Sure enough, he spotted the photo feature of him and Jason outside the hotteok shop. "Shit."

Jason moved behind Tae Hyun and looked over his shoulder. "Oh, wow. They even got me wiping honey off your chin."

Tae Hyun huffed. "Damn it. We never should've come here."

Jason took Tae Hyun's phone from his hand and turned off the screen. "It's fine. I've seen you and your fellow idols do that kind of thing all the time."

"It's not that." Tae Hyun frowned. "I mean, it's not just that. But the shop is clearly visible in the photos, so it's probably about to be mobbed with *Dreamers*. If it isn't already."

"Dreamers?"

"We called our fan club the *Dream*," Tae Hyun explained, "and our fans are *Dreamers*. But we should go find this café. Ji Hoon said it was close."

Jason nodded. "Yes, sir."

13

Jason followed Tae Hyun up the alley until they spotted a small sign for the café his manager had told him about. Jason's rage at the photographer had faded after Tae Hyun's dominance display behind the fragrance store. But he hadn't forgotten about the asshole photographer or their brazen use of the flash. It was a taunt, daring Jason to break character and show his true colors. But Tae Hyun's angry admonishments were foremost on Jason's mind.

Tae Hyun had taken Jason seriously after he agreed that they should slow down. The idol's walls went back up as soon as they left the bathroom and got dressed. But that was okay. Jason had already gotten a thorough look behind them and liked what he saw. And the more often Tae Hyun brought them down, the easier it would get. So Jason went easy on him for the rest of the evening. Even if he spent the entire time remembering the idol's enchanting naked form.

Of course, the walls were up again as they sat at the rearmost table in the café Ji Hoon had directed them to. The woman Tae Hyun spoke with delivered a pair of tall beers and a tray of fried snacks to hold them over while they waited. The rest of the café's staff pretended the pair wasn't there. And they couldn't be seen from the front windows.

Jason watched Tae Hyun as he sipped from his beer. The idol's thoughts may as well have been written on his face. But Jason knew his familiarity was an illusion. Despite their recent physical intimacy, he still barely knew Tae Hyun. Jason had assumed that his icy facade was just that–a front. But Tae Hyun could've easily just been like that all the time. That would've been disappointing were it true. As the prolonged silence grew uncomfortable, he decided to drag Tae Hyun out of his head.

"I'm sorry about earlier."

Tae Hyun's far-off gaze quickly focused on Jason. "Are you?"

"Of course. Just because I have a temper doesn't mean I'm proud of it."

Tae Hyun nodded. "Okay."

Jason reached for a handful of french fries. "Any word on when your handlers will get here?"

Tae Hyun glanced at his phone, sitting next to his beer on the table, and tapped the screen to wake it. "They're nearly here."

"Okay," Jason said after swallowing his fries. "So, can we talk about that photographer?"

"You already apologized for that."

Jason snorted. "I don't want to talk about me. I want to talk about the photographer. Like, why did he use his flash? We may not have even spotted him otherwise."

Tae Hyun frowned. "I don't know. I assumed it was an accident."

"No way." Jason shook his head. "It couldn't be. Not after he managed to get those shots of us eating together." He picked up a few pieces of dried squid and inspected them before putting them in his mouth. It wasn't calamari, but it was still good. "If he hadn't given himself away like that, he could've followed us all around this damn place."

"So, what's your theory?"

"Provocation."

Tae Hyun tilted his head in confusion. "You think he was trying to provoke us?"

"Not us. Me."

Tae Hyun pushed his brows together. "As in, he knew you'd get mad?" He shook his head. "That seems a little far-fetched."

Jason quietly chuckled as he recalled the incident at the dive bar on Van Nuys. That could've easily been the same sort of setup by two surfer boy posers looking for a quick score. "You'd be surprised how often that happens."

Tae Hyun looked away for a moment. "Oh. They're here."

Min Jun and two unknown KBR handlers approached the table from the back entrance. Or maybe they were bodyguards. It was hard to tell.

Min Jun offered them a quick bow. "We have a van waiting nearby. We'll take you to it via the alley." He held up a pair of shopping bags. "But first, you should change."

Jason's bag contained a dark gray hooded sweatshirt and a red baseball cap to replace the black one he'd been wearing. "Subtle," he joked as he put on the hoodie.

"It's a simple misdirection," Min Jun admitted. "But we only have to get you to the van."

Jason snorted as he put his black hat into the bag. Then he handed the bag to Min Jun. "Don't lose this."

Min Jun stared at the bag for several moments before taking it from Jason. "I will not lose it, sir," he agreed with a tone that suggested he'd definitely leave the bag sitting on the sidewalk.

After Tae Hyun changed and Min Jun settled up with the café manager, the handlers led Min Jun, Jason, and Tae Hyun through the back door to the alley. Calling it an alley was generous. There was barely room to walk, and several times Jason had to turn sideways to fit around century-old utility pipes. It terminated in a fire door that led to a sidewalk next to a regular street. A maroon minivan sat idling just ahead with its hazard lights flashing. One of the handlers opened the side door to allow Tae Hyun and Jason inside. Then the handlers took the rearmost bench seat while Min Jun climbed into the passenger seat. Min Jun had barely closed his door before the van pulled away.

Jason felt his phone vibrate and pulled it from his pocket to see a message from Naomi.

I see you've already made the local gossip blogs

Jason snorted and typed out his reply. *KBR just sent a security detail to sneak us out of there in a van with curtains on the windows*

I know you'll never do it, but you need to be more careful

Jason rolled his eyes. He assumed he was on his way to get yelled at by Tae Hyun's manager. Jason didn't need to hear it from his, too.

Noted. Be a dear and save copies of those pics for me

"Everything alright?"

Jason turned to a suspiciously present Tae Hyun. "Yeah. My business manager saw the pics, too."

Tae Hyun smiled. "Naomi?"

Jason chuckled. "Oh, yeah. You two are friends now."

"I don't know about that. But I like her."

Jason laughed when he saw Naomi's reply.

I'm sure Steven already has

"Of course you do." Jason put his phone back in his pocket.

"She's amazing."

The drive back to Gangnam was short enough that Jason didn't mind being unable to see out the windows. They soon pulled off the street into the KBR parking garage, stopping at the same underground entrance Ji Hoon's driver had taken Jason to after picking him up from Incheon. The handlers stayed with the driver in the van, leaving Min Jun with escort duty. Ji Hoon's assistant took them and their bags to the twelfth floor and deposited them at Ji Hoon's office door before returning to his desk. Ji Hoon was on the phone but waved the pair inside.

While Tae Hyun sat down, Jason spied a new addition to Ji Hoon's bar and walked right over. A brand new, unopened bottle of Kingston sat there among the other unmarked bottles. Jason was impressed. He picked up the bourbon bottle and offered it to Tae Hyun, who shook his head. Jason shrugged, cracked the seal as he opened the bottle, and poured himself three fingers into a low ball. Then he grabbed his drink and took the seat next to Tae Hyun.

Ji Hoon finished his call as Jason sipped his Kingston. He frowned as he hung up his phone. "I see you've already helped yourself."

"What? Did you get this for someone else?"

Ji Hoon shook his head. "No, of course not." He pushed back from his desk, got up, and went to pour something for himself. "I bought it as a bribe for you."

"A bribe for what? You're already paying me."

"Your business manager suggested that it would smooth things over between us," Ji Hoon offered as he returned to his desk with his drink.

Jason snorted. "Is this the kind of meeting where I need to

be smoothed over, Ji Hoon?"

Tae Hyun quietly chuckled, which earned him a frown from Ji Hoon. "It's only been two days," Ji Hoon said, "and I've already had to rescue you from photographers when you should've been working."

Jason sat forward and set his empty low ball on the edge of Ji Hoon's desk. "Who says we weren't working? Did you take some acting classes I don't know about?"

Ji Hoon shook his head. "I expect this sort of behavior from you, Jason. But, you, Tae Hyun?" He directed a stern gaze toward the idol. "I thought more of you than this."

Tae Hyun was about to respond, but Jason cut him off. "No. You're not doing that." Tae Hyun and Ji Hoon turned to Jason with dual looks of surprise. "You said I had a free hand with this. Or was your helpful assistant lying when he told me that?"

Ji Hoon's firm expression melted after a few moments. "No, my assistant did not lie."

"Alright." Jason sat back in his chair, leaving his empty glass behind. "Then the only problem I can see is that your office has a leak."

Ji Hoon huffed. "What makes you say that?"

"It's obvious, sir," Tae Hyun said. "Why was a professional photographer at Ikseon-dong in the first place if he wasn't following us? I was masked, except for when we were eating."

"Which is when he took those pictures," Ji Hoon added.

"But only because he was there in the first place, sir," Tae Hyun countered.

Ji Hoon shook his head. "No, I fear you're both being paranoid. It was a coincidence, nothing more."

"So there's no real problem with our being there," Jason

said. "If no one knew I was here yet, I mean."

Ji Hoon slowly nodded, unsure if he'd won their argument. "Which brings us to the real purpose of our meeting. Now that we've finalized the main cast, we're moving up the official movie announcement to this evening."

Tae Hyun frowned. "Finalized the cast?"

"I mean your costar, of course. We decided to hold off on officially announcing the movie until we signed her. But the contracts have been signed, so we're moving our press conference to this evening."

"My costar?"

Ji Hoon confidently smiled as he nodded. "Yes. You'll be starring opposite Sang Yoo Mi."

Jason hadn't expected to be surprised by that. Clearly, neither had Tae Hyun, by the sound of his gasp. "What? How long has that been in the works?"

"Since the beginning. She was available. And it seemed a perfect pairing, given your history."

Tae Hyun's breathing had grown shallow. And he gripped the arms of his chair so hard that Jason saw his knuckles turn white. "And her fiance is okay with that?"

Ji Hoon tilted his head in confusion. "Why wouldn't he be? It's a movie role. You're not dating her again."

Tae Hyun frowned. "Well, I don't know if I'm okay with this, sir."

"Why wouldn't you be?" Ji Hoon shook his head. "We've already given you everything you asked for."

Jason was reluctant to intervene, but his attempt to silently will Tae Hyun to relax wasn't working. "He's right. This is a good thing, Tae Hyun. You already have chemistry with Yoo Mi. I think it'll make things easier for you."

"See?" Ji Hoon gestured toward Jason. "Even the American agrees."

Jason glared at Ji Hoon's othering of him as *the American*. Then he decided maybe he did need more smoothing. So he retrieved his glass and returned to the bar. "I assume you're done with me for the day since you need to prep for your press conference."

"No," Ji Hoon replied. "You'll need to be there, as well. We're announcing you as a production consultant."

Jason snorted as he poured himself another glass of Kingston. "A what?"

"A production–"

"I heard what you said," Jason interrupted as he returned to his chair. "I was asking what you meant. As far as I know, you're paying me to be an acting coach."

Ji Hoon frowned. "It's merely a title."

"No, it's a promotion."

Ji Hoon's frown deepened. "You're already being well paid, Jason."

Jason couldn't really dispute that. But the whole thing still felt like a bait and switch. "Okay, sure. But now I want a producer credit."

"I'm not sure–"

"If you're announcing me as a production whatever, that makes me part of production. Which makes me a producer."

Ji Hoon sighed and swallowed the rest of his bourbon. "The CEO will need to authorize that."

Jason smiled, knowing that the negotiations were over and he'd won. If he was getting dragged to hell by KBR and their damn movie, then he sure as hell was getting a producer credit out of it. That would look a lot better than acting coach on his resume. "Then you'd better get him on the phone. If you want me at your press conference, that is."

"Alright. Go get ready. It'll be done by then." Ji Hoon picked up his phone receiver. "Tae Hyun, take him down to the stylists and wardrobe. The press conference is in two hours."

Ji Hoon put the phone to his ear as Tae Hyun stood. Then the idol took Jason back to the elevator. "I could really learn a lot from you," Tae Hyun said as the doors closed.

Jason snorted. "That's why I'm here, right?"

"I could never talk to Ji Hoon like that. Believe me, I've tried."

"Of course not. He's your elder and your superior. You want to see me crumple like a wet napkin? Put me in front of my mother. Or, worse. My father."

Tae Hyun chuckled. "I think that's a universal truth." He sharply inhaled as the elevator doors opened. "Shit. I just realized that Yoo Mi will be at the press conference."

"I assume so, yeah."

Jason followed Tae Hyun from the elevator to a corridor on the fifth floor. Then Tae Hyun abruptly stopped and turned around to face Jason. "You can't tell her about us, hyung."

Jason frowned. "Of course, I won't tell her. I don't even know her. But I'm curious about why you think I would."

"I–" Tae Hyun sighed. "I don't know. Just paranoia, I suppose."

"You don't need to worry about me like that. I'm not Chang Min."

Tae Hyun scoffed. "Oh, I know. You're a total saint."

Jason gently took hold of Tae Hyun's arm and smiled. "No, I'm just awful in completely different ways. Besides, why are you even worried about Yoo Mi, considering she already knows about you."

Tae Hyun frowned. Jason could see the idol's struggle to maintain his emotional equilibrium. "I know. But why didn't she tell me about the movie?"

"Did you tell her?"

"No. But I didn't know that she'd be involved."

"Maybe she didn't know about you."

Tae Hyun reluctantly nodded. "Maybe. Please just let me talk to her first."

"I will." Jason gently squeezed Tae Hyun's arm. "Remember, I know a thing or two about keeping secrets."

The KBR style team was waiting for Jason and Tae Hyun when they arrived. Jason hadn't sat in a makeup chair since they shut down production on his last movie. And he'd never sat for an idol glam squad before. But he wasn't there to get the full glam treatment–just enough to look good on camera. At least that would wipe away the vestiges of his waning jet lag. Then his makeup artist started giving him a full boy beat anyway.

Min Jun and a handful of people from the KBR PR team arrived as Jason's stylist gave his cheeks a dusting of translucent shimmer powder. Min Jun handed Jason a pair of note cards printed in Korean and English. "These are your talking points, sir," Min Jun shared. "Remember, your contract prevents you from deviating from these responses."

"My contract says no such thing yet," Jason countered.

"Well, it will say that."

Jason snorted, earning him an irritated cluck from his makeup artist. "You'd better hope so."

Once his makeup artist declared him to be done, she hustled

Jason from his chair and told him to visit wardrobe next.

"I'm almost finished," Tae Hyun told Jason. "I'll take you over in a minute."

"Okay."

Jason retreated to the wall next to the door to read through his cards as the makeup artists and hair stylists finished with Tae Hyun's transformation. They were simple talking points. And Jason didn't imagine he'd take many questions. But he was sure he knew what his questions would be and looked over the cards to see what KBR wanted him to say. Then he frowned. The Korean and English answers didn't match.

"Tae Hyun," Jason called out. "Can you read English?"

"Better than I can speak it."

Jason walked up behind him and snuck a card through the wall of stylists. "Take a look at this and tell me what you think."

Tae Hyun waved the stylists away and turned his chair to face Jason. "What do you mean?"

"Just read it."

Tae Hyun looked down at the card, nodding as he read the printed text. "It looks–Oh. Yeah, I see what you mean. The translations are wrong."

Jason frowned. "Are they? Or did someone give me two different sets of talking points?"

Tae Hyun pursed his lips as he reread the card. "I'm sure it's probably nothing. This is all so last minute." He looked up and handed the card back to Jason. "But to be safe, stick with what's printed in Korean. It matches what's on my cards."

Jason nodded. "Alright."

"And remember to stick with formal Korean."

"I will."

"Good." Tae Hyun got up from his chair. "Let's go next door."

Next door was an impressive, two-story wardrobe department that would be the envy of fashion magazine editors everywhere. One of the wardrobe stylists immediately grabbed Jason to take a quick set of measurements while he quietly stewed about the situation. Tae Hyun was right. Everything felt too last minute. That morning, he was just an acting coach, a decidedly behind-the-scenes role. Cut to the late afternoon when he was being measured for a press conference wardrobe as a film producer. Jason's ability to go with the flow was being sorely tested.

After taking his measurements, the stylist presented Jason with an indigo suit with satin black tuxedo lapels. She'd paired it with a steel gray, collarless dress shirt and shiny, black ankle boots. She had to clip the back of the shirt to fit Jason's narrow waist, but the jacket and pants fit well enough.

"I hope everyone's decent," came an unknown voice from the doorway behind Jason. He turned around to see Sang Yoo Mi walk into the room with a pair of minders in tow. "Or, at least dressed," she added with a wink. Yoo Mi gave Jason a quick once over before smiling and offering her hand. "Hello! I don't know if you remember me—"

"Of course," Jason replied, gently shaking her hand. "New York Fashion Week."

Yoo Mi's smile grew brighter. "Yes! At the Maximilien Cuvier afterparty, I believe. How are you, Jason? You look very smart in that suit."

Jason couldn't help but smile. Yoo Mi's charm was highly infectious. "You look lovely, as well." Yoo Mi was dressed in a bright red business suit with a highly tailored jacket accentuating her figure. "Congratulations on joining the cast, by the way."

Yoo Mi offered Jason a quick bow. "Thank you. It's exciting to be starring opposite my Tae Hyun. And I hear the two of you have been getting on very well," she added with a wink. Jason wondered what exactly she'd heard. Or was she referring to their photos that had just been posted online? "Where is he, by the way?"

"I'm here," Tae Hyun said as he emerged from between two rows of clothing racks. He changed into an oversized, black sweater with narrow, horizontal white stripes and tight black jeans. "You and I need to talk."

Yoo Mi pouted. "I'm sorry, Tae Hyun. I didn't–"

"Not here," Tae Hyun interrupted. He walked over, took her hand, and led her back between the clothing racks.

Jason watched them walk off. As much as he was curious about what Tae Hyun would say, he was glad he wasn't a part of the conversation. Jason needed to spend some time memorizing his talking points anyway. His instincts suggested he was about to get ambushed, and he wanted to be ready. But his vibrating phone told him someone had other plans. Jason checked to see that Naomi was calling and considered ignoring it. But there were too many pieces in motion, and what she had to say might be important.

"What's up, Naomi?"

"Wow. You actually answered your phone? I was already mentally composing the voicemail I was about to leave you."

Jason snorted. "Well, I can hang up and–"

"Don't you dare. I'm looking at a new contract KBR's lawyers just sent over."

"Yeah, that tracks. I did some renegotiating earlier when I

found out that–"

"Jason. Stop and listen. There's something you need to know."

14

Tae Hyun dragged Yoo Mi down the narrow gap between the long clothing racks until they were far enough away from the others to comfortably speak.

"Are you taking me back here to ravish me, ex-lover?"

Yoo Mi's amused expression said she didn't believe that for a second. But Tae Hyun wasn't in the mood for silly wordplay.

"Why didn't you tell me?"

Yoo Mi allowed a small pout to break through her merry facade. "I could ask you the same thing."

"It's not the same thing." Tae Hyun let out an exasperated sigh. "I only even found out you'd be involved an hour ago."

Yoo Mi frowned. "They didn't tell you we were in negotiations?" Tae Hyun shook his head. "Oh. Well, I guess that explains why you were so closed-lipped about it. I assumed you were trying to be coy. At least now I know why you asked me about Jason Park." Then she smirked. "How was he, by the way?"

Tae Hyun nearly choked on his sudden panic. "What do you mean?"

Yoo Mi chuckled. "I'm kidding. Unless–" She gasped. "Wait. Did you two really–"

Tae Hyun cut her off with a finger to her glossy lips. "Don't."

He lowered his finger. "Keep your voice down."

"Seriously?" Yoo Mi dropped her amused facade long enough for Tae Hyun to see her genuine surprise. "Damn. I was only teasing you. I never for a moment thought he'd sleep with you."

Tae Hyun quietly scoffed. "What? I'm not good enough?"

"No, not that." Yoo Mi shook her head and smacked Tae Hyun on the arm. "Of course, you're good enough. I didn't know he was even into guys, silly."

"Oh." Tae Hyun felt his ears getting warm. He'd walked right into that one. "Well, for the record, we haven't slept together yet. We just fooled around a little."

"Yet?" Yoo Mi chuckled. "I admire your confidence."

Tae Hyun frowned. He knew his ears were probably bright red. "Please don't tease me. I can't handle it today."

Yoo Mi nodded. "I'm sorry. I'll be good. And you can tell me everything at my party later."

"Your party?"

"Yes. That's why I stopped in to see you before the press conference. To let you know that Seong Woo is hosting a little celebration for us tonight."

Tae Hyun's eyes narrowed into a suspicious glare. "Will the press be there?"

"Of course not." Yoo Mi casually shrugged. "But, you never know."

Tae Hyun frowned. "I don't know, Yoo Mi. I don't think I can handle that right now."

"What?" Yoo Mi huffed. "No." She put a hand on Tae Hyun's chest and pushed him back into the wall behind him. "Can't handle it? No, you listen to me right now. I don't know what's gotten into you, but you and I are filming a fucking movie together. And that's a big fucking deal. So you need to suck up whatever's making you so shaky and throw it away right now. Understand?"

Tae Hyun nodded. "Alright."

"Good." Yoo Mi shook her head. "The Tae Hyun I know wouldn't be intimidated by a few gossip queens at a little party."

Tae Hyun huffed. "It's not that."

Yoo Mi furrowed her brows for a moment before she remembered herself and smoothed her forehead. "Shit. You actually like him, don't you?"

"I don't know." Tae Hyun sighed. He'd been wondering that very thing all day. "Maybe. I mean, we don't get along all that well. We've spent half our time together arguing. He's rude, forward, and has a temper."

"And he's hot."

Tae Hyun breathed out hard through his nose. "So hot. But it's more than that, Yoo Mi. He's kind, too. In his own way. And he's more genuine than anyone else I know." He shook his head. "I don't know. I'm sure he's got some hidden agenda like the rest of us."

Yoo Mi grabbed Tae Hyun's chin and pointed his face toward hers. "Look at me. You're fine. I know this is a lot. But I know you can handle it."

Tae Hyun smiled. "Thanks, Yoo Mi."

Yoo Mi nodded. "Let's get back out there before someone comes looking for us."

Tae Hyun followed Yoo Mi as she returned to the dressing area. Jason was on the phone, which thankfully meant he hadn't heard anything they'd said. Jason acknowledged Tae Hyun with a quick nod before returning to his call. It didn't look like he was enjoying it.

Yoo Mi leaned in close enough that Tae Hyun was nearly overwhelmed by her floral perfume. "So, tell me. How big is it?"

Tae Hyun almost choked on his own spit. "If you don't stop, I'll–"

"I'll stop," Yoo Mi said, chuckling. "I'll stop."

Jason huffed and shoved his phone into his pocket. "Stop what?"

"It's nothing–" Tae Hyun started.

"I'm being a bad girl," Yoo Mi interrupted. "I've been teasing him."

Jason snorted. "Oh. Yeah, he doesn't like that."

"Excuse me, everyone," Min Jun politely called out. "Please take some time to review your talking points. We'll be headed down to the press conference in a few minutes."

With all the excitement of Yoo Mi's arrival, Tae Hyun hadn't even looked at his cards since they were handed to him. He pulled them from his back pocket and began reading them. The movie's name and director. Very excited about this opportunity. Happy to work with Yoo Mi. It was all what he'd expected. There was even a line about having an experienced professional like Jason onboard.

Yoo Mi was right. Tae Hyun was letting the situation with Jason get to him. He'd dealt with far more complicated and emotionally precarious scenarios when dating Chang Min during his *XTC* days. Tae Hyun looked up at Jason to see the actor scrolling through something on his phone. Jason's expression was neutral, verging on negative, and his shoulders looked stiff. Something was bothering him. Had Tae Hyun come off too harshly when he demanded that Jason keep their sexual relationship a secret from Yoo Mi?

Ji Hoon arrived just as Tae Hyun replaced his cards in his pocket. Jason didn't bother looking up from his phone. But Yoo Mi offered the KBR manager a gracious bow. "Managing Director Choo, sir. I can't tell you how excited I am to be working with KBR."

"Not as excited as we are," Ji Hoon replied. "I assure you. Is everyone ready? It's time to head down."

"Please, everyone," Min Jun called as he gestured toward the door. "If you could kindly head this way."

Yoo Mi and her handlers followed Min Jun, Ji Hoon, and the KBR publicists into the hallway. Tae Hyun figured they were holding the press conference in one of the media rooms on the building's second floor. He followed Jason into the corridor, then grabbed his sleeve.

"Hyung," Tae Hyun quietly said. "Is everything alright?"

Jason shrugged. "Sure. What makes you think something's wrong?"

"I don't know. You seem a bit more guarded than I'm used to."

"Oh." Jason smiled, but it looked a little forced. "It's nothing. Just an unexpectedly long day."

"This will be over quickly," Tae Hyun assured Jason. "The press has all been vetted by KBR."

Jason nodded. "Sure. Did you get things worked out with Yoo Mi?"

"I did. By the way, her fiance is having a small celebration tonight in our honor. But I'm sure she'll invite you herself."

Jason raised a single, curious eyebrow. "A celebration?"

"Seong Woo is wealthy, so I'm sure it'll be fancy."

"Ah, of course. We'll see."

Tae Hyun frowned. "We'll see what?"

"If I feel like going."

"You see, that makes me think something's wrong."

Jason stopped before getting into the elevator. Min Jun reached out to keep the doors from closing, but Jason shook his head. "That's okay. We'll take the next one."

Min Jun looked like he wanted to protest, but Ji Hoon pulled his assistant's hand back and let the doors close. Jason turned to face Tae Hyun and smiled.

"Look, you're right. I've got something on my mind. But it's not you or anything to do with you. At least not directly. I had a great time today. Okay?"

Tae Hyun frowned. Jason's reassurance was nice, but it wasn't all that reassuring. "Okay. But?"

"But, nothing." The elevator doors opened, and Jason turned to walk inside. "We can talk more after all this if you want. But let's get this over with."

Tae Hyun swallowed his irritation at getting the brush off, knowing that Jason was right. "Okay, fine."

Min Jun was waiting for them when they got to the second floor. He led Jason and Tae Hyun to an anteroom between two of the floor's media rooms. Everyone else was already inside.

"Ah, good," Ji Hoon said. "You're here. The press is ready and waiting, so I'll get things started. Min Jun will let you know when to follow."

Min Jun opened the door leading to the media room for Ji Hoon, then closed it behind him, cutting off a storm of flash bulbs. Tae Hyun tried to keep his breathing calm as he silently stewed. So many things were in flux. Tae Hyun was still reeling from Ji Hoon's announcement about Yoo Mi.

And he didn't like Yoo Mi's explanation for keeping her movie role from him. Of course, she may have been prevented from doing so for any number of reasons. But that didn't mean Tae Hyun had to like it.

Then there was Jason. The actor was obviously deep into his thoughts about something. And it wasn't something he was willing to share. That was entirely reasonable. But it still bothered Tae Hyun. And it bothered him even more that he was bothered by it. While he claimed to be unsure about how he felt about Jason when he talked to Yoo Mi, Tae Hyun was having an increasingly difficult time denying the truth–at least to himself. He was developing feelings for Jason. Shit.

"Excuse me, sir." Tae Hyun turned to Min Jun, who stood nearby with an older man. He looked to be in his late thirties or early forties, with close-cropped, graying black hair, a well-trimmed mustache, and thick, black-rimmed glasses. The man's handsome face looked vaguely familiar. "Please let me introduce you to the esteemed Director Han Soo Jin, who will be directing the movie."

Of course! Tae Hyun immediately smiled. "Director Soo Jin! It's a pleasure to see you again."

Soo Jin smiled. "I wasn't sure you'd remember."

Min Jun looked confused. "Do you already know one another?"

"Of course," Tae Hyun replied. "Soo Jin directed *XTC*'s first music video. How could I forget that? Let me introduce you to Jason."

Soo Jin's eyebrows shot up with surprise. "So, that really is Jason Park?"

Jason looked up at the sound of his name, and Tae Hyun beckoned him over. "It really is. Jason, this is Director Han

Soo Jin. He directed the music video for *Random Geography*."

Jason smiled. "Really? That was a masterpiece. I loved how you used the split screen effect in that one."

Soo Jin bashfully smiled. "Wow, thank you. That means a lot coming from you. I didn't realize you were attached to this project."

"I am," Jason replied. His smile seemed a little more mysterious than usual. Then he put his hand on Tae Hyun's shoulder. "I'd warn you that you'll have your hands full with this one, but I suppose you already know that."

Soo Jin chuckled. "Tae Hyun could be twice as difficult as he was in that video, and he'd still be less than half as troublesome as most of the actors I've worked with."

Tae Hyun smiled at Soo Jin's compliment, despite knowing it wasn't necessary. And he could see that Jason and Soo Jin were posturing. But Tae Hyun didn't know why. Or for what.

"It's time, everyone," Min Jun suddenly announced.

Tae Hyun took a deep breath as Min Jun put everyone in order. Tae Hyun went out first–careful to already have a smile on his face–followed by Yoo Mi, Soo Jin, and finally, Jason. The flashes immediately started, riding the room's gentle rolling murmur like a wave. Tae Hyun guessed that there were maybe twenty reporters in attendance. Tae Hyun briefly wondered if anyone from *K-Star Daily* was there, then pushed the thought away as he took the first available seat next to Ji Hoon. Once the flashes slowed, he found the video cameras in the back of the room. Ji Hoon introduced everyone at the table, then called for questions. The assembled reporters erupted into chaos until Ji Hoon chose someone from the front row.

"Thank you. Han Ji Min, *Crash Boom Bang Magazine*. Tae

Hyun, can you tell us how you feel about officially working with Sang Yoo Mi for the first time."

Tae Hyun smiled as he looked at the reporter. "Of course! I'm so happy to work with someone as talented and beautiful as Sang Yoo Mi. I hope to learn a lot from her during the project."

"A follow-up question, please. Is that why you and Yoo Mi were spotted out together two weeks ago?"

It sounded like a gotcha question, but Tae Hyun had already seen it on his prep cards. "No, that truly was a chance for us to catch up."

"You can imagine our surprise," Yoo Mi cut in, putting her hand on Tae Hyun's arm, "when we found out afterward that we'd be working together."

The reporters politely chuckled as the flash storm resumed. Yoo Mi made her charm sound so effortless.

Ji Hoon fielded several questions for Tae Hyun and Yoo Mi that came in almost in the order they'd been printed on Tae Hyun's prep cards. Then Ji Hoon shifted to questions for the director, Soo Jin. Strangely, there didn't seem to be any questions for Jason. Tae Hyun began to wonder why Jason had even been asked to be there.

When it seemed like things were nearly wrapped up, Ji Hoon made a final call for questions. A single reporter raised their hand. "Director Choo, sir!"

Ji Hoon frowned. "Um, yes. Please go ahead."

"Thank you. Kwon Ji Woo, *K-Star Daily*. Jason, is it true that this movie is being financed by your father, Gerald Park, to help you break into the Korean film industry?"

Ji Hoon immediately growled. "That's not–"

"It's true," Jason interrupted, "that my father is helping to finance this project. But it would be a frivolous thing for him to do so just to—how did you put it? Help me break into the Korean film industry? And anyone who knows my father knows that he's never frivolous with his money. No. Gerald Park never spends his money unless he intends to make a profit." Then Jason smiled. "I'd say that speaks pretty highly of this film to have his support."

The reporters erupted in a flurry of calls for follow-up questions. But Ji Hoon immediately stood and announced that was all the time they had. Tae Hyun barely heard any of that. He made sure to smile as Min Jun tapped him on the shoulder and led him and the others from the media room. He finally understood what was on Jason's mind. Had Jason known about his father's involvement the whole time? No, he couldn't have. Jason must've found out during his last phone call. No wonder he'd been so mysterious about it.

But there was no mystery about how Ji Hoon felt. As soon as the door to the anteroom closed, he marched right up to Jason, his neck veins prominently bulging. "What the hell was that in there?"

Jason scowled as he puffed out his chest and went nose-to-nose with Ji Hoon. "You'd better back off, old man."

Ji Hoon wisely stepped away. "Fine. But you owe me—"

"I owe you shit," Jason spat. "If anyone here owes anything, it's you, uncle." Jason's words were formal, but his tone was acid. Tae Hyun was impressed. "As in, you owe me the fucking truth." Alright, not so formal. But it was still impressive. "You didn't call the CEO. You called my fucking father."

Ji Hoon threw up his hands in exasperation. "Fine. Yes, I called your father. Yes, your father's company is helping to finance this film. Alright? Are you happy now?"

Jason stepped up to Ji Hoon so fast that Tae Hyun thought they'd collide. But Jason stopped short of knocking the man over. And Ji Hoon, to his credit, only took a single step back. "You and I must have seriously different definitions of happiness. Maybe if you'd just told me the truth from the start—"

"Is that why you leaked it to the press?"

Jason snorted. "You've got to be kidding me. You think I leaked it to the press? To the *K-Star* fucking *Daily*? The same blog that just published photos of me palling around with my new best friend? Why the fuck would I do that? How the fuck would I do that? I only found out a half-hour ago. I'd never even heard of the *K-Star Daily* before today. And I don't know anyone in this fucking country except the people in this room." Jason shook his head and pointed at Ji Hoon. "No. The leak is in your office."

"I thought he handled it well." Everyone turned to Yoo Mi in surprise. "What? I did. It was an excellent response. It made that reporter sound like an idiot."

"He absolutely did," Soo Jin said.

"I agree," Tae Hyun added. As much as it bothered him when Jason lost his temper, Tae Hyun liked seeing him do it to Ji Hoon. He liked it a lot. "I read Jason's prep cards. There was nothing on there for a question like that. And I thought you'd vetted all the reporters, too."

Ji Hoon frowned and turned to Min Jun. "That's right. How did they even get in here?"

"I don't know, sir," Min Jun answered. "There was no one from the *Daily* on our press list."

"Well, find out." Min Jun nodded as Ji Hoon turned his attention back to Jason. "As for you—"

"Oh, no," Jason said, cutting Ji Hoon off. "We're not doing that again. You heard these two. I handled it fine. And, since it's my father's money paying for this shit show, I'd say you need me more than I need you. Yeah? So plug your fucking leaks. In the meantime–" Jason turned to Yoo Mi. "–I believe I heard something about a party?"

15

The last thing Jason expected was for Tae Hyun to ambush him the moment they returned to their apartment. The door had hardly closed before Tae Hyun pinned Jason against the wall in the apartment entryway–just like he'd done in that tiny alleyway. And Jason liked it just as much.

They'd hardly spoken on the ride back from the KBR building. Not that they didn't have anything to say. But Jason and Tae Hyun were both conscious of the potential leaks coming from KBR. Until those leaks were plugged, no one could be trusted.

Back at the apartment, Tae Hyun pressed his mouth onto Jason's as he pushed Jason against the wall. His kisses were voracious. Jason had suspected that Tae Hyun would be a little wild the more he unwound. It was nice to know he was right. As Tae Hyun worked his way across Jason's face to his neck, Jason grabbed hold of Tae Hyun's firm behind and pulled him close enough to feel their erections push against each other. He gasped from the ticklish brush of Tae Hyun's lips on his neck. Then Tae Hyun's hands found the zipper on Jason's pants. But Jason pulled his hands away.

"Oh, no." Jason grabbed Tae Hyun by the shoulders, flipped them around, and pressed him against the wall. "It's my turn."

Jason knelt before Tae Hyun, lifting his sweater to unfasten the idol's jeans. Then he slid Tae Hyun's pants and underwear down, releasing his stiff cock. Jason took a moment to admire it. He hadn't gotten a good look the day before. It was as long as Jason's–maybe seven inches or so–but a bit thinner. And Tae Hyun had a thick foreskin that let the tip peek out when he was hard. Jason smiled and licked the glistening drop of precum waiting for him. Then he grabbed Tae Hyun by the hips and put his mouth around it.

Tae Hyun loudly groaned as Jason inhaled him, swallowing him until he poked the back of his throat. Jason pulled back enough to breathe before taking the whole thing back in. He didn't have anywhere near Tae Hyun's mastery of breath control. But the taste of Tae Hyun's precum dripping down the back of his throat drove Jason wild. He tightly pressed his lips around the shaft and rolled out his tongue like a red carpet, forcing the idol's hips back and forth as his moans grew louder. Then Tae Hyun cried out as he launched an explosion of cum down Jason's throat.

Jason let Tae Hyun's cock fall from his lips so he could catch his breath. But Tae Hyun had other ideas, grabbing Jason by his jacket lapels and dragging him to his feet. He quickly licked the remnants of his orgasm off Jason's chin before pressing their mouths together. Tae Hyun pushed his tongue past Jason's lips as he reached down, undid Jason's pants, and slid them down. Then he pulled Jason's still-hard cock from his underwear and began to stroke it. His tongue played along the roof of Jason's mouth as he worked his hand to the furious rhythm of Jason's stuttered breathing. Despite already cumming twice the day before, Jason barely lasted another minute or so, erupting all over the bottom of Tae

Hyun's oversized sweater.

Tae Hyun kissed Jason one last time before letting his head fall back against the wall. Jason balanced his hand on the wall, panting as he rode the lingering chemical wave of his climax. Then he chuckled.

"Do you think they'll still want these clothes back?"

Tae Hyun snorted. "I know a good dry cleaner if they do."

Jason stepped out of his pants and slipped off his jacket, letting them both fall to the floor. "Come on," he said as he unbuttoned his shirt. "Let's get washed up. We've got a party to attend."

Tae Hyun lifted his sweater over his head and took it off. "So, you really want to go?"

Jason nodded. "I do. Although I'll need to eat something, too. I haven't eaten since those stuffed pancake things."

"Hotteok." Tae Hyun slipped off his jeans and underwear, allowing Jason to marvel again at his lithe dancer's frame. "And if you want to skip out on it, I'm–"

"It's fine." Jason silenced Tae Hyun with a quick kiss. Tae Hyun's walls were fully down during his post-orgasm bliss, and Jason could hear the concern in his voice. It was adorable. And totally unnecessary. "I was annoyed before about the shit with my father. But that's all out in the open now, so there's no reason to stress about it." He took Tae Hyun's hand and led him toward the bathroom and its standing shower.

"Was it true? What you said earlier, I mean."

Jason turned on the water and waited for it to warm up before stepping inside. "Fuck if I know. No one's telling me shit." He grabbed a bath sponge and squirted some body wash onto it. "Come on in and turn around."

Tae Hyun stepped into the shower and presented Jason

with his back. He quietly purred as Jason gently rubbed the soaped-up sponge across his shoulders. Jason felt himself get hard again but ignored it. There'd be plenty of time for more of that later, hopefully.

"Naomi's the one who noticed," Jason continued. "It was in the new contract the KBR lawyers sent her. Or, more specifically, the email chain included the Brightstar Group legal department."

Tae Hyun turned around so Jason could wash his front. He'd gotten hard again, too, Jason noticed. "That's your father's company?" Jason nodded as Tae Hyun took the sponge from him and rubbed it on his chest. "What are you going to do?"

"I'm under contract." Jason shrugged. "So, I'll do what the contract says." Then he grinned. "Of course, my contract is with KBR, not Brightstar. If KBR wants to get into bed with Brightstar, that's up to them."

Tae Hyun chuckled and glanced at Jason's erection. "Was that innuendo?"

Jason smiled and shook his head. "No. I mean, I like that you're as horny as I am. But I'd rather wait if that's okay."

"Of course." Tae Hyun grabbed the shower nozzle and rinsed Jason's body. "Can I ask you something?"

"Sure."

"What are we doing?"

Jason grabbed the shower nozzle from Tae Hyun and began to spray him down. "You mean besides washing each other?" Tae Hyun nodded. "I don't know. I know that I like you. But things are complicated, right?"

"I suppose."

Jason saw the briefest shadow of a frown cross Tae Hyun's face. He reached out and lightly grasped Tae Hyun's chin. "I'm not giving you the brush off here. I really do like you. But you can't deny that every day seems to bring a new challenge for us."

Tae Hyun seemed to consider that. Then he nodded as he hung the shower nozzle and turned off the water. "You're right. We already agreed to go slow, and I'm being pushy."

Jason leaned forward and gave Tae Hyun a gentle kiss. "No, you're not. I get it. I've had so much change in my life lately that I wouldn't mind having something I could count on. Or someone. But–" Jason sighed and stepped out of the shower.

Tae Hyun frowned. "But what?"

"I've never had that before," Jason quietly admitted. It was a fact that he usually wore as a badge of honor. But it felt like a fault under his current circumstances. "I don't know that I'm even capable of it."

Tae Hyun stepped from the shower, grabbed a towel from the nearby rack, and began to rub Jason dry. "Oh. Really?"

Jason looked away, suddenly unwilling to maintain eye contact for fear of reopening a long-darkened chapter of his past. "Really."

Tae Hyun put his finger under Jason's chin and turned him back. And Jason felt the electric connection as he looked into Tae Hyun's lustrous, deep brown eyes–a connection beyond their physical chemistry.

"I can't say that things will always be easy between us," Tae Hyun admitted. "But, if you ever think you might want something more, I think I'd like that, too."

Jason smiled. "I have to say–I think you're pretty amazing."

"That's because I am," Tae Hyun replied with a wink. Then he handed Jason the towel. "Let's get dressed. As fucked up as this day has been, we could use a good party."

Jason took the towel back to his room to finish drying himself. Then he pulled his hanging bag out of his suitcase, cringing at the thought of what its contents must look like after several days of being folded. If there was one thing he knew about Korean nightlife, it was that you could never dress up too much. It wasn't much different than going out in Hollywood or DTLA in that way. And Jason also knew he probably hadn't brought anything that would be up to standard. He'd spent too long embracing his bad boy image to bother dressing to impress. Jason impressed people with his body and attitude. The clothes were just a formality. But he could always lean into that. He was the American movie star, after all. Seoul may have taken the crown as the world's newest pop culture capital. But American pop culture would always reign supreme. It was one of the few positive things his fucked up home still contributed to the world.

Jason pulled a charcoal, short-sleeve, collared shirt from his hanging bag. He'd bought it for a party that he ended up skipping, so he knew there weren't any photos of him wearing it. It was summer-weight Italian wool, so it was thin enough for the temperate Seoul weather and stylish enough for Yoo Mi's wealthy fiance. Jason paired it with slim, dark, Japanese-label jeans that went with practically anything. And they made his ass look amazing.

Jason chuckled at that thought. Who was he trying to impress? He'd pretty much already admitted his feelings to Tae Hyun. And Tae Hyun had pretty much done the same. Were they being foolish? They'd only just met and were from different countries. Hell, they may as well have been from different planets. But Jason couldn't deny the spark between them. He guessed that meant he was trying to impress Tae

Hyun. Jason's cock agreed, already in the beginning stages of another hard-on.

"Not now, damn it. I've got things to do."

"I'm sorry?"

Jason whirled around to see Tae Hyun standing in his room. He'd changed into a plum-colored silk shirt he'd left halfway unbuttoned over light-gray, stonewashed jeans. "Wow. You look fantastic."

Tae Hyun smiled. "You don't need to flatter me. I've already put your dick in my mouth."

Jason's dick flexed as if it heard and accepted the implied offer on its own. "I know. It's still true."

Tae Hyun's ears started turning red like they always seemed to. "Thank you." Then he held up the phone in his hand. "I messaged Yoo Mi, by the way. She said they'll have food at the party."

Jason nodded as he sat on the bed and slipped on the boots he'd worn for the press conference. They fit well and matched his look. "Good. That's one less thing to worry about." Jason stopped. Seeing Tae Hyun's phone gave him a thought. "Where'd you get your phone?"

"KBR, of course."

Jason nodded. "Ah. That must be how they found us today."

Tae Hyun frowned. "What are you saying?"

"That's how Naomi finds me. KBR tracked us to Ikseon-dong with your phone. You should leave it at home tonight."

Tae Hyun looked at his phone like it was about to explode. "Shit. I suppose that's easier than tailing us around the city." Then he frowned. "I'm probably not supposed to go anywhere without it."

Jason shrugged. "Just say you forgot it if anyone asks. I'll have mine, and we'll be together."

"We will?"

Jason snorted as he stood up. "You know what I mean."

Since they were avoiding KBR, that meant figuring out another way to get to the party. Tae Hyun typically would've arranged a driver from KBR. But that would've required him to bring his phone. Tae Hyun solved that by calling Yoo Mi, who offered to send a car. It wasn't foolproof–Tae Hyun supposedly trusted Yoo Mi, but Jason wasn't convinced that her motives were entirely altruistic. Jason would ask Naomi to find him a better option once she was back in the office. At least arriving with Yoo Mi's driver meant they'd get through security faster.

A half-hour later, Jason and Tae Hyun were in the back of a glossy black Korean luxury sedan being whisked across the Han River to the Hannam-dong penthouse Yoo Mi's fiance owned.

"I assume you haven't been there before," Jason said.

"No, I've never met Seong Woo. They got engaged when I was still serving. But I know of him. His family is very wealthy."

"Chaebol?"

Tae Hyun snorted. "No, not like that. Just ordinary, exclusive, high-security compound wealthy."

Jason laughed. "Yoo Mi's a lucky girl."

"I'm sure luck had very little to do with it."

That may have been true, but it was lucky they'd chosen to ask Yoo Mi to send a driver. The gated complex Seong Woo lived in had serious security. After finally being dropped off, they took the private elevator to Seong Woo's penthouse apartment and were greeted by Yoo Mi herself.

"Hello, boys!" Yoo Mi hugged Tae Hyun before offering Jason the same. She changed to a more cocktail party-appropriate, low-cut, glittery silver dress that fell just beyond the top of her thighs. "Come in. Let me introduce you to Seong Woo."

Cho Seong Woo was tall, handsome, and athletic. He had great hair and a chest that Jason could hardly take his eyes off of. He was also charming, almost to the point of deference. Yoo Mi had chosen well. Jason was immediately jealous of her. Then Yoo Mi pulled Tae Hyun away to bring him to a nearby group of young women that Jason was pretty sure were a K-pop girl group. That left him alone with her hunky fiance.

"I gotta confess," Seong Woo said in English with a flawless California accent, "that I'm a big fan of yours."

"You are? Thank you."

Seong Woo nodded. "I went to school in the Bay Area," he said, answering Jason's unasked question about his English, "but I went to grad school in LA. Although we've never met, we were at the same party once."

Jason laughed. Seong Woo had to be a fan to remember something like that. "Was it a good party?"

Seong Woo smiled and nodded. "It was Raven Wilde's afterparty the year Sunshine Sage won Best New Artist at the Music Video Awards."

Jason's eyebrows shot up. That had been a total rager. Jason vaguely remembered making out with one of the rappers from *Ghost Hoax* in Raven's pool house. "Wow. That was a good party."

"I was dating Amanda Child at the time," Seong Woo explained. "Before she got married." Seong Woo gestured toward the nearby bar. "Would you like a drink?"

Jason nodded. "Absolutely." He followed Seong Woo to the bar, which featured an impressive selection of top-shelf liquors. "You have a nice place."

"Thanks." Seong Woo pulled a bottle from under the bar. "Kingston, right?"

Jason laughed. "How'd you know?"

"Yoo Mi, of course. Once she found out you were in town, she had her assistant run a profile on you. She wanted you to feel at home."

Jason took the glass Seong Woo offered and sipped from it. "Does that also mean there's a room here filled with cherry gelatin and whipped cream?"

Seong Woo laughed. "It's lime, I'm afraid." He glanced at something over Jason's shoulder and nodded. "Looks like you're being summoned. Please don't let me forget to ask you for a selfie before you leave."

"For sure."

Seong Woo delivered Jason to Yoo Mi and Tae Hyun, who were talking with a pair of women from *Sapphire Emblem.* They were a girl group represented by one of KBR's competitors. Maybe that meant Tae Hyun was the only KBR performer present? The intimate affair was more sparsely attended than Jason had expected. But, the party's overall beauty quotient was off the charts between the musical artists and the other models from Yoo Mi's agency.

By the time Jason was on his third bourbon, Soo Jin, the movie's director, and his wife arrived. Jason went to say hello and ask him about his vision for the film, but Yoo Mi pulled Jason aside instead.

"Let me give you a tour," Yoo Mi smoothly requested as she

slipped her arm around Jason's. It was a surprisingly intimate maneuver that meant Seong Woo was either very secure with their relationship or already knew Jason wasn't competition.

"You bought me a bottle of Kingston," Jason replied. "You can do whatever you like with me."

Yoo Mi laughed. "It's nice to know how easy it is to earn your good graces." She guided him through the expansive main room to an open, sliding glass door on the far side. The broad outdoor balcony overlooked the Han River and the distant lights of the Gangnam skyline.

"Wow. This view is spectacular," Jason commented before turning to Yoo Mi. He wasn't sure how she intended to use their alone time. Would it be a serious conversation? Frivolous wordplay? Both? Jason pulled out his cigarette pack and showed it to Yoo Mi. "Is this alright?"

Yoo Mi smiled. "Of course."

"Great." Jason lit one of his cigarettes and took a long drag. "I'm surprised it's allowed here."

"Darling, this is the penthouse. Everything's allowed."

Jason laughed. "Is that how it works here?"

Yoo Mi quietly snorted. "Don't be silly. That's how it works everywhere. Whoever has the most makes the rules. No one in this building would dare complain about what happens in Seong Woo's penthouse."

"I suppose you're right. Your fiance is amazing, by the way. Good idea to lock that one down."

Yoo Mi laughed. "He was a little too excited when he learned you'd be coming by. I should be jealous."

"Perhaps," Jason agreed before taking a sip of his bourbon. "But I doubt you're the jealous type."

"No, I'm not."

Jason nodded. "So, is this the part where you warn me against hurting your friend?"

Yoo Mi's laugh had a musical quality that Jason enjoyed. "No. Tae Hyun's already hurt. So, if you can still somehow work your way into his heart, you've earned my good graces."

Jason snorted. "I guess yours aren't as cheap as mine."

"I think we both know that yours are far more expensive than just a bottle of American bourbon."

Jason laughed. "I'd love to hear what you think you know about me."

Yoo Mi took a languorous sip from her wine glass. The red she drank had an intense, almost floral bouquet that Jason could even smell over his whiskey. "I don't know anything about you, Jason. But I know your type." She turned her back to the view and faced her party guests. "After all, I dated one for a year."

"You think Tae Hyun and I are alike because we're both gay? That's rich. The gays aren't a monolith, you know."

Yoo Mi shook her head. "No, it's not that. I think you're both tortured, damaged artists forced into a position where you have to lie to stay in the game."

So much for frivolous wordplay. "Are we still talking about me? Because it sounds like you're looking into a mirror."

"Perhaps." Yoo Mi quietly sighed. "Is this the part where you accuse me of being the KBR leak?"

Jason shook his head. "No, not at all. I know it isn't you. You wouldn't hurt this project because it would hurt you more than the rest of us."

Yoo Mi frowned. "While I'm glad to hear that you trust me, I'm curious to know why you think that."

"I didn't say I trusted you." Jason turned to face Yoo Mi's

striking profile. She truly was a lovely woman. Based on her blossoming career and impending marriage, she was probably the envy of all the other women at her party. "But I know you wouldn't out me because it would out Tae Hyun. And, yes, outing Tae Hyun would make things harder for him. But nobody would blame an idol for wanting to keep that a secret. You, on the other hand? You'll either be seen as oblivious enough to miss it or vicious enough to use it as a weapon against someone you supposedly care about."

Yoo Mi nodded. "I suppose that's all true."

"It's nothing personal. Besides, Tae Hyun likes you and, more importantly, trusts you. So I'm willing to accept that you're a good person based on that alone. But I've been in this business long enough to see a lot of good people do things they end up regretting later."

Yoo Mi looked at Jason with a half grin. "Are we still talking about me?"

Jason snorted. "You got me there." He paused long enough to swallow the remaining liquor in his glass. "I like Tae Hyun. I don't know what that means for us. And I can't promise I won't hurt him. But I can tell you that I don't want to hurt him, for what that's worth."

"Considering whose footsteps you're following?" Yoo Mi shrugged. "I'd say that's a big step up." Then she looked at his empty glass. "Let's head back inside. It looks like you need a refill."

"Does that mean I have your blessing?"

Yoo Mi laughed. "As if that would matter. But, yes. You do."

Jason followed Yoo Mi inside but left her behind when she was stopped by a pair of tall, willowy model types. He went for the bar to help himself to his fourth and probably final Kingston. Jason had a comfortable buzz going and no desire to push that into being actually drunk. He'd expected to get cornered by Yoo Mi, but their chat went much better than he'd anticipated. Jason understood why Tae Hyun liked her. She was gifted with a cunning that, when combined with her keen observation skills and effortless charm, was very attractive.

"So, how'd that go?"

Jason snorted as he turned at the sound of Tae Hyun's voice. The pair had hardly spoken since arriving. But Jason was surprised at how comforting it felt to have Tae Hyun nearby. "She told me if I ever tried anything with you, she'd come after me with a baseball bat."

Tae Hyun laughed and slapped Jason on the arm. He must've been drunk. Then he wobbled a little before regaining his balance. Definitely drunk. "Yoo Mi doesn't need a bat to hurt you."

"That's true. But I see why you like her."

"Yeah." Tae Hyun's smile was warm and friendly. "She's the best. Oh, hey. I was thinking–"

"Are you sure that's wise in your condition?"

Tae Hyun snorted. "Whatever. I was thinking we should get out of here."

Jason raised a curious eyebrow. "Oh, really?"

"Not for that." Tae Hyun leaned in close enough to whisper. Jason could smell the alcohol on his breath. "We already did that today."

"I know. I was there."

Tae Hyun shared a sly grin. "Yeah," he said, chuckling. "But no. We should go because I'm tired and drunk." Then he

15

leaned in close. "And also, I'm having a hard time keeping my hands off you, hyung."

Jason grinned back. "Okay. Then let's go."

16

"Good. Hold your poses just like that."

Tae Hyun struggled to maintain his awkward stance as the flashes went off. He was bent over Yoo Mi in a way that the photographer said evoked true romance.

"Perfect. Just one more. And, okay. You can relax."

Tae Hyun let out the breath he'd been holding and stood before his back muscles protested any further. He was no stranger to photo sessions. But he'd never posed like that with Chang Min or Xiang. At least not in front of an audience. But Yoo Mi didn't seem bothered at all.

"How are you holding up?"

"Don't tell me you're getting tired already." Yoo Mi grinned. "I'm used to shoots that last hours."

Tae Hyun snorted. "Sure. Talk to me after you do a two-hour stage show with a dozen choreographed dance routines."

"Alright, alright. It's not a competition." Yoo Mi turned to the photographer. "Photographer Ahn? Can we take five?"

"Let's just call it lunch," the photographer replied. "We've got to reset for the next background anyhow."

Yoo Mi smiled at Tae Hyun. "There. Happy?"

"I'll be happy when I get to take this off." Tae Hyun tugged at the durumagi he'd been given as part of his hanbok. It was heavy and itchy. "I couldn't imagine having to wear this every day."

"Better get used to it since it'll be part of your character's wardrobe." Yoo Mi glanced around the studio. "Any idea where the boys got off to?"

Tae Hyun shook his head. "No." He was surprised when Jason agreed to come to the photo shoot. Tae Hyun had expected Jason to avoid returning to the KBR building after the disastrous press conference. Maybe his opinion of KBR has mellowed in the days since then. "I'd call if I had my phone. Are you going to eat?"

"No way." Yoo Mi huffed. "I can barely breathe in this corset. There's no way I'm stuffing any food in this body. But I could–" Yoo Mi frowned. "Shit."

Tae Hyun snorted. "You could what?"

"Don't be gross." Yoo Mi tilted her head toward Tae Hyun. "We have a visitor."

Tae Hyun had a sudden sinking feeling. He turned around to see Chang Min chatting with the photographer. "Shit."

Chang Min must've noticed the attention. He looked at Tae Hyun and waved before walking over. "Hello, sunbae-nim. Yoo Mi, you're looking especially lovely. It's too bad I don't see you more often."

Yoo Mi forced an insincere smile. "Yes, well, you're looking especially healthy, no matter how often I've wished you would drop dead."

Chang Min frowned. "Can't you at least pretend you're not a raging bitch for one conversation?"

"No. And fuck you." She looked at Tae Hyun. "Want me to call security?"

Tae Hyun shook his head. "No. What do you want, Chang

219

Min?"

"You told me we could have a conversation, sunbae-nim."

Tae Hyun let out a heavy breath. Chang Min was the last person he wanted to see. But maybe it was better to get their talk over with. At least he wasn't being overly familiar. "Fine. We can talk." Tae Hyun turned to Yoo Mi. "Would you mind tracking down Jason and Seong Woo?"

"Are you sure you want me to leave you alone with the asshole?"

Tae Hyun nodded. "I'll be fine." He leaned over and kissed Yoo Mi on the cheek. "This won't take long," he whispered.

Chang Min shook his head as Yoo Mi left them alone. "Is that what you call me? The asshole?"

"Yes. And you get one conversation, Chang Min," Tae Hyun answered. "Is that what you want to talk about?"

Tae Hyun watched Chang Min's anger lurking under the surface of his stony facade. "No," Chang Min finally said. "I want to apologize."

"Alright. I'll hear your apology as long as you understand that it won't change the situation at all."

"Why not?" Chang Min huffed. "I don't understand why you've cut me off like this?"

"Do you really not understand?" Tae Hyun felt his cheeks warming as the fires of his anger quickly stirred. "Do you really not know how much you hurt me?"

Chang Min huffed again. "I was young and stupid. I made a dumb mistake, and I'm sorry." He put a cautious hand on Tae Hyun's arm, but Tae Hyun stiffened and turned from his reach. Chang Min sighed and dropped his arm. "Isn't there any way you can give me another chance?"

Tae Hyun frowned. "What are we even talking about right

now? I already told you there's no way I'll ever work with you again."

"I know. I'm not talking about that." Chang Min swallowed hard. "I'm still in love with you."

"What?" Tae Hyun's wild rage surged to the point he could no longer control it. "How can you even say that?" He pushed forward, stopping just short of Chang Min. "You've had two fucking years to think about what you've done," he growled. "And this is the best you can do? You were never even in love with me in the first place. And I might consider forgiving you someday if I ever believe you're truly sorry for what you did. But I will never go back to that." Tae Hyun poked his finger into Chang Min's chest. "You and I are through. We're nothing. And the sooner you get that through your thick fucking skull, the sooner we can both move on!"

Chang Min snarled and shoved Tae Hyun away. "You'd better be careful. Or, I'll–"

"You'll what?" Tae Hyun cut Chang Min off, stepping right back into his face. "Because if you want to fight me–"

"Hey, that's enough." Seong Woo grabbed Chang Min from behind while Jason stepped between Chang Min and Tae Hyun.

"Let it go," Jason implored Tae Hyun. "He's not worth all this."

Chang Min struggled against Seong Woo's firm grip on his arms. "What the hell do you know, asshole? This is none of your fucking business."

Jason snorted as he turned around to face Chang Min. "What do I know? Well, I know you might want to think about what picking a fight with me really means." Jason's voice was low and tight with unleashed aggression. Chang

Min scowled but stopped struggling. "Yeah, that's what I thought. No one wants you here. So, why don't you leave before you do something else you'll regret?"

Chang Min let out a long, staggered breath. "So, that's how it's going to be, Tae Hyun. Him over me?" He tried pulling himself from Seong Woo's grip, but Seong Woo held firm. "Let me go, dammit."

"It's alright, Seong Woo," Jason said. "I don't think Chang Min will cause us any more trouble."

Seong Woo let go. Chang Min stood there for several moments, rubbing his arms where Seong Woo had held him. "I wish it didn't have to be like this. Goodbye, Tae Hyun."

Tae Hyun had already had enough of Chang Min's theatrics. "Just go. And don't talk to me again."

Chang Min shook his head and walked away.

Jason turned back to Tae Hyun. "Are you okay?"

"Yeah." He shook his head. "No. Shit, I don't know. But thank you."

Jason smiled. "Hey, if one of us is gonna get into a fight, it should probably be the one that's already got the reputation."

Tae Hyun snorted. "Yeah, I suppose. But that's not what I mean. You were right. I need to let this go. He's had this hold over me all this time, but he's not worth it."

Jason grinned as he reached up and rubbed the back of his head. It was an adorably transparent flirt that still had its intended effect on Tae Hyun. "Yeah, well, it turns out I know a thing or two about letting go of the past. But maybe I could—"

"Excuse me, Jason, sir." Min Jun approached the group with something in his hand. "I believe this is yours." He held out a phone.

Jason patted his empty back pocket. "Shit." He smiled and took the phone from Min Jun. "I set it down and then forgot about it. Thanks."

"It's my pleasure. Tae Hyun, sir? The stylists are waiting for your next wardrobe change whenever you're ready." Min Jun offered a quick bow before walking away.

Jason sighed as he tapped his phone to wake it and began to scroll.

"Is there anything there?" Tae Hyun asked, thinking about their conversation the morning after Yoo Mi's party.

You realize Min Jun's probably the leak, Jason said as he lay shirtless in bed next to Tae Hyun. Min Jun had woken them that morning with a call to Tae Hyun, complaining that he hadn't answered his phone all evening. *Right?*

Despite how unlikely it felt, Tae Hyun couldn't fault Jason's reasoning behind suspecting Min Jun as the source of KBR's leak. It fit the facts they had, at least. But Tae Hyun couldn't imagine what would possess someone like Min Jun to do that. He had a highly coveted position in the entertainment industry. And he'd lose a lot more than his job if Jason's accusation turned out to be true. CEO Pak may have gotten his college degree in the US, but his business sense was decidedly old-school Korean. Getting fired would probably be the least of Min Jun's consequences for disrupting KBR's business interests.

"I don't see anything," Jason replied without looking up from his phone. "But I'll probably reset it anyway, just in case." He stuffed the phone in his back pocket and looked at Seong Woo. "Thanks for your help. Remember, you didn't see or hear any of that, right?"

"See or hear what?" Seong Woo smiled. "And you're

welcome."

As hard as he tried to let it go, Tae Hyun couldn't get the confrontation out of his head during the rest of the photo shoot. Thankfully, he at least had enough modeling experience to keep his feelings from showing. Mostly. Yoo Mi had to prod him to pay attention more than once when his mind drifted back to what happened.

"Hey, what's with you?" Yoo Mi unwound herself from Tae Hyun's grasp after the photographer called an end to their day-long session. "It's like you're somewhere else."

"Didn't you hear what happened?"

Yoo Mi rolled her eyes. "Please. You've been fighting with Chang Min for longer than you and I dated. This is something else."

"I don't know." Tae Hyun knew the answer, even if he wasn't willing to admit it. It wasn't because of Chang Min. He'd been mad at that asshole for literal years. Those feelings were old and familiar. No, it was because of Jason, who'd jumped in to calm Tae Hyun and then immediately stood up for him to the asshole. Tae Hyun already knew he liked Jason. And he'd already confessed as much to Jason and Yoo Mi. But the feelings that experience kindled were more than like and attraction. They were new and unfamiliar. And they were a little scary. "It's just been a long day. And I'm not used to all this yet."

Yoo Mi shook her head. "It's fine if you don't want to tell me, Tae Hyun. But don't lie to me."

Tae Hyun quietly accepted his rebuke, knowing their friendship was strong enough to withstand a little white lie. And he started smiling as he changed back into the clothes he'd worn to the studio, thinking about Jason fearlessly getting in Chang Min's face, heedless of how that might turn out. It wasn't that Tae Hyun couldn't handle himself in a fight with Chang Min. He'd already gotten physical with the asshole when he had to. But he couldn't remember the last time someone had defended him like that. And thinking about it brought an unexpected and nearly forgotten stirring within.

Tae Hyun decided it was finally time to take things with Jason to the next level. They'd already fooled around several times. And they'd been sharing a bed for several nights. Tae Hyun grabbed his phone and hurriedly placed a delivery order. Then he went to find Jason, who'd been waiting for him to change.

"Thanks for earlier," Tae Hyun said. "And for sticking around."

Jason shrugged. "It's no problem. I've had plenty to do while I was here. Are you okay?"

Tae Hyun smiled and nodded. "I am. Especially now that we're done. Want to get out of here?"

"Absolutely. I'm starving."

Tae Hyun started walking with Jason toward the elevator. "What have you been doing all day?"

"Besides watching all the ways you wrapped yourself around Yoo Mi? Booking a commercial."

Tae Hyun stopped. "What? No way! What's it for?"

Jason grinned. "CheezyFish."

"What? That's great!

"I know, right? I almost can't believe I'm doing another CheezyFish ad."

Tae Hyun could see Jason trying to look excited. He frowned. While Jason had confessed to doing a CheezyFish commercial as his first acting gig, he hadn't yet told Tae Hyun about what happened during that visit to Seoul that made him swear never to return. And Tae Hyun had no intention of dragging the information out of him, no matter how much he wanted to know. But he still wanted Jason to know he cared.

"Are you sure you're okay with it?"

"Yeah." Jason nodded. "They're paying me more than I'm getting from KBR. And it's just one day's filming. Not even a full day."

"When is it?"

"Next week."

"Can I go?"

Jason frowned. "You want to come?"

Tae Hyun shrugged. "You came with me today, right?" Jason nodded. "Okay. Then yeah, I want to go."

KBR had a driver waiting for Jason and Tae Hyun in the garage. Jason and Tae Hyun traded ideas for having dinner delivered on the way back to the apartment. Tae Hyun struggled to keep himself composed, especially when they stopped in the lobby to pick up Tae Hyun's package.

"What did you get?" Jason asked as they got into the elevator.

"This?" Tae Hyun answered, trying to sound casual. "Oh, it's just some skin care products that Yoo Mi recommended. You're welcome to try them." That part was true. Tae Hyun really had ordered skin care products. But he'd also ordered a couple things he hadn't used in a very long time.

"I'm gonna take a shower," Tae Hyun announced as they walked into the apartment.

"What should I get for dinner?"

"Surprise me," Tae Hyun said as he closed the bathroom door.

Tae Hyun tore open the package and set the contents on the bathroom counter. He'd gotten moisturizers for daytime and nighttime, an under-eye cream that Yoo Mi said worked miracles, a package of single-use face masks, a bottle of lube, and a squeeze bottle. Tae Hyun stared at the squeeze bottle for at least a minute, wondering if he was ready to commit to it.

"Fuck it," he muttered and unscrewed the top. After an awkward but successful thirty minutes, Tae Hyun was showered and clean. He stood naked in front of the bathroom mirror, attempting to psych himself up. "Fuck it," he muttered again as he wrapped a clean towel around his waist.

After delivering the lube to his bedroom, Tae Hyun found Jason in the kitchen drinking his Kingston. He smiled and nodded toward Tae Hyun as he set the glass down. "Hi, sexy. Good shower?"

"Yeah." Tae Hyun smirked. "Now I'm ready."

"Ready for what?"

"I want you to fuck me, hyung."

Tae Hyun's breath caught in his throat as he waited for Jason's reaction. Would it be more flirty wordplay? Or maybe a look of shock? But Jason simply set his glass down, walked over to Tae Hyun, and kissed him. Tae Hyun hungrily pushed his tongue into Jason's mouth, slipping it between lips tasting of salt and bourbon. He felt Jason's hands trace the muscles of his naked back as they roamed from his shoulders to his waist.

Tae Hyun broke off their kiss just as Jason's hands reached the towel wrapped around him. "Not here." He backed free of Jason's grasp and took his hand. "Come on."

Jason let Tae Hyun bring him to the bedroom they'd been sharing. When Tae Hyun stopped near the bed, Jason gripped him by the waist and pushed himself against Tae Hyun's ass. Then Tae Hyun felt the warm caress of Jason's breath on his neck before Jason kissed the top of his shoulder. Tae Hyun quietly moaned as Jason's kisses continued along his shoulder to his neck.

"Are you sure about this?" Jason purred below Tae Hyun's ear. Tae Hyun nodded. Jason gripped his waist and turned him around. "I need to hear you say it."

Tae Hyun nodded again. "I'm sure."

"How long has it been?"

"Since I've been fucked?" Tae Hyun swallowed as he felt his mouth go dry. "Chang Min was the last time."

Jason reached up to brush Tae Hyun's bangs from his forehead. "Alright." He let out a long breath through his nose as he ran his tongue along his lower lip. "If it ever feels uncomfortable, or you want to stop for any reason, just say so, and we'll stop. Okay?"

Tae Hyun lightly bit down on his lower lip and nodded. Chang Min had never shown that much concern for his enjoyment or well-being before. It was such a turn-on he could barely contain himself. "Okay, I will."

Jason stepped back and lifted his shirt over his head. Then he undid his pants and slid them off. Jason's cock strained against the front of his gray boxer briefs. A dark spot stained the front where his precum had already soaked through the fabric. Although Tae Hyun had seen Jason's body multiple times, he was still mesmerized. Even in the bedroom's dim lighting, Jason was stunning, with large, well-defined muscles stretched over his broad-shouldered frame.

Jason grinned as he stepped up to Tae Hyun, undid his towel, and grabbed his cock. Tae Hyun moaned as Jason gently pushed the foreskin back and rubbed his thumb around the tip. Then Jason put a hand on Tae Hyun's chest and pushed him back onto the bed.

"Wanna suck it?"

Tae Hyun nodded as he reached out to pull Jason's boxers down. Jason's stiff cock popped up from under the waistband. Tae Hyun took hold of it at the base, pointed it at his mouth, and licked the thick drop of precum glistening at the tip. Then Tae Hyun opened his mouth and inhaled Jason until his lips reached his hand. Jason quietly moaned as Tae Hyun bobbed up and down on him. The woodsy remnants of their shared body wash mingled with the musky scent of Jason's balls and drove Tae Hyun wild.

"My god," Jason exclaimed in English. "You're so fucking good at that."

Tae Hyun chuckled and sat back. "I know. Now let's see what your tongue can do." He lay back onto the towel on the bed and pulled his legs into the air, exposing everything to Jason.

"Gladly." Jason knelt between Tae Hyun's legs, leaned forward, and pushed his tongue against Tae Hyun.

Tae Hyun let out a deep groan as Jason swirled the tip of his tongue around, sending surges of ticklish pleasure through his body. Then Jason took hold of Tae Hyun's hips and plunged his tongue inside.

"Fuck!" Tae Hyun cried out. His cock throbbed, bouncing in time to Jason's rhythmic tongue barrage. Chang Min rarely agreed to put his mouth anywhere near Tae Hyun's ass, despite how much he enjoyed it when Tae Hyun did it to him. But Chang Min was soon the farthest thing from his mind as wave after wave of ecstasy crashed over him. "I can't stand it anymore. I want you inside me!"

Jason chuckled. "Let's see if you're ready." He stuck his index finger in his mouth to wet it before pressing it against Tae Hyun. Tae Hyun felt the pressure from Jason's finger and forced himself to relax. Jason slowly pushed his finger until Tae Hyun felt it slip inside. "Breathe," Jason commanded, and Tae Hyun let go of the breath he'd been holding. Jason worked his finger inside Tae Hyun until the tip brushed against the underside of Tae Hyun's prostate.

Tae Hyun pressed himself into the bed as exploding stars burst around him. "Yeah! Don't stop!"

"Damn." Jason chuckled. "Okay, I think you're ready." He pulled his finger out, got up, and grabbed the bottle of lube Tae Hyun had left out. "You just got this, eh?"

"Yeah?" Tae Hyun turned his head to see Jason struggling to open the seal. "Oh, shit. Sorry."

"It's okay," Jason replied. "Perfect sex only happens in porn because they edit this shit out."

Tae Hyun snorted and lowered his legs before they cramped. While he was anxious to get on with things, Tae Hyun appreciated how easy Jason made it to be human. As much as he hated constantly comparing Jason with Chang Min, it was unavoidable. Sex with Chang Min often felt rushed and sometimes like a chore. With Jason, things could go wrong, and it was only part of the process.

Once Jason got the seal open, he opened the bottle and applied a generous amount of lube to each of them, slipping a lubed finger inside Tae Hyun for good measure.

Tae Hyun bucked and groaned as Jason's finger brushed his prostate again. Then he chuckled. "Stop teasing me, hyung!"

"You're such a bossy bottom." Jason grinned. "I really like that."

Jason stood, lifted Tae Hyun's legs, and balanced them against his shoulders. Tae Hyun felt Jason position himself and press against him. Then the pressure increased as Jason pushed. Tae Hyun closed his eyes in anticipation, his breath again caught in his throat.

"Breathe," Jason reminded him. "It'll help you relax."

Tae Hyun exhaled the breath he'd been holding, then forced himself to breathe again. "Now, who's bossy?"

"That's better. Okay, here goes."

Tae Hyun felt the pressure build until Jason finally poked inside him. "Oh, shit." He closed his eyes again, remembering to breathe, as Jason slowly slid inside. It felt tight but not painful. Then he felt the pressure against his prostate again. "Hyung! That feels so good."

"You're so tight," Jason said as he pulled back. Then he slowly pushed forward until he was all the way inside. Tae Hyun's cock twitched as it leaked precum onto his already slick stomach. Jason pulled back a third time, then pushed forward again. This time he didn't stop, plunging in and out with increasing force and speed.

"Yeah," Tae Hyun moaned as he clutched the towel underneath him. "Fuck me, hyung. Fuck me!"

Tae Hyun grunted in time to Jason's thrusts as the curling wave of bliss grew from deep within him. Each motion attacked his senses, slipping over the walls of mere touch in a riot of color and noise. Tae Hyun craved that fuck with such intensity that he would've opened up and taken Jason into him whole if he could.

Tae Hyun came almost without warning. He hadn't even touched himself. His cum splattered warm and wet on his chest and chin as he cried out with delirious joy. Jason kept on fucking him, each thrust extending the animal pleasure of Tae Hyun's orgasm a little longer. Jason fell out of his rhythm soon after that, grunting and moaning with each thrust as he neared his own climax. Then he pulled out, took himself in his hand, and shot his load on top of Tae Hyun's.

Jason stood there, his heavy breath singing a ragged duet with Tae Hyun's before Tae Hyun lowered his legs and let them relax. Then Jason leaned forward and crawled on the bed, straddling Tae Hyun on his hands and knees. He wordlessly bent and licked the cum from Tae Hyun's chin, swallowing it before he planted his mouth on Tae Hyun's lips. Tae Hyun wrapped his arms around Jason's shoulders, holding him in place while their tongues danced. Tae Hyun's heartbeat pounded in his ears as a bead of sweat fell from Jason's forehead onto his. Then he felt Jason's arms begin to shake before he collapsed onto Tae Hyun's chest, still wet and sticky from their dual deposits. Tae Hyun gladly accepted Jason's warmth and weight atop him.

"You said it's been years?"

Tae Hyun chuckled. "I feel like maybe I was saving up."

Jason rolled off Tae Hyun and lay next to him. "I'd believe that if I hadn't already made you cum several times."

"Well, I'd still say it was worth the wait."

"For sure." Jason's chuckle was low and deep. "I can't wait until it's my turn."

Was Jason versatile? Tae Hyun had assumed he was a top. "You want me to fuck you?"

Jason laughed. "Not right now. But, yeah, I very much want that."

"Oh. Well, I can count the times I've topped on one hand."

Jason shifted, rolled onto his elbow, and rested his head on his hand. "It's fine if you don't want to top. You're an excellent bottom."

Tae Hyun snorted. "So I've been told. But it's not that I don't want to. Chang Min didn't like to bottom, and none of my partners since him have been anything but blow jobs and hand jobs. Until now."

Jason reached out with his free hand, twirled a finger in the mingled puddle floating on Tae Hyun's chest, then put his cum-coated finger in his mouth. "Mmm. Well, I'd love to bottom for you when you're ready. Your cock looks like it will feel amazing."

Tae Hyun laughed. "That's a new one for me. But I'd love to fuck you, hyung." He craned his neck to reach Jason's mouth and kissed him. "Until then, let's clean up and get something to eat. I'm fucking starving."

17

Jason gazed at the majestic triple peaks of Bukhansan from the roof of the Frostfire Productions building in Seongsu-dong. He technically wasn't allowed to smoke up there, but one of the Production Assistants told him it was where everyone went to smoke anyway. It was his first cigarette of the day and would probably be his last. To his surprise, he'd hardly smoked at all since arriving in Seoul. But the filming work–even for a simple commercial shoot–stressed him out.

Shooting the CheezyFish campaign had reawakened many of Jason's feelings from a critical part of his troubled past. It didn't help that the Director had been a PA during his original shoot more than a decade ago. Jason didn't remember him at all, but the former PA turned Director couldn't get enough of seeing Jason as a grown and allegedly successful actor. And, as much as he hated to admit it, Jason owed much of his career to that first job. But he'd already said his famous catchphrase a hundred times that day. He'd be happy to go another decade before saying *get in my tummy* again.

Jason's vibrating phone dragged him from his melancholy reverie. He saw it was a video chat from Naomi and tapped the connect button right away. "What's up?"

"Just checking in." Naomi looked great, as usual, in a silky, teal, spaghetti-strap top. She'd pulled her bushy curls into a pair of afro puffs tied with matching teal ribbons. "How's the commercial coming?'

"It's fine. It's a commercial. But I'll be happy if I never eat another CheezyFish cracker."

Naomi laughed. "Yeah. They're damn good, though.'

"You've tried them?"

"They sent a whole case to the office. I've been eating them for days."

Jason snorted. "Better you than me. Did I get paid?"

"Mm-hmm." Naomi turned away, and Jason heard a distinctive crunch that probably meant she was enjoying her surprise Korean treat as they spoke. "The wire hit your account yesterday."

Jason smiled. Between that and the money from KBR, things would be okay for a while. At least until the next crisis, hopefully. "Sweet. If that's all, I should–"

"How's everything else?"

Jason frowned. "What do you mean?"

"I mean, how are things with the idol?

"Oh." Jason smiled. "Tae Hyun's good. He's here with me, actually. Well, not right here. I think he went to find some lunch, but–"

Naomi groaned. "Oh, my god. You fucked him? Damn it, Jason, I told you–"

"Jesus, Naomi." Jason scoffed. "First of all, it's none of your fucking business who I fuck. Second, how the fuck do you even do that?"

Naomi snorted. "I could see your smile. Besides, I've known you since you were eighteen. I know everything about you. I know you better than your mother."

"Hell, that's not saying much. My old bartender Josie probably knows me better than my mother."

"That's probably true." Naomi sighed. "But that doesn't change the fact that he's your client and–"

"No, KBR is my client."

"That's a difference with no distinction, Jason. And stop interrupting me. We can't afford to–" Naomi paused. "No. You can't afford to–"

"I like him, Naomi."

Naomi went silent as she massaged the bridge of her nose. "Say that again."

"I'm not saying it again."

"Say it again, so I know you're being honest with me."

Jason huffed. "Fine. I like him, okay. I like Tae Hyun. Sure, he's beautiful. But he's also smart, talented, and fun to be around. He's thoughtful and kind. And he doesn't put up with my shit. As crazy as it sounds, I think there might be something there."

More silence. It had been a long time since Jason had rendered Naomi speechless twice in the same conversation. "Huh," she finally said.

"That's all you've got to say?"

"I don't know, Jason. I honestly never thought I'd hear you talk about someone other than yourself that way."

"Oh."

"Listen to me, Jason. Don't fuck this up. He's not some WeHo fuckboy."

Jason snorted. "You think I don't know that?"

"But don't settle, either. You deserve happiness just as much as the rest of us. Maybe even more than some."

"Stop it," Jason deadpanned. "You're gonna make me cry."

"You see? That's why people think you're an asshole."

Jason snorted again. "No, people think I'm an asshole because I'm an asshole. And where's all this motherly concern coming from anyway? If you're worried about your job, don't. I'm rich again, remember? Hell, you should give yourself a raise."

Naomi scoffed. "Who says I didn't? Do you even know how much you pay me?"

"Nope. I pay you so I don't have to know stuff like that."

"Shit. You're lucky I'm trustworthy. I could've drained you dry and disappeared by now."

Jason laughed. "Go ahead. I'll just shack up with my new secret lover."

"Speaking of which, how's your actual job coming along?"

"The coaching?" Jason shrugged. "Really well, to be honest. Don't tell Ji Hoon I said this, but they probably didn't need to hire me. Tae Hyun's a natural, so I'm just helping him refine his technique a bit."

"And that's not innuendo?"

Jason laughed. "No way. That technique doesn't need any refining, believe me."

"Oh, lord." Naomi softly chuckled. "Well, it sounds like you've finally met your match, mister." She cleared her throat. "Congrats."

Jason chuckled. "Thank you."

"Of course. If you're going to work out there—"

"What?" Jason frowned. "Who says I'm going to keep working out here?"

"I've had calls from three different production companies since that damn press conference. You're a hot commodity right now. There might actually be a bidding war."

"Are you serious?"

Naomi smiled. "Jason. Ethan called me."

His agent? Jason hadn't heard from that asshole since before he'd been fired from that BigCloud movie. "I hope you told him to go fuck himself."

"You know it. But that's how much things have turned around for you. If this keeps up, you could end up in a series."

Jason had never done television. There was a while when he considered it beneath him. But that was long before he'd resorted to working on direct-to-streaming action movies and TV commercials. "I'm not sure how to feel about that." Jason frowned. "Why am I suddenly so popular?"

"Your reputation isn't nearly as damaged there as it is here. People remember your old CheezyFish commercial. *Moon Shines Madly* did well in Korean and East Asian theaters. And you've recently gotten the KBR blessing, which is a pretty big deal."

A message notification popped up with a text from Tae Hyun.

They're asking for you on the set

"Okay. I gotta go. But let me know if we get any serious offers."

"I will."

Naomi disconnected. Jason tapped on Tae Hyun's message and typed out a reply. *I'll be right there*

Tae Hyun waited for Jason in the space Frostfire had set up as his dressing room. It was a smaller production company that had essentially lucked into the CheezyFish gig before casting Jason in their campaign. But Jason had dressed in a lot worse places. At least it was private. And inside. He'd spent the morning shooting all the video spots. The next hour or two were set aside for the print campaign's still photos.

"You were up there for a while," Tae Hyun said from his seat on the room's tiny couch.

"I was doing a check-in with Naomi. Did you find anything to eat?"

Tae Hyun held up the bag that sat next to him. "Yeah. There's a deli on the ground floor. I gotta bunch of stuff in case you're hungry."

Jason shook his head. "No, thank you. I've eaten so many crackers that I feel a little nauseous. Maybe when we're done, though."

Someone knocked on the dressing room door before cracking it open. The PA who'd sent Jason to the roof ducked her head inside. "Oh, good. You're back. We'll start with the outfit you're in and work back in reverse order whenever you're ready."

Jason smiled. "Thanks. I'll be right there." The PA nodded and closed the door behind her. Jason turned to Tae Hyun. "What do you say? Want to watch them take a thousand pictures of me?"

Tae Hyun chuckled. "Let's go."

The set was still dressed as a generic, upscale office from the previous video shoot. The director had Jason mimic several of the video shoot's poses, attempting to extol the virtues of CheezyFish as the perfect office snack. Jason and the director fell back into their rhythm right away, with the director calling out for new poses or expressions between every five or ten photos. Jason hadn't shot many commercial campaigns in his career beyond movie promos. Every time he did, he was grateful he'd never become a model. Jason found the work to be a little mind-numbing.

Every so often, Jason would glance over to the director's chair one of the PAs had provided for Tae Hyun to see the idol intently watching him. Although Jason had never officially introduced Tae Hyun to everyone, most of the young production team knew him and quietly asked him for autographs or to pose for selfies. Only the director seemed oblivious to the presence of a K-pop idol in his studio. But Jason was glad Tae Hyun had come along. Jason could sense Tae Hyun's calming presence even when he stared into the bright key lights and blinding flash.

The rest of the day's shoot felt like it dragged on. But only an hour had passed when Jason checked the time. They'd already shot the office and kitchen scenes and were breaking while the production team redressed the set to look like a park, complete with realistic fake grass and a picnic table. Jason changed into the scene's wardrobe on set just to keep from delaying the end of the shoot. He stepped into his jeans, pulled them up, and noticed a young stranger on the other side of the set with their phone pointed at him. At first, Jason thought she was one of the production assistants. Then he frowned as the stranger realized she'd been busted and quickly lowered her phone.

"What the hell are you doing?" Jason called out. He didn't care if people watched him change. There were already plenty of pics of him in his underwear on the internet. But he certainly didn't want some spy filming him while he changed without his permission. "Hey! I said–"

The stranger quickly turned and walked away.

"God damn it." Jason's anger quickly exploded beyond his control as he took off after the spy. Then Tae Hyun grabbed his arm and stopped him.

"What's happening?"

Jason turned to Tae Hyun and nearly growled at him, only just stopping himself in time. "Someone was just filming me while I changed." He looked down at Tae Hyun's hand and hopefully made it clear just how easily Jason could transfer his anger to the idol.

"Shit." Tae Hyun let Jason's arm go. "Sorry."

Jason stormed across the set. He couldn't see the spy anywhere but spotted an exit door. Jason rushed through the door to an empty corridor beyond the set. There was no sign of his spy. "Damn it!"

"Hey," Tae Hyun said. He put his hand on Jason's shoulder. "Please calm down."

Jason scowled and shook Tae Hyun's arm off. "She's gone already! She was filming me and–"

"Jason." Tae Hyun grabbed Jason's arm and squeezed hard enough to get his attention. It was a good reminder for Jason that just because Tae Hyun was smaller didn't mean he wasn't strong. "You need to calm down before you do something you may regret." Tae Hyun held Jason's gaze until his point pricked the fiery balloon of Jason's rage. "And you don't need to handle this yourself. Talk to the director. Find out who that person was."

"I–" Jason stopped and took a breath. Tae Hyun was right. What could Jason do beyond threatening violence? Would he fight this stranger and steal their phone? "Okay. You're right." He took another breath. "Thanks."

Tae Hyun nodded and released Jason's arm. "Come on."

Jason followed Tae Hyun into the studio and approached the director. He was speaking to a pair of PAs–probably wondering where Jason had gone.

"Ah," the director said when he saw Jason approaching. Then he frowned. "Where did you get off to? Are you alright?"

"No, I'm not fucking alright," Jason spat, his tone sharp enough to cause the director to step back. He pointed to where he'd seen his spy. "Someone stood right there in front of you all and fucking filmed me while I was changing."

"What?" The director shook his head. "Who would do that?"

"I don't fucking know." Jason tried taking a deep breath, but he was too worked up. "When I tried talking to her, she ran away. You need to find her right now and delete that video, or we're done here."

The director frowned. "That's a grave accusation, Jason. I can hardly believe someone would–"

"I saw her," said the PA who'd told Jason where to smoke. "I thought she was here with you." She bowed her head. "I'm sorry, sir."

"With me? Tae Hyun is the only person here with me. I thought this was a closed set? What kind of amateur operation are you clowns running here?"

The director looked at the PA, who bowed again. "You didn't know her?" The PA shook her head, and the director sighed. "I'm sorry, Jason. I have no idea how someone like that even got into the building. I'll contact security and have them conduct a search of the building. Will that be alright?"

Jason frowned. He recalled the aging, disinterested security guard sitting at a desk in the building lobby and realized that there was nothing anyone could do. This wasn't KBR, with its layered security and omnipresent video cameras and biometric scanners. It was a backwater production studio shooting outside their league. They'd probably never had a real celebrity on-site before and had no idea what that meant. And the spy's video was probably already online. "Fine. You do that. I need a few minutes to calm down before we can shoot again."

"Very well." The director turned to the PA. "Contact the front desk and–"

"No," Jason interrupted. He was tired of his needs being pawned off on the PAs. "You're the director. This is your set. You handle this yourself, or I walk."

The director nodded. Then he bowed. "Of course, sir. You're right. I'll handle it and return shortly. Please excuse me."

Jason, Tae Hyun, and the PA watched the director walk away. Then the PA turned to Jason and opened her mouth to speak.

"Ah," Jason said, holding up his finger to quiet her. "Just because I made him do that doesn't mean you're off my shit list. Remember that next time you see a stranger on a closed set. Now go get me a damn coffee."

"Of course, sir. Right away."

Jason sighed as the PA walked away. "Bunch of fucking clowns," he murmured in English.

"Hey." Tae Hyun put his hand on Jason's arm and gently turned Jason to face him. "I'm sorry."

"For what? You're the only person here who's got any fucking sense. I would've torn this place apart if you hadn't been here."

Tae Hyun carefully smiled. "But I was here. And you didn't tear this place apart."

Jason remembered his conversation with Naomi on the roof, where he confessed his feelings for Tae Hyun to her. No one had ever managed to get through Jason's wall of anger the way Tae Hyun could. The way Jason wanted him to. The way Jason needed him to. "I really want to kiss you right now."

Tae Hyun's careful smile widened as his ears reddened. "Yeah, well, I don't think that's a good idea."

"I know," Jason said, nodding. "But I would if I could."

Tae Hyun swallowed. Then he carefully surveyed their surroundings before leaning forward and quickly kissing Jason on the cheek. "You can get a real one later," he whispered. When Tae Hyun stood back, his ears were bright red.

Jason smiled. "I'll hold you to that."

The PA returned a short time later with Jason's coffee, followed by the director, who promised they were conducting a thorough search of the premises and reviewing the security cam footage from the main entrance. Jason knew that was all he could hope for, so he agreed to finish the shoot. Once the director called it a day, Jason and Tae Hyun returned to his dressing room so Jason could change. As soon as he was fully dressed, someone knocked on the door.

"It's open."

The Production Assistant came just inside the threshold and bowed. "I'm sorry, sir, but the video is trending online."

Jason huffed. "Of course, it's online already." Then he shrugged. "At least it's trending." He took out his phone and composed a message to Naomi to search for the video and get it taken down.

"That's not all, sir." Jason raised a curious eyebrow as he looked up from his phone. "A crowd has gathered outside the building. I think they're here to see him."

Jason frowned. "Why would they be here to see him? How does anyone even know–" Shit. "Show me the video."

17

The PA nervously shook her head. "I don't think–"

"Do it. I know you've got it on your phone." Jason's tone was firm and final. The PA reluctantly handed over her phone. The browser tab displayed a k-pop fan site's post about the video. Jason tapped the play button and watched the short clip. But he ignored his own presence. He already knew what he looked like. Then he saw what he was looking for. Tae Hyun was in the background watching him change. "Shit."

Jason's rage at the absurdity of the situation threatened to reappear. But he held it back, remembering Tae Hyun's efforts to calm him. Jason focused instead on his immediate need to get out of there. He handed the phone back to the PA.

"I'm in the video, too, aren't I?"

Jason looked at Tae Hyun and nodded. "You are."

Jason had a lot of questions about what was happening. The most critical was how someone even knew when and where he was filming that day. But the most urgent was what to do about getting out of the building. If Jason had been alone, he could've easily ducked out the back way and been gone before anyone even noticed. Not that he would've actually done that. He'd march right through the crowd out front if he was alone. Because fuck those people. But Jason wasn't alone, and there was no way he'd act like that in front of Tae Hyun.

"You can go," Jason instructed the PA as he grabbed his phone.

The PA silently stood in place for a moment before nodding and leaving the room.

"What are you gonna do?" Tae Hyun asked.

"All things being equal, a crowd wouldn't bother me," Jason replied as he did a web search for hashtags related to his name.

245

It only took a moment of scrolling to find a live feed of the people gathered before the Frostfire building. Jason could see at least fifty people. Then the camera panned, and Jason counted three times that many. "But things aren't equal. And somebody's trying to provoke me into acting out on camera."

Tae Hyun nodded. "It really feels like that, doesn't it?" He frowned. "What if we called KBR?"

Jason shook his head. "I don't trust them. And I don't want to hear a lecture from Ji Hoon." He opened the contacts app and scrolled until he found a number. "I'm gonna call Seong Woo. He gave me his number at your promo shoot."

"Yoo Mi's fiance? You trust him?"

"For this?" Jason nodded. "Yeah. He's highly protective of Yoo Mi's interests. And you're one of her interests."

Tae Hyun frowned. "Are you serious?" He shook his head. "I don't know."

Jason lowered his phone and looked Tae Hyun in the eyes. "You're also one of my interests." He reached up and gently caressed Tae Hyun's cheek. "But I won't call him if you don't want me to."

Tae Hyun gently bit down on his lower lip as he gazed into Jason's eyes. Jason almost kissed him right then. "Alright. Let's do that."

Jason hit the call button on Seong Woo's contact. Yoo Mi's fiance answered after the second ring.

"Hey Jason," Seong Woo said in English. "What's up?"

"Hi. I'm sorry to bother you, but I've got a favor to ask." Jason briefly explained the situation and what he wanted from Seong Woo. "I hope you can help."

"Yeah, for sure. Just gimme a minute." Jason heard the muffled sounds of Seong Woo speaking to someone with his

17

hand over the phone. "Alright, it's done. I'm sending Min Kyu to your location with a couple of his boys. He's my head of security. He'll get you both sorted."

Jason smiled. "Just like that? Thank you. I'm happy to–"

"If you're about to insult me by offering to pay for this, please don't."

"Pay you?" Jason snorted. "Hell, I'm planning on sending you a bill."

Seong Woo chuckled. "That's more like it. I'll give Min Kyu your number as soon as I hang up so he can arrange to meet you. He'll take you wherever you need to go. Afterward, we can talk about setting you up with proper security."

"Alright, then I'll let you go. I appreciate this, Seong Woo. Really."

"I know. I'll talk to you again soon."

18

Tae Hyun nervously fidgeted when he saw Seong Min and Seong Hyeon patiently waiting by the door. The brothers were part of the arrangement Jason had made with Seong Woo and Min Kyu, Seong Woo's security chief, to prevent any further incidents after Jason's commercial shoot.

Despite Jason's reassurances, Tae Hyun was convinced that the two would be forced to face a growing mob of people who were there to get a glimpse of Jason and Tae Hyun. Then Min Kyu arrived. The security chief appeared ordinary and unassuming in his simple, dark suit and vaguely military-inspired haircut. He was pleasant but never smiled. He was confident but never pushy. And his obvious self-assuredness made Tae Hyun feel better about how things would work out.

The first thing Min Kyu did when he arrived at Frostfire was check for alternate exits. The building had a pair of alley entrances, but those also had crowds camped out nearby. That wasn't surprising. Tae Hyun had checked his socials while he waited. An anonymous account claiming to be a member of Tae Hyun's fan club shared that Jason and Tae Hyun were at Frostfire to secretly film the music video for an upcoming, unreleased solo track. Of course, Tae Hyun had no fan club he knew of–only the *Dreamers* who had Tae

Hyun as their bias. But the post had drawn out many nearby *Dreamers*. And including the video of Jason changing onset only made it seem legit.

Tae Hyun expected that Min Kyu and his men would take him and Jason out through the back door anyway. But one of Min Kyu's men found an old utility tunnel he could access from the basement. The tunnel led all the way up the block, allowing Min Kyu, Jason, and Tae Hyun to exit into a seafood restaurant up the street, much to the surprise of the kitchen workers. From there, they snuck into a van waiting in the alley. Min Kyu also made Jason and Tae Hyun hand over their phones and put them in a specially lined bag that kept them from being tracked. But he gave them back once they reached their apartment and promised to send over a dedicated security team that evening.

That security team was the Song brothers, Song Seong Min and Song Seong Hyeon. Their names apparently sounded funny to Jason's American ear, if the way he kept chuckling every time he said them was any indicator. Jason tried explaining that they had a running joke in Hollywood that half the biggest stars were white men named Chris that people couldn't tell apart. But Tae Hyun didn't get it and chalked the whole thing up to his inability to understand American humor.

Seong Min and Seong Hyeon had watched over them in the days since then, even going so far as to take an apartment in the same building and sleep in shifts. Tae Hyun didn't quite understand who was paying for that. He knew he wasn't and that KBR wasn't, either. But Jason's company had hired a Korean PR firm owned by Cho Seong Woo's family to help manage the fallout from the illicit video, which sort of figured into the deal. It also turned out that the Cho family's company somehow owned CheezyFish. Or, they owned the Imperative Group, which owned Essential Foods, which owned AttackSnax, the company that made CheezyFish. And that made them responsible for what happened to Jason. It was complicated. And, while Tae Hyun still knew that the Cho family wasn't a chaebol, he was no longer sure they were that far off.

Once Jason finished getting ready, he walked up behind Tae Hyun and put a hand on his shoulder. Tae Hyun immediately stiffened as he felt the heat rising in his ears. He understood that the Songs knew about Jason and Tae Hyun and had no opinion on the matter. But that didn't make him any more comfortable showing affection in front of them.

Jason quickly pulled his hand away. "Sorry. I forgot." Jason suffered from no such hang-ups. "Boys, we're ready. Could you go fetch our ride?"

"Yes, sir," Seong Min answered. He was the younger and larger of the two. "I'll go."

"I'll wait for you in the hall," Seong Hyeon added as he followed his younger brother out the door.

"I'm sorry," Tae Hyun said. He turned to face Jason, who looked striking in the indigo Maximilien Cuvier tuxedo he'd picked up the day before after visiting the KBR stylists to touch up his haircut.

"It's okay." Jason smiled. "You're adorable when you pout like that."

Tae Hyun quickly sucked in his lower lip. He hadn't realized he'd been pouting. "Are you sure you want to do this?"

"I'm sure I want to kiss you," Jason replied before leaning in and planting his thick, luscious lips on Tae Hyun's mouth.

Tae Hyun reveled in the moment of private intimacy—especially how Jason's cologne mingled with his natural, musky scent. "That's not what I meant," he said after their kiss.

"I know." Jason used his thumb to wipe the edge of Tae Hyun's lower lip. "And, yes. I'm sure I want to go. I haven't been to a party like this in years." Then he grinned. "And I want to watch you looking this hot while you mingle with everyone knowing that you're coming home with me."

Tae Hyun chuckled, remembering his reunion with Yoo Mi. "You could at least pretend to be jealous."

"I'm insanely jealous." Jason shrugged. "But you're not my property. You can talk to whoever you want."

"As long as I go home with you."

"I'd hold your hand the entire time if I thought we could get away with it."

Tae Hyun felt his ears warming again as he stared into Jason's shimmering cinnamon eyes. Chang Min would've sooner cut off his hand than offered it to Tae Hyun in public. Not that Tae Hyun entirely blamed him for that. It would've ruined both their careers. But Jason at least acknowledged that he wanted to. "I'd love that."

Their moment of privacy ended when Seong Hyeon quietly knocked on the door. The car was ready. Tae Hyun tore himself from Jason's gaze to check his appearance in the entryway mirror one last time. He'd dressed in the shiny, burgundy Maximilien Cuvier sharkskin suit, black shirt, and black tie Jason had picked up for him. Tae Hyun leaned in close to ensure that his eyeliner looked good enough.

"I knew that would look stunning on you," Jason assured him. "But if we don't leave now, I'm gonna tear that expensive suit off you and fuck you right here."

"Promises, promises." Tae Hyun gently bit down on his lower lip as he considered the repercussions of skipping out on the party. But it was Xiang's video release party, and Xiang was a fellow KBR artist, which made the event important. And Xiang was also a friend, which made it even more so. "But I have to be there, so let's go."

Seong Hyeon brought the pair down to the building's garage, where his brother sat waiting behind the wheel of the pearl-white German sedan provided by the Vital Agency, Jason's PR firm, as part of their agreement. It was a short drive across Gangnam-gu to the party at the Park Grand Hotel that held Tae Hyun's last KBR event. Seong Min dropped them off at the hotel's garage entrance, and Seong Hyeon waited with Jason and Tae Hyun while his brother parked the car. Then everyone went inside.

Xiang's party had merited a grander ballroom than the *DoubleDown Boys* event to accommodate the much larger crowd. Tae Hyun suspected at least five hundred people were milling about the room. The decor was pure Xiang–literally–with ten-meter-tall promos of him for his new Chinese-language single hung like banners throughout the space, punctuated by dozens of giant video screens displaying clips of his previous videos. Red and gold lights splashed across the walls and ceiling, highlighting a giant fabric sculpture of a Chinese dragon that hung in the center of the room.

"Wow," Jason commented in English. "You guys don't fuck around with this shit."

Tae Hyun laughed. "This is nothing. You should've seen the release party for *Blossom*. Let's see if we can find Xiang so I can introduce you."

Jason's eyes were suddenly weighed down with concern.

"Are you sure that's a good idea?"

Tae Hyun nodded. "Yes. We're here, and I'm not going to avoid Xiang at his own party. Besides, I'm sure he'll love you." Tae Hyun turned to Seong Min, who lurked behind them. He couldn't see Seong Hyeon but assumed that the security guard was still watching them from somewhere. Ji Hoon had initially objected to Jason using his own security service. But Jason countered that he'd practically been stalked by photographers the moment he set foot outside and didn't feel safe–a fact he was more than happy to share with his father if need be.

"Seong Min? Do you know what Kim Xiang looks like?" Since Seong Min was half a head taller than Tae Hyun, he figured the guard had a better view of the party.

"I do, sir." Seong Min's head swiveled as he scanned the room. Then he gestured to Tae Hyun with his chin. "I see him over there."

"Great. Lead the way, please."

"Of course, sir."

Tae Hyun grabbed Jason by the sleeve as they followed Seong Min through the crowd. The partygoers seemed to sense Seong Min's looming bulk as he approached and cleared a path for him. Then Seong Min stepped aside at the last moment to allow Tae Hyun and Jason to approach Xiang directly.

The former *XTC* maknae was dressed in a scarlet silk shirt open to below his chest and tight, dark pants. He'd also gone platinum blonde since Tae Hyun had last seen him. Tae Hyun hated his own blonde phase, with the constant bleaching, toning, and root touch-ups. Just maintaining his purple streak was already a chore.

Xiang smiled the moment he saw Tae Hyun. "Hyung! I'm so glad you made it!" He threw his arms open wide.

Tae Hyun gladly stepped into Xiang's hug, figuring he'd officially become a hugger. "Of course, I'm here," he said as he tightly squeezed Xiang. "You know I wouldn't miss it."

Xiang nodded as he released Tae Hyun and noticed Jason. "And this must be the infamous American actor I've heard so much about." He offered Jason a quick bow. "I'm Kim Xiang. Welcome to my party." Then he frowned. "I'm sorry. Do you speak Korean? My English isn't very good.

Jason smiled and bowed in return. "Jason Park. And yes, I speak Korean. Congrats on your single. Tae Hyun played it for me. It's a real banger, even if I don't understand it. I never learned to say more than a dozen words in Mandarin."

Tae Hyun chuckled. He was pretty much the same. "Yeah," he agreed. "It's terrific."

"Thanks! I'm glad you like it," Xiang said. "I hope you're both enjoying the party."

Tae Hyun nodded. "Yeah. I mean, we just got here, so–"

"So we could use a couple drinks," Jason added.

Xiang smiled again. "Of course. I was actually hoping you wouldn't mind if I spoke to Tae Hyun alone for a bit."

Jason shot Tae Hyun a glance, but Tae Hyun patted him on the arm. "It's fine. Maybe go find us those drinks?"

Jason nodded. "Sure. No problem." Jason turned to Seong Min. "Come on. You can let your invisible brother keep an eye on Tae Hyun."

Tae Hyun watched Jason melt into the crowd before turning back to Xiang. "Before you say anything, we're just–"

"Hyung," Xiang interrupted. "Can we stop pretending I didn't know about you and Chang Min now?"

Tae Hyun frowned. "You knew?"

Xiang's chuckle was a little sad. "I'm not blind. Of course, I knew. We were together all day, every day. I knew every time you both snuck off to be alone together. I figured you'd tell me if you wanted me to know, so I pretended not to."

"I'm sorry, Xiang. That wasn't fair of us."

Xiang shook his head. Tae Hyun could see the hurt in his eyes. Xiang was always the most private of the three. Now Tae Hyun knew why. "I get why you had to keep it a secret. And it's not like you weren't my friend, so it was fine. Although I couldn't for the life of me understand what you saw in that asshole."

Tae Hyun grunted. "I wish you'd talked me out of it back then. Not that it would've worked."

"I was so mad when he pulled that shit in Tokyo. And I'm sorry about that."

Tae Hyun couldn't contain his surprise and felt his ears warming. "You knew about that, too?"

Xiang nodded and frowned. "I knew he was fooling around behind your back. I assumed you did, too. I'm sorry that I never said anything."

Tae Hyun sighed. Dating Chang Min had made a mess of everything, including his friendship with Xiang. "No, I understand why you kept that from me." He shook his head. "I kept everything from you. Shit. I'm sorry I never talked about it with you."

Xiang shook his head. "It's done and over with. I've moved on." Then he grinned. "And I can see that you have, too."

Tae Hyun's eyebrows shot up. "You can see that?"

Xiang chuckled. "Relax. You're not broadcasting it or anything. But I can see how much different you are today than the last time I saw you. You're more, I don't know. Relaxed, maybe? You're definitely not as angry."

Tae Hyun tried to keep from smiling but soon gave up. "Jason is a lot–" He paused before comparing Jason to Chang Min. "A lot different than I'm used to."

"Does he treat you well?"

Tae Hyun nodded. "He does."

"Good." Xiang smiled. "Now, if only I could find someone like that, too."

"Do you even have time for that? I saw that you're about to head out on another tour."

Xiang nodded. "Yeah. Tokyo, Manila, Bangkok, Beijing, Shanghai–"

"Sounds like you're gonna be busy," Jason interrupted as he returned to stand near them. He handed Tae Hyun a tall cocktail. "I don't know how you can stand all that flying. It took me days to adjust after flying here from LA."

"That's a much longer flight," Xiang agreed. "I remember when *XTC* last flew there. We still had to perform that same night. In fact, I think–"

"I like him, Naomi."

Tae Hyun instinctively turned at the sound of Jason's voice. "What did you say?"

Jason shook his head. "I didn't say anything. That's–"

"Say that again."

That was a new voice, also speaking English. The music had stopped, and–

Tae Hyun knew that voice. It was Naomi.

"I'm not saying it again," Jason's voice responded.

Tae Hyun whirled around, frantically searching for the source of the audio. A fist of cold dread gripped him as he caught a glimpse of Jason's red-faced, rock-hard grimace. Tae Hyun hadn't seen him that upset since the commercial shoot.

Seong Hyeon burst from the crowd. "Jason, sir. What do you want to do?"

Jason scowled. "Find the fucking sound booth and stop that playback."

"Fine. I like him, okay," Jason's ghost voice continued. Seong Hyeon shoved his way back into the crowd with Jason on his heels. *"I like Tae Hyun. Sure, he's beautiful. But he's also smart, talented, and fun to be around. He's thoughtful and kind. And he doesn't put up with my shit. As crazy as it sounds, I think there might be something there."*

Tae Hyun ignored the curious and surprised looks of the people around him as he pushed through the crowd on Jason's tail. His conflicting feelings fought for dominance. On the one hand, he'd dreamed of someone saying those things about him. To hear Jason say it was almost magical. But it was the wrong place and time. And there would undoubtedly be English speakers at the party who might understand what was happening. Jason was admitting his feelings for another man. For Tae Hyun.

Xiang suddenly gripped Tae Hyun's arm. "I see Chang Min in the DJ booth."

Chang Min? How did he figure into things? Xiang firmly held onto Tae Hyun as he dragged him through the crowd.

"I don't know, Jason," Tae Hyun heard Naomi say. *"I honestly never thought I'd hear you talk about someone other than yourself that way."*

"Oh."

Tae Hyun cringed as he listened to the end of Jason's career. And his own. He silently willed the sound system to shut off or the power to go out.

"Listen to me, Jason," Naomi continued. *"Don't fuck this up. He's not some WeHo fuckboy."*

"You think I don't know that?"

Tae Hyun finally spotted Chang Min standing in the DJ booth with an absolutely evil grin. He'd done it, Tae Hyun realized. He had no idea how, but somehow Chang Min had recorded Jason saying those things to his business manager and was broadcasting them to Xiang's party guests.

"But don't settle, either. You deserve happiness just as much as the rest of us. Maybe even more–"

The sound system finally shut down with a loud pop. Small comfort that it was, Tae Hyun still exhaled with relief. That was one problem dealt with. It was time to deal with Chang Min.

The asshole made eye contact with Tae Hyun as he approached, leering like the sadistic piece of shit he was. Tae Hyun automatically curled his hands into tight fists, ready to unleash his fury on the man who continued to ruin his life. But Jason got there ahead of him. He stormed across the sound booth platform, stopping just short of knocking Chang Min down. Jason poked his finger into Chang Min's chest, but Tae Hyun was too far away to know what he was saying.

Tae Hyun ignored the gasps and murmurs rolling through the nearby crowd as he climbed onto the platform and got close enough to hear Jason.

"–or we can fucking handle this right here," Jason said. "It's up to you."

Chang Min's leer slipped into a frown. "You wouldn't dare hit me."

Jason's grin was shockingly unhinged. "If you really know who I am, you know that's absolutely not true."

"Excuse me, sir." Seong Min pushed past Tae Hyun and grabbed Jason's arm. "Don't, sir. You can still recover from this. But not if you assault him in front of everyone."

Jason snarled. "Recover? How the fuck can I recover from–" Then he spotted Tae Hyun and stopped. "Fine. Take this piece of shit backstage. We can settle things there."

"What did you do!" howled a voice behind Tae Hyun. Ji Hoon shoved past Tae Hyun to join the growing crowd behind the DJ booth. "I'm going to–"

Tae Hyun grabbed Ji Hoon's arm. "Not here, sir."

Ji Hoon wrenched his arm free from Tae Hyun's grip. "What? Can't you see–"

"Jesus Christ," Jason exclaimed in English. "Everyone's looking at us," he added, switching back to Korean. "Seong Min, Seong Hyeon, get these two out of here." He looked at Tae Hyun. "Come on. Let's go."

Seong Hyeon and Seong Min formed a dark-suited cocoon around Chang Min and Ji Hoon and marched them toward the nearest exit. Jason and Tae Hyun followed behind them. Tae Hyun knew making a quick exit was the right thing to do. If he stayed, he'd have to address some uncomfortable questions to which he didn't have the answers. It was all a big mess, especially with Ji Hoon involved. And Tae Hyun couldn't stop thinking about Chang Min's ugly leer.

The turbulent currents of Tae Hyun's confused feelings swirled beneath those thoughts. Namely, what he'd just heard Jason say over the room's speakers. Tae Hyun already knew that Jason liked him. But Jason had privately admitted to Naomi that he maybe felt more–that maybe there was something between them. Then Chang Min had gone and made Jason's private confession public. Tae Hyun tightly pressed his lips together as he felt a surge of sudden rage. He'd deal with the asshole as soon as they were out of sight.

The Songs led them through the exit door into a service corridor. A handful of wheeled, metal serving carts stood parked against the corridor walls, and Tae Hyun could hear the muffled crash of pots and pans clanging in the nearby kitchen. He also heard Ji Hoon furiously berating Chang Min as the Song brothers led them down the corridor and around the first corner. Tae Hyun saw Jason say something to the guards but ignored it as they backed away to let Ji Hoon have his way with Chang Min. He finally had his chance to act. Chang Min's jaw dropped when he spotted Tae Hyun's angry approach. Then he held up his hands in defense and started backing away.

"You can't touch me," Chang Min desperately implored Tae Hyun. He fearfully looked to Ji Hoon for support. "You can't let him touch me, sir."

Ji Hoon shook his head and tried to block Tae Hyun's path. "Think about what you're doing, Tae Hyun. Let's just—"

But Tae Hyun hardly heard Ji Hoon as he pushed past him. He ignored the growing tension in his shoulders and jaw and squeezed his hands into fists. "You've fucked me over for the last time, asshole!"

"Hyung, just stop and think—"

Tae Hyun feinted a strike to Chang Min's face. Chang Min raised his hands to protect himself, exposing his torso, and Tae Hyun swung low with his left hand and nailed Chang Min hard in the gut. Chang Min doubled over in agony before Tae Hyun shoved him, knocked him to the floor, and kicked him in the stomach. Chang Min wailed as he curled into a ball. Then Tae Hyun felt a hand on his shoulder.

"That's enough," Ji Hoon commanded Tae Hyun. "I'll take care of him. And I'll deal with you later." He turned to Seong Hyeon. "You, whoever you are. Get these two out of here. And make sure they're not seen."

Tae Hyun felt a tug on his sleeve.

"Come on," Jason said. "It's time to leave."

Tae Hyun let out a long breath as he watched Chang Min sobbing on the floor. "Fine. Take me home."

19

Jason stared out the car window at neon-splashed streets still wet from an earlier rain shower. His mind aimlessly followed the bright trails of painted light while processing everything that had just happened.

Jason had another name to add to his growing conspiracy list. Chang Min must've been working with Min Jun somehow to take down Tae Hyun by taking down Jason. His motivations were clear. Min Jun's were less so, but Jason had a few ideas about that. But Jason didn't know how they'd gotten a copy of his video call with Naomi. Or, at least, the audio from it. Had Min Jun managed to install some spyware on his phone? Still, it was sloppy work. Without the video, the audio had no context and could hopefully be explained away as something other than Jason confessing his feelings for Tae Hyun. Hopefully.

However that all worked out, Jason was sure of one thing. He was fucking done with Seoul. Never had another place managed to so thoroughly fuck with him as Seoul had. And not just once but twice. Of course, the second time was Jason's fault. He should never have come back. But then, he never would've met Tae Hyun.

Jason turned from the window to look at the idol, who was

lost in his thoughts. His expression was carefully composed and neutral. After all that time and effort, the walls were back up. Fucking Chang Min. But Tae Hyun still looked fantastic in the suit Jason had bought. And Jason's icy hatred for Seoul melted a little. Things hadn't quite worked out the same way they had the last time he'd been to Korea. Not yet.

"How do you feel?"

Tae Hyun turned to Jason in surprise. "How do I feel? I wasn't the one–"

"I mean, how's your hand. You gave Chang Min quite a wallop. Did you hurt yourself?"

Tae Hyun lifted his hand from his lap and examined his knuckles. "No." He shook his head. "I learned more than how to cook in the army."

Jason snorted. "It's hot when you're aggressive like that."

"That's not fair." Tae Hyun sighed. "Did you mean all that?"

"Mean what?"

Tae Hyun huffed. "You know."

Jason took Tae Hyun's hand and gently massaged the knuckles with his thumb. It was warm despite the chill in the evening air. "Absolutely. Obviously, I planned to talk about it with you, too. I mean, once I was sure."

"Oh? But you talked about it with your business manager first?"

Jason quietly sighed. He knew Tae Hyun wasn't purposely trying to push his buttons. He was mad at the situation, too. And Chang Min. "You know Naomi's more than that to me. She's a friend. Sometimes, she's a mother. And she's one of the few people I've had in my life who genuinely care about me. If only because I pay her."

Tae Hyun shook his head. "It's not because you pay her."

"Maybe not." Jason took a heavy breath. "But it wasn't how I wanted you to find out."

"Find out what?"

Jason glimpsed the hurt and fear lurking behind Tae Hyun's stone wall gaze. He gently massaged Tae Hyun's hand again. "That I'm completely crazy about you."

Tae Hyun's facade cracked as his lips spread into a smile. "I'm crazy about you, too."

Jason smiled. Tae Hyun's confession unexpectedly warmed his heart. That made what he wanted to do next a lot easier. "Good. Seong Min?"

The burly security guard turned from the front passenger seat. "Yes, sir?"

"Let me use your phone."

"Of course, sir." Seong Min reached into his pocket and took out his phone. Then he unlocked it and handed it back to Jason.

Jason made three calls. The first was to Naomi. He left her a message explaining what happened and demanding that she find out how that audio leaked. The second was to the Vital Agency so they could start managing the PR and social media fallout from the party. The third was to his mother's assistant. To his surprise, she answered right away.

"Hello?"

"Myra? It's Jason. I'm sorry to bother you so late. Or, early, I guess."

"It's no bother, dear." There was a point when Jason was younger that Myra filled the role Naomi had taken as Jason's surrogate mother figure. His mother's assistant wasn't exactly loving, but she cared enough about Jason to look out for him when he'd needed it. "What can I do for you? Your mother tells me you've finally gone back to Seoul."

Jason's breath caught in his throat. Did Myra know what had happened back then? She had to. She was there, after all. But Myra had never said anything to indicate that. "That's right. In fact, that's why I'm calling. Is the Koh Sirey villa available? I thought I'd spend a little time there since I'm already out this way."

"It is. Your parents had intended to visit. But your father's been forbidden from traveling for the time being because of the stroke."

Shit. Jason had forgotten about that. "Oh, yeah. Sure."

"When would you like to visit?"

"Right away."

Jason swallowed his automatic wince as he waited for an irritated response. But Myra, used to dealing with his mother's highly spur-of-the-moment habits, didn't hesitate.

"Of course. I'll let the Sakdathorns know to expect you. Is this a good number to reach you at?"

"No. It's only temporary. Thank you, Myra."

"My pleasure. I'll give your best to your parents."

Jason snorted once Myra had disconnected. She knew him well enough to volunteer that sentiment without asking. He handed the phone back to Seong Min, who shook his head.

"Keep it. I only got it for this job. Min Kyu and Seong Hyeon are the only people who have that number."

Jason nodded. "Thanks." Of course, Seong Min knew why Jason had wanted to borrow it. He no longer trusted his old phone.

"What's Koh Sirey?"

Jason smiled at Tae Hyun. "It's where my family's villa is in Thailand. Koh Sirey is an island next to Phuket."

Tae Hyun frowned. "You want to go to Thailand?"

Jason nodded. "Yes. I can't–" He sighed. "I can't deal with all this, Tae Hyun. I need a fucking break."

Tae Hyun's frown deepened. "So you're leaving? Just like that."

Jason had intended to ask Tae Hyun about it but only then realized he should've done it before he called Myra. Stupid. "Yes. Come with me."

"What?" Tae Hyun shook his head. "I can't just up and leave."

"Do you have a passport?"

"Of course."

"Then, yes. You can just leave. It's not forever. Just for a few days. Maybe a week." Jason grabbed Tae Hyun's hand again. "Look. I realize now I should've talked to you first. I'm no good at this sort of thing because I don't have any experience." Jason knew he'd fucked up. It was time to fix that. He quickly made a new choice. "But I want to be with you, so I won't go without you. If you want to stay here, I'll stay."

Jason wondered for a moment if he'd meant that or just said it because it was convenient. The latter was more his style. But Jason felt like he'd really meant it, so he let the offer hang. He'd probably just make things worse if he said anything else.

Then Tae Hyun smiled. "Alright. Let's go."

A half-day, a dozen phone calls, and a hastily arranged private flight later, Jason reclined in a lounge chair next to the pool at his family's villa on Koh Sirey Beach. Run Sakdathorn had just brought him a fresh glass of Kingston before returning to the kitchen to help his wife Del finish preparing lunch. The Sakdathorns had been caretakers at the villa and lived in the guest house since they were a young couple Jason's age. To their credit, neither of them batted an eye when Jason presented Tae Hyun as his guest. They were probably relieved. The first time Jason had stayed there without his parents, he'd come with the *Monday Night Club* cast for a week-long party binge.

Seong Min and Seong Hyeon were another matter, immediately drawing skeptical looks from Del. Then Seong Hyeon spoke with them in Thai for a few minutes. Jason had no idea what he'd told them, but it seemed to work. And having them around made it less likely that Jason would be in a situation where he was tempted to fight. That alone made it worth the trouble of bringing them to Thailand.

Jason had no idea where the Song brothers had gone. He guessed they were probably assessing the villa's strategic security or something. That was fine. It made the pool feel less crowded. Jason usually would've been captivated by the view of Koh Sirey Bay beyond the disappearing edge of the villa's infinity pool while he lounged. But he couldn't take his eyes off Tae Hyun. The idol relaxed in the chair next to Jason's, wearing only a pair of Jason's skimpy swim briefs. Tae Hyun's bulge alone made it difficult for Jason not to be continually hard in his presence. And his lightly tanned skin almost glistened in the midday sun as he sipped the gin and tonic Run brought him. Jason grinned as he thought about them having sex later.

Tae Hyun glanced Jason's way in time to catch the tail end of his grin. "What's that look for?"

"Oh, just enjoying the view."

Tae Hyun chuckled. "I guess I should be flattered that you'd rather look at me than that gorgeous ocean."

"I've seen the ocean before. This is the first time I've seen you like this."

Tae Hyun rolled his eyes and took another sip of his drink. "This is good."

Jason smiled. "It's my mother's drink of choice. Run makes them almost as good as I do. But he didn't learn how to make them from her like I did."

Tae Hyun frowned. "Your mother taught you how to mix drinks? We obviously had very different upbringings."

Jason laughed. "I loved it. It was one of the few things she bothered to teach me herself. And it was one of the few times she seemed willing to welcome my presence instead of just tolerate it." He snorted. "How fucked up is it that ten-year-old me looked forward to cocktail hour just so he could talk to his mother?" Jason shook his head, hoping to shed the memories. "Are you close to your family? I've hardly heard you talk about them."

"Just my sister. She's amazing. I'm sure you'd love her. My parents–" Tae Hyun sighed as a brief shadow of sadness crossed his face. "My parents are very proud to have a successful son. But they have no idea who I really am."

"Well, my parents would probably love you. Right up until the moment they found out we're fucking."

Tae Hyun's eyes darted to the villa behind them. "Jason!"

Jason laughed. "Oh, relax. Run and Del have seen and heard far worse from me." He glanced over his shoulder to see Del approaching them from behind. "Isn't that right, Del?

"I'm sure I don't know what you mean, Khun Jason," Del responded. Even speaking English, she defaulted to Thai honorifics. "Lunch is ready. Would you like me to serve it out here, ka?"

Jason nodded as he sat up. "Yes, please." He put on the shirt and shorts that hung from the back of his chair before moving to the table where Del served their food. After a light lunch of spicy papaya salad, BBQ chicken skewers, and sticky rice, Jason asked Tae Hyun if he wanted to walk on the beach.

"Really?" Tae Hyun's bright smile and animated body language made Jason grin. "I'd love to!"

Jason slipped on his sandals and sunglasses before sending a message to Seong Hyeon, letting him know where they were headed. Then he offered Tae Hyun his hand. Tae Hyun reached out to grab it but stopped short.

"Are you sure it's okay?"

Jason nodded and took Tae Hyun's hand. "Positive. This stretch of beach is technically public. But the only access is through the properties surrounding us, so it's effectively private. Besides, there are tons of other beaches for people to visit around here already, anyway."

Jason took Tae Hyun down the stairs past the guest house and onto the beach. A broad horseshoe carpet of clean, white sand bordered the turquoise waters of Koh Sirey Bay. The beach was framed on both sides by tall rock formations covered in dense jungle greenery. It genuinely felt private. In all the times Jason had visited, he'd only seen the neighbors twice.

Jason held Tae Hyun's hand as they strolled along the sand. A mild, salty breeze caressed Jason's shoulders as it wandered off the water. Being there with Tae Hyun, hand in hand, felt magical after the mess from the night before. He should've suggested visiting sooner.

"I'm glad I didn't insist we stay home," Tae Hyun said, echoing Jason's thoughts.

"Me, too." Jason quietly sighed as the weight of everything

suddenly descended on him. "After all that shit yesterday and everything before it, it's nice to just be with you and not worry about who's watching and waiting to hurt us."

"It is." Tae Hyun let his hand slip from Jason's grasp so he could drape it around Jason's shoulders. "Are you ready to tell me now?"

"Tell you what?" Jason thought he knew what Tae Hyun meant. But he'd kept the truth of his last visit to Seoul hidden for so long that he wasn't sure he could talk about it even if he wanted to.

"It's alright if you're not," Tae Hyun added. "And it's okay if you never tell me. But you can, if you want to. Or need to."

Jason nodded, quietly stewing in the brew of his complicated reality. The life he'd built since his first visit to Korea was more than he could've hoped for. Yet, somehow, the damage from that time in his life continued to haunt him. Jason hadn't even told the story aloud since the studio pushed his sixteen-year-old self into mandated therapy after he started acting out on set. Since then, he'd locked up the memories behind vague descriptors like *the incident*, content to settle for a firm vow to never return. A vow he'd since broken and suffered for.

"I–" Jason stopped. "I need to sit down." He turned to face the water and sat on the loose, hot sand. Jason waited until Tae Hyun settled next to him before continuing. Then he waited some more, unsure how to even start the story. He finally gave up and just let it come out. "His name was Joo Won. We met at a garden party in Seongbuk-dong my parents brought me to. My father was looking for investors like his father for a new Brightstar venture."

Jason paused as he thought about Joo Won again. Even

after a decade, his rosy memories of Joo Won's lovely face and goofy smile were fresh and distinct. "We had so much in common. We were the same age. We were the spoiled, only children of new wealth." Jason smiled. "He was so beautiful. His smile would light up a whole room. He had this laugh–" Jason shook his head. "Anyway, we snuck away from the party. He brought me up to his room to play video games. Our parents didn't care, thinking they could get down to business without us around." Jason grinned. "I'm not sure which of us initiated the kiss. But it felt like gravity pulled us together. I don't think either of us could've stopped it."

Jason paused to listen to his breathing in time to the ocean waves lapping against the warm sand. Tae Hyun gently rubbed Jason's back.

"It was like magic. Our fathers made a handshake deal, which meant we could keep seeing each other. Joo Won and I were together nearly every day for the next three weeks. We kissed a lot, but neither of us had the courage to push for anything more. I didn't care. Just being with him was enough oxygen to fuel the fires of my young crush."

Jason paused again, knowing he was near the point where he'd have to say the words aloud. The sounds of the beach suddenly fell away. All he could hear was his breathing and his heart's furious pounding as tears gathered in the corners of his eyes.

"One evening, we were at his house for another dinner meeting. After dinner, everyone split up. Our fathers went outside to smoke cigars. Our mothers stayed in the lounge for cocktails. And we went up to Joo Won's room. Something felt different about that night. He felt it, too. There was an urgency–some kind of force pushing us to go further.

We were making out with our shirts off when our parents found us. I don't even know why they'd come upstairs. All I remember is the shouting. Our fathers dragging us apart. My furious sobbing and Joo Won's stoic acceptance of his mother's vicious slap."

A tear broke free from the others and ran down Jason's cheek. "I never saw Joo Won again. My mother made me delete his number and all his pictures from my phone. My father ranted about good family values and military school. He also canceled the deal with Joo Won's father. Or maybe Joo Won's father canceled it. I don't know. But I became a zombie, sleepwalking through the remaining weeks of our summer visit."

Jason's tears fell in earnest. He reached up to wipe some from his face. "My mother visited me the night before we left Seoul. Maybe something about my behavior had broken through her alcoholic haze. But she was crying when she came to me. Then she told me Joo Won had killed himself. Hearing that was a dagger to my heart. Before that night, I could've counted the times my mother hugged me on both hands. But she held me then while I sobbed. And I let her, as much as I hated her and my father for what they'd done. That night, I promised myself I would never come back. And I didn't. Until now."

Tae Hyun reached up and ran his fingers through the hair on the back of Jason's head. "That's an awful thing to go through. I'm sorry."

Jason closed his eyes and breathed. He'd expected to feel more than the profound sadness in his heart. But there was no rage. No guilt. None of the emotions that typically attacked him on the rare occasions he unpacked those memories.

Perhaps he'd finally moved on. "It was a beautiful moment in my life that destroyed so much. I'd say it ruined things between my parents and me, but it's hard to be sure since things were so awful, to begin with. But I've never forgiven my parents for it. Or his." Jason paused for a deep breath. "I forgave Joo Won, though. I was so angry at him for what he did. But I understood when I got older. I've never felt that hopeless, but there were times when I came awfully close." He snorted. "My therapist told me I was too narcissistic to consider suicide."

Tae Hyun chuckled. "What an asshole."

Jason shrugged. "He was right, though. Joo Won and I were different that way. The experience broke him. But it became my armor. It made me bold and reckless. What could the world take away from me that was worse than what it already had?" He put his hand on Tae Hyun's thigh. "Now it's given me something new."

"That's why you've been alone all this time?"

Jason shook his head. "No. I just haven't met anyone else who made me feel like that." He turned to look at Tae Hyun. "Until now."

"I promise I won't let anything–"

"Don't." Jason shook his head. Then he gently stroked Tae Hyun's thigh. "You know you can't promise that. We're two closeted gay celebrities from different continents. There's still so much that could come between us."

Tae Hyun frowned. "How can you say that?"

Jason shrugged. His story was enough to back up that sentiment. "Would you give it all up? The fame? The career? If it came to that?"

"Of course, I would. If it came to my happiness, I'd give it up in a second."

Jason smiled at Tae Hyun's confident tone. It was easy to say that when the idea of giving everything up was fiction. But would Tae Hyun feel the same when push came to shove? Maybe he would, Jason reasoned. He'd already done it once before.

"What would we do? How would we support ourselves?"

Tae Hyun smiled. "I can cook. You mix drinks. We could open a restaurant."

Jason chuckled. "Yeah, I guess we could." He leaned back to stretch his arms. "We should think about heading back so we can get cleaned up for dinner."

"Wait." Tae Hyun grabbed Jason's arm, pulled him in close, and kissed him. "Thank you for trusting me with that." He kissed Jason a second time. "And for bringing me here."

"I'm glad you're here with me." Jason smiled. "And I'm glad you like it. Maybe you could show me your appreciation after dinner, too."

Tae Hyun grinned. "I'd like to see you try to stop me."

20

Even as Tae Hyun sat for dinner, he couldn't stop thinking about Jason's story on the beach. He'd known Jason was damaged, just like him. But he'd never suspected the full extent of Jason's trauma. Tae Hyun could hardly imagine what that must've felt like. To be dragged from your lover's arms and forbidden any future contact only to learn afterward that he'd taken his own life? Tae Hyun didn't blame Jason for not wanting to return to Seoul. He wouldn't have either. Tae Hyun still hadn't been back to Tokyo because of Chang Min.

After cleaning up and changing, Tae Hyun tried his best to be present for the meal. Seong Hyeon and Seong Min had joined them at Jason's invitation. And dinner was a delightful sweet clam soup with lemongrass and stir-fried minced pork with basil–a pair of Del's specialties, according to Jason. While his guests ate, Run pulled out his older but well-loved guitar and serenaded the group with some traditional southern Thai folk songs. The music helped wrestle Tae Hyun's mind from the dark places it was touring. Once he was done eating, Tae Hyun asked if he could play something, too. Run, ever the gracious host, quickly agreed. He stood and offered his stool and guitar to Tae Hyun.

"I didn't know you could play," Jason commented.

Tae Hyun nodded as he sat and took the guitar from Run. "I can play piano, too. But I'm out of practice. I only had access to my guitar when I was in the army." Tae Hyun strummed a few chords before nodding again. "Any requests?"

"My favorite *XTC* song is *Blossom*," Jason suggested.

"I bet you've never heard the acoustic version, have you?" Jason shook his head. Tae Hyun smiled. "Then you're in for a treat."

Tae Hyun improvised the song's intro since *Blossom* was usually a quick, bass-heavy dance number. But he slowed it to more of a ballad tempo appropriate for Run's old guitar. Then Tae Hyun closed his eyes and began to sing. Even raw and unamplified, his voice was still a powerhouse. Singing it over a naked guitar reminded him of when he was in the recording studio. It was one of the last songs *XTC* recorded for the album, and he hadn't been in a studio since. If only he'd known then what would soon happen to his career, he might've appreciated the experience more.

Tae Hyun sang through the first verse and bridge before opening his eyes again. He looked right at Jason as he sang the chorus. *"I'm so happy you're mine. You look at me, and I cry. And our love's blossom burns like the fires in my mind."*

Tae Hyun had always secretly sung *Blossom* to Chang Min. It was a love song, after all. And his fellow idol had supposedly been the love of his life. But the more Tae Hyun sang, the less he felt like that had ever been true. Sure, he and Chang Min had passion. But it turned out Chang Min had passion with a lot of other guys, too. The love blossom burning for Chang Min in Tae Hyun's mind had only been imaginary. But the flames sparking for Jason were another matter. His feelings for Jason were different, at once more careful and more uninhibited. And Tae Hyun was older, more experienced, and more mature.

Tae Hyun closed his eyes after the chorus, afraid that Jason's piercing gaze would make him forget the words. And he had to fight to keep from rushing the song. If he'd only had an audience of one, Tae Hyun would've set the guitar down and jumped Jason where he sat. Even singing, Tae Hyun could only focus on what Jason told him on their way back outside for dinner.

I want you inside me tonight.

Everyone applauded Tae Hyun when he finished the song. Run even joked that Tae Hyun was good enough to sing professionally. Tae Hyun wasn't sure he was kidding until Run added a wink. Then the Song brothers excused themselves from the table while Run and Del cleared the dinner dishes. That left Jason and Tae Hyun alone with their drinks and the dimming firelight of the recent sunset.

"That was fucking amazing." Jason sipped at his bourbon before setting the glass down and standing from his chair. "I've never been serenaded before."

Tae Hyun bashfully grinned as Jason approached, ignoring the rising warmth in his ears. "If you're planning to–"

Jason straddled Tae Hyun's stool, sat on his lap, and leaned in close. "If I'm planning to what?" he purred in Tae Hyun's ear. Then he sucked Tae Hyun's ear lobe into his mouth and lightly bit down.

Tae Hyun let a low moan escape his lips before remembering himself. "Hyung. Everyone will see us."

Jason released Tae Hyun's earlobe and kissed the side of his neck. "No one's watching us," he replied. The feel of his warm breath on Tae Hyun's neck made the hair on his arms stand up. "Besides, I thought you liked performing for an audience."

Tae Hyun put his hands on Jason's chest and gently pushed him back. "Not for this."

"Then you'd better take me to the bedroom right now." Jason grinned. "Or I'm gonna rip those shorts off and sit on that thing I can feel between my legs right here."

"Alright." The villa's main suite was on the upper floor, away from prying eyes and ears. Tae Hyun would more easily feel alone with Jason in there. "Let's go."

A cool breeze snuck in through the open balcony doors as Tae Hyun lifted Jason's shirt off and pushed him down onto the bed. Then he took off his own shirt and climbed on top of Jason. Jason tried to sit up, but Tae Hyun held him down.

"You stay right there," Tae Hyun commanded as he leaned down and took one of Jason's nipples in his mouth. Jason groaned as Tae Hyun flicked his tongue across the top of it. Then he bucked and nearly threw Tae Hyun off when he began sucking it.

"Oh, fuck." Jason took hold of Tae Hyun's head and held it in place. Then he bucked again when Tae Hyun switched to Jason's other nipple. Jason's groaning crescendoed as Tae Hyun reached back to pinch the first one, too. When Jason tried to swat Tae Hyun's hand away, Tae Hyun let go and sat up.

"Too much?"

Jason shook his head. "My nipples aren't usually that sensitive," he panted. "I guess you just got me turned on that much."

Tae Hyun could feel Jason's erection pulsing underneath him. He grinned as he rubbed himself on top of it. "That's sure what it feels like to me."

Jason grunted and rolled to his side, knocking Tae Hyun onto the bed. Then he climbed onto his knees and straddled Tae Hyun's hips. "Oh yeah? Two can play at that game."

Jason leaned down and sucked on one of Tae Hyun's nipples, making him uncontrollably squirm. Then Jason switched to the other one. Electric fire shot through Tae Hyun as Jason twirled his tongue around the tip. Just when Tae Hyun thought he would black out, Jason relented, kissing Tae Hyun in the middle of his chest before scooting backward to draw a crooked line of kisses down Tae Hyun's belly. Then he grabbed the waistband of Tae Hyun's shorts and yanked them down, exposing Tae Hyun's cock.

"Oh, hyung," Tae Hyun moaned as Jason took him into his mouth. He reached down and ran his fingers through Jason's hair. Then he grabbed hold as Jason bobbed his head up and down on him.

"Damn," Jason said when he eventually came up for air. "That thing is leaking like a precum factory. I almost think we won't need any lube."

Tae Hyun took a heavy breath as he tried to calm his pounding heart. "That's because your mouth feels amazing."

Jason grinned. "Just wait until you find out what my ass feels like."

"Are you sure you want me to fuck you?" Tae Hyun tried not to frown. But he couldn't deny the anxiety he suddenly felt. "I really don't have any experience as a top."

"Says the guy who just mouth fucked me?" Jason chuckled as he stood on the bed, pulled his shorts off, and began stroking himself. "You'll be fine."

Tae Hyun nodded and tried to focus on Jason's primal

display. But his doubts crept up from the dark places of his mind to chill the heat between them. It wasn't technically true that he had no experience topping. Chang Min had bottomed for him once after Tae Hyun had incessantly nagged him about it. But he clearly didn't enjoy it and complained so much afterward that Tae Hyun never asked him to do it again. Tae Hyun assumed Chang Min didn't like to bottom until he caught him getting pounded by that callboy. That's when he knew Chang Min just didn't like bottoming for him.

"Hey, what's up?"

Tae Hyun looked up at Jason, not realizing that he'd tuned out. "I'm sorry. I was just–" He finally allowed himself to frown. "I was thinking about Chang Min. I tried not to go there, but–" Tae Hyun sighed. He felt his cock softening and knew he'd ruined the mood between them.

Jason frowned. "Hey, it's alright." He offered Tae Hyun his hand. "Could you sit up?" Tae Hyun nodded, took Jason's hand, and let Jason help him up. Jason let go to kneel in front of him. Then he pulled Tae Hyun into an embrace. "I know you come with a past," he said, holding Tae Hyun's cheek against his chest as he softly stroked his hair. The gentle throb of Jason's heartbeat immediately calmed him. "And I know that means you might have some hangups. But those are totally okay. They're normal and allowed." Jason put his hands on Tae Hyun's cheeks and pointed his face up. "And, yeah, I want you to fuck me." Tae Hyun looked up into Jason's soft, caring eyes. "But only when you're ready. Until then, we can do something else. Or, we can stop for now. Okay?"

Tae Hyun's heart warmed so much that he couldn't help smiling. Sometimes, Jason had this uncanny ability to say exactly the right things. He couldn't remember the last time someone had made him feel so seen and supported. Tae Hyun nodded. "Okay. I want to do it. I think I maybe just need a little direction."

"That's fine." Jason grinned. "I can be a bossy bottom, too." He reached down and took hold of Tae Hyun, gently stroking him while looking him in the eyes. "You know, I have a confession? When I first met you years ago at that concert, I had such a crush on you that I jerked off to pics of you for weeks after that."

Tae Hyun gasped as he felt his erection grow from Jason's touch. "I had a huge crush on you after I saw you in *Moon Shines Madly*. I talked about you so much it made Chang Min jealous."

Jason leaned down and nibbled on Tae Hyun's earlobe again. "Naughty boy," he purred. "Did seeing me in my underwear turn you on?" Tae Hyun moaned as Jason strengthened his grip. "Did you imagine what it would be like to be naked in bed with me?"

"Yeah," Tae Hyun whispered, unsure if he'd even said it aloud.

Jason kissed Tae Hyun's neck again. "And here I am right in front of you."

Jason let go of Tae Hyun and gently pushed him back onto the bed. Then he reached over to the nearby nightstand to grab the bottle of lube. He poured some on his hand and reached for Tae Hyun. Tae Hyun's whole body lit up as Jason ran his slick hand along his erection.

"Fuck!"

Jason chuckled. "That's the plan, sexy." He poured some on his fingers to apply it to himself. Then he returned to straddling Tae Hyun's hips. Jason pushed himself back against

Tae Hyun as he leaned down and brushed his lips against Tae Hyun's mouth. "Are you ready?" Tae Hyun nodded. Jason reached back and grabbed Tae Hyun's cock again. "I need to hear you say it."

"I'm ready," Tae Hyun moaned as his body shuddered.

Jason positioned his ass until Tae Hyun felt himself pressing against it. The pressure increased until he was inside. Jason softly hissed as he pushed himself back onto Tae Hyun, wrapping him in soft, velvety warmth until Jason rested his weight on Tae Hyun's hips.

"Fuck," the pair muttered in near unison. Jason remained still for a few moments, his grip on Tae Hyun so tight that he wondered if it might hurt. Then Jason moved, slowly lifting himself until Tae Hyun's cock was halfway out. Jason stayed there and took several heavy breaths.

Tae Hyun began to be concerned. "Are you okay?"

Jason nodded. "Oh, yeah." He let out a long breath as he lowered himself again. "This feels fucking amazing."

Tae Hyun closed his eyes as Jason took him inside. It felt so much better than when he'd fucked Chang Min. He almost gasped as Jason lifted and lowered himself again. Tae Hyun expected him to stop, but Jason continued, increasing his speed bit by bit until he rode Tae Hyun's hips. Tae Hyun's breath quickened in time to his thrusts. When Jason finally began to slow, Tae Hyun grabbed hold of Jason's thighs and pushed himself back in.

"Oh, yeah," Jason gasped. "Fuck me."

Tae Hyun took over, flexing his torso to fuck Jason from underneath him. Jason began stroking himself, and his ass contracted around Tae Hyun like a vise.

"Oh, fuck," Tae Hyun muttered. "Keep jerking yourself

while I'm fucking you."

Jason grunted as he fell forward onto his free hand, still stroking himself in time to Tae Hyun's thrusts. Tae Hyun struggled to keep his eyes open and observe the unreal vision of Jason riding him. But there he was–the troubled and troublesome American actor who came into his life and turned everything upside down. Tae Hyun's ass twitched at the memory of Jason fucking him as he pounded Jason harder. Jason's contractions grew stronger and more frequent in response, and Tae Hyun knew he would finish soon.

"Hyung, I'm gonna cum," Tae Hyun said and tried to pull out.

"No." Jason sat back down on him. "I want it inside me."

Tae Hyun didn't argue. He kept right on fucking Jason until the sensation nearly overwhelmed him. Then he unleashed an animal cry as the white flames of pleasure surged through him. He remained still, afraid to move, until Jason cried out a few moments later as he came on Tae Hyun.

Jason immediately fell on Tae Hyun's chest, slick with his sweat and Jason's cum. He kissed Tae Hyun, greedily sucking Tae Hyun's tongue into his mouth. Tae Hyun ran his hands along the muscles of Jason's back while they kissed. Then Jason pushed himself to his hands and knees. He stared down at Tae Hyun, his eyes glistening, with a crooked smile on his face.

"I love you, Tae Hyun."

Tae Hyun's breath caught in his throat at Jason's unexpected confession. Well, not entirely unexpected. Jason had already admitted he was crazy about Tae Hyun. But that was implying love. This was outright saying it. And Tae Hyun knew he felt the same way. "I love you, too."

Jason snorted. "For a second, I thought you wouldn't say it back." He leaned down and kissed Tae Hyun again. But it was slow and gentle. The urgency was gone. "But I'm glad you did." Then he pushed himself back up and carefully rolled off Tae Hyun to lay next to him. "And that was amazing."

It was Tae Hyun's turn to snort. "Which part? The fuck or the *I love you*?"

"Why not both?" He rolled onto his side and propped himself up on his elbow. "I'm glad you let yourself go there toward the end. I thought maybe you were too worried about someone hearing us."

"What?" Tae Hyun's mouth fell open as he turned to look at Jason. "Do you think someone heard us?"

Jason chuckled. "I think they heard us in Phuket Town." He reached out and gently caressed Tae Hyun's chest. "Don't worry about it. You're on vacation, remember? If it's any consolation, I've heard Run and Del go at it plenty of times. Those two definitely have an active sex life."

Tae Hyun shook his head. "I've never once had sex without worrying that I might get caught."

"That's real." Jason rolled to the other side, grabbed a pair of hand towels from the nightstand, and started wiping down Tae Hyun's chest. "I don't think we gotta worry about that here. If Run and Del were out to get me, they've already had plenty of opportunities to do that. Besides, Del's younger brother is gay."

"Really?" Jason nodded and handed the towel to Tae Hyun, who started to wipe himself. He needed a shower but was in no hurry to get up from their love bed. "And they're okay with that?"

Jason nodded again. "Yeah. I mean, there's still plenty of

homophobia in Thailand, but it's not as bad as in Korea. And the Sakdathorns love Beam no matter what. I'm kinda jealous, to be honest."

There was that word again. Love. The fact that they'd both said the words *I love you* to each other still hadn't quite sunk in. But hearing Jason say it first meant so much to Tae Hyun. He'd been the first one to say it to Chang Min and often wondered if it was what eventually drove them apart.

"I can't imagine telling my parents," Tae Hyun confessed.

Jason shrugged. "Not all parents are the Sakdathorns. Mine in particular. But I gotta admit that not having to come out to them at least gives me one less thing to stress about." He smiled. "I need to go clean up. But you're welcome to join me in the shower in a few minutes."

"Okay."

Jason rolled off the bed and started walking toward the bathroom. Tae Hyun sat up to watch him.

"Hyung."

Jason turned back with a curious eyebrow raised. "What's up?"

"Say it again."

Jason smiled. Tae Hyun expected Jason to say something sarcastic or ask him to be more specific. But he didn't hesitate. "I love you."

21

Clear morning light streamed through the window to settle in a bright stripe across Jason's legs. He had no idea what time it was as he extended his body in a great, long stretch. But the time didn't matter. Jason was on vacation and could lay in bed next to Tae Hyun all day if he wanted.

Jason felt a moment of panic when he rolled over to face Tae Hyun and saw that idol's side of the bed was empty. Then he heard the distant sounds of conversation and kitchen utensils. Tae Hyun must've already gotten up. He always rose before Jason. Why would a vacation with his lover be any different? Jason resisted the urge to call out for Tae Hyun, not wanting to interrupt whatever the idol was up to in the kitchen. Instead, he lay still and considered what happened the night before. He'd confessed his love for Tae Hyun, and the idol had done the same in return. Everything felt utterly perfect right then. He knew things wouldn't stay like that, but it was nice to feel that way for the moment.

Jason wasn't sure which part was more unbelievable. That he'd said the words *I love you* to Tae Hyun or that he actually felt that way. Not that either fact was in dispute. Jason knew he was in love. He'd known it since he told Joo Won's story on the beach. But Joo Won was the last person to hear those words from Jason, whispered in the dark under a shared blanket for fear that they might be seen or overheard. Well, until the night before. Sure, Jason's characters had uttered those fateful words plenty of times. But that was just reading from a script. He'd never felt that way himself about anyone after Joo Won died. And Jason had made another secret vow, perhaps without realizing it. He would never say those words again. But Jason had believed then that he'd never feel that way about anyone else. It turned out he was wrong.

A delicious aroma climbed in through the open balcony door, prompting Jason to finally get up. After a quick trip to the bathroom, he put on his swim briefs, followed by a pair of loose shorts, and went downstairs. He saw Tae Hyun and Del laughing and chatting in the kitchen as they prepared whatever Jason had smelled. Tae Hyun wore Jason's *Midnight Club* t-shirt and left his hair unstyled. Even in his natural, unmade-up state, Tae Hyun's beauty was as bright and blinding as the morning light that had woken Jason. Grinning, Jason made a beeline for the large french press filled with coffee that sat on the near edge of the kitchen island.

Del smiled when she noticed Jason's approach. "Good morning, Khun Jason, ka. Sleep well?"

Jason nodded as he poured some coffee into an empty mug. "I did, thanks." He pulled out a stool and took a seat at the island. "What are you two up to? I never thought I'd see Del let someone else into her kitchen."

"If Nong Jason ever offered to help like his faen," Del smoothly replied, "I certainly would allow him into my kitchen."

Tae Hyun snorted. "Don't listen to him, Del. Jason's just

jealous that you like me better."

Jason smiled. He wondered if Tae Hyun knew that faen was the Thai word for lover. But it was nice to finally see Tae Hyun relaxed and comfortable around someone who had almost certainly heard them fucking the night before. "That's fine if you want to gang up on me." He took a quick sip of his coffee. "As long as you make me breakfast while you're doing it."

Del frowned. "Perhaps Khun Jason would enjoy having his coffee by the pool, ka?"

"Alright, alright." Jason held up his hand in mock surrender. "I can tell when I'm not wanted." He got up from the stool, walked around the island, and offered Tae Hyun a quick kiss on the cheek. "Good morning," he said in Korean. "Sleep well?"

Tae Hyun grinned as his ears reddened. "I did. I hope you don't mind that I let you sleep. You looked so peaceful I didn't want to disturb you."

Jason shook his head. "It's only fair since you're the one who wore me out." Jason grinned as Tae Hyun's cheeks reddened to match his ears. "But I'll leave you with the kitchen boss now."

Jason took his coffee out to the patio and sat at the table near the pool. The weather was almost perfect, with golden sunlight streaming down from a nearly cloudless sky. Jason gazed beyond the pool toward Koh Sirey Bay, where he saw a yacht anchored. He wondered if it was one of the neighbors. Maybe some tourists had chosen to snorkel there.

"Good morning, sir."

Jason turned to see Seong Hyeon standing near him and nearly choked on his coffee. The elder Song brother wore a blue and white Hawaiian print shirt and khaki shorts. It was the first time Jason had seen him not wearing a dark suit. "Sorry, Seong Hyeon. I see you've updated your uniform."

Seong Hyeon frowned. "Is this not okay? I can–"

Jason waved off Seong Hyeon's apology. "It's fine, it's fine. Just surprising. Are you and your brother enjoying yourselves?"

Seong Hyeon relaxed his frown and nodded. "Yes, sir. This area is beautiful. And mostly secure." He reached into his pocket and pulled out a phone. "I have a message from Cho Seong Woo asking if you'd call him at your earliest convenience."

Jason rolled his eyes. He'd gone almost a day without the outside world requiring his attention. "Is that a demand or a request?"

"I work for you, sir. I'm merely relaying the message."

"Is that the phone I got from your brother?" Seong Hyeon nodded. "Alright, fine."

Jason took the phone and powered it on. A handful of new message alerts popped up, including several from Seong Woo and one from Naomi. Jason snorted. His business manager really did know everything if she'd somehow dug that number up already. Once he was sure Seong Hyeon had left him alone, Jason tapped on Naomi's number and hit call. She answered on the second ring.

"Fucking Thailand, Jason?"

Jason snorted. "Considering where I am and what I've been doing, I'd say that's accurate."

Naomi sighed. "Of course. The whole world goes to hell, and you jet off to Phuket for some fun in the sun, eh?"

"Can we please skip to the part where you tell me what's

up? Cuz, if I wanted to be scolded, I would've stayed in the kitchen with Del."

Naomi paused. "You don't know?"

"I mean, I know that Chang Min's still got a boner for Tae Hyun and tried to use me to take him down like some bad K-drama revenge plot. But Vital should be handling that."

"Oh, Jason. You really have disconnected." Naomi sighed. "Shit. Alright. Are you sitting down?"

Jason felt a sudden jab of worry. "Just tell me, damn it."

"I'm sorry, Jason." It was Steven, Naomi explained. Her (now former) assistant had leaked the audio from their call to Chang Min. But he'd also gone to the *Hollywood Hush* blog claiming that Jason was gay and handed over some of his records to prove it, including details of his payments to Diego. Of course, because Jason was connected to Tae Hyun, the *K-Star Daily* had run the story, too. "I've sent C&Ds to everyone I could think of," Naomi added. "And Vital had the story pulled from *K-Star*. But I've had my phone ringing non-fucking stop all day. Everyone wants a statement from you, and I don't know what to say."

Jason reached for his cigarettes before remembering that he didn't have any. It had been a week since he'd last smoked, and he hadn't even brought a pack. "Well, that's just fucking great. I wouldn't fuck Steven, so the evil twink decided to out me to the fucking press? Didn't he sign an NDA?"

"Of course, he did. And we can sue him to high heaven, along with anyone who illegally prints any confidential records. But you can't put this horse back in the barn. The story's out, and it's not going away."

Jason huffed. Why didn't he have any goddamned cigarettes? Someone there had to have some, right? Didn't

Run smoke? Maybe he could–

"Jason."

"Sorry. I just realized I picked a shitty week to quit smoking."

"What? You quit? I–uh. Wow."

"Fuck, Naomi. Let's not make a thing out of it, please." Jason sighed. "So, what else?"

"What do you mean?"

Jason shook his head. "My fucking security guard just strongly suggested that I call my new friend who owns the Vital Agency. So, what else?"

"Oh. Well, CheezyFish pulled the campaign. They're exercising your contract's morals clause.

"My what? You let me sign a contract with a morals clause?"

"All your contracts have a morals clause. Especially your contracts, I imagine."

Jason huffed. "Yeah, yeah. You're fucking hilarious." Jason sat up and took several deep breaths, hoping to calm down. It wasn't smoking, but maybe he could fool his body for a bit into thinking it was. "And the money?"

"They haven't made any moves for it yet. I don't know enough about Korean contract law to be sure, but I don't think they have grounds to ask for it back. Of course, that doesn't mean they won't."

Jason pursed his lips. Maybe that was Seong Woo's influence? "What about KBR?"

"I don't know. I have a call into Ji Hoon's office, but there's the time difference and everything. So–" Naomi let the rest of her thought hang.

Jason guessed that Ji Hoon was probably furious and would cut Jason loose if it were up to him. But Gerald Park was involved and wouldn't allow Ji Hoon or KBR to do anything that might smear his family name. What a fucking mess. "Alright. I need to talk to Tae Hyun."

"No, Jason. This is too im–"

"I said I need to fucking talk to Tae Hyun. He's part of this, too."

Naomi fell silent. Jason could almost hear her stewing. "You're right. I'm sorry. I'm not used to you being like this."

"Like what?"

"I don't know. In love? I mean, you quit smoking. And I bet you haven't had a drink yet today, have you?"

Jason frowned. "No, but I'm strongly considering it."

"Don't do it. Talk to Tae Hyun. Enjoy another day in paradise. I can hold things off for the time being."

Jason took another deep breath. His body wasn't fooled, but he still felt better. "Okay. Thanks, Naomi."

Jason disconnected and set the phone next to his coffee. He stared at it, tempted to go online and see what people were saying about him. Jason had imagined for years what might happen if he were outed. Would the calls of *I knew it* and *no wonder* drown out any misguided supporters who insisted someone like him couldn't possibly be gay? Jason also knew he should call Seong Woo, who knew he was gay but didn't care. Too bad that didn't extend to his family's company. And Diego. Jason should call Diego. Shit.

"Breakfast is ready." Tae Hyun set a plate in front of Jason before sitting next to him. "It's three-mushroom pancakes and steamed eggs. Although it's really just two-mushroom pancakes, but–" He stopped and frowned. "Is something wrong? I know it's probably not what you're used to, but–"

"It's wonderful." Jason switched on his smile and picked up

his fork. "It smells delicious."

Tae Hyun smiled and nodded, but Jason could see his lingering uncertainty. "Okay, good." He scooped up a bite of egg and put it in his mouth. "So," he added after swallowing, "did I see you talking on the phone?"

Jason nodded, careful to keep his face neutral. He was well aware of the irony that he was doing the same annoying thing that Tae Hyun had done to him. "I talked to Naomi. She wanted to let me know what's been going on since Chang Min pulled his little stunt."

"Oh." Tae Hyun's smile slipped. "I'm sorry again. I had no idea–"

"It's fine. It wasn't your fault." Jason cut into the mushroom pancake, which was closer to a fritter, and took a bite. It was crunchy, savory, and a little spicy. He probably would've loved it under different circumstances. But his conversation with Naomi heavily weighed on him, overriding his enjoyment of simple things like a home-cooked meal.

"Well?"

Jason saw Tae Hyun's expectant gaze and forced himself to smile. "It's delicious."

Tae Hyun's frown meant Jason wouldn't be winning any awards for his mealtime performance. "I can tell something's bothering you." He set down his fork. "If you want to take back what you said, that's okay."

"What? Shit." Jason shook his head and grabbed Tae Hyun's hand. "No, that's not it at all. My feelings haven't changed. Have yours? Do you want to take it back?"

"No." Tae Hyun let out a heavy breath. "I'm sorry. I thought you were regretting it. It was the heat of the moment and everything. You know?"

Jason gave Tae Hyun's hands a gentle squeeze. "No way. I meant what I said. I love you. Regardless of everything, I need you to know that."

"What does that mean? Regardless of what?"

Jason explained what Naomi had shared. It was hard to say everything aloud. It wasn't quite as real when it only existed in his head. "So now I gotta decide how I want to handle it. But you're a part of things, so I wanted to discuss it with you first."

Tae Hyun had gone stone-faced as Jason spoke, making Jason afraid that he was about to get shut out. Then Tae Hyun's face softened again as he turned toward the bay. "Wow. I don't even know how to process all that."

Jason nodded as he let go of Tae Hyun's hand and sat back in his chair. They remained silent for several minutes. Jason fought to keep from pressing Tae Hyun for an answer, knowing how much that irritated him when Tae Hyun did it.

"It's so beautiful here," Tae Hyun finally said. "Could we just stay here like this?"

Jason wasn't sure if Tae Hyun meant specifically there, together, at the villa, or generally where they were as a new couple. Either way, he thought he understood the sentiment. "Of course. If that's what you want."

Tae Hyun snorted. "You don't need to humor me."

"I'm not. When I wasn't sure how things would go between us back at the beginning? This was my fallback plan."

"Oh." Tae Hyun nodded. "I can see why." He turned back toward Jason. "What would you do if it was just you?"

Jason shrugged. "I don't know. I mean, the last time I went through something like this, things didn't work out so well for me. And this time, it's not just me. There's you.

And there's no action I can take here that doesn't impact you somehow." Jason sighed. "I could officially deny everything, but the damage is done. Still, I'm pretty sure I can live without the CheezyFish money if they try to come for it. And I'm guessing I gotta drop the KBR gig."

"You'll give that up? Just like that?"

Jason shrugged. "Think about it. What would happen if you got outed? Like, if Chang Min came clear about your history or something?"

Tae Hyun frowned. "KBR would drop me for sure."

"Right? And, even if I deny everything, people will always wonder about you–and us–if they keep me around. Hell, they'll wonder anyway. But that'll eventually go away as long as I do."

"What?" Tae Hyun angrily shook his head. "So you're gonna–what? Just fuck off into the sunset? But what about us?"

Jason sighed. That was the actual conversation they needed to have. But he wasn't ready for it. He'd had no time to prepare–emotionally or otherwise. Jason had assumed they'd have at least a couple more months to come up with a plan. Instead, they had less than a day. "This is about us. Don't you see that?"

"I don't see how your leaving would do us any good."

Jason shook his head. "Because I'd have to leave when my contract was up anyway. I'm not from Korea, remember?" He pointed toward the horizon. "And I still have a life back home. Yeah, it wasn't much of one at this point. But it needs to be dealt with."

Tae Hyun started chewing on his bottom lip. Jason couldn't remember ever seeing him do that. "I suppose so."

"But it's not like I'd be gone forever," Jason explained. "I could get a place in Seoul, although I couldn't stay full-time. And you could come to LA. Hell, we could even meet up here." Jason paused, letting the silence linger while Tae Hyun considered the implications of what he'd just said.

"Is that what our future looks like?" Tae Hyun leaned forward and put his palms on the table. "Flying back and forth between our homes?"

"I don't know what else you expected." It wasn't an ideal situation, but it wasn't that bad. At least compared to the alternative. Jason frowned. He didn't think Tae Hyun would like their other option, but it was still something he knew they should consider. "Of course, we could also just come out."

Tae Hyun's eyebrows shot up. "What? Are you serious?"

"Yesterday, you said you'd give it all up for your happiness. You'd be a cook, and I'd be a bartender, remember?"

Tae Hyun shook his head. "But I didn't–" He stopped and shook his head again.

"You didn't mean it?"

Tae Hyun huffed. "I didn't think I'd have to do it the next fucking day."

The idol silently looked down and stared at the half-eaten meal on his plate. As much as Jason wanted to shake him and remind him they were supposedly in love, he let Tae Hyun have his time. Not everyone was like Jason. It took some people time to process difficult decisions.

Besides, Jason had always known that love was never in the cards for him. Even having just one day's worth of it was probably more than he could've hoped for.

"It's alright," Jason finally spoke into the quiet, keeping his voice even while his heart sank. It was alright. Everything had happened so fast. They'd obviously rushed things, especially considering the forces clearly working against them. "We don't have to decide anything right now. Let's just–"

Tae Hyun smacked the table, startling Jason into silence. "It's not fucking alright. Nothing about this is alright. How can you just–?" Tae Hyun stopped, leaving his question unfinished. "Why aren't you more upset about this?"

Jason snorted. "I am fucking upset. I'm just trying to deal with this situation without making it worse like I usually do. But I can have a tantrum, too, if you think that'll help."

"A tantrum?" Tae Hyun scoffed. "Oh, sure. Call me childish. That's really fucking helpful." He pushed back from the table and stood up. "Of course, you're willing to come out. What would you even be giving up? Day drinking and picking fights with the press?"

Jason frowned. He knew Tae Hyun was just lashing out because he was upset. But that didn't make it hurt any less. "I know you don't really mean that."

Tae Hyun snorted. "Don't I?" He slammed his hands on the table hard enough to rattle the dishes, jarring Jason's nerves and testing his self-control. "I'm the one with a career. I'm the movie star who's in an actual movie. I'm the fucking k-pop idol with a solo album on the way. And you want me to give all that up?"

Jason folded his arms across his chest to keep from doing something he knew he'd regret. Tae Hyun was clearly doing more than lashing out at Jason. He was trying to provoke him. But maybe he didn't realize he was. "What are you doing?"

"What?"

"You heard me. Why are you acting like this? I get that

you're upset, but we're supposed to be in love. Or did you not mean that, either?"

"Are we? Is that what this is?" Tae Hyun leaned in closer. "Because it doesn't really feel like that right now."

Jason quietly chuckled. After all that worry and everything they'd done to get to that point, Tae Hyun still wouldn't let Jason in, no matter how much Jason wanted in. Maybe he never would. "I see how it is with you. Love only applies until the first sign of trouble. Then you're out. Just like with Chang Min."

Tae Hyun's wall went up so fast it almost made Jason dizzy. He knew he'd scored a deadly hit and immediately regretted it.

Tae Hyun scowled. "Fuck you. I need to be alone for a while. Don't follow me."

Tae Hyun turned away without waiting for a reply. And Jason silently sat and watched him march across the pool deck to the stairs leading down to the beach. He let out a long breath, hoping to release some of the tension in his neck. But he was losing that battle, just like he was losing the will to not smoke. Maybe if–

A sudden shadow fell across Jason's face. "Khun Jason, krub?"

Jason looked up at Run, a look of fatherly concern on his face. Jason almost sneered until he remembered that Run might have cigarettes. "What?"

"Are you alright? Is there anything I can get you?"

A cigarette? A drink? A fucking time machine so he could go back and stop Chang Min, Steven, Min Jun, and everyone else who'd made it their mission to fuck with him? Or, better yet–turn down the fucking KBR job in the first place. "No,

P'Run," he replied, adding the Thai honorific. "I think I'd better start packing."

22

Tae Hyun aimlessly drifted along the beach, surrounded by scenery so gorgeous it was stifling. He had to be a ghost. He felt so hollowed out he couldn't possibly have been alive. And anyone who might've witnessed their fight would assume Jason's words had killed him.

I see how it is with you. Love only applies until the first sign of trouble. Then you're out. Just like with Chang Min.

But those witnesses would've been wrong. Tae Hyun had done it to himself, flinging his knife-edged words into the universe only to have them come right back at him. It was fitting. Twice he'd fallen in love, and twice he'd angrily walked away from it.

Tae Hyun wandered far enough into the water to get his ankles wet. The bathwater-warm waves lapped at his shins as he stared at the distant horizon. His home was out there somewhere. And Jason's was beyond that, past the Korean Peninsula and across the great Pacific. Jason, who Tae Hyun loved.

You said you'd give it all up for your happiness. Tae Hyun had said as much on that very beach. And he'd meant it, hadn't he? He shook his head, trying to shake the sharp feelings from that memory loose. It was an easy promise to make

22

when it was an empty one. Tae Hyun was so caught up in his self-assuredness that he hadn't believed he'd ever have to follow through. Then the universe used Jason to speak Tae Hyun's lie back to him.

Tae Hyun may have been lying–consciously or not–but at least he wasn't asking Jason to give up everything he'd spent his life building. His career and his fans were all Tae Hyun had left. Surely Jason could understand how that would all come crashing down if Tae Hyun came out. It wasn't even hyperbole. Everyone knew about the rare idols who'd come out, voluntarily or otherwise. To a one, they'd been shunned by the industry and its fans alike. Is that what Jason wanted for them? Did he really believe they'd be happy as a bartender and a cook?

How could Tae Hyun have ever thought things would work out with Jason? He was no lovesick starry-eyed youth, smitten beyond recognizing the basic facts. Tae Hyun had been burned by that kind of ignorant innocence once before when he fell for a selfish asshole. Jason and Tae Hyun had started at a disadvantage, coming from different countries on opposite sides of the ocean. Then Tae Hyun's spurned former love conspired to exact his revenge by ruining Tae Hyun and Jason's lives. And that was before someone who'd worked for Jason did the same thing. Tae Hyun imagined that Chang Min would've been delighted to see how things worked out.

Tae Hyun resumed marching the length of the beach, finally turning back when he reached the great rocky promontory covered in jungle plants. But the walk had done him no good. He felt just as empty climbing the steps back to the villa as he had when he first walked off. Jason had left the table while Tae Hyun was gone. Maybe he'd gone inside.

Seong Hyeon walked out to the pool deck as Tae Hyun approached the villa. His face was grim.

"Tae Hyun, sir?"

Tae Hyun stopped, wondering what fresh trouble he was about to discover. "Yes?"

"He's gone, sir." Seong Hyeon held out a small, folded note with both hands. "But he asked me to give you this."

Gone? What did that even mean? Tae Hyun took the note and opened it.

I'm sorry things worked out like this. I wish they hadn't. But we both know how much wishes are worth. The Songs will make sure you get home. Love, Jason

Tae Hyun looked up at Seong Hyeon, not entirely understanding what he'd just read. "What is this?"

"I haven't read it, sir. But I assume it's a goodbye note."

Tae Hyun's jaw dropped. "Goodbye? You mean he's really gone? As in, he left Thailand?" Tae Hyun shook his head. How was that possible? How long had he been down at the beach?

"Jason wanted you to know that you're welcome to stay here as long as you like, sir. And he asked us to get you home when you're ready."

Tae Hyun looked down at the note again. *Love, Jason.* Love? How was any of it love when his last words to Jason were *fuck you*? "Well, that's just fucking great." He looked up at Seong Hyeon. "Fine. Then take me home right now."

Once he'd finished packing–studiously ignoring the bed where he and Jason had recently proclaimed their love for one another–Seong Hyeon and Seong Min drove Tae Hyun to the Phuket Airport's private jet terminal. After their jet touched down in Seoul, the brothers escorted a still-hollow

Tae Hyun back to the apartment he shared with Jason. Or used to share. Tae Hyun still carried the weight of his dread as he walked inside. It was clearly empty, to Tae Hyun's unexpected surprise. Had he honestly thought he'd find Jason there, waiting to welcome Tae Hyun back with a warm hug and soft kiss? It seemed so. But Tae Hyun was only met with the cold darkness of rooms that had gone unoccupied for days. And his broken-hearted anguish bounced around the empty apartment like a sad echo.

As he walked by Jason's room, Tae Hyun did his best to ignore the open door. Then, after delivering his luggage, Tae Hyun swallowed his dread and went into Jason's empty bedroom. The bed was unmade, despite Jason having slept in Tae Hyun's bed since soon after his arrival. And pieces of Jason's life were strewn about. A watch sat on the dresser. A single sock stuck out from under the unmade bed. A suitcase, no doubt filled with the clothes Jason hadn't taken to Phuket, sat near the closet. What did that mean? Had Jason left all that behind in Tae Hyun's care? Or had he simply abandoned it? Worst of all, Jason's smell still permeated the space, causing a deep ache in Tae Hyun's chest.

Tae Hyun sighed and closed Jason's door on his way out. Then he showered and changed. Once he'd dried his hair and dressed in his sweats, Tae Hyun finally turned his phone on. He sat on his bed while the message notifications poured in. Yun Seo, Yoo Mi, and Ji Hoon had all sent him dozens of messages. That told him much about how things had gone in his short absence. First came the messages wondering where he was. Then about Jason's news. And finally, the pleas for him to call them back. Tae Hyun was tempted just to turn the phone back off. But he knew that would only be putting off the inevitable. So he called Ji Hoon, who answered right away.

"Is this really you?"

"Of course, sir. Who else would it be?"

"Then please help me understand what's going on. Because the Tae Hyun I know wouldn't disappear for two fucking days without so much as a word."

The fact that Ji Hoon was already swearing didn't bode well for the rest of the call. But Tae Hyun was in no mood to get scolded. "The Tae Hyun you know now absolutely would, sir. Tell me about Chang Min."

Ji Hoon sighed. "What a fucking mess that's turned out to be. But it's my fault for not acting sooner."

"Acting sooner, sir?"

"I knew Chang Min was a moderately talented loose cannon, but I hoped your return would push him into greater things."

Tae Hyun snorted. "Maybe now you'll understand why I refuse to work with him."

"Indeed. What I don't understand is what's happening with Jason. I spoke with his business manager, who assured me Jason would make a public statement soon. But that's all she would say. Meanwhile, he's not taking my calls. You're not taking my calls. And CEO Pak is furious with me. Please tell me something, Tae Hyun."

"Something, sir?"

"You know what I mean. You've spent a great deal of time with Jason. Is what this person said about him true?"

Tae Hyun absently chewed on his lower lip, then noticed what he was doing and stopped. He knew he should deny the rumors if only to cover his own ass. And he certainly had no qualms about lying to Ji Hoon about that. He'd been doing it for years. But he had no idea what Jason's public statement would be, and he didn't want to contradict what he might say. Damn it. "Of course, it's not true, sir."

Ji Hoon sighed. "Alright. Thank you. I'm sure you can understand the difficulties this situation has caused."

Tae Hyun almost laughed. "I can, sir."

"And, unfortunately, it would be best if Jason stepped away from the project for the time being. Is he with you? I'd like to talk to him if that's possible."

Tae Hyun realized he'd been chewing on his lip again and made himself stop. "No, sir. Jason's not here. He's gone back home."

Ji Hoon loudly scoffed. "What? He's left the country?"

"Yes, sir."

Ji Hoon remained silent save for the ragged sounds of his breath. "I see." He sighed. "I need to call the CEO, so I'll have to go. I'll call you again in the morning. Please don't turn off your phone again."

"I understand, sir. I won't."

Ji Hoon disconnected without saying goodbye. Tae Hyun sat and stared at his darkened phone. His conversation with Ji Hoon had gone about as well as it could've. He sighed and looked back at his bed, imagining sleeping there alone for the first time in weeks. Tae Hyun didn't think he could do it. So he sent a message to his sister. *I'm coming over.* Then he got up to change. He'd just finished putting on his pants when he heard a knock on the door.

Tae Hyun nervously peered through the front door peephole to see Seong Min standing outside. He quickly opened the door, then found himself at a loss for words.

"Uh—"

"I was about to go get some food, sir." Seong Min had changed from his resort wear into jeans and a dark sweatshirt. His military haircut was covered by a baseball cap for a team Tae Hyun didn't know. "Would you like me to get you anything?"

"Why didn't you call?"

Seong Min shrugged. "I didn't know if you'd turned your phone back on yet."

"Thank you for the offer. But would it be okay to ask you for a ride somewhere instead?"

"Of course. It's my job."

Tae Hyun frowned. "I thought your job was to protect Jason."

Seong Min shook his head. "No, sir. Our job is to protect you. At least, it is until Cho Seong Woo says otherwise."

That was a surprise. Tae Hyun had assumed he'd already seen the last of the Song brothers. So he asked Seong Min to take him to his sister's place in Changcheon-dong. Hopefully, she was home. If not, Tae Hyun still had a key. He refused Seong Min's offer to walk him inside. It didn't matter if Min Jun, Chang Min, or whoever knew he was there. They'd played their hand already. There was nothing more they could do. But Seong Min requested that Tae Hyun call or message him when he was ready to leave. And Tae Hyun suspected Seong Min would probably be waiting for him outside.

Tae Hyun knocked before he tried his key. Yun Seo quickly opened the door and ushered her brother inside. Tae Hyun made it three steps beyond the threshold before he started crying. Yun Seo pulled him into a hug as he tearfully tried to explain what had happened.

"I'm sorry, oppa," Yun Seo said as she gently stroked the back of Tae Hyun's head. "Do you want to stay here tonight?"

"Yeah. I can't go back there right now."

"Was he there?"

Tae Hyun shook his head. "No. But that's almost worse."

Yun Seo nodded. "Of course. Come in and tell me everything." She took her brother's hand. "I just opened a bottle of wine."

After pouring them both glasses of the red she was drinking, Yun Seo joined Tae Hyun on her small couch. Tae Hyun took a sip of his wine. He wasn't much of a wine drinker, but it tasted nice. "Thanks, Yun Seo."

"Of course. So, how are you feeling?"

Tae Hyun sighed. He hated being so dramatic. But he'd just spent the past eight hours with only his security guards, so he'd felt compelled to keep his feelings to himself. "I feel like this is the opposite of how I expected today to go. This morning I was in Thailand and in love. Now I'm here with you."

Yun Seo snorted. "Thanks a lot."

"You know what I mean." Tae Hyun shook his head. "I can't believe he just left like that."

"Oppa." Yun Seo frowned. "Do you want me to just listen and commiserate? Or are you looking for advice?"

"Why? What advice have you got for me?"

"Well, we talked about this before, right? You know, your habit of driving people off when they get too close?"

Tae Hyun scowled. "I didn't drive him off. He left."

"I'm not saying this is entirely your fault, oppa. It's not like Jason hasn't run off before. And I can see that you're hurting.

But I'm not sure it's because of Jason."

"Of course it's not!" Tae Hyun shook his head. "It's because of Chang Min and whatever fucked up games he's been playing. If he'd just left us alone, things would be fine."

"Would they? Because you two have had plenty of rocky moments already." Yun Seo put her hand on her brother's leg. "And here comes the part you won't want to hear."

Tae Hyun snorted. "I can hardly wait."

Yun Seo didn't quite roll her eyes, but it was close. "You've had two years to get over what happened, but you haven't. You just ignored it because it was easier. And now you're paying for it."

Tae Hyun scoffed. "So you think this really is my fault?"

"No, I think your asshole ex is being an asshole. But I also think how you've reacted to everything is entirely your fault. It's been two years, and you're still the same hurt boy scared that any time he opens his heart to someone, he'll get hurt again." Tae Hyun frowned but stayed silent. "So," Yun Seo continued, "are you really sure you didn't say anything to push Jason away?"

"You mean besides, *I love you?*" Yun Seo tilted her head to the side with her typically judgmental eyes. "Alright, fine. Maybe. I may have said something about how only one of us has anything to lose if we came out."

Yun Seo quietly hissed. "Ouch."

"What? Was that not true?"

Yun Seo reached out and patted her brother's arm. "There's truth, and there's ruthless honesty." Then she poked his bicep. "And that was cold. Even for you."

Tae Hyun frowned as he replayed his argument with Jason. His confused rage from that morning had faded to the point where he almost didn't understand why he'd even felt it. But he'd said a lot of hurtful things then. And Jason let Tae Hyun keep pushing him until he'd finally gone too far. Then Jason struck back. *Love only applies until the first sign of trouble. Then you're out.* Was Jason right? Yun Seo had basically just told him the same thing.

Yun Seo snorted. "I take it from your stunned silence that you might agree with that?"

"I think maybe I fucked up, Yun Seo."

"I know." Yun Seo patted his arm again. "Have you eaten? I'm hungry."

Tae Hyun had lunch on the plane, but that was hours ago. "I could eat."

Yun Seo reheated some leftover dakgangjeong and japchae, which paired surprisingly well with the wine they'd been drinking. Tae Hyun, anxious to stop thinking about his day and the disastrous state of his relationship with Jason, finally asked his sister how she'd been.

"I know you're just tired of talking about yourself," Yun Seo said. Then she smiled. "But I'll take it."

Tae Hyun half-listened to his sister talk about the classes she was taking and the boys who'd been unsuccessfully hitting on her. It wasn't that he wasn't interested. But, between the argument with Jason and the flight back home, it had been a long day, and Tae Hyun was tired. He hoped it wasn't too obvious.

"Are you even listening to me?"

Shit. "Sorry. I guess I'm just tired."

Yun Seo sighed. "Alright. I did just stuff you with food and wine after a long day. What do you want to do?"

Tae Hyun shrugged. "What I want doesn't much matter,

does it? I know I need to call him, but–"

"You've got Jason on the brain, oppa." Yun Seo quietly chuckled. "I meant do you want to go to bed? Because you can sleep here if you want."

"Oh. Right." Tae Hyun smiled. "Thanks."

Tae Hyun's mind spun as he lay on the guest bed he'd slept on after first coming home from the army. Whether it was the wine or the whirlwind set of days he'd just had, he didn't know. But the unfocused rage he'd felt that morning–and that he'd unfortunately directed at Jason–had mellowed to a more manageable anger. Tae Hyun also didn't know what the days ahead had in store for him. But he still had the movie and then his album to work out. Maybe being left alone on a Thai beach would be a good thing. Tae Hyun snorted at his own wishful thinking before he rolled over and tried to ignore the fact that he already missed lying next to Jason.

23

"I guess I just don't see why it's anyone's business who I sleep with." Jason stopped himself before he rolled his eyes and refocused on the phone camera. "So, that's my response. Steven is a bitter, spiteful–" Jason almost said twink. "–person who's got no business talking about anyone but himself. And to everyone else he hurt with his malicious allegations–" Jason felt himself tearing up. Good. That would help. "–I'm sorry you got dragged into this." Jason blinked, and a tear rolled down his cheek. "You don't deserve it. You haven't done anything wrong."

Naomi waved at Jason and made the kill sign. He nodded. "I guess that's all for now." Jason tapped the stop button, ending the live video feed. Then he set his phone down, picked up his glass, and took a drink. The bourbon's smooth fire warmed his throat as it went down.

"That wasn't bad."

"Not bad?" Jason scoffed. "That was fucking amazing." He reached up to wipe the tears from his face. "Award-worthy, even."

Jason and Naomi had spent the past hour on Jason's veranda going over the potential statements from Vital awaiting his sign-off before Jason gave up and decided to wing it. Well, not exactly wing it. He'd spent nearly an entire day flying back to LA and had plenty of time to think about things.

His first thought was that he wished things with Tae Hyun had ended differently. Despite how much pain Tae Hyun's words had caused him, Jason knew that the idol was only hurt and scared and took that out on the closest target.

His second thought was that he may have left too soon. But he didn't really believe that. Once he'd realized that Tae Hyun was nowhere near ready to come out, it was obvious what Jason had to do. After all, it was Jason that Chang Min and Steven had targeted. So it was Jason who needed to go. Sticking around would've only made his denials feel like the lies they were.

His third thought was how much he already missed Tae Hyun.

"Alright, fine. You really are a damn good actor." Naomi swiped at something on her tablet before flipping it around to face Jason. "Now, we should discuss what you need to say to your father." She frowned. "Are you sure you still want to do that?"

Jason rolled his eyes and sipped his bourbon. "You know it's long past time he and I had this conversation, Ms. Bell. None of this would've happened if he hadn't fucked with me again." Naomi had spent most of Jason's flight time going back through the paper trail for his deal with KBR. They'd hidden it from her well, but, in the end, she discovered that everything pointed to Brightstar. At Gerald Park's request, one of his company's East Asian subsidiaries had approached KBR about producing the movie in the first place, which set everything in motion. Of course, Jason's father couldn't have predicted that Jason's situation would end up worse than it was before. "And I'm fucking sick of his two-faced lies. One minute he's supposedly cutting me off when he's actually pulling the strings to get me back to Seoul." Jason sighed and slumped back in his chair as a light breeze tousled his hair. He drank the rest of his bourbon and set the empty glass on the table. "So, fuck him."

"Hey. Are you okay?"

Jason snorted. "No, I'm not fucking okay. I'm tired, angry, and broken-hearted."

"Have you heard from him yet?"

Him, meaning Tae Hyun, of course. "No. But I haven't reached out yet, either."

Naomi nodded. "Give it a little time, Jason. If it's meant to be, he'll come around."

"I can hardly think of a relationship that was less meant to be. Maybe something from a Greek tragedy?" Jason chuckled. "At least we're not related."

Naomi reached out and took Jason's hand. "Don't do that. Your anger is totally justified here. But so is your love. Tae Hyun brought out sides of you I never thought I'd see. That's pretty special."

Jason resisted the urge to tug his hand away. Maybe his manager was right. But her words did nothing to address the situation or his pain. He nearly said so before Naomi's phone buzzed.

"Your car's here."

Jason nodded and sat up. "Okay. Wish me luck."

Naomi frowned. "Are you sure you don't want me there with you?"

"No. I want you to do what we talked about."

"Alright. As long as you're sure."

"Yeah." Jason smiled. "I've never been more sure of anything."

Jason was surprised to discover that the driver was the same one who'd taken him to Naomi's office the day he'd signed KBR's contract. Jason had never bothered to learn his name, so he settled for a friendly nod and hello as he got into the back of the black SUV. Once he confirmed that the driver had the correct address, Jason settled back and made the call he'd dreaded making since landing at LAX.

"Hey, J," Diego said. "I wondered when I'd hear from you."

"I'm sorry. I've been away for a while and was just in the air for eighteen hours."

"Yeah, I've been following the news about you. Korea, eh?" Diego quietly chuckled. "I thought I heard you tell me once that you'd sworn never to go back there."

Leave it to Diego to remember something like that. He was a true professional.

"I guess now you know why."

"Did this happen to you before?"

"Not this exact thing, no." Jason appreciated Diego's instinctive caring, but they were getting away from why he called. "Look, I want to apologize. I'm sorry you got hit with all this."

"It'll be okay. I was thinking about taking a break, anyway. I haven't had a proper vacation in years."

"Really?" Jason was surprised by how laid-back Diego seemed. "That's awfully generous of you.

"Is it? I don't know. I mean, I know this isn't your fault, and it seems like you're getting the worst of it, anyway. Me?" Diego snorted. "I'm a sex worker. I was already out."

"I guess that's true. Still, I'm sorry."

"I know. And thanks. But how are you? I watched your live broadcast. Were those real tears?"

Jason chuckled. "I'm a Best Actor winner. They're always real tears."

Diego laughed. "Of course, of course." He quietly sighed. "He's a lucky guy, this idol of yours. I really hope you two figure everything out."

Jason swallowed hard. Of course, Diego would know that all the rumors were true. He'd know it better than just about everybody. "I don't think it's in the cards for us," Jason replied, knowing the driver could hear him. "But it was good while it lasted."

Diego sighed. "I assume you're somewhere you can't really talk. It's too bad we can't see each other in person."

"Yeah. That feels like asking for trouble we don't need right now."

"For sure. But, if we did, I'd remind you of how fond I am of you. And I'd tell you how happy I am that you found someone you liked as much as they liked you. That's a rare thing in this world, J. Believe me."

Jason thought back to their last hookup when Diego had asked Jason to eat together afterward. And Jason had blithely dismissed him for fear of being seen with an escort in public. "Shit, Diego. I really am an asshole, aren't I?"

"Don't sweat it, J. I'm in the biz, and I know the score." Diego snorted. "If this was a movie, I'd probably give you some big speech about how love matters over everything else and to hold onto it with everything you've got."

Jason chuckled. "I've given that speech myself. But this isn't a movie."

"Nope. But I still like you, J. Don't be a stranger."

"Same to you, man."

Jason disconnected and used the rest of the drive to get himself into character. He'd be playing the role of the angry, black sheep son coming to seek revenge on his scheming parents. It was the part he was born for. Literally.

Jason was ready by the time the driver pulled up to the gate at the Park's Bel Air estate. The uniformed security guard opened the gate and waved them onto the drive. And one of the house staff was waiting to open Jason's door when the driver pulled up. Say what you would about the excesses of Gerald Park. But he ran his estate like a well-oiled machine.

Jason was about to climb out of the SUV when he stopped and turned back. "What's your name, driver?"

"Esteban, sir."

Jason nearly chuckled. He had a lot of Stevens in his life lately. "Thanks for the ride, Esteban. And don't go too far. This won't take very long."

"No problem, Mr. Park. Ms. Bell was very clear that I wasn't to leave unless you were in the truck with me."

Jason snorted. "Yeah. Let's you and me both try staying on her good side."

The house staff handed Jason over to Myra at the door. Jason forgot how much of a production visiting the family could be. But Myra seemed happy enough to see him. She looked nearly the same as when Jason had last seen her, having reached that age where she didn't get older so much as she just shrank a little every year.

"Welcome home, Jason," Myra said with a wide smile. Her voice echoed through the home's enormous marble foyer as she walked him inside. "Will you be staying long?"

Jason chuckled. "I think you already know the answer to

that."

Myra clucked her tongue. "Your parents won't live forever, young man. Don't you think you'll regret all the times you could've seen them?"

Jason shook his head. "I think you already know the answer to that, too. Where are they?"

"I believe they're in your father's study waiting for you."

Waiting for him? Well, fine. If that's how they wanted to play things. "Great. That'll make this easier."

"Jason." Myra grabbed his arm to stop him. "I know you're angry. But go easier on Mr. Park today. He won't admit this to you, but the stroke took a hard toll on him. He hasn't been a hundred percent since."

Jason snorted. "Fifty percent of Gerald Park is still twice as much as anyone else."

Myra shook her head. "I'm serious, Jason."

"So am I."

Myra wisely dropped the subject and let Jason go. She hadn't won an argument with him since the first time he returned from Seoul. And Jason wasn't about to let her start. He made his way to his father's study unaccompanied. He knew the room well. Or at least the door to it. He'd been forbidden from entering before he turned eighteen and then afterward allowed in only when his father was present. The fact that his parents chose to meet him in there most likely meant they were planning to ambush him. Having recently survived a run of ambushes from all sides, Jason was ready and willing to take whatever they thought they could throw his way.

Jason knocked before opening the study door to avoid the inevitable argument about manners. When he walked in, he saw his father sitting at the massive, marble-topped mahogany desk with his mother standing beside him. And Jason could see what Myra meant. Gerald Park looked exhausted. His skin was red and blotchy. And he looked like he hadn't showered in days. It had been more than a year since Jason had last seen his father. But he looked at least ten years older. Had Jason been a responsible, dutiful son, he wouldn't have needed Myra's warning. But those days had long since passed.

Jason's mother looked as put together as always in a blush vintage Mario Bellomo jacket and skirt accented by a string of knuckle-sized pearls. She'd sprayed and blow-dried her dyed-black hair into the same streamlined helmet she'd worn for as long as Jason could remember.

Both of them watched Jason enter. Neither one smiled at him.

"Dad. Mom." Fresh off his weeks of speaking Korean every day, Jason almost reverted to formal Korean speech. While that might've unnerved his parents since it was unexpected, Jason figured it was better to stick with the dynamic they'd already established. "Wow, Dad. You look like hell."

"Jason!" His mother didn't waste any time, going straight to outrage. "You will not–"

His father clucked his tongue, interrupting her. May Mi Young Park, ever the doting wife, immediately shut her mouth. "Come closer, Jason," he said. His voice sounded weaker than usual. "I'd prefer not to shout across the room."

"No, because shouting is so much easier up close." Jason strolled across the thick, patterned rug and sat in one of the high-back leather chairs facing his father's desk. Jason's father frowned, not having actually invited his son to sit. "Alright.

Let's have it."

His mom made a little mewling noise as she struggled to keep quiet. But Jason's father nodded. "I'm not sure what there is to say, Jason, beyond how you managed to royally screw up such an easy job."

Jason chuckled. His father was so predictable. "That's right. An easy job that you arranged for me behind the scenes without telling me."

"Would you have taken it if I had?"

"Maybe. Maybe not. But being upfront with me would've at least earned you a little respect. Considering you've currently got exactly none from me, that's a precious commodity."

"Sons should respect their fathers," his mother spat, unable to control herself.

"You both know why I don't respect you," Jason cooly replied. "And why I never will." He leaned forward and put his hands on his knees. "You meddled in my life back then, too. I thought a smart guy like you would've learned his lesson the first time, Dad."

"What you and that boy did," Gerald growled, "was unnatural. If you had no intention of changing your ways, then you should've taken his example."

Jason's jaw nearly dropped. He'd known his whole life that his father would've preferred having a dead son to the fucked-up gay son he'd been saddled with. But he'd never before said such a thing aloud.

His mother actually gasped. "Gerald!"

"Don't bother, Mom." Jason shook his head and sat back in the chair. "It's how he's always felt, and you know it." He snorted. "And I'm sorry to disappoint you by continuing to live, Dad. At least, by the looks of things, I can be sure I'll outlive you."

Jason's mother turned her shocked face to him. "Jason! If you only came here to spit in our faces, then–"

"Oh, sure," Jason said, cutting her off. "It's fine when Dad wishes I was dead. But when I do it, it's spitting in your faces." He leaned forward again. "But I've got good news. That's not the reason I came here." Then he stood and smacked his hands on the cool marble desktop hard enough to make his parents jump. "I'm here to tell you that I'm cutting you off. The moment I walk out the front door will be the last moment I'm your son. I never want to see or hear from you again. And, just so we're clear, the only reason I didn't publicly come out today and admit that I'm gay is to protect the man I love from people like you. You can both go to hell, as far as I'm concerned."

Jason looked between his father's scowl and his mother's frown. Had either of them really expected anything different from him? Had they honestly thought he'd come to them contrite and begging their forgiveness this time? He smiled. "And, if you ever decide to intrude on my life again, just know that I'll go public with everything, starting with Joo Won."

His father huffed. His cheeks were bright red with barely contained fury. "You would turn down your inheritance?"

Jason laughed as he stood up. "Come on, Dad. If you think I believe for one second you ever intended to leave all this to me, you're a bigger fool than you take me for. Besides, I've been doing just fine without your money. You can let this all die with you, as far as I'm concerned."

His father's face had gone entirely red by that point. Jason almost wondered if he was having another stroke. If so, Myra would be pissed. His mother had started crying. Maybe she'd finally realized that Jason was serious. But he was done with them regardless. So, he shrugged and turned around to leave. When he'd gotten a few steps away, he stopped and dramatically turned back. "Oh. And if you really wanted to avoid all this, you should've just paid off Steven when you had the chance."

After firing Steven, Naomi went through his chat and call history. That's when she discovered multiple calls from his company cell phone to Gerald Park. It didn't take a genius to figure out what those were for. Steven obviously knew of Gerald's tendency to pay Jason's way out of trouble and tried taking advantage of it. Unfortunately for him, it was after he'd already cut Jason off. Naomi still hadn't figured out how Steven got connected with Chang Min. Jason figured it was through Min Jun, somehow. But Jason had Seong Woo's security team working on that part.

Jason smiled. Then he flipped his parents off before turning toward the door and walking out.

24

"If this is what your acting looks like, I think we're gonna be in trouble."

Tae Hyun made an irritated frown as he looked up at Yoo Mi. "What?"

"This." Yoo Mi rolled her eyes and gestured toward his script. "Pretending you're reading when your mind is obviously somewhere else."

"What?" Tae Hyun huffed. "I'm not pretending."

"You're obviously not reading either." Yoo Mi's sigh was masked by the leather couch's squeak as she sat next to Tae Hyun. "I'd ask what you're thinking about, but I'd be surprised to hear you say anything except—"

"Don't." Tae Hyun flipped the script closed and looked at Yoo Mi. "Don't say it."

Yoo Mi snorted. "Not saying his name isn't going to make him stop existing."

Tae Hyun anxiously scanned the conference room to ensure no one else was within earshot. Director Soo Jin was across the room speaking with the pair of actors who'd been cast to play Tae Hyun's character's parents. Since they'd taken a break from the table read, none of the other cast members were in the room. "I'm not trying to wipe him from existence.

I'm just trying to make what he did worth the trouble."

What he did. Jason had left Tae Hyun alone in Thailand a week ago, sacrificing any chance at a relationship with him to avoid harming Tae Hyun's career. It's what Tae Hyun had claimed he wanted–choosing his career over Jason.

Yoo Mi nodded. "Have you heard from him?"

"No." Tae Hyun shook his head. "We haven't spoken." That much was true, but it wasn't what Yoo Mi had actually asked him. In fact, Jason had begun messaging Tae Hyun the same day he'd done his live broadcast denying–well, not exactly denying–the accusations of his manager's former assistant.

I'm sorry you got dragged into this. You don't deserve it. You haven't done anything wrong.

Tae Hyun had watched Jason's live broadcast along with the hundreds of thousands of other viewers who'd tuned in. But he knew Jason had been speaking directly to him, letting him off the hook for the terrible things he'd said that day in Phuket. Then Jason sent his first message a few hours later.

I know you probably don't want to hear from me. But I hope you safely made it back to Seoul

Jason hadn't asked a question or even asked for a reply. And he'd sent Tae Hyun a message every day since then. They were simple, innocuous things, asking him to ensure he got enough rest or had eaten well for the day. Every message made Tae Hyun briefly smile before making him sad again. His sister told him he should either reply or block Jason's number. Otherwise, he was just torturing himself. But torture was what he deserved, so Tae Hyun kept reading them.

"Remember what I said about lying?"

Tae Hyun grunted. "Fine. Yes, I've heard from him. But we haven't spoken."

"Oh, Tae Hyun." Yoo Mi frowned and put her hand on his arm. "Why don't you just call him?"

"You know why." Tae Hyun tapped his script. "It's because of this. But I don't expect you to understand."

Yoo Mi snorted. "First, you lie to me, and now you insult me?"

"How is that an insult? You don't have to—"

"Have to what?" Yoo Mi leaned in close enough that Tae Hyun could feel her breath on his face. "I don't have to live a lie so I can stay in the industry? Or don't you recall how we met?" She nodded in response to Tae Hyun's frown. "That's right. Even the idea that I might be having sex with someone was enough to nearly sink my whole career. I'm lucky that you and I got along. Because don't think for a second that I wouldn't have kept right on dating you anyway."

"It's not the same thing."

"How is—"

"It's not!" Tae Hyun took a breath and tried very hard to calm down. "You did it for a year. And now you're engaged to the person you love. I have to keep doing it for as long as I want this career.

Yoo Mi frowned. "Okay, maybe you're right. I'm sorry."

Tae Hyun nodded and put his hand on top of hers. "I'm sorry, too." He sighed. It sounded much more dramatic than he'd expected. "Besides, he lives in another country. It would've been tough to make that work under any circumstances."

Yoo Mi's narrowed eyes said she didn't believe that for a second. But she nodded. "I'm sure."

Tae Hyun swallowed his groan. He hated when people humored him like that. He hated it even more that he knew

Yoo Mi's unspoken accusation was true. He was only making excuses.

"Excuse me, Yoo Mi." Ji Hoon's new assistant, Hyun Woo, approached the pair with a phone in hand. "You asked me to alert you if your fiance called, ma'am."

"Thank you." Yoo Mi stood and took the phone. "I'll be right back," she said to Tae Hyun.

Hyun Woo turned his attention to Tae Hyun. "Is there anything I can get for you, sir?"

Tae Hyun shook his head. He didn't know what Hyun Woo knew or had been told about his predecessor, Min Jun. But he'd been almost embarrassingly deferential to Tae Hyun since Ji Hoon introduced them a week ago. Ji Hoon wouldn't tell Tae Hyun what happened with Min Jun other than to say that he was no longer part of the KBR family. So he had Seong Hyeon do a little digging and discovered that the former assistant had gone back to live with his parents in Oegwang-ri near Ulsan. A top executive assistant like him would've ordinarily been picked up by a competitor right away. But Tae Hyun was sure Ji Hoon had put the word out about what Min Jun had done. Only KBR's desire to save face probably prevented them from going to the police.

KBR's other significant departure had been Song Chang Min, who'd been officially released from his contract. Tae Hyun heard he'd already been signed by Star Infinity, a smaller label out of Busan. That was fine. Since it was on the other side of the country, Tae Hyun didn't expect to run into him again for a long while.

Tae Hyun reopened his script and looked for the page he'd last been reading when he felt his phone buzzing. He pulled it from his pocket to see a message from Yun Seo.

You need to see this

Tae Hyun clicked on the link she'd included in her message and opened a news video clip featuring a typically white, blonde, American news reporter. He paused the video long enough to put in his earbuds, then hit play.

"*Perpetual bad-boy actor Jason Park, who was recently the subject of a minor scandal initiated by a disgruntled former employee, was among those subpoenaed by the LA County District Attorney in the case against director Marvin Lindsay. Lindsay, known for his infamous physical confrontation with Park on the set of The Long Evening Sunset, was arrested this week on charges of attempted rape and aggravated assault. Prosecutors have accused Lindsay of allegedly assaulting Best Actress winner Camilla Khan on the set of his latest film, The Burners. Following Lindsay's arrest, actress Amber Merritt testified during her deposition that Lindsay had also attempted to assault her on the set of The Long Evening Sunset. She added that it was after she'd shared the incident with Park that he'd confronted Lindsay on her behalf. Park's attorney offered no comment on the matter, but a source close to Park privately shared that the actor was anxious to put the whole horrible episode behind him. Up next on the—*"

Tae Hyun smiled as he stopped the video. After weeks of incident after incident, something finally went their way. Well, Jason's way. But Tae Hyun was happy for him. Jason deserved the vindication he was due for what had happened. And he considered sending Jason a message. But Tae Hyun had no idea what to even say. It had only been a week, but it may as well have been a year. He messaged Yun Seo instead.

Wow, that's great news. Thanks for sharing it

Yun Seo's reply came a few moments later. *Don't tell me that, dummy. Tell him*

24

Tae Hyun knew she was right. But he wasn't ready to reach out to Jason. And the rest of the movie's cast had already begun filtering back into the conference room. It would have to wait.

Soo Jin had arranged everyone so that Tae Hyun and Yoo Mi sat at the head of the table, with him at the opposite end and everyone else in between. They'd already read through the first few scenes that morning. So, after some explanation from Soo Jin, he asked them to pick up where they'd left off.

"Exterior, Suwon, Night," Soo Jin said, reading the scene's slugline. "Legend: Suwon, 1795. Ji Hae frantically runs up the desolate street, lantern in hand, looking for his love, Sora. He must find her before he's captured by Jeongjo the Great's royal guards. Then he spots her."

"Sora!" Tae Hyun called out.

"*Ji Hae!*" Yoo Mi answered.

"Ji Hae rushes to Sora and takes her hand," Soo Jin said.

"Quickly," Tae Hyun said. "There's no time."

"My love–" Yoo Mi began.

"No," Tae Hyun interrupted, "don't speak. I must say this before the coming dawn steals my courage." Tae Hyun stopped, suddenly struck with the memory of Jason taking his hands and saying that line to him. He shook off the memory and forced himself to continue reading aloud. "I've dreamed of you since the night we first met. But I've never dared to speak of it, to open the floodgates for fear of drowning in my emotions. To say love is to fail–" Tae Hyun stopped again, a rush of tears blurring his vision. He quickly wiped them away. "–for the word cannot begin to bind the ocean of my feelings. You've trapped me. You've ensnared my heart. My captured soul–"

Tae Hyun's voice broke, forcing him to stop. The deep, plunging ache had returned, weighing down his heart to the point where he feared it might stop. He turned to Yoo Mi, close to sobbing. "I can't," he whispered. "I can't do this."

Yoo Mi nodded as she stood. "Director Soo Jin, sir." She put her hands on Tae Hyun's shoulders and pulled him back from the table. "I think we'll need a minute."

"Uh, of course," a clearly confused Soo Jin replied. "Take whatever time you need. We'll just skip ahead a bit."

Yoo Mi pulled Tae Hyun to his feet and marched him out to the corridor. His breathing had become erratic to the point where he thought he might hyperventilate. "I–I need to sit down," he stammered.

Yoo Mi grunted and led him into the next meeting room. A pair of KBR staffers had set up in there to work. Yoo Mi put Tae Hyun in the closest chair, looked at the two office workers, and pointed to the door. "Out."

"But–" one of the workers began.

"Now."

Unwilling to argue with Yoo Mi, both workers grabbed their laptops and hurried from the room. Once the door closed, Yoo Mi sat in the chair next to Tae Hyun and turned to face him. "Breathe, Tae Hyun. Breathe."

Tae Hyun nodded. Hearing her command the others from the room had helped him focus on where he was. "Thank you. That was–" He stopped and suffered through another ragged breath. "Jason read that passage to me. It was–" Tae Hyun frowned. "It was right before I first kissed him."

Yoo Mi let out a long breath. Then she shook her head. "Damn it, Tae Hyun. Is the whole movie going to be like this for you?"

"I don't know. I didn't expect–"

"No," Yoo Mi interrupted. "We're not doing this anymore. You need to make your choice. Either admit that you still love him and are willing to do whatever it takes to be with him, or let him go. Because I'm not watching you spend the next two years pining after him."

"You don't understand." Tae Hyun turned away. "I can't just–"

Yoo Mi grabbed Tae Hyun by the arms. "Look at me," she commanded, leaving Tae Hyun powerless to disobey. "I understand well enough what it feels like to be in love. And if Ji Hoon marched in here and told me right now I had to choose between this movie and Seong Woo, I know damn well what I'd choose."

"But–"

"No," Yoo Mi interrupted again. "No buts. If you choose to go on with this movie, your album, and whatever else you've got in mind, then you need to really choose it. Because you're just going through the motions right now. Hell, we're not even halfway through the first table read, and you've already gone to pieces."

Tae Hyun let out a long breath through his nose. "I don't know if I can do it."

"And I know you can do whatever you fucking need to. Remember Manila?"

Tae Hyun didn't know what she'd meant at first. Then he remembered. It was during their second world tour. An earthquake struck near Manila, briefly knocking out the power to the arena where they were performing. The crowd, still holding their *XTC* light sticks, began to grow restless. So, Tae Hyun borrowed a bullhorn from a nearby security staffer and used it to call out to the sections closest to the stage. Then he started singing their second album's title track, *Fireside*, a cappella, asking the crowd to join in. He ended up singing the song three times over, with the whole stadium eventually singing along, before the power came back on and they could continue the concert. *Dreamers* still talked about that night, and the *XTC* fan site had a whole page dedicated to the Manila concert.

Where had that Tae Hyun gone? So much had happened since then. Chang Min. The army. And Jason. But Yoo Mi was right. That Tae Hyun was still inside him, buried under another who desperately clung to circumstances he was no longer sure he even needed, let alone wanted.

"Shit. I haven't thought about that in years." Tae Hyun nodded as he felt the weight on his heart lift away. "You're totally right."

"You're damn right I am." Yoo Mi let go and leaned back. "It felt like that was one more thing that asshole Chang Min stole from you."

Tae Hyun frowned. "What if this turns out the same way?"

"Are you kidding?" Yoo Mi scoffed. "Jason is nothing like Chang Min. Sure, he's loud, rude, and forward. But he's also sweet, honest, and kind." She chuckled. "You should've heard what he said to me at Seong Woo's party." She gently rested her hand on Tae Hyun's leg. "I'm not saying that man is perfect. Or even that he's perfect for you. But, when you're with him, you're more like the old Tae Hyun than I've seen in a long time."

Tae Hyun nodded. Yoo Mi was right. Just like she and his sister had been right all along. "Okay. I'm gonna do it."

"You'll call him?"

Tae Hyun smiled. "Better." Suddenly energized, he quickly stood up. "I need the room. Could you go back and buy me some time? Tell them I went to get some fresh air or something."

Yoo Mi's finely-shaped brows fell with concern. "What are you planning?"

Tae Hyun shook his head as he reached out to take Yoo Mi's hand. "Trust me." He pulled her to her feet and ushered her toward the door. "And help me, please."

"Alright, alright." Yoo Mi brushed his hands away. "No need to push. I'll tell them something." She stopped halfway out the door. "Are you sure?"

"Yes. Just go."

Tae Hyun locked the door behind her, partly to keep from being interrupted and partly to keep from being stopped once he got started. Then he went to the far side of the room and opened the blinds, flooding the space with midday light. After taking out his phone and using the camera to check his lighting–perfect–he sat at the edge of the table and opened his live-streaming app. He took a deep breath and started broadcasting.

"Hey, *Dreamers* and everyone else who may be watching. This is Tae Hyun, formerly of *XTC*. I'm at the KBR building doing a table read with the cast of *Lover's Time Soul's Journey*. Here, I'll show you."

Tae Hyun panned the camera around the conference room, pointed it toward the window to show he was really in the KBR building, then turned it back on himself.

"Anyway, we were just reading through the scene where my character declares his love for Yoo Mi's character, and I had to stop." Tae Hyun smiled. "You see, I got emotional–partly because of my character's lines and partly because of the memories that scene brought up. Now, I'm gonna ramble here for a bit, but it's important. So, please bear with me."

Tae Hyun glanced down at the viewer count as it steadily climbed. It was an unannounced stream, so he'd started at practically zero. But, as word spread that he was live streaming, he'd already hit a thousand viewers. No, two thousand. And, as soon as it hit people's social media feeds, that number would skyrocket.

"Here's a little backstory. I fell in love with someone a few years ago. We were already very close, so it felt right for us to be together. Plus, I was young and inexperienced, so I didn't know any better." The stream of commenters started asking if he was talking about Yoo Mi. "No, it wasn't Yoo Mi. I mean, I love her very much. But only as a friend." Tae Hyun chuckled at the flurry of hearts and *I love you*'s coming from his viewers. "Awe, I love you all, too," he added and made a finger heart. "I always have."

Tae Hyun took a breath as he saw the viewer count hit twenty-five thousand.

"Unfortunately, that relationship was a horrible mistake. It ended badly, and it's been affecting me ever since. It's why I left *XTC* and joined the army."

Tae Hyun hadn't mentioned anyone but Yoo Mi by name, but he'd said enough to send the *Dreamers'* heads spinning. People were already commenting, wondering if he was talking about Xiang or Chang Min.

"But that was all in the past, so it's time for me to leave it there. I need to focus on the future. And that future includes the person I'm in love with now."

Tae Hyun grinned as he felt a surge of fresh feelings he

24

couldn't identify. He knew he could still back out. He hadn't yet committed to anything he couldn't back away from or deny. But it was time to stop backing away. It was time to stop fighting against his own nature.

"That's why I'm talking with you all. Because I want you to know I'm in love with Jason Park."

25

Jason would've skipped the photographers if he had a choice. Between the incidents with Steven and Chang Min and Amber's testimony during the Marvin Lindsay trial, Jason's public approval ratings had skyrocketed. Now everyone wanted a piece of him. But he needed to be seen and photographed in his custom, scarlet and cobalt-blue Kimi Wakari tuxedo as part of the deal he'd made with Kimi's design studio. And he didn't really mind being quizzed by style reporters. It was a huge step up from the paparazzi that used to tail him, waiting for the inevitable trouble he'd get himself into. So Jason waved and posed for their photos, ensuring he dropped Kimi Wakari's name whenever he could before finally heading inside.

Sophie Gibson and her fiance rented the main ballroom at West Hollywood's infamous Sunset Grand Hotel for their engagement party. Jason wanted to think his longtime friendship with his former *Monday Night Club* co-star earned him an invite to her event. But he knew it was more likely his resurgent popularity. Friendship was one thing. But it was Hollywood, and image mattered more than anything else. At least the ballroom was a far more elegant choice than the dressing room trailers Jason and Sophie used to trash during their teens.

Jason grabbed a champagne flute from a roaming server and took a sip. It was sweeter than he liked but a better bet than anything stronger. Jason knew many eyes would be on him and wanted to be on his best behavior. He said hi to the people he knew as he wandered the ballroom and posed for another set of photos for a *Zigzag Magazine* photographer working the party. Jason made sure to offer them his designer's name but excused himself before they could ask him about anything else. Then he heard Sophie calling out his name.

"Jason Fucking Park!" Sophie trotted up to Jason as quickly as she could in her black and white satin mini-dress and four-inch spike heels. "I can't believe you actually came!"

Jason accepted Sophie's air kisses before offering her a quick hug. "Of course, I came. Congratulations on the engagement, by the way."

Sophie's pale, freckled face blushed as she tucked a few strawberry-blonde curls behind her ear. "Thanks. Be honest, J. You thought this would work out like all the other ones, right?"

Jason chuckled. "I don't know what you mean. But let me see that rock." Sophie offered her hand so Jason could inspect her diamond and emerald engagement ring. "Damn, girl. Isn't your hand tired holding that thing up?"

"J!" Sophie quickly leaned in close enough that Jason could smell the Kingston on her breath. "Don't tell anyone," she said in a bourbon-scented stage whisper, "but it's a fake. We keep the real one in the safe at home."

"Good plan," Jason replied with a wink. "Your secret's safe with me."

"Speaking of secrets, it looks like some evil fucking twink's been out there trying to spill yours."

Jason snorted. You could put Sophie in as many couture dresses as you wanted, but she'd never change. "Yeah. I gotta admit, it's been a helluva week."

"Then I'm even happier you came. I still miss the old days, sometimes. You know, we should—" Sophie suddenly frowned. "Not that I mind the attention, but why is everyone looking at us like that?"

"Like what?" Jason hadn't been paying attention to anyone but Sophie. He looked around to see some other guests glancing at them with their phones in hand. No. They were looking at him. "It looks like one of us must've made the news again." Cold uncertainty wormed in through the confident seams of Jason's Wakari tux. It couldn't have been the Lindsay trial. It was too late in the day, and his deposition wasn't even scheduled for another two weeks. Had something happened to his parents?

Sophie huffed. "Don't you have your phone?"

The subtle glances had transitioned into open stares and pointing. "I'm almost afraid to check it now." But Jason pulled out his phone anyway and nearly scoffed when he saw a half-dozen messages from Naomi. Shit. He'd put his phone on silent in the car on the way over. He tapped the most recent message.

You missed the live broadcast but here's the replay link

Live broadcast? Jason tapped the link and opened a video of Tae Hyun sitting inside a KBR conference room. His uncertainty fractured into equal parts excitement and fear. But he couldn't hear Tae Hyun over the party noise. And he didn't have his earbuds with him. "Shit."

"What is it?" Sophie leaned around to see Jason's phone.

"Oh! Isn't that your idol friend? What's he saying?"

"I don't know. I can't hear it."

A new message from Naomi popped up. *Here's a link to the news story since you probably can't watch the video*

There was Naomi reading his mind again. Jason tapped the link to open a fresh post from the *Hollywood Hush* blog. He had to read the headline three times to wrap his head around it. *K-pop Star Tae Hyun Woo Comes Out, Declares Love for Jason Park*

"What the fuck?"

"What now?" Sophie leaned in again. "Oh. Shit."

Jason scrolled to the post's first paragraph. *Breaking: Former XTC leader Tae Hyun Woo stunned the world with a surprise live broadcast from KBR's headquarters today. "I need to focus on the future," Woo said in his live stream. "And that future includes the person I'm in love with now. That's why I'm talking with you all. Because I want you to know I'm in love with Jason Park."*

Sophie gasped as she read over Jason's shoulder. "Awe, J. That's fucking beautiful. Congratulations."

But Jason barely heard what she said. His mind refused to process the words he'd just read. Tae Hyun came out? He told everyone about Jason? How could any of that be–

"J!" Sophie tugged at his shoulder.

Jason looked up from his phone to see Sophie's giant fiance looming over them. He'd never met the man and couldn't remember his name. Anthony? No, Antony. Whatever his name, his football lineman's build gave him an imposing presence in person. Jason hoped her fiance's scowl wasn't directed at him. Jason didn't relish the idea of fighting someone so big, especially if they were his friend's fiance. Or maybe Jason was just projecting.

"Some reporters are crashing the party looking for you," Antony said in a disturbingly deep voice.

Jason frowned. "I'm sorry about that." He waved his phone at them. "But I need to hear this. Is there somewhere I can go?"

Antony nodded. "Yeah. Follow me."

Jason and Sophie fell in line behind her fiance as the crowd magically parted before him. Jason heard his name at least a dozen times as they marched toward a pair of doors on the far side of the ballroom. A gray, concrete service corridor sat beyond the doors, giving Jason unwelcome flashbacks to his fateful evening at the hotel party in Seoul.

Antony pulled a card key from inside his white tuxedo jacket. "Take this. It's for our room. Number 1107."

Jason nodded and took the card. "Thanks."

"Of course. Use the room as long as you need to. Just leave the key card when you're done. I've got another."

"Hey, I've got to get back," Sophie announced. "They'll miss me."

Jason nodded again. "This is perfect. Thank you both." He leaned in and gave Sophie a kiss on her cheek. "Congrats again."

Jason went to the nearby service elevator while Sophie and her fiance returned to the party. The ride to the eleventh floor felt like it took an hour. Thankfully, the hallway was empty when he stepped out. Sophie's room was a corner suite with a panoramic view of the distant DTLA skyline. The couple had obviously used it as a dressing room. It looked like someone's glam squad exploded inside. Jason ignored the mess and the view, saving his attention for his phone. His first thought was to watch the video. But he could do that later. He needed to talk to Tae Hyun.

Jason called Tae Hyun's phone, waiting for the international ringtone to start. But he was immediately transferred to the automated message stating the caller wasn't available. Jason tried again with the same result. Was Tae Hyun's phone turned off? Was he in trouble? Even if he'd recorded that video inside the KBR building, there was no way he'd done it with anyone's blessing. And there was no telling how Ji Hoon would've reacted when he saw it. But how he'd reacted to Chang Min's party sabotage was a big clue.

Jason tried Seong Hyeon next. As far as he knew, the Song brothers were still taking care of Tae Hyun. And Jason was spending a lot of money with The Vital Agency for that. The phone rang long enough that Jason was about to hang up and try Seong Min. Then Seong Hyeon finally answered.

"Jason, sir." Seong Hyeon sounded like he was out of breath. "Are you calling for Tae Hyun?"

"Seong Hyeon! Is he there? If anything happened to him, I'll–"

"He's here, sir. And he's fine. One moment."

Jason noticed he'd started pacing as he listened to the muffled sounds of the phone being passed to someone else. He made himself stop.

"Jason?"

Cool relief flooded through Jason, riding the warm tones of Tae Hyun's voice. "Are you alright? I tried calling your phone–"

"Ji Hoon confiscated it after he saw the live stream." Tae Hyun sighed. "Jason, I'm sorry I haven't reached out since you left. And I'm sorry that I didn't talk to you first. Once I'd realized what I had to do, I just–"

"It's alright. Everything's–" Jason's voice cracked. He took a ragged breath, ignoring the tears welling in the corners of his eyes. "Everything's fine as long as you're alright. And I love you."

"I love you, too." Tae Hyun sighed again. Or was he catching his breath?

"What happened?"

"It was quite the scene. But that's not important. I don't know what to do now. I'm here in Seoul, and you're in LA."

"I'll head for the airport right now. I can be there tomorrow. Do you have a place to stay?"

"No. I mean, yeah. I have a place to stay. But, no. Don't come. I should go there."

Was Tae Hyun really offering to come to LA? Jason almost laughed, remembering the trouble he had convincing the idol to visit Thailand. "Are you sure?"

"Yeah. I need to be with you, and it's better that we see each other there. For now, at least. Things are complicated here."

"I can only imagine." Jason took a deep breath, trying to steady his pounding heart. Tae Hyun had completely thrown Jason for a loop. Deep down, he'd known that Tae Hyun would come around at some point. And he'd been determined to wait, only sending short daily messages to remind Tae Hyun that he was there but never asking for a response. But the idol had come around in such a big way. It was almost a complete reversal from when he'd angrily stormed off to the beach in Phuket. Or when he'd quit *XTC* and joined the army. Obviously, when Tae Hyun committed to something, he committed fully. And immediately. "I don't know what possessed you to do it like this. But I'm so happy right now."

Tae Hyun chuckled. "I'm glad to hear that. I was worried

that I'd fucked things up again."

"No, you didn't fuck anything up, then or now. Things happened how they happened. What's important now is we get you here. Could you put me on with Seong Hyeon again?"

"Okay. Should I be worried?"

"No. We'll decide everything together. I just want to get some information first."

"Alright. I love you."

Jason smiled. "I'll never get tired of hearing that."

Once Jason, Tae Hyun, and Seong Hyeon came up with a halfway decent plan, Jason called Lily and had her deliver a change of clothes to the Sunset Grand. She'd reluctantly agreed to come work for him again earlier in the week after he'd apologized and explained his new business plans. Jason figured she would after he heard from Naomi that Lily had already been fired from her new job. It helped that Lily also felt terrible about what Steven had done. Not that she could've prevented it. But she'd taken to calling him the evil twink, too, after she'd heard Jason say it.

After Jason had changed his clothes, Lily helped sneak him out through the hotel's kitchen entrance and took him home in her car.

"I watched the video," Lily shared on the drive back to Jason's house. "It made me cry. If nothing else had convinced me that you'd changed, that definitely would've."

"I wasn't that bad before."

"No, you weren't." Lily chuckled. "But you're not that much better now, either. So make sure you're worth what he did for you."

"He didn't do it for me, Lil. But yeah, I hear you."

Once he was home, Jason spent the next few hours ensuring

Tae Hyun got on his plane and would be allowed into the country when he arrived. He called in every favor he could think of and ended up owing a few more. But it all worked out, and after a tearful call with Tae Hyun before he boarded his plane, Jason finally went to bed.

Jason woke the next morning feeling like he'd barely slept. And he looked like it, too. He spent an hour in his gym sweating out all the toxins from his lingering anxiety. Then he spent another hour showering and getting dressed. He could hardly believe Tae Hyun was on his way there and how nervous that made him feel. Once he was ready, Jason called Esteban to pick him up and drive him to LAX. He'd debated buying himself a ticket just so he could meet Tae Hyun at the gate. But, in the end, he decided against it. His plans were tricky enough as it was.

Esteban dropped Jason outside International Arrivals with plenty of time to complete all his final preparations. Then Jason spent the rest of the time obsessively checking the arrivals board and the flight tracker on his phone, periodically posing for photos with fans daring enough to approach him, and answering the few questions he could to the reporters he'd alerted to Tae Hyun's arrival. Then, finally, his phone rang.

"We just landed, and we're taxiing to the gate."

"Okay. We're waiting for you outside baggage claim." Shit. He'd said we. Hopefully–

"We?"

Shit. "You don't expect me to carry all those bags myself, do you?"

Tae Hyun laughed. "No, I guess not. I can't wait to see you."

"Me either."

It felt like Tae Hyun took as long to get off the plane as it took him to fly there. Jason briefly worried that he'd face trouble at customs. Then he finally saw black hair streaked with purple and grinned.

"He's here."

As Tae Hyun emerged from the baggage claim area, the *Dreamer* mob assembled around Jason erupted into wild cheering and applause. Tae Hyun stopped, clearly shocked at his fans' presence and unexpected show of support. When Jason had infiltrated the *XTC* fan site's message boards the night before, he'd worried that Tae Hyun's coming out would drive many of his fans away. And there were several long threads debating whether or not Tae Hyun being gay was okay. But the longest thread was an outpouring of *Dreamer* support for their bias and former *XTC* leader. So Jason posted a request for any *Dreamers* in LA to meet their idol when he arrived at LAX. He'd expected a dozen or so to show up. But he'd counted at least a hundred waiting at the airport when he got there.

Jason gave Tae Hyun a few moments to bask in his fan's adoration before approaching him. His heart nearly burst at the sight of Tae Hyun's loving smile. Then Tae Hyun dropped his bags and pulled Jason into a hug.

"I'm so sorry," Tae Hyun said over Jason's shoulder as he tightly squeezed him. He smelled like sweat, first-class bathroom soap, and whatever cologne he'd applied before deplaning. Jason couldn't get enough of it.

"Me, too. But we're together now." He pulled back to gently cup Tae Hyun's face in his hands. "Can I kiss you?"

Tae Hyun nodded, and the *Dreamers* erupted into another chorus of cheers as Jason kissed the man he loved. Tae Hyun pulled away after a moment. "I can't believe they're all here. Did you do that?"

Jason nodded. "I wanted you to see that your fans still love you when you're being the real you." He took Tae Hyun's hand, turned to face the *Dreamers*, and triumphantly raised their hands. The delighted *Dreamers* broke into their third round of cheers, finally drawing some concerned looks from the airport security who'd gathered nearby.

After Tae Hyun spent some time thanking his fans, signing autographs, and posing for photos under Seong Hyeon and Seong Min's watchful eyes, Jason finally got them all to the SUV outside. Esteban helped them load up Tae Hyun's luggage—including Jason's bags, rescued from the KBR apartment with Tae Hyun's things before they made their mad dash to the airport. Jason and Tae Hyun held hands as they rode back to Jason's house. And Tae Hyun finally shared what happened at KBR.

"It was complete madness," Tae Hyun explained. "After I went back to the table read, Ji Hoon stormed into the conference room with a pair of security guards. He took my phone back, then told me I wasn't leaving the KBR building until I posted another video taking back what I'd said about you."

"Are you serious?" Jason knew Ji Hoon could be hardcore. But that was next-level shit. It was essentially kidnapping.

"Yeah. It was scary. But Yoo Mi stood up to him. So did Director Soo Jin and the rest of the cast, even though none of them knew what was really happening. So security called in more men. It was almost like some kind of TV drama standoff."

"Shit. How did you get out?"

Tae Hyun smiled. "Yoo Mi, of course. She recorded a video of Ji Hoon threatening me, which she used to threaten him right back. Meanwhile, a mob of *Dreamers* showed up outside the building looking for me." Tae Hyun shrugged. "By that point, my story had made the news. In the end, Ji Hoon had to let me go."

"What about the Songs?"

"We were in our own standoff," Seong Min offered from the seat behind Jason's. "KBR security tried to throw us out of the building, but we refused to leave without Tae Hyun." He grinned. "We almost came to blows."

"Damn." Jason shook his head. "Fucking KBR. So, what's gonna happen?"

Tae Hyun shrugged again. "I don't know. I imagine they'll just release me from my contract. Otherwise, I'll have to sue."

Jason watched Tae Hyun as he turned to look out the window at the passing LA scenery. Esteban had taken them up La Brea to avoid the early rush hour on the 405. Even so, it was slow going. "I can hardly believe you're here."

Tae Hyun turned back and smiled. "I can hardly believe it myself. Yesterday I was struggling to get through my first table read." He gently squeezed Jason's hand. "It was my character's speech to his lover that did it. You know, the one you did for me that first day?"

Jason chuckled. "Yeah, it's quite the speech. It's supposed to leave a lasting impression so she'll remember it in her next life."

Tae Hyun smiled. "I'm sure I'll remember it in mine."

Jason basked in the warm glow of Tae Hyun's lovely face, still reeling from them being together once again. "Well, I'm happy you remembered it in this one. I'll settle for that."

<u>26</u>

Tae Hyun cuddled up to Jason in the pale, predawn light while the actor quietly slept. He hadn't meant to be awake that early, but his body thought it was mid-afternoon. Still, it was nice to finally share a bed again after a week of sleeping alone. It was an unexpected sentiment for someone who'd spent years sleeping by himself before he'd taken to sharing his bed with Jason. He smiled as he gently brushed the hair from his sleeping lover's face. The last time he'd seen Jason look so peaceful was their final morning in Phuket before they'd fought, and Jason had gone back home.

Never again, Tae Hyun promised himself. Not that he was naive enough to think the pair would never argue. He was sure they would. But he resolved to never again use their arguments as an opportunity to push Jason away. For better or worse, Tae Hyun was committed. And the whole world was watching.

Tae Hyun's restlessness and urge to visit the washroom finally forced him out of bed. After taking care of things and washing up, Tae Hyun padded barefoot to the main room in Jason's house. He was still amazed at how big it was. As he looked out through the expansive window wall, he saw silvery light peeking over the rooftop as it crept toward the twinkling lights of the distant skyline. He couldn't imagine ever tiring of that view, just as he couldn't imagine owning a home that large. Then he heard a noise and headed for the kitchen. When he rounded the corner, he saw Seong Min pouring coffee from a french press. The younger Song brother looked up as Tae Hyun approached.

"Good morning, sir. Coffee?"

Tae Hyun nodded. "Yes, please. You couldn't sleep either?"

Seong Min shook his head as he filled a second mug. "No, sir. I've been up for more than an hour. So I tried out Jason's gym." He grinned. "I could get used to living like this."

Tae Hyun chuckled as he accepted the mug from Seong Min. "It'll do for now." He sipped his coffee and nodded in thanks. "But, if you want to stay here, you'll have to practice your English."

Seong Min nodded. "I know. How long do you think we'll be here, sir?"

"I don't know. But I appreciate that you and Seong Hyeon came along."

Seong Min nodded. "It's our job, of course. But we like you, too. And I think what you did was very brave."

Tae Hyun felt his ears warming. Coming out shouldn't have to be a matter of bravery, but it was how the world worked. He tried to accept the praise anyhow. "I suppose. But it cost me my job."

"Maybe." Seong Min shrugged. "But it's just a job. You're still you. And you already saw that your fans still love you." He smiled and filled another cup. "Unless you need anything else, sir, I'll take this down to my brother."

"No, I'm good."

Seong Min nodded and left with his mugs in hand, so Tae

Hyun went back to the main room and out to the veranda. The autumn air's surprisingly wet chill energized him as he walked to the railing on the opposite side and stared out to the distant ocean. He remembered standing on the Thai beach far across the ocean and thinking about Jason's home. And then he was there. Tae Hyun snorted and sipped his coffee.

"What's that you're humming?"

Tae Hyun nearly jumped and spilled his coffee at the sound of Jason's voice. He'd been so lost in his thoughts he hadn't realized he was humming. "Oh, nothing. But you scared me. Why aren't you sleeping?"

"Sorry for sneaking up on you." Jason walked up behind Tae Hyun and wrapped his arms around him, bathing him in comforting warmth. "I'm up because your phone kept ringing. So I answered it and had a short but interesting chat with your sister."

"My sister?" Shit. Tae Hyun had forgotten to call her last night. "Sorry."

"It's fine." Jason rested his chin on Tae Hyun's shoulder. "I told her you made it here safely and you're sorry you forgot to call." He chuckled. "Then she realized who I was and gushed a little bit."

Tae Hyun snorted. "She probably likes you better than me."

"No way, not even for a second. After she gushed, she told me if I didn't take proper care of you, she'd fly over here and make me regret it."

Tae Hyun grinned as he thought about how well Jason had taken care of him in the shower before they went to bed. "Well, you're doing an excellent job so far."

Jason chuckled. "I aim to please. How are you holding up? You know, considering everything?"

"Well enough, I suppose." Tae Hyun sighed. "I'm so scared and confused I can hardly wrap my mind around everything. Two days ago, I was a musician and soon-to-be actor. Now, what am I?"

Jason turned Tae Hyun around and looked him in the eyes. "You're still a musician and soon-to-be actor." He brushed a section of Tae Hyun's bangs off his face. "And you're also my boyfriend."

Tae Hyun felt his ears warming as he bashfully smiled. "Is that what we are? Boyfriends?"

"I'd say so. I mean, we met, got together, broke up, and got back together, so yeah." Jason grinned. "Hell, we've had sex in three different countries."

"Does last night count as sex?"

Jason nodded. "As far as I'm concerned, yeah. Besides, you declared your love for me to the whole world. That alone makes us boyfriends." He leaned in and nuzzled Tae Hyun's neck, sending a ticklish rush down his spine and making him quietly moan. "But, if you're still concerned about our qualifications," he purred, "I'm happy to properly take care of you right now."

Tae Hyun blushed when Jason pulled them closer together, and he felt Jason's stiff cock press against him. Then he grinned. "As long as it's proper. We wouldn't want my–"

Jason silenced Tae Hyun with a finger. "New boundary. No mentioning anyone's family members when we're about to fuck."

Tae Hyun gasped as Jason bent down, slipped an arm behind his legs, and hoisted him up. "Hyung!"

Jason turned to carry Tae Hyun inside. "Stop struggling, or I'll drop you."

Tae Hyun snorted as he wrapped his arms around Jason's shoulders and allowed himself to be carried to the bedroom. "Fine. But don't get hurt."

Jason gently kicked the bedroom door closed as they went by, carried Tae Hyun across the room, and set him down on the bed. "There you go. And no idols were harmed in the making of this romantic gesture."

Tae Hyun started chuckling. "Alright. But I suppose you expect a reward now?"

"No way. Just you being here is reward enough for me."

Tae Hyun got up on his knees and grabbed Jason's shirt. "For you, maybe." He pulled Jason close, leaned down, and briefly suckled on Jason's lower lip. "But I want more."

Jason grinned as he lifted Tae Hyun's t-shirt off him. Then he leaned in to put his mouth on Tae Hyun's naked chest and left a meandering series of kisses while he ran his fingers up and down Tae Hyun's back. And Tae Hyun's pulsing erection strained at the fabric of his shorts. Jason moved his kisses up Tae Hyun's body, stopping when he reached Tae Hyun's neck before he looked up.

"Better?"

Tae Hyun nodded. "It's a start." He threaded his fingers through Jason's thick hair and gently pushed his head downward. "But you're going the wrong way."

Jason snorted as he neared Tae Hyun's waist. Then he looped his fingers under the waistband of Tae Hyun's shorts and underwear and tugged them down. "Wow. What's all this then?"

Tae Hyun gasped again as he felt himself quickly enveloped in the wet, warm pocket of Jason's mouth. He held onto Jason's hair, as much to keep himself upright as for the connection, and Jason's head pistoned back and forth along his cock. Then he nearly squealed when he felt Jason tickle the tip with his talented tongue. He pulled Jason off him, tilting his head back to look at his face. "How are you so good at that?"

Jason chuckled. "I'm just naturally gifted, I guess." He grabbed his shirt and pulled it off before nodding toward Tae Hyun's shorts. "You should get rid of those."

Tae Hyun lay back and slipped off his shorts and underwear while Jason did the same. Tae Hyun tried to sit up, but Jason crawled on top of him first, balancing over him on his hands and knees. Tae Hyun softly chuckled. "Hi."

"Hi there." Jason smiled. "I don't know if I've said this before." He gently brushed Tae Hyun's bangs from his forehead. "But I love you."

Tae Hyun couldn't help but grin. "I think you may have mentioned it."

"It's the truth." Jason leaned down and kissed Tae Hyun's forehead. "I love you here." He kissed Tae Hyun's cheek. "And here." He kissed Tae Hyun's earlobe. "And here, too." Then he pushed himself back up. "I love your smile. I love your honesty. I love your stubbornness. I love your talent. I love your courage." He smiled again. "I love every piece and part of you."

Tae Hyun beamed at the radiant vision of Jason gazing down as he once again declared his love. "You're the most amazing person I've ever met," he said in English. "I'm so lucky to have you in my life."

Jason leaned down again, this time kissing Tae Hyun on the lips. And Tae Hyun poured his mounting passion into their kiss, pushing his tongue into Jason's mouth to twirl with its opposite. Then he reached down and grabbed Jason's cock, tightly squeezing it before pushing the foreskin back. Jason let out a deep moan and rolled onto the bed. Tae Hyun followed, turning to his side as Jason took hold of him and began stroking. The two continued their kiss, their tongues gleefully dancing as they fell into a mutual rhythm rubbing each other. After minutes that felt like hours, Tae Hyun finally groaned as the pressure of his impending climax rose from deep inside to burst forth between them. Then he squealed as Jason gave him a final post-cum stroke, sending shock waves through his body.

"You're gonna pay for that, hyung," Tae Hyun threatened as he jumped away.

Jason chuckled. "Go ahead. Make me suffer."

Tae Hyun grinned as he leaned over and took Jason into his mouth. He gently caressed Jason's balls with one hand and stroked the base with the other, all while pumping his head up and down to the increasing intensity of Jason's moaning.

"I'm gonna cum," Jason called out. Tae Hyun's mouth was soon filled with warm, wet thickness. He quickly swallowed. Then he teased his tongue along the tip of Jason's cock, making Jason squirm. "I surrender! I surrender!"

Tae Hyun laughed as he sat up. "Told you so." He leaned down and kissed Jason again. "I love you, too, by the way. I'm sorry I don't have a romantic speech prepared."

Jason chuckled. "I watched your video. I'd say you're good on that front."

Tae Hyun lay down and let out a contented sigh, enjoying the feeling of being next to Jason again. And he never wanted it to stop. "Promise me something."

"Okay. Anything."

"Promise you'll never leave me." Tae Hyun waited for the scoff or joke. He remembered trying to promise that he'd never hurt Jason, and Jason shut him down. *You know you can't promise that. There's still so much that could come between us.* But Jason didn't even hesitate.

"Alright. I promise I'll never leave you."

Tae Hyun quickly turned to his side. "Are you being serious?"

"Of course. When have I ever lied to you?"

Tae Hyun pressed his lips together, remembering the very recent example where he'd unintentionally lied to Jason. "I–"

"I didn't mean that to be a dig against you." Jason turned on his side and put his hand on Tae Hyun's chest. "I know why you said all that. It's okay. We're together now, right?" Tae Hyun nodded, cautiously mollified. "In fact, maybe we should get married."

Tae Hyun furrowed his brows, heedless of the lines that made on his forehead. "Married? You mean, as in, actually married?"

"Yeah. It's legal here, remember? And you could get a green card."

"So I'd become an American? Why would I want that?"

Jason chuckled. "I know, right? But, no. That doesn't make you a citizen. It just means you could stay here."

Tae Hyun felt his arm tingling and lay back down. He'd never imagined something like marriage for himself, especially after all that shit with Chang Min. But Jason had just promised to never leave him. Wasn't that sort of the same thing? "Okay."

"Really?"

Tae Hyun nodded. "Yeah, really. Not today, of course. But,

yes. Someday I'll marry you." He turned his head to see Jason and his bright, beaming smile. "I want to be with you forever."

Jason kissed Tae Hyun before laying back down. Then he threaded their fingers together. "I'm so happy right now. I almost can't stand it. You know?"

Tae Hyun grinned. He could keep lying naked next to Jason, hand in hand, forever. "I think I do. I feel a bit less uncertain about my future now."

Jason gently squeezed Tae Hyun's hand. "About that. You should let me produce your solo album."

"What?" Tae Hyun let go of Jason's hand and rolled back onto his side. "Are you serious? How would you even do that?"

"Of course, I'm serious." He turned to face Tae Hyun. Then he reached up and gently caressed Tae Hyun's cheek. "I've been talking with Naomi about converting my business to a production company. I'm pretty fucking sick of getting fired every time I sneeze too loud, so I thought I could start producing my own projects." He smiled. "Guess what it's called."

"I'm almost afraid to ask now."

Jason grinned. "Big Hammer Entertainment."

"For real?" Tae Hyun chuckled. "I should charge you for that."

"Sure. Or, you could let me produce your album instead. Seong Woo may be interested in investing, too. If I brought him a project like your album, I bet he'd for sure say yes."

Tae Hyun frowned. Then he saw a shadow of uncertainty darken Jason's smile.

"It's just a thought. You don't have to–"

"Yes." Tae Hyun smiled. "I'll do it."

Jason's jaw dropped. "Really? You will?"

Tae Hyun chuckled as he put his hand on Jason's chest. He could feel the excitement of Jason's pounding heart. "I left KBR so I could make my own decisions without worrying about offending my seniors or fans. And that's my decision. Besides, I'll need investors to record and promote an album, anyway. And I can't stand the thought of contracting with another big entertainment company–not after working with KBR." He snorted. "Not that any of them would have me."

Jason's sunshine smile lit up his whole face. "Well, I'll have as much of you as you'll give me."

Tae Hyun leaned down and kissed him. "And I'll give you all of me."

27

"How's it sounding, Gordo?" Jason pointed his phone's camera at Gordo Hong, the maestro behind Red Lightning Studios, sitting at the giant soundboard.

"Are you kidding?" Gordo replied in English, knowing they were live streaming to an international audience. "This song's gonna be a masterpiece."

"You heard it, *Dreamers*," Jason enthused as he swung the camera back to Tae Hyun in the sound booth. "Gordo just called it a masterpiece. And he would know."

Hiring Gordo had been a stroke of genius–and luck–on Jason's part. The famed, award-winning Korean music producer had worked with everyone from K-pop legends like *H34RTB34T* and *5alive* to international stars like *Pluto's Orbit* and Raven Wilde. Jason had used his connection with Raven to score an introduction to Gordo, who'd agreed to help record and produce Tae Hyun's album. It helped that Gordo was a *Dreamer*. And he was forward-thinking enough to know that KBR had shot themselves in the foot when they fired Tae Hyun. Hopefully, their album sales would justify Gordo's high price tag.

Jason leaned forward and pressed the button for his studio mic. "Tae Hyun, give the fans a wave before we sign off for the day." Tae Hyun looked at Jason and made a finger heart before waving. Jason glanced at the follower comments as a stream of thumbs and hearts burst forth. Then he tapped the screen to switch to the front-side camera. "And that's it for us today, *Dreamers*. Don't forget to tune in for our next live broadcast, where Tae Hyun will answer some of your fan questions. And be sure to visit the Big Hammer store to pick up your exclusive *Boy Without Shame* merch." Jason waved to the camera. "Bye for now."

Gordo chuckled. "You're way too good at that. Tae Hyun's lucky he's got you."

"Nah, I'm definitely the lucky one." Jason took a screenshot of the post-stream analytics to send to Naomi and Seong Woo. "I only have to be goofy on camera. And I could do that all day if it meant listening to Tae Hyun perform."

Of course, Jason had done much more behind the scenes to promote Tae Hyun's work. Having Seong Woo and The Vital Agency onboard helped. Tae Hyun had decided to record *Boy Without Shame* in English to capitalize on the global market, which was generally receptive to gay artists. But there were still exceptions to that. And the Korean market was heavily divided, with many Netizens speaking out against Tae Hyun for being gay. KBR's marketing machine had gone into overdrive, rendering Tae Hyun's history virtually invisible while putting significant pressure on the news outlets they worked with to keep him out of their publications. KBR also prevented Xiang from publicly speaking about Tae Hyun, even though he privately supported him. But most of the former *XTC Dreamers* stood solidly behind him to become Tae Hyun's *Dreamers*. And *K-star Daily* ran a lot of favorable coverage for Tae Hyun after Jason and Tae Hyun sat with them for their first official interview as a couple.

"How was it?" Tae Hyun excitedly emerged from the sound booth. It seemed like no amount of time in front of the microphone would dampen his enthusiasm. "It felt great!"

"It sounded great," Gordo assured him. "Once you figured out those triplets, you nailed them every time. I'm impressed."

"Yeah," Jason added. "What he said."

Tae Hyun playfully frowned. "Do you even know what a triplet is?"

Jason shrugged. "A fun threesome?" He glanced at his phone to check the time. "How are you feeling? We've still got dinner with Yoo Mi and Seong Woo."

"I wouldn't miss it," Tae Hyun assured him. "Hey, you should come, Gordo."

Gordo chuckled and shook his head. "Oh, no. I've got plenty to do here. But you kids have fun."

Jason stood up, went to Tae Hyun, and put his hands on his waist. "You sounded great." Then he leaned in and kissed Tae Hyun's cheek. "Really. But we should get going if we want time to change. Traffic is already a mess." Jason had rented an apartment in Nonhyeon-dong, across the river from the studio and close to Cheongdam-dong's nightlife. But Seoul traffic was what it was.

"Alright," Tae Hyun agreed. "Just let me get my stuff."

On their way out, Tae Hyun stopped to visit the fans gathered outside the studio, drawn there by Jason's live broadcast. Tae Hyun was consistently kind and generous with his time when it came to his fans. Jason was impressed and swallowed his jealous complaints. He knew it was part of the business. He also knew that Tae Hyun genuinely cared about them. But they didn't have much time, so he gave Seong

Min the signal to collect Tae Hyun and get him into their car.

After stopping at the apartment to shower and change, Jason had the Songs drive them across Gangnam to Veil, where they'd meet Yoo Mi and Seong Woo. Jason held Tae Hyun's hand in the car as he often did.

"You look so sexy," Jason said, despite knowing it would turn Tae Hyun's ears red. The idol kept the purple streak in his hair, although he'd been talking about changing it. And he obviously enjoyed being in control of his own wardrobe again. That night he'd chosen an oversized sweater with a jumbo, black and white herringbone print, tight black trousers, and chunky black leather boots.

"Thanks. So do you. I'm glad you went with the blue."

Jason smiled and nodded. He'd taken to letting Tae Hyun advise his fashion choices, too. Jason knew he looked good in pretty much whatever, and it made Tae Hyun happy. "You were right."

"Jason, sir," Seong Min said from the front. "It looks like the press is waiting outside the restaurant."

Tae Hyun snorted. "Yoo Mi, of course."

"We're early," Jason said. "We've got time if you want to talk with them."

"That's assuming they'll want to talk to me."

Some members of the press had taken KBR's threats seriously. But not all. More prominent outlets like *Crash Boom Bang Asia* and *Flipside Korea* didn't care, knowing that KBR needed them more than the other way around.

Jason and Tae Hyun posed for photos and answered a few questions before letting the Songs escort them inside. Jason appreciated having the Songs still watching out for them. And the brothers were still essential, given the number of nasty and violent threats he and Tae Hyun had gotten since coming out. The restaurant's host brought the four of them up to the mezzanine where Yoo Mi and Seong Woo already waited, offering Seong Hyeon and Seong Min seats at a nearby table per Jason's request.

"Well, don't you two look so handsome," Yoo Mi said as she stood to greet them. She glanced at Seong Woo. "You could learn from them."

"I think Seong Woo looks very handsome," Tae Hyun countered.

"And you're a fucking knockout tonight, Yoo Mi," Jason added. "You put us all to shame." The model and actress wore a glittery silver, body-hugging dress featuring a set of black straps accentuating her figure in a not-quite-bondage look.

Yoo Mi politely bowed before taking her seat. "I'm sitting with the three most handsome men in Seoul. If I don't stand out, no one will see me."

A server took Jason and Tae Hyun's orders while dropping off Yoo Mi and Seong Min's drinks. Then they returned a few minutes later with Jason's Kingston and Tae Hyun's gin and tonic.

"How'd the recording session go?" Seong Woo asked after taking a sip from his glass.

"Gordo said it's gonna be a masterpiece," Jason replied.

"Of course, it will be," Yoo Mi agreed. "Remember when I said you'd be three times the performer on your own?"

Tae Hyun chuckled. "Yeah, yeah. I never imagined this is how that would work out." He reached over to take Jason's hand. "But I'm glad it did."

"Well, I'm very proud of you," Yoo Mi assured him. "Even if it cost me my first movie role." After Tae Hyun got fired, Yoo

Mi's support for him got her fired from *Lover's Time Soul's Journey*, too. But it didn't matter because Brightstar soon cut off their funding for the project. And Yoo Mi picked up a role in a new paranormal mystery series called *Bullet Time Memory* anyway.

"At least you bounced back just fine," Tae Hyun offered. "Are you enjoying the new series?"

Yoo Mi excitedly nodded. "It's so much fun! The other day I filmed a scene where I got thrown by someone with telekinetic powers. I had to wear a harness and everything."

Jason raised his eyebrows in surprise. "You're doing your own stunts?"

"That's what I said," Seong Woo agreed. "Especially this close to the wedding."

Yoo Mi cheerfully scoffed. "Whatever. It was nothing. I once did a runway show walking a tightrope. Speaking of weddings, have you set a date yet?"

Jason gave Tae Hyun's hand a gentle squeeze, knowing the idol's ears were reddening without having to look. While Yoo Mi had kept their engagement a secret as promised, she still constantly hounded them about their unplanned wedding.

"You know we're too busy," Tae Hyun said.

"Yeah," Jason agreed. "Between working on the album and planning Tae Hyun's tour, we've got no time. We may end up just eloping in Las Vegas."

Yoo Mi frowned. "If you do, I'll kill you. I want to be Maid of Honor."

"Sorry." Tae Hyun shook his head. "That'll be my sister, but you can be a bridesmaid.

"Hell, you can be my Maid of Honor," Jason offered.

Tae Hyun turned to him in surprise. "What about Naomi?

"She says marriage is for fools. Oh, and something about the patriarchy."

Yoo Mi shrugged. "She's probably right. And yes, I'll happily be your Maid of Honor."

"Does that mean I can't be your Best Man?" Seong Woo asked, pretending to pout.

"No way. You two can be both. Like the Best Couple, I suppose."

"Second best couple," Tae Hyun corrected. "You and I are the best."

Seong Woo lifted his glass to make a toast. "To the best couples."

"And to lovely friends," Jason added, " and happy lives."

Acknowledgments

I'm proud to present my debut novel, *Idol Minds*, a K-pop-inspired contemporary gay romance that explores the complexities of fame and the struggles of finding love as a queer person under a heteronormative spotlight. As a longtime K-pop fan, I was drawn to the fast-paced and high-stakes entertainment world and the unique challenges faced by those in the public eye. I wanted to create a story that delves into the emotions and experiences of gay characters challenging societal norms and prejudices. Set amidst the glittering world of Hollywood and K-pop, *Idol Minds* is a tale of love, growth, and redemption, following Jason and Tae Hyun's journey as they navigate the treacherous waters of fame, desire, and love. It's a story that will make you believe in the power of communication, self-reflection, and the resilience of the human heart. And it's my privilege to share it with you.

Thanks to Robert, Owen, Eric, and José for their help on this journey. And a special thank you to Jetspace Studio for making this book real.

About the Author

KT Salvo (he/they) is a queer romance novelist and artist with a passion for gaming, anime, and K-pop. With a love for diverse and inclusive storytelling, KT's stories explore the complexities and joys of modern queer relationships. When not writing, KT can be found honing their artistic skills or enjoying a hearty, home-cooked, vegan meal. With a distinctive voice and a talent for crafting relatable and realistic characters, KT is quickly becoming a rising star in the world of queer romance fiction.

You can connect with KT at:
- ktsalvo.com
- twitter.com/ktsalvo

Made in the USA
Middletown, DE
23 August 2023